Gems from World Literature

Gems from World Literature

The Greatest Russian Classics

from

Pushkin

to

Sologub

Edited by

J.A. Hammerton

CREST PUBLISHING HOUSE

G-2, 16 Ansari Road,

Darya Ganj, New Delhi-110 002

Published by Crest Publishing House
G-2, 16 Ansari Road
Darya Ganj, New Delhi - 110 002

The Greatest Russian Classics
from Pushkin *to* Sologub
ISBN 81-242-0483-7

First Crest Impression : 2004

Printed by Saurabh Printers Pvt Ltd
A-16, Sector IV, NOIDA 201 301

Editorial Board

Editorial Note

A SHORT story may be a mere anecdote of three hundred words or a work of ten or fifteen thousand. In content it may be anything from a glimpse of character, an incident, to a highly finished picture of life. But it should be a complete work of imagination, its effect achieved with a minimum of personages and events.

To select the best thousand examples was a task that could be achieved only on arbitrary lines. As to length, three thousand words was the ideal average, but this excluded some of the finest stories, so exceptions had to be allowed. National characteristics also had consideration. Another test was the value of a story as illustrating the development of the art.

PROBLEMS of arrangement were not entirely solved by classification according to the country of each writer's origin. This puts Richard Steele into the Irish volume and separates those ideal literary partners Agnes and Egerton Castle. But it is the best possible arrangement for the work, and the index makes reference easy. The inclusion of a series of stories of the War became possible when the War itself ruled out all modern German work.

A WORD as to the method of selection. The general editor prepared a trial list of titles, which was submitted to all the members of the Editorial Board, who rejected and added according to their individual tastes and knowledge, These individual lists were then collated and the final list evolved. The thousand stories selected are therefore representative of the combined opinion of the whole group of editors. A very few modifications of the final list were made necessary by difficulties of copyright and considerations of Anglo-Saxon taste in certain translations from foreign literatures.

MOST of the foreign stories have been specially translated, and all copyrights, in both stories and translations, the use of which authors and publishers have courteously permitted, are duly credited at the end of each volume.

J.A. HAMMERTON

Contents

CONTENTS

The Russian Story-Tellers

From Pushkin to Sologub

RUSSIAN literature was revealed to the Western reader through the works of Russia's greatest masters—Turgeniev, Tolstoy, and Dostoyevsky—whose novels, true epics of Russian life and thought, are vast in bulk and purpose. Their extensive proportions seem, in a way, an essential element of Russian art in its variety of observation and deep search after truth and the aims of existence.

Russia is a vast country. It includes a greater divergency of human types and modes of consciousness than any other State in Europe. Russia is comparatively young, too. She began cultured life at a much later period than the rest of Europe, and from a certain point in her history made gigantic strides to overtake the level of Western culture. In some respects she is ahead of it, though many remnants of an uncultured past are latent in the steady and sometimes feverishly hasty growth of her inner development.

RUSSIAN life seems to extend over a simultaneous range of several centuries, to contain conditions and conceptions which are almost mediæval, while the psychology and idealism of Russian intellectuals as well as the spontaneous spirituality of the Russian masses are in many cases in advance of the normal and gradual progress of Western Europe. This accounts for the complexity of Russian problems, both individual and social. Until the consummation of its wonderful revolution, the nation's creative power had not had sufficient opportunities to apply itself to active and constructive work in the way of social progress. Until then, by a sort of instinct, and for historic reasons, too, it had been centred on inner development. It is too early yet to discern how Russia's new political freedom may react on her intellectual progress. The spirit of the nation had already achieved higher standards than those manifested in pre-Revolution realities. The outstanding, all-embracing problem is how to fulfil in the actual conditions of life all that the Russian spirit has gained in its long trials and through its endurance.

THIS problem is at the bottom of all Russian literature, and accounts for the high idealism of Russian writers, combined with a strong realistic vein and an all-pervading spirit of humanity. It forms that peculiar atmosphere of tense inner life, longing to assert itself in action, which is so characteristic of Russian novels, and makes them so fascinating to the Western reader.

The same atmosphere, the same problems are characteristic of the Russian short story. As a distinct type of literature the short story made its first appearance in Russia towards the end of the nineteenth century with Garshin and Chekhov, who excelled in the art of story-telling and specialised in it. From the very beginning of the nineteenth century, however, at the outset of Russia's literary life, and all through the succeeding periods of its further development, all the best Russian novelists, as well as Russia's greatest poets, wrote short stories in the same spirit, many of which possessed the same literary value as their works of a much wider scope. A series of representative short Russian stories such as those contained in this volume affords in consequence a general view of Russian literature with its successive tendencies, pervaded with the one and same spirit peculiar to Russian art.

Pushkin

ALEXANDER PUSHKIN (1799-1837), the greatest Russian poet, the founder of both Russian prose and poetry in its classic form, is the first link between Russian and Western literature. His deepest inspiration came from the very heart of Russia—from Russian folk-lore. He was the first to reveal the imaginative power and intuitive moral force of the Russian peasant. In the mainsprings, however, his genius was akin to Western culture and influenced to a large extent by the romantic school of his time. He was under the spell of Byronic "Titanism," which took a markedly Russian form in his works. His story "The Pistol Shot" is very representative in this respect. The Western romantic spirit of it blends originally and naturally with the Russian motive of pity, which solves, by a sort of inner revelation, the most complex problems. The hero of the story is distinctly "Byronic" in his cool aloofness, in his gambling with fate, but in the supreme moment, when his "Satanic" disposition is brought to a test, the instinct of humanity and pity triumphs over his romantic intellectuality.

The best of Pushkin's stories—a gem of romantic literature—is "The Queen of Spades," perfect in its artistic finish. It is a fantastic ghost story, told with an entrancing power of imagination, yet with sufficient psychological motives to make it real. Its background is strongly realistic. It gives a true picture of high society life under Alexander I., with significant details of the home of the period. The old countess is a curious remnant of eighteenth-century grandeur, a court beauty, Russian to the core despite her adventurous Parisian past, despotic, yet generous by impulse. It is an afterthought of compassion for the victim of betrayed love that moves her soul to disclose the fatal secret to the unfortunate gambler. Lisa, the young lady-companion, is a type created of social conditions, a poor victim of self-indulgent, idle surroundings, dragged into a luxurious life in which she remains a lonely stranger, half-lady, half-servant, fed on romantic dreams which lead her fatally to ruin—crushed in her human dignity as a plaything of the idle rich. There is a great human truth in this type, the more remarkable as revealed by a romantic poet.

Lermontoff

MICHAIL LERMONTOFF (1814–41) was Pushkin's younger contemporary, and ranks next to him as Russia's second great poet. Lermontoff's short stories are purely romantic. Many of them show a Byronic vein like those of Pushkin. He dwells in preference on characters of wild beauty, of irresistible personality, cruel, yet justified by their inner tragedy and their defiant attitude to life. The Russian element in them consists in the passionate instinct of inner freedom, that justifies even the outlaws, as we see in the picturesque Cossack story, "The Fair Smuggler." The heroine and her associates are desperate characters, yet the victim of their conspiracy is ready to forgive his loss and the fair lady's deception on account of the beautiful instincts of freedom he observes in the gang. The "Fair Smuggler" cheats him unscrupulously, but remains true to her freely chosen lover. The woman and her lover, as well as the boy who pretends to be blind, have their own moral standards and are true to them. The atmosphere of inner freedom in this story has a psychological value and is representative of the Russian mind.

Gogol

REALISM, that great force of Russian art, makes its appearance in Russian literature with Nicolai Gogol (1809–52). His genius of observation and true representation of life was united to the romantic soul of the Ukranian. He became the poet of Russian reality. Absolute truth to life is combined in Gogol's works with the utmost simplicity of invention. He never flatters life, nor does he slander it. He is happy to show all that is beautiful and humane in it, but does not hide its ugly sides. His novels and stories contain a gallery of immortal types of Russian officials demoralised by the arbitrary power they possess, monstrous in their pettiness and inhumanity; of idle, self-indulgent, narrow-minded land- and serf-owners before the emancipation, and of all the social deformities created by excess of power on the one hand and total defencelessness on the other. With a grim humour does he paint these portraits of depravity, but alongside he gives us a world of beauty, poetry, light and colour in his masterful stories of peasant life, of pure innocent souls, as well as in his broad emotional pictures of Russian scenery—the steppes, the rivers and the woods.

The peculiar atmosphere of peasant life appears in the story "The Eve of St. John," with its tale of superstitions influencing the life and psychology of the simple souls. The minute rendering of the village types, the happy tone of a fairy tale that makes the fantastic appear real, the genuine, deep emotions running through it form the beauty of the story. The plot of "The Carriage" is of the simplest—a mere incident of daily life—yet Gogol's humour mirrors in it a wonderful picture of petty life with its lack of activity, idle rivalries and amusements.

Turgeniev

IVAN TURGENIEV (1818–83), the great master of Russian prose, gives a vast picture of Russian conditions in his novels. He was the first to reveal the new social types created by the transitionary period of the abolition of serfdom, which transformed the old Russia, as she used to live and to feel and to reason before the great reform of Alexander II. His short stories, especially those included in "Memoirs of a Sportsman," rank among his masterpieces, both as perfect works of art and as the expression of his higher humanitarian ideals. Turgeniev revealed in them the poetic beauty of the Russian landscape, and, above all, the soul of the Russian serfs, the peasants with their reserved but deep emotions, and the spiritual treasures hidden in their simple hearts.

There is nothing sentimental or artificial about Turgeniev's peasants. He does not idealise them for the purposes of mere social propaganda. He gives them to us with all their peculiarities and limitations resulting from their uncultured state, the more striking because of the revelation of their rich and deep emotions in the sober, simple pictures of their lives. "The Singers" is one of Turgeniev's particularly interesting tales. In it he reveals the artistic temperament of the Russian peasant, his delight in music, showing what a world of passion, of harmony with the universe is concealed in his soul. He pours out his inmost self in the weird strains of Russian songs, then resumes his humble existence and works like a slave, or gets drunk, as he does in the end of the story. "The Rendezvous" is a pathetic story of disappointed love, deeply humane, showing the genuine emotions of a simple peasant girl and the demoralising effect of half-cultured town life on her lover. "Visions" discloses a mystic side in Turgeniev, to be met with in other stories of his. Others of his tales might well have found places in this collection, but with few exceptions they exceed the average length of story admitted in this compilation, while others, again, of the desired length are less stories than sketches.

Dostoyevsky

FIODOR DOSTOYEVSKY (1822–81) is Russia's great mystic, whose vision of the world is that of a contest between the questioning and often rebellious human mind and the mystery of divine omnipresence revealed to the enlightened in the very midst of life's bitterest wrongs and agony. The outcome of Dostoyevsky's mystic teaching is his message of pity, manifested in all his work. "The Honest Thief" is one of this author's tales of pity, in which he reveals that compassionate sympathy of the Russian mind for all suffering. All human relations in Dostoyevsky's story are based on intuitive pity, which discovers a pure and wide-awakened conscience in the fallen man. Pity as revealed in this story is active, and brings spiritual beauty and light into what would have seemed abject and ugly seen without that compassionate love for humanity.

Schedrin

ALONG with those great masters, prophets of religious and spiritual truth, Russia possesses story-tellers chiefly concerned with social ideals and struggles. Nicolai Schedrin, the *nom de plume* of Michail T. Saltickov (1826–89), is the greatest of them. A satirist of remarkable force and rich invention, Schedrin lashes with his inexhaustible wit the self-complacency, self-indulgence and cruelty of the higher administrative power. He has a particular genius in drawing portraits of the bureaucratic caste which covers it with contempt and ridicule. These portraits have to a large extent revealed the psychology of the Russian bureaucratic mind, and the names of many of Schedrin's ridiculed heroes have become the nick-names of certain types of officials. The pathetic tale, "Two Little Moujiks," shows the grim side of Schedrin's talent in the story of the two children who are animated with the desperate desire to avenge their humiliation, to assert their human dignity against despotic cruelty. Their only means to that end is suicide—a grim symbol of social wrongs. Schedrin's sarcasm, however, does not spare those who are too weak to oppose evil, as we see in the delightful story "The Self-sacrificing Rabbit."

Tolstoy

LEO TOLSTOY (1828–1910), the genius of world-wide fame, needs little introduction to the Western reader. His short stories were a part of his life-work from the very outset of his literary career and all through the first half of his life, when his moral teaching, though asserting itself strongly in his vast psychological and artistic conceptions, had not yet crystallised into a positive message. From 1881, when his religious crisis resolved itself into active moral teaching, Tolstoy made the short story a means to convey his ideas to simple minds. He put all his artistic power and inspiration into the tales written for the peasants, but read by the whole cultured world. "How Much Land does a Man Need?" is simple in its teaching, and convincing as a true and symbolic picture of unreasoned and instinctive greed. "The Three Hermits" contrasts journalistic dogmatism with genuine faith and the moral force it brings—a favourite subject of Tolstoy's. The remaining stories in the present volume are typical of his peculiar vein of story-telling—clear and strong in their purpose, simple and full of artistic details, so characteristic of Tolstoy's work as a whole.

Leskov

OF a different type from any of the preceding writers in this volume is Nicolai S. Leskov (1831–95). A strong enemy of the revolutionary movement of the 'sixties, his early work was chiefly concerned in attacking it. It was only towards the latter half of his career that he left the bitterness of politics behind him and began to devote himself to pure literature. He has given us numerous stories, unique in both style and conception. His subjects were largely the clergy, the church, the beliefs—dogmatic and otherwise—of the people, and their superstitions. Rich in invention, his language full of colour, he could give us in five or six pages the content of a whole volume. He had a wonderful way of creating an atmosphere, so admirably illustrated in "The Ghost of the Engineers' Castle."

Uspensky

NICOLAI USPENSKY (1837–89), one of the minor Russian writers, could tell a good realistic story without any deep psychological problems. He began life as a schoolmaster, then developed a taste for literature, which paid him so badly at first that, owing to his extreme poverty, he was forced to live in common doss-houses—an experience that stood him in good stead afterwards, and afforded him many types for his stories.

Mamin-Sibiriak

Dmitri Mamin-Sibiriak (*b.* 1852) was born in the Urals—the background of many of his novels and stories. Mining, greed, the severity of the military authorities formed the principal subjects of his plots. The story "In the Heart of the Urals" shows us what an immense amount of love and sympathy he felt for the simple people—primitive and unspoiled by civilisation—whose lives were disturbed by the first shriek of a train that broke the stillness of their forests, to the wonder of the boy Pimka, the disgust of old grandfather Tit, and the delight of the soldier. We see Mamin-Sibiriak in a different vein in the story "There is no Reply," with its atmosphere of tragedy.

Korolénko

Vladimir Korolénko (*b.* 1853) is a Little Russian, whose work is coloured by Polish romanticism and Ukranian poetry and sadness. His prose is like music, singing now of nature, now of human emotions. Even in moments of greatest tragedy he is utterly devoid of bitterness, as we see in the story "Easter Eve," and in the quieter story of "The Old Verger" called to his eternal rest.

Garshin

VSEVOLOD GARSHIN (1855–88) did not live long enough to write more than about ten stories, but they rank him as one of the greatest masters of Russian prose. Every line was wrung out of him from his deep inner experience. We see the spiritual nature of the man in the wonderful realistic story, depicting the horrors of war, "Four Days," and in the powerful story "The Red Flower," a tale that was largely biographical; for Garshin used to suffer from fits of madness (the cause of his tragic death), during which he dreamt of destroying all evil in the world at one fell swoop. His melancholy nature, however, had little faith in the force of good, or in the destruction of evil, and still less belief had he in that the attainment of his dreams could bring him either peace or happiness. "Is this all?" asks the palm, in the charming, poetic story "Attalea Princeps," when after all her tremendous efforts she emerges into freedom, the goal of her desires.

Ignati Potapenko (*b.* 1856) had the curious career of being first a Uhlan officer and then a priest. Some of his best stories are about the rural clergy. He has a wonderful power of observation and a ready style. In the story "Bigger than Yourself" we have an ordinary, average young man who lets his present opportunities of action and happiness slip by for some illusory ideas of greatness.

Potapenko

ANTON CHEKHOV (1860–1904), the chronicler of the Russian period of depression and pessimism, was the leader of the realistic school of the Russian short story. Many writers have compared him to Guy de Maupassant in his masterful manner of creating an atmosphere and reaching a climax. He seizes a given moment in his heroes' lives and reveals their souls in two or three pages. Mediocrity, the tragedy of pettiness, commonplaceness, the emptiness and meaninglessness of everyday life form the principal themes of his stories. He reveals the rottenness of the social structure, yet, unlike most great Russian writers, has no doctrine to teach. The few stories of his given in this volume are remarkably characteristic of his work. "The Avenger," "The Chameleon," "A Work of Art," "The Slanderer," show him to us as a humorist, the rest show him in his more artistic vein.

Chekhov

Feódor Sologub (*b.* 1863), mystic and realist, is a writer of long novels in the Dostoyevsky school, and many short stories, of which those included in this volume are very representative. A favourite theme of his is reincarnation, which he uses very powerfully in the three stories, "The White Mother," "The Invoker of the Beast," and "A Soothing Dream."

Sologub

R. S. T.

ALEXANDER S. PUSHKIN
1799–1837

THE PISTOL-SHOT

WE were in camp in a small Russian village. Every one knows the life of an officer of the line: in the morning, drill and horseback exercise; then comes dinner with the colonel of the regiment, or else at the Jewish restaurant; and at night, drinks and cards. At this place, however, there were no entertainments of any kind, for no one had a marriageable daughter to bring out. We spent our time in one another's quarters, and at our evening gatherings there were uniforms only.

However, there was one man in our set who was not a soldier. He must have been about thirty-five, and, consequently, we looked upon him as quite old. His experience had great weight with us; and besides, his reserve, his grand air, and his sarcastic manner made a deep impression on us young men. There seemed to be something mysterious about his life. He looked like a Russian, though he bore a foreign name. In days gone by he had been in a regiment of hussars, where he was quite prominent at one time; but suddenly he had sent in his resignation, no one knew why, and had retired to this poor, out-of-the-way village, where he fared very badly, while at the same time he spent much money. He always wore a shabby overcoat, and still he kept open house, where every officer was made welcome. To tell the truth his dinners generally consisted of two or three simple dishes prepared by his servant, an old discharged soldier, but the champagne always flowed. No one knew anything of his affairs or his means, and no one dared ask him any questions on the subject. There were plenty of books in his house—mostly military—among them a few novels. He lent them willingly and never asked for them again.

On the other hand, he never returned those he borrowed. His one pastime was pistol-shooting. The walls of his room were riddled with bullets, giving it the appearance of a honeycomb. A rich collection of pistols was the only luxury to be seen in the miserable house which he occupied. The accuracy of his aim was remarkable, and if he had taken a bet that he could shoot the pompom on a helmet, not one of us would have hesitated to put the helmet on. Sometimes we talked of duelling, but Silvio (I will give him that name) never opened his lips on the subject. If some one asked him if he had ever fought a duel, he answered shortly that he had, and that was all. He never entered into any particulars, and it was evident that he disliked being asked such questions. We surmised that the death of one of his victims had left a blight on his life. Never for a minute would any of us have thought that he could have been guilty of faint-heartedness. There are some people whose very appearance precludes such an idea.

One day eight or ten of our officers were dining at Silvio's. We drank as much as usual—that is, excessively. When dinner was over we begged of our host to take the bank in a game of faro. After refusing to do so, for he seldom played, he finally called for cards, and laying fifty ducats on the table before him, he sat down and shuffled. We formed in a circle about him and the game began. When playing Silvio never uttered a word, neither objecting nor explaining. If a player made a mistake he paid out exactly the amount due to him or else credited it to himself. We were all familiar with his manner of playing, and always let him have his own way. But on the day I speak of there was with us an officer newly arrived who, through absent-mindedness, doubled his stakes on a certain card. Silvio took the chalk and marked down what was due to him. The officer, convinced that there was a mistake, made some objections. Silvio, still mute, went on dealing as if he had not heard. The officer, out of patience by that time, took the brush and wiped off the figures. Silvio picked up the chalk and wrote them down again. At this the officer, excited by the wine, by the play, and by the laughter of his comrades, and thinking he had been insulted, took up a brass candlestick and hurled it at Silvio, who by bending aside averted the blow. Great was the uproar! Silvio rose, pale with rage, and with eyes blazing.

"My dear sir," he said, "you will please leave this room, and be thankful that this has happened in my house."

Not one of us doubted the outcome of this affair, and we all looked upon our new comrade as a dead man. The officer went out, saying he was ready to meet the banker just as soon as it was convenient. The game proceeded a few minutes longer, but it was evident that the master of the house was not paying much attention to what was going on. We all left, one by one, and returned to our quarters, discussing the while the vacancy in our ranks which was sure to take place.

Next morning, while at riding exercise, we all wondered if the poor lieutenant were dead or alive, when, to our surprise, he appeared among us. We plied him with questions, and he answered that he had had no challenge from Silvio, which caused us all much surprise. We called on Silvio and found him in his yard, firing bullet after bullet at an ace nailed to the door. He received us in his usual manner, never mentioning the scene of the night before. Three days went by and the lieutenant was still alive. We kept saying to each other, " Will Silvio not fight ? " amazed at such a thing. But Silvio did not fight. He simply gave a very lame explanation, and that was all that was said about the matter.

This forbearance on his part did him much harm among us young men. Youth never quite forgives a want of courage, for to youth fearlessness is the greatest quality one can possess, and it excuses many faults. Still, after a while all this was forgotten, and by degrees Silvio regained his old ascendancy over us.

I alone could never feel the same toward him. Being of a romantic turn of mind I had loved this man whose life was an enigma to us all more than any one else, and I had made him, in my thoughts, the hero of some mysterious drama ; and he liked me—of this I felt sure. For when we were alone, dropping his sharp and sarcastic speeches, he would converse on all sorts of subjects and unbend to me in a fascinating manner. Ever since that unlucky evening of which I have spoken, the fact that he had been insulted and had not wiped out the offence in blood worried me to such an extent that I never could feel at ease with him as in the days gone by. I even avoided looking at him, and Silvio was too clever and quick not to notice it and to guess at the reason. He seemed to me to feel it deeply. On two occasions I thought I had detected a wish on his part to explain matters, but I avoided him, and he did not pursue me.

Those happy mortals who live in cities, where there is so much to see and to do, can never imagine how important certain small happenings can become in an out-of-the-way village or town. One of these is the arrival of the mail. On Tuesdays and Fridays the offices of our regiment were besieged with men ; one expected money, another a letter, and again others looked for newspapers. As a rule everything was opened and read on the spot. News was given, and the improvised post-office was full of animation. Silvio's letters were addressed to the care of our regiment, and he called for them with us. One day a letter was handed to him, the seal of which he broke hurriedly. While reading it his eyes flashed with suppressed excitement. None of the officers except myself noticed this, as they were all busy reading their own letters.

" Gentlemen," said Silvio, " business compels me to leave town immediately. I must go to-night. I hope none of you will refuse to dine with me for the last time. I shall expect you," said he, turning to me pointedly. " I hope you will not disappoint me."

After saying this he went away in great haste, and we all retired to our own quarters, agreeing to meet at his house later.

I arrived at Silvio's at the hour he had named, and found almost the whole regiment there. Everything he possessed was packed, and the bare walls, riddled with bullets, stared back at us. We sat down to dinner, and our host was in such a jovial mood that before long we were all in the greatest of spirits. Corks flew about, the froth rose in our glasses, which we refilled as rapidly as they were emptied. We all felt great affection for our host, and wished him a pleasant journey, with joy and prosperity at the end of it. It was very late when we got up from the table, and while we were all picking out our caps in the hall, Silvio took me by the hand and detained me as I was about to leave.

" I must speak to you," he said in a low tone.

So I remained after the others went away; and, seated facing each other, we smoked our pipes for a while in silence. Silvio seemed worried, and there was no trace of the feverish gaiety he had displayed in the earlier part of the evening. His dreadful pallor, the brilliancy of his eyes, and the long puffs of smoke he blew from his mouth gave him the appearance of a fiend. After a few moments he broke the silence.

" It may be," he said, " that we shall never see each other again. Before we part I wish to explain certain things to you. You have noticed, perhaps, that I attach very little importance to the average man's opinion; but I like you, and I feel that I cannot leave without having you think better of me than you do."

He stopped to shake the ashes out of his pipe. I remained silent and avoided looking at him.

"It may have seemed strange to you," he continued, "that I did not ask any satisfaction from that drunkard—that young fool Rassinoff. You will admit that, I having the choice of weapons, he was at my mercy, and that there was not much chance of his killing me. I might call it generosity on my part, but I will not lie about it. If I could have given Rassinoff a good lesson without in any way risking my life, he would not have been rid of me so easily."

I looked at Silvio in the greatest surprise. Such an admission from him was astounding. He went on:

"As it is, unhappily, I have no right to risk my life. Six years ago I received a blow, and the man who struck me is still alive." This excited my curiosity to an unusual degree.

"You did not meet him?" I asked. "Surely some extraordinary circumstance must have prevented your doing so?"

"I did meet him," answered Silvio, "and here you see the result of our encounter."

He rose and drew from a box near him a cap of red cloth with a gilt braid and tassel, such as Frenchmen call *bonnet de police*.[1] He put it on his head, and I saw that a bullet had pierced it about an inch above the forehead.

"You know," said Silvio, "that I was in the Imperial Hussars, and you also know what kind of a disposition I have. I like to rule every one. Well, in my youth it was positively a passion with me. In my day brawlers were in fashion, and I was the foremost brawler of the regiment. To get drunk was then considered a thing to be proud of. I could outdrink the famous B——, celebrated in song by Davidoff. Every day brought its duel, and every day saw me either the principal actor in them or else taking the part of a second. My comrades looked up to me; and our superior officers, who were constantly being transferred, considered me a plague of which they could not be rid.

"As for me I kept on quietly—or, rather, riotously—in my glorious career, when one day a young fellow who was very wealthy and of good family was transferred to our regiment. I will not give you his name, but never have I met a fellow with such unheard-of luck. Imagine having youth, a fine figure, no end of spirits, a daring which is utterly indifferent to danger, a great name, and unlimited means to do with as one likes, and you may have a faint idea of the impression

[1] A *bonnet de police* is a small cloth cap worn with undress uniform.

he created among us. My power was gone in an instant. At first, dazzled by my reputation, he tried to make friends with me, but I received his advances very coldly, seeing which he quietly dropped me without showing any annoyance whatever.

"I took such a dislike to him when I saw his popularity in the regiment, and his success with the ladies, that I was driven almost to despair. I tried to pick a quarrel with him, but to my sarcastic remarks he answered with caustic and unexpected wit that had the merit, besides, of being more cheerful than mine. He was always in jest, while I was in dead earnest. Finally, one night while at a ball in a Polish house, seeing how much the ladies admired him, especially our hostess, with whom I had been very friendly, I whispered in his ear some insulting remark, which I have long since forgotten. He turned around and struck me. We grasped our swords, some of the ladies fainted, and a few officers parted us. We went out immediately in order to fight it out right then and there.

"The three witnesses and myself reached the meeting-place, and I awaited the coming of my adversary with no ordinary impatience. The sun rose and its intense heat was being felt more and more every minute, when I finally saw him coming in the distance. He was on foot, and in his shirt-sleeves, carrying his uniform over his arm; he was attended by only one witness. I went forward to meet him, and I noticed that his cap, which he carried in his hand, was full of cherries. Our witnesses placed us twelve paces from each other. It was my privilege to shoot first, but with passion and hatred blinding me I feared my aim would be poor, and to gain time to steady my hand I offered to let him fire first. He refused to do so, and it was then agreed we should leave it to chance. Luck was, as usual, with this spoiled child of fortune. He fired and pierced my cap. It was then my turn, and I felt that he was at my mercy. I looked at him with eagerness, hoping to find him at least a little uneasy. Not at all, for there he stood within range of my pistol, coolly picking the ripest cherries out of his cap and blowing the pips in my direction, where they fell at my feet.

"'What shall I gain,' thought I, 'by taking his life, when he thinks so little of it?'

"A diabolical thought crossed my mind. I unloaded a pistol.

"'It seems,' I said, 'that you care very little whether you die or not at the present moment. You seem more anxious to breakfast instead. It shall be as you please. I have no wish to disturb you.'

"'You will be kind enough to attend to your own business,' answered he, 'and please to fire; but, after all, you may do as you like. You can always fire your shot when and where you like. I shall always be at your call.'

"I went away with my witnesses, to whom I said that I did not care to shoot just then, and the thing ended there.

"I sent in my resignation, and retired to this out-of-the-way village. From that day to this I have thought of nothing but revenge. And now the time has come!"

Silvio drew from his pocket the letter received that morning. Some one, his lawyer, it seemed, had written from Moscow that the *person in question* was soon to be married to a young and pretty girl.

"You can guess, I have no doubt," said Silvio, "who is the *person in question.* I am leaving for Moscow, and we shall see if he will look at death in the midst of bridal festivities with as much coolness as he did when facing it with a pound of cherries in his cap!"

After saying these words he rose, and throwing his cap viciously on the floor, walked back and forth the length of the room like a caged tiger. I had listened to him without saying a word, stirred by very contradictory feelings.

A servant entered, saying the carriage was at the door. Silvio grasped my hand, which he shook with all his might. He entered a small open carriage in which were two boxes, one containing his pistols and the other his baggage. We said good-bye once more, and he was driven away.

II

Years went by, and family matters compelled me to live in an obscure village in the district of Yerna. While looking after my interests I often sighed for the enjoyable life I had led until then. The long, solitary evenings of winter and spring were the hardest to bear. I could not become reconciled to their lonesomeness. Until the dinner-hour I managed somehow to kill time by chatting with the landowner, visiting my workmen, and watching the new buildings being erected. But as soon as night came I was at a loss to know what to do. I knew by heart the few books I had found in the ancient bookcases and in the garret. All the stories known to my old housekeeper, Kirilovna, I had asked her to tell me over and over again, and the songs of the peasants saddened me. I drank everything at hand, until my head ached. I will even admit that at one time I thought I should become a drunkard from sheer desperation—the worst kind of drunkard—of which this district offered me a good many examples.

My nearest neighbours consisted of two or three of these confirmed inebriates, whose conversations were ever interspersed with sighs and hiccups, so that even complete solitude was to be preferred to their society. I finally got into the habit of dining as late as possible and retiring as early as I could afterward, and in that way I solved the problem of shortening the evenings and lengthening the days.

About four versts from my house was a beautiful estate belonging to the Countess Birovna. It was occupied by her steward, the countess herself never having lived in the place except for a month at one time, and that in the first year of her marriage.

One day, in the second year of this lonely existence of mine, I heard that the countess and her husband were to occupy their residence during the summer months. In the early part of June they arrived with all their household.

The coming of a rich neighbour is always an event in the life of country people. The owners of property, and their servants also, speak of it two months before they arrive, and it is still a topic of interest three years after they have left. For my part, the fact that a young and pretty woman would live so near upset me very much. I was dying to see her, and the first Sunday after they had settled I walked over, after dinner, to pay my respects to the lady and introduce myself as her nearest neighbour and devoted slave.

A footman led me to the count's library and left to announce me. This library was large and magnificently furnished. Against the walls were shelves filled with books, and on each one was a figure in bronze; above a marble mantelpiece stood a large mirror. The floor was covered with a green carpet, over which were thrown rich Persian rugs. Unused as I was in my hovel to any kind of luxury, it was so long since I had seen anything like this display of wealth that I actually felt timid and experienced inward tremblings while waiting for the count—such nervousness as a country solicitor might feel when asking an audience of a minister. The door opened and a young man about thirty-two years of age entered. He greeted me in a most cordial and charming manner. I tried to appear at ease, and was going to make the usual commonplace remarks about being delighted at having such neighbours, when he forestalled me by saying how welcome I was.

We sat down and his manner was so cordial that it soon dispelled my unusual timidity. I was just beginning to feel like myself again when the countess appeared in the doorway, and once more I grew desperately shy. She was a beauty. The count introduced me, and the more I tried to be natural and quite at ease, the more I looked awkward and embarrassed. My hosts, in order to give me time to recover from my bashfulness, chatted together as if to show that they already considered me an old acquaintance and one to be treated as such, so that while walking about the library I looked at the books and pictures. So far as pictures are concerned I am no connoisseur, but there was one there that attracted my attention. It represented a Swiss scene, and the beauty of the landscape did not attract me quite as much as did the fact that the canvas was pierced by two bullets, evidently fired one over the other.

"That is a pretty good shot!" I cried, turning to the count.

"Yes," said he, "and rather a peculiar one. Are you a pistol-shot?" he added.

"Why, yes, a fairly good one," I answered, delighted to have a chance to speak of something with which I was familiar. "I think I could hit a card at thirty paces—with my own pistols, of course."

"Really?" said the countess, seeming much interested. "And you, my dear"—this to her husband—"could you hit a card at thirty paces?"

"I don't know about that," answered the count, "but I was a pretty good shot in my day, though it must be four years now since I used a pistol."

"In that case, sir," I continued, "I'll bet you anything that even at twenty paces you could not hit a card; because to excel at pistol-shooting constant practice is necessary. I know this from experience. At home I was considered one of the best shots in the regiment, but it happened once that I was a month without using a pistol, mine being at the gunsmith's. We were called to the shooting-gallery one day, and what do you think happened to me, sir? I missed a bottle standing twenty-five paces away four times in succession. There was with us, at the time, a major of cavalry, a good fellow, who was for ever joking : ' Faith, my friend,' he said to me, ' this is too much moderation. You have too great a respect for the bottle.' Believe me, sir, one must practise all the time. Otherwise one gets rusty. The best marksman I ever knew practised every day, firing at least three shots before his dinner ; he would have no more missed them than he would have omitted his cognac before eating."

Both the count and his wife seemed pleased to listen to me.

" And how did he shoot ? " asked the count.

" How ? Let me tell you. He would see a fly on the wall. You laugh ! Madame, I swear to you, this is true. ' Eh, Kouska ! a pistol ! ' Kouska would bring one loaded. Crack ! there lay the fly flattened against the wall."

" What consummate skill ! " cried the count. " And what was this man's name ? "

" Silvio, sir."

" Silvio ? " cried the count, starting to his feet. " You have known Silvio ? "

" Have I known him ? Well, rather. We were the greatest of friends ; he was like one of us in the regiment. But it is now five years since I heard of him. And you, also, knew him ? "

" Yes, I knew him well. Did he ever tell you a peculiar thing which happened to him once ? "

" How he received a slap in the face one evening from a cad ? "

" And did he tell you the name of this cad ? "

" No, sir, he did not. Ah ! " I cried, guessing at the truth. " Forgive me, sir, I did not know. Can it be you ? "

" Yes, it was I," answered the count, in an embarrassed manner, " and that picture with a hole in it is the souvenir of our last interview."

" For God's sake, my dear," said the countess, " don't speak of it. The thought of it terrifies me to this day."

" No," said the count, " I feel I ought to tell this gentleman. He knows how I offended his friend, and it is only fair that he should learn how he revenged himself."

The count drew up an armchair for me to sit in, and I listened with the greatest interest to the following story :

" Five years ago we were married. We spent the first month of our honeymoon here in this house, and to it clings the memory of the happiest days of my life, coupled with one of the most painful experiences I have ever had.

"One evening we had both gone out riding. My wife's horse became very restless, and she was so frightened that she begged me to lead him to the stables and she would walk back by herself. On reaching the house I found a travelling-coach at the door, and was told that a man was waiting in the library. He had refused to give his name, saying he wished to see me on business. I came into this room, and in the half-light I saw a man with a beard standing before the mantelpiece, still in his dusty travelling-clothes. I drew nearer to him, trying to place him in my memory.

"'You do not remember me, count?' said he, in a voice that shook.

"'Silvio!' I cried.

"And, to be candid with you, I felt as if my hair were standing on end.

"'Exactly,' he continued, 'and it is my turn to shoot. I have come to fire. Are you ready?'

"I saw a pistol sticking out of his left pocket. I measured twelve paces, and stood there in that corner, begging him to be quick about it, as my wife would return in a few moments. He said he wanted a light first, and I rang for candles.

"I closed the door, after giving instructions not to admit any one, and once more I told him to proceed. He raised his pistol and took aim. I was counting the seconds. I was thinking of her. All this lasted a full minute, and suddenly Silvio lowered his weapon.

"'I am very sorry,' he said, 'but my pistol is not loaded with cherry-pips, and bullets are hard. After all, come to think of it, this does not look much like a duel. It is more like a murder. I am not in the habit of firing on an unarmed man. Let us begin all over again. Let us draw lots to see who will shoot first.'

"My head was in a whirl, and it turned out that I at first refused. Finally, we loaded our pistols, and put two pieces of paper in the very cap I had once perforated with a bullet. I took one of the pieces; and, as luck would have it, I drew number one.

"'You are devilish lucky, count!' said he, with a smile I will never forget.

"I cannot to this day understand it, but he finally compelled me to fire, and my bullet hit that picture there."

The count pointed to the landscape with the hole in it. His face was crimson. There was the countess, as white as a sheet, and as for me, I barely suppressed a cry.

"I fired at him," continued the count, "and, thank God, I missed him."

"Then Silvio—at that moment he was positively hideous—stood back and took aim. Just then the door opened. My wife came in, and seeing us facing each other, threw herself in my arms. Her presence gave me back my courage.

"'My dear,' I said, 'do you not see we are only jesting? How frightened you are! Go, now, get a glass of water, and come back to us. I will then introduce my old friend and comrade to you.'

"But my wife knew better than to believe my words.

"'Tell me, is what my husband says true?' she asked the terrible Silvio. 'Is it true that this is only a jest?'

"'He is always jesting, madam,' replied Silvio. 'Once upon a time he gave me a slap in jest; again, in jest, he pierced my cap with a bullet; and a few minutes ago, still jesting, he just missed me. Now it is my turn to laugh a little.'

"Saying which, he took aim once more, with my wife looking on. She fell on her knees at his feet.

"'Get up, Macha,' I cried, enraged. 'Are you not ashamed of yourself? And you, sir, do you wish to drive this poor woman crazy? Will you please fire—yes or no?'

"'I will not,' answered Silvio. 'I am satisfied. I saw you falter. You were pale with fright, and that is all I hoped to see. I compelled you to fire on me, and I know you will never forget me. I leave you to your conscience.'

"He walked toward the door; and, turning round, he glanced at the picture with the bullet-hole, and without aiming at all he fired and doubled my shot. Then he went out. My wife fainted—none of the servants dared stop him, and the doors opened before him in great haste. In the porch he called for his carriage; and he was already some distance away when I recovered from my bewilderment."

The count stopped.

It was thus I heard the end of a story, the beginning of which had interested me much. I never saw Silvio again. It was said that at the time of the insurrection of Alexander Ypsilanti he was at the head of a regiment of rebels, and that he was killed when the enemy was routed at Skouliani.

THE SNOW-STORM

ALEXANDER S. PUSHKIN

TOWARDS the end of 1811, at a memorable period for Russians, lived on his own domain of Nenaradova the kind-hearted Gavril R. He was celebrated in the whole district for his hospitality and his genial character. Neighbours constantly visited him to have something to eat and drink, and to play at five-copeck boston with his wife, Praskovia. Some, too, went to have a look at their daughter, Maria, a tall pale girl of seventeen. She was an heiress, and they desired her either for themselves or for their sons.

Maria had been brought up on French novels, and consequently was in love. The object of her affection was a poor ensign in the army, who was now at home in his small village on leave of absence. As a matter of course the young man reciprocated Maria's passion. But the parents of his beloved, noticing their mutual attachment, forbade their daughter even to think of him, while they received him worse than an ex-assize judge.

Our lovers corresponded and met alone daily in the pine wood or by the old roadway chapel. There they vowed everlasting love, inveighed against fate, and exchanged various suggestions. Writing and talking in this way, they quite naturally reached the following conclusion :—

If we cannot exist apart from each other, and if the tyranny of hard-hearted parents throws obstacles in the way of our happiness, then can we not manage without them ?

Of course this happy idea originated in the mind of the young man ; but it pleased immensely the romantic imagination of Maria.

Winter set in and put a stop to their meetings. But their correspondence became all the more active. Vladimir begged Maria in every letter to give herself up to him that they might get married secretly, hide for a while, and then throw themselves at the feet of their parents, who would of course in the end be touched by their heroic constancy and say to them, " Children, come to our arms ! "

Maria hesitated a long while, and out of many different plans proposed, that of flight was for a time rejected. At last, however, she consented. On the appointed day she was to decline supper and retire to her room under the plea of a headache. She and her maid, who was in the secret, were then to go out into the garden by the back stairs, and beyond the garden they would find a sledge ready for them, would get into it and drive a distance of five miles from Nenaradova, to the village of Jadrino, straight to the church, where Vladimir would be waiting for them.

On the eve of the decisive day Maria did not sleep all night; she was packing and tying up linen and dresses. She wrote, moreover, a long letter to a friend of hers, a sentimental young lady; and another to her parents. Of the latter she took leave in the most touching terms. She excused the step she was taking by reason of the unconquerable power of love, and wound up by declaring that she should consider it the happiest moment of her life when she was allowed to throw herself at the feet of her dearest parents. Sealing both letters with a Toula seal, on which were engraven two flaming hearts with an appropriate inscription, she at last threw herself upon her bed before daybreak and dozed off, though even then she was awakened from one moment to another by terrible thoughts. First it seemed to her that at the moment of entering the sledge in order to go and get married her father stopped her, and with cruel rapidity dragged her over the snow and threw her into a dark bottomless cellar—down which she fell headlong with an indescribable sinking of the heart. Then she saw Vladimir, lying on the grass, pale and bleeding; with his dying breath he implored her to make haste and marry him. Other hideous and senseless visions floated before her one after another. Finally she rose paler than usual and with a real headache.

Both her father and her mother remarked Maria's indisposition. Their tender anxiety and constant inquiries, "What is the matter with you, Masha—are you ill?" cut her to the heart. She tried to pacify them and to appear cheerful; but she could not. Evening set in. The idea that she was passing the day for the last time in the midst of her family oppressed her. In her secret heart she took leave of everybody, of everything which surrounded her.

Supper was served; her heart beat violently. In a trembling voice she declared that she did not want any supper, and wished her father and mother good-night. They kissed her, and as usual blessed her; and she nearly wept.

Reaching her own room she threw herself into an easy-chair and burst into tears. Her maid begged her to be calm and take courage. Everything was ready. In half an hour Maria would leave for ever her parents' house, her own room, her peaceful life as a young girl.

Out of doors the snow was falling, the wind howling. The shutters rattled and shook. In everything she seemed to recognise omens and threats.

Soon the whole home was quiet and asleep. Maria wrapped herself in a shawl, put on a warm cloak, and, with a box in her hand, passed out on to the back staircase. The maid carried two bundles after her. They descended into the garden. The snow-storm raged; a strong wind blew against them, as if trying to stop the young culprit. With difficulty they reached the end of the garden. In the road a sledge awaited them.

The horses, from cold, would not stand still. Vladimir's coachman was walking to and fro in front of them, trying to quiet them. He helped the young lady and her maid to their seats, and packing away the bundles and the dressing-case, took up the reins, and the horses flew forward into the darkness of the night.

Having entrusted the young lady to the care of fate and of Tereshka the coachman, let us return to the young lover.

Vladimir had spent the whole day in driving. In the morning he had called on the Jadrino priest, and, with difficulty, came to terms with him. Then he went to seek for witnesses from amongst the neighbouring gentry. The first on whom he called was a former cornet of horse, Dravin by name, a man in his forties, who consented at once. The adventure, he declared, reminded him of old times and of his larks when he was in the Hussars. He persuaded Vladimir to stop to dinner with him, assuring him that there would be no difficulty in getting the other two witnesses. Indeed, immediately after dinner in came the surveyor Schmidt, with a moustache and spurs, and the son of a captain-magistrate, a boy of sixteen, who had recently entered the Uhlans. They not only accepted Vladimir's proposal, but even swore that they were ready to sacrifice their lives for him. Vladimir embraced them with delight, and drove off to get everything ready.

It had long been dark. Vladimir despatched his trustworthy Tereshka to Nenaradova with his two-horsed sledge, and with appropriate instructions for the occasion. For himself he ordered the small sledge with one horse, and started alone without a coachman for Jadrino, where Maria ought to arrive in a couple of hours. He knew the road, and the drive would only occupy twenty minutes.

But Vladimir had scarcely passed from the enclosure into the open field when the wind rose, and soon there was a driving snow-storm so heavy and so severe that he could not see. In a moment the road was covered with snow. All landmarks disappeared in the murky yellow darkness, through which fell white flakes of snow. Sky and earth became merged into one. Vladimir, in the midst of the field, tried in vain to get to the road. The horse walked on at random, and every moment stepped either into deep snow or into a rut, so that the sledge was constantly upsetting. Vladimir tried at least not to lose the right direction; but it seemed to him that more than half an hour had passed, and he had not yet reached the Jadrino wood. Another ten minutes passed, and still the wood was invisible. Vladimir drove across fields intersected by deep ditches. The snow-storm did not abate, and the sky did not clear. The horse was getting tired and the perspiration rolled from him like hail, in spite of the fact that every moment his legs were disappearing in the snow.

At last Vladimir found that he was going in the wrong direction. He stopped; began to reflect, recollect, and consider; till at last he became convinced that he ought to have turned to the right. He did so now. His horse could scarcely drag along. But he had been more than an hour on the road, and Jadrino could not now be far. He drove and drove, but there was no getting out of the field. Still snow-drifts and ditches. Every moment the sledge was upset, and every moment Vladimir had to raise it up.

Time was slipping by; and Vladimir grew seriously anxious. At last in the distance some dark object could be seen.

Vladimir turned in its direction, and as he drew near found it was a wood.

" Thank Heaven," he thought, " I am now near the end."

He drove by the side of the wood, hoping to come at once upon the familiar road, or, if not, to pass round the wood. Jadrino was situated immediately behind it.

He soon found the road, and passed into the darkness of the wood, now stripped by the winter. The wind could not rage here; the road was smooth, the horse picked up courage, and Vladimir was comforted.

He drove and drove, but still Jadrino was not to be seen; there was no end to the wood. Then, to his horror, he discovered that he had got into a strange wood! He was in despair. He whipped his horse, and the poor animal started off at a trot. But it soon got tired, and in a quarter of an hour, in spite of all poor Vladimir's efforts, could only crawl.

Gradually the trees became thinner, and Vladimir drove out of the wood; but Jadrino was not to be seen. It must have been about midnight. Tears gushed from the young man's eyes. He drove on at random; and now the weather abated, the clouds dispersed, and before him was a wide stretch of plain covered with a white billowy carpet. The night was comparatively clear, and he could see a small village a short distance off, which consisted of four or five cottages. Vladimir drove towards it. At the first door he jumped out of the sledge, ran up to the window, and tapped.

After a few minutes a wooden shutter was raised, and an old man stuck out his grey beard.

"What do you want?"

"How far is Jadrino?"

"How far is Jadrino?"

"Yes, yes! Is it far?"

"Not far; about ten miles."

At this answer Vladimir clutched hold of his hair, and stood motionless, like a man condemned to death.

"Where do you come from?" added the man. Vladimir had not the courage to reply.

"My man," he said, "can you procure me horses to Jadrino?"

"We have no horses," answered the peasant.

"Could I find a guide? I will pay him any sum he likes."

"Stop!" said the old man, dropping the shutter; "I will send my son out to you; he will conduct you."

Vladimir waited. Scarcely a minute had passed when he again knocked. The shutter was lifted, and a beard was seen.

"What do you want?"

"What about your son?"

"He'll come out directly: he is putting on his boots. Are you cold? Come in and warm yourself."

"Thanks; send out your son quickly."

The gate creaked; a youth came out with a cudgel, and walked on in front, at one time pointing out the road, at another looking for it in a mass of drifted snow.

" What o'clock is it ? " Vladimir asked him.

" It will soon be daylight," replied the young peasant. Vladimir spoke not another word.

The cocks were crowing, and it was light when they reached Jadrino. The church was closed. Vladimir paid the guide, and drove into the yard of the priest's house. In the yard his two-horsed sledge was not to be seen. What news awaited him !

But let us return to the kind proprietors of Nenaradova, and see what is going on there.

Nothing.

The old people awoke, and went into the sitting-room, Gavril in a night-cap and flannel jacket, Praskovia in a wadded dressing-gown. The samovar was brought in, and Gavril sent the little maid to ask Maria how she was and how she had slept. The little maid returned, saying that her young lady had slept badly, but that she was better now, and that she would come into the sitting-room in a moment. And indeed the door opened and Maria came in and wished her papa and mamma good morning.

" How is your headache, Masha ? " (familiar for Mary) inquired Gavril.

" Better, papa," answered Masha.

" The fumes from the stoves must have given you your headache," remarked Praskovia.

" Perhaps so, mamma," replied Masha.

The day passed well enough, but in the night Masha was taken ill. A doctor was sent for from town. He came towards evening and found the patient delirious. Soon she was in a severe fever, and in a fortnight the poor patient was on the brink of the grave.

No member of the family knew anything of the flight from home. The letters written by Masha the evening before had been burnt ; and the maid, fearing the wrath of the master and mistress, had not breathed a word. The priest, the ex-cornet, the big moustached surveyor, and the little lancer were equally discreet, and with good reason. Tereshka, the coachman, never said too much, not even in his drink. Thus the secret was kept better than it might have been by half a dozen conspirators.

But Maria herself, in the course of her long fever, let out her secret. Nevertheless, her words were so disconnected that her mother, who never left her bedside, could only make out from them that her daughter was desperately in love with Vladimir, and that probably love was the cause of her illness. She consulted her husband and some of her neighbours, and at last it was decided unanimously that the fate of Maria ought not to be interfered with, that a woman must not ride away from the man she is destined to marry, that poverty is no crime, that a woman has to live not with money but with a man, and so on. Moral proverbs are wonderfully useful on such occasions, when we can invent little or nothing in our own justification.

Meanwhile the young lady began to recover. Vladimir had not been seen for a long time in the house of Gavril, so frightened had he been by his previous reception. It was now resolved to send and announce to him the good news which he could scarcely expect : the consent of her parents to his marriage with Maria.

But what was the astonishment of the proprietors of Nenaradova when, in answer to their invitation, they received an insane reply. Vladimir informed them he could never set foot in their house, and begged them to forget an unhappy man whose only hope now was in death. A few days afterwards they heard that Vladimir had left the place and joined the army.

A long time passed before they ventured to tell Masha, who was now recovering. She never mentioned Vladimir. Some months later, however, finding his name in the list of those who had distinguished themselves and been severely wounded at Borodino, she fainted, and it was feared that the fever might return. But, Heaven be thanked ! the fainting fit had no bad results.

Maria experienced yet another sorrow. Her father died, leaving her the heiress of all his property. But the inheritance could not console her. She shared sincerely the affliction of her mother, and vowed she would never leave her.

Suitors clustered round the charming heiress ; but she gave no one the slightest hope. Her mother sometimes tried to persuade her to choose a companion in life ; but Maria shook her head, and grew pensive.

Vladimir no longer existed. He had died at Moscow on the eve of the arrival of the French. His memory was held sacred by Maria, and she treasured up everything that would remind her of him : books he had read, drawings which he had made, songs he had sung, and the pieces of poetry which he had copied out for her.

The neighbours, hearing all this, wondered at her fidelity, and awaited with curiosity the arrival of the hero who must in the end triumph over the melancholy constancy of this virgin Artemis.

Meanwhile the war had been brought to a glorious conclusion, and our armies were returning from abroad. The people ran to meet them. The music played by the regimental bands consisted of war songs, " Vive Henri-Quatre," Tirolese waltzes and airs from Joconde. Nourished on the atmosphere of winter, officers who had started on the campaign mere striplings, returned grown men, and covered with decorations. The soldiers conversed gaily among themselves, mingling German and French words every moment in their speech. A time never to be forgotten—a time of glory and delight ! How quickly beat the Russian heart at the words, " Native land ! " How sweet the tears of meeting ! With what unanimity did we combine feelings of national pride with love for the Tsar ! And for him, what a moment !

The women—our Russian women—were splendid then. Their usual coldness disappeared. Their delight was really intoxicating when, meeting the conquerors, they cried, " Hurrah ! " And they threw up their caps in the air.

Who of the officers of that period does not own that to the Russian women he was indebted for his best and most valued reward ? During this brilliant period Maria was living with her mother in retirement, and neither of them saw how, in both the capitals, the returning troops were welcomed. But in the districts and villages the general enthusiasm was, perhaps, even greater. In these places the appearance of an officer became for him a veritable triumph. The accepted lover in plain clothes fared badly by his side.

We have already said that, in spite of her coldness, Maria was still, as before, surrounded by suitors. But all had to fall in the rear when there arrived at his castle the wounded young captain of Hussars—Bourmin by name—with the order of St. George in his button-hole, and an interesting pallor on his face. He was about twenty-six. He had come home on leave to his estates, which were close to Maria's villa. Maria paid him such attention as none of the others received. In his presence her habitual gloom disappeared. It could not be said that she flirted with him. But a poet, observing her behaviour, might have asked, " S' amor non è, che dunque ? "

Bourmin was really a very agreeable young man. He possessed just the kind of sense that pleased women : a sense of what is suitable and becoming. He had no affectation, and was carelessly satirical. His manner towards Maria was simple and easy. He seemed to be of a quiet and modest disposition ; but rumour said that he had at one time been terribly wild. This, however, did not harm him in the opinion of Maria, who (like all young ladies) excused, with pleasure, vagaries which were the result of impulsiveness and daring.

But above all—more than his love-making, more than his pleasant talk, more than his interesting pallor, more even than his bandaged arm—the silence of the young Hussar excited her curiosity and her imagination. She could not help confessing to herself that he pleased her very much. Probably he too, with his acuteness and his experience, had seen that he interested her. How was it, then, that up to this moment she had not seen him at her feet ; had not received from him any declaration whatever ? And wherefore did she not encourage him with more attention, and, according to circumstances, even with tenderness ? Had she a secret of her own which would account for her behaviour ?

At last Bourmin fell into such deep meditation, and his black eyes rested with such fire upon Maria, that the decisive moment seemed very near. The neighbours spoke of the marriage as an accomplished fact, and kind Praskovia rejoiced that her daughter had at last found for herself a worthy mate. The lady was sitting alone once in the drawing-room, laying out grande-patience, when Bourmin entered the room, and at once inquired for Maria.

" She is in the garden," replied the old lady : " go to her, and I will wait for you here." Bourmin went, and the old lady made the sign of the cross and thought, " Perhaps the affair will be settled to-day ! "

Bourmin found Maria in the ivy-bower beside the pond, with a book in her hands, and wearing a white dress—a veritable heroine of romance. After the first inquiries Maria purposely let the conversation drop ; increasing by these means the mutual embarrassment, from which it was only possible to escape by means of a sudden and positive declaration. It happened thus. Bourmin, feeling the awkwardness of his position, informed Maria that he had long sought an opportunity of opening his heart to her, and that he begged for a moment's attention. Maria closed the book and lowered her eyes, as a sign that she was listening.

"I love you," said Bourmin, "I love you passionately!" Maria blushed and bent her head still lower.

"I have behaved imprudently, yielding as I have done to the seductive pleasure of seeing and hearing you daily." Maria recollected the first letter of St. Preux in *La Nouvelle Héloïse*. "It is too late now to resist my fate. The remembrance of you, your dear incomparable image, must from to-day be at once the torment and the consolation of my existence. I have now a terrible secret to disclose, which will place between us an insurmountable barrier."

"It has always existed!" interrupted Maria; "I could never have been your wife."

"I know," he replied quickly; "I know that you once loved. But death and three years of mourning may have worked some change. Dear, kind Maria, do not try to deprive me of my last consolation; the idea that you might have consented to make me happy if——. Don't speak, for God's sake don't speak—you torture me. Yes, I know, I feel that you could have been mine, but—I am the most miserable of beings—I am already married!"

Maria looked at him in astonishment.

"I am married," continued Bourmin; "I have been married more than three years, and do not know who my wife is, or where she is, or whether I shall ever see her again."

"What are you saying?" exclaimed Maria; "how strange! Pray continue."

"In the beginning of 1812," said Bourmin, "I was hurrying on to Wilna, where my regiment was stationed. Arriving one evening late at a station, I ordered the horses to be got ready quickly, when suddenly a fearful snow-storm broke out. Both station-master and drivers advised me to wait till it was over. I listened to their advice, but an unaccountable restlessness took possession of me, just as though some one was pushing me on. Meanwhile, the snow-storm did not abate. I could bear it no longer, and again ordered the horses, and started in the midst of the storm. The driver took it into his head to drive along the river, which would shorten the distance by three miles. The banks were covered with snowdrifts; the driver missed the turning which would have brought us out on to the road, and we turned up in an unknown place. The storm never ceased. I could discern a light, and told the driver to make for it. We entered a village, and found that the light proceeded from a wooden church. The church was open. Outside the railings stood several sledges, and people were passing in and out through the porch.

"'Here! here!' cried several voices. I told the coachman to drive up. 'Where have you dawdled?' said some one to me. 'The bride has fainted; the priest does not know what to do; we were on the point of going back. Make haste and get out!'

"I got out of the sledge in silence, and stepped into the church, which was dimly lighted with two or three tapers. A girl was sitting in a dark corner on a bench; another girl was rubbing her temples. 'Thank God,' said the latter, 'you have come at last! You have nearly been the death of the young lady.'

"The old priest approached me, saying, 'Shall I begin?'

"'Begin—begin, reverend father,' I replied, absently.

"The young lady was raised up. I thought her rather pretty. Oh, wild, unpardonable frivolity! I placed myself by her side at the altar. The priest hurried on. Three men and the maid supported the bride, and occupied themselves with her alone. We were married!

"'Kiss your wife,' said the priest.

"My wife turned her pale face towards me. I was going to kiss her, when she exclaimed, 'Oh! it is not he—not he!' and fell back insensible. The witnesses stared at me. I turned round and left the church without any attempt being made to stop me, threw myself into the sledge, and cried, 'Away!'"

"What!" exclaimed Maria. "And you don't know what became of your unhappy wife?"

"I do not," replied Bourmin; "neither do I know the name of the village where I was married, nor that of the station from which I started. At that time I thought so little of my wicked joke that, on driving away from the church, I fell asleep, and never woke till early the next morning, after reaching the third station. The servant who was with me died during the campaign, so that I have now no hope of ever discovering the unhappy woman on whom I played such a cruel trick, and who is now so cruelly avenged."

"Great heavens!" cried Maria, seizing his hand. "Then it was you, and you do not recognise me?"

Bourmin turned pale—and threw himself at her feet.

THE QUEEN OF SPADES

ALEXANDER S. PUSHKIN

I

THERE was a card party at the rooms of Naroumoff, a lieutenant in the Horse Guards. A long winter night had passed unnoticed, and it was five o'clock in the morning when supper was served. The winners sat down to table with an excellent appetite; the losers let their plates remain empty before them. Little by little, however, with the assistance of the champagne, the conversation became animated, and was shared by all.

"How did you get on this evening, Surin?" said the host to one of his friends.

"Oh, I lost, as usual. I really have no luck. I play *mirandole.* You know that I keep cool. Nothing moves me; I never change my play, and yet I always lose."

"Do you mean to say that all the evening you did not once back the red? Your firmness of character surprises me."

"What do you think of Hermann?" said one of the party, pointing to a young Engineer officer. "That fellow never made a bet or touched a card in his life, and yet he watches us playing until five in the morning."

"It interests me," said Hermann; "but I am not disposed to risk the necessary in view of the superfluous."

"Hermann is a German, and economical; that is the whole of the secret," cried Tomski. "But what is really astonishing is the Countess Anna Fedorovna!"

"How so?" asked several voices.

"Have you not remarked," said Tomski, "that she never plays?"

"Yes," said Naroumoff, "a woman of eighty, who never touches a card; that is indeed something extraordinary!"

"You do not know why?"

"No; is there a reason for it?"

"Just listen. My grandmother, you know, some sixty years ago, went to Paris, and became the rage there. People ran after her in the streets, and called her the 'Muscovite Venus.' Richelieu made love to her, and my grandmother makes out that, by her rigorous demeanour, she almost drove him to suicide. In those days women used to play at faro. One evening at the Court she lost, on *parole*, to the Duke of Orleans, a very considerable sum. When she got home, my grandmother removed her beauty spots, took off her hoops, and in this tragic costume went to my grandfather, told him of her misfortune, and asked him for the money she had to pay. My grandfather, now no more, was, so to say, his wife's steward. He feared her like fire; but the sum she named made him leap into the air. He flew into a rage, made a brief calculation, and proved to my grandmother that in six months she had got through half a million roubles. He told her plainly that he had no villages to sell in Paris, his domains being situated in the neighbourhood of Moscow and of Saratoff; and finally refused point blank. You may imagine the fury of my grandmother. She boxed his ears, and passed the night in another room.

"The next day she returned to the charge. For the first time in her life, she condescended to arguments and explanations. In vain did she try to prove to her husband that there were debts and debts, and that she could not treat a Prince of the blood like her coachmaker.

"All this eloquence was lost. My grandfather was inflexible. My grandmother did not know where to turn. Happily she was acquainted with a man who was very celebrated at this time. You have heard of the Count of St. Germain, about whom so many marvellous stories were told. You know that he passed for a sort of Wandering Jew, and that he was said to possess an elixir of life and the philosopher's stone.

"Some people laughed at him as a charlatan. Casanova, in his memoirs, says that he was a spy. However that may be, in spite of the mystery of his life, St. Germain was much sought after in good society, and was really an agreeable man. Even to this day my grandmother has preserved a genuine affection for him, and she becomes quite angry when any one speaks of him with disrespect.

"It occurred to her that he might be able to advance the sum of which she was in need, and she wrote a note begging him to call. The old magician came at once, and found her plunged in the deepest despair. In two or three words she told him everything; related to him her misfortune and the cruelty of her husband, adding that she had no hope except in his friendship and his obliging disposition.

" 'Madam,' said St. Germain, after a few moments' reflection, 'I could easily advance you the money you want, but I am sure that you would have no rest until you had repaid me, and I do not want to get you out of one trouble in order to place you in another. There is another way of settling the matter. You must regain the money you have lost.'

" 'But, my dear friend,' answered my grandmother, 'I have already told you that I have nothing left.'

" 'That does not matter,' answered St. Germain. 'Listen to me, and I will explain.'

"He then communicated to her a secret which any of you would, I am sure, give a good deal to possess."

All the young officers gave their full attention. Tomski stopped to light his Turkish pipe, swallowed a mouthful of smoke, and then went on.

"That very evening my grandmother went to Versailles to play at the Queen's table. The Duke of Orleans held the bank. My grandmother invented a little story by way of excuse for not having paid her debt, and then sat down at the table, and began to stake. She took three cards. She won with the first; doubled her stake on the second, and won again; doubled on the third, and still won."

"Mere luck!" said one of the young officers.

"What a tale!" cried Hermann.

"Were the cards marked?" said a third.

"I don't think so," replied Tomski gravely.

"And you mean to say," exclaimed Naroumoff, "that you have a grandmother who knows the names of three winning cards, and you have never made her tell them to you?"

"That is the very deuce of it," answered Tomski. "She had three sons, of whom my father was one; all three were determined gamblers, and not one of them was able to extract her secret from her, though it would have been of immense advantage to them, and to me also. Listen to what my uncle told me about it, Count Ivan Ilitch, and he told me on his word of honour.

"Tchaplitzki—the one you remember who died in poverty after devouring millions—lost one day, when he was a young man, to Zoritch about three hundred thousand roubles. He was in despair. My grandmother, who had no mercy for the extravagance of young men, made an exception—I do not know why—in favour of Tchaplitzki. She gave him three cards, telling him to play them one after the other, and exacting from him at the same time his word of honour that he would never afterwards touch a card as long as he lived. Accordingly Tchaplitzki went to Zoritch and asked for his revenge. On the first card he staked fifty thousand roubles. He won, doubled the stake, and won again. Continuing his system he ended by gaining more than he had lost.

"But it is six o'clock! It is really time to go to bed."

Every one emptied his glass and the party broke up.

II

The old Countess Anna Fedorovna was in her dressing-room, seated before her looking-glass. Three maids were in attendance. One held her pot of rouge, another a box of black pins, a third an enormous lace cap, with flaming ribbons. The Countess had no longer the slightest pretence to beauty, but she preserved all the habits of her youth. She dressed in the style of fifty years before, and gave as much time and attention to her toilet as a fashionable beauty of the last century. Her companion was working at a frame in a corner of the window.

"Good morning, grandmother," said the young officer, as he entered the dressing-room. "Good morning, Mademoiselle Lise. Grandmother, I have come to ask you a favour."

"What is it, Paul?"

"I want to introduce to you one of my friends, and to ask you to give him an invitation to your ball."

"Bring him to the ball and introduce him to me there. Did you go yesterday to the Princess's?"

"Certainly. It was delightful! We danced until five o'clock in the morning. Mademoiselle Eletzki was charming."

"My dear nephew, you are really not difficult to please. As to beauty, you should have seen her grandmother, the Princess Daria Petrovna. But she must be very old, the Princess Daria Petrovna!"

"How do you mean old?" cried Tomski thoughtlessly; "she died seven years ago."

The young lady who acted as companion raised her head and made a sign to the officer, who then remembered that it was an understood thing to conceal from the Princess the death of any of her contemporaries. He bit his lips. The Countess, however, was not in any way disturbed on hearing that her old friend was no longer in this world.

"Dead!" she said, "and I never knew it! We were maids of honour in the same year, and when we were presented, the Empress"—and the old Countess related for the hundredth time an anecdote of her young days. "Paul," she said, as she finished her story, "help me to get up. Lisabeta, where is my snuff-box?"

And, followed by the three maids, she went behind a great screen to finish her toilet. Tomski was now alone with the companion.

"Who is the gentleman you wish to introduce to madame?" asked Lisabeta.

"Naroumoff. Do you know him?"

"No. Is he in the army?"

"Yes."

"In the Engineers?"

"No, in the Horse Guards. Why did you think he was in the Engineers?"

The young lady smiled, but made no answer.

"Paul," cried the Countess from behind the screen, "send me a new novel; no matter what. Only see that it is not in the style of the present day."

"What style would you like, grandmother?"

"A novel in which the hero strangles neither his father nor his mother, and in which no one gets drowned. Nothing frightens me so much as the idea of getting drowned."

"But how is it possible to find you such a book? Do you want it in Russian?"

"Are there any novels in Russian? However, send me something or other. You won't forget?"

"I will not forget, grandmother. I am in a great hurry. Good-bye, Lisabeta. What made you fancy Naroumoff was in the Engineers?" and Tomski took his departure.

Lisabeta, left alone, took out her embroidery, and sat down close to the window. Immediately afterwards, in the street, at the corner of a neighbouring house, appeared a young officer. The sight of him made the companion blush to her ears. She lowered her head, and almost concealed it in the linen. At this moment the Countess returned, fully dressed.

" Lisabeta," she said, " have the horses put in ; we will go out for a drive."

Lisabeta rose from her chair, and began to arrange her embroidery.

" Well, my dear child, are you deaf ? Go and tell them to put the horses in at once."

" I am going," replied the young lady, as she went out into the ante-chamber.

A servant now came in, bringing some books from Prince Paul Alexandrovitch.

" Say I am much obliged to him. Lisabeta ! Lisabeta ! Where has she run off to ? "

" I was going to dress."

" We have plenty of time, my dear. Sit down, take the first volume, and read to me."

The companion took the book and read a few lines.

" Louder," said the Countess. " What is the matter with you ? Have you a cold ? Wait a moment, bring me that stool. A little closer ; that will do."

Lisabeta read two pages of the book.

" Throw that stupid book away," said the Countess. " What nonsense ! Send it back to Prince Paul, and tell him I am much obliged to him ; and the carriage, is it never coming ? "

" Here it is," replied Lisabeta, going to the window.

" And now you are not dressed. Why do you always keep me waiting ? It is intolerable ! "

Lisabeta ran to her room. She had scarcely been there two minutes when the Countess rang with all her might. Her maids rushed in at one door and her valet at the other.

" You do not seem to hear me when I ring," she cried. " Go and tell Lisabeta that I am waiting for her."

At this moment Lisabeta entered, wearing a new walking dress and a fashionable bonnet.

" At last, miss," cried the Countess. " But what is that you have got on ? and why ? For whom are you dressing ? What sort of weather is it ? Quite stormy, I believe."

" No, your Excellency," said the valet ; " it is exceedingly fine."

" What do you know about it ? Open the ventilator. Just what I told you ! A frightful wind, and as icy as can be. Unharness the horses. Lisabeta, my child, we will not go out to-day. It was scarcely worth while to dress so much."

"What an existence!" said the companion to herself.

Lisabeta Ivanovna was, in fact, a most unhappy creature. "The bread of the stranger is bitter," says Dante, "and his staircase hard to climb." But who can tell the torments of a poor little companion attached to an old lady of quality? The Countess had all the caprices of a woman spoilt by the world. She was avaricious and egotistical; and thought all the more of herself now that she had ceased to play an active part in society. She never missed a ball, and she dressed and painted in the style of a bygone age. She remained in a corner of the room, where she seemed to have been placed expressly to serve as a scarecrow. Every one on coming in went to her and made her a low bow, but this ceremony once at an end no one spoke a word to her. She received the whole city at her house, observing the strictest etiquette, and never failing to give to every one his or her proper name. Her innumerable servants, growing pale and fat in the ante-chamber, did absolutely as they liked, so that the house was pillaged as if its owner were really dead. Lisabeta passed her life in continual torture. If she made tea she was reproached with wasting the sugar. If she read a novel to the Countess she was held responsible for all the absurdities of the author. If she went out with the noble lady for a walk or drive, it was she who was to blame if the weather was bad or the pavement muddy. Her salary, more than modest, was never punctually paid, and she was expected to dress "like every one else"; that is to say, like very few people indeed. When she went into society her position was sad. Every one knew her; no one paid her any attention. At a ball she sometimes danced, but only when a *vis-à-vis* was wanted. Women would come up to her, take her by the arm, and lead her out of the room if their dress required attending to. She had her portion of self-respect, and felt deeply the misery of her position. She looked with impatience for a liberator to break her chain. But the young men, prudent in the midst of their affected giddiness, took care not to honour her with their attentions, though Lisabeta Ivanovna was a hundred times prettier than the shameless or stupid girls whom they surrounded with their homage. More than once she slunk away from the splendour of the drawing-room to shut herself up alone in her little bedroom, furnished with an old screen and a pieced carpet, a chest of drawers, a small looking-glass, and a wooden bedstead. There she shed tears at her ease, by the light of a tallow candle in a tin candlestick.

One morning—it was two days after the party at Naroumoff's, and a week before the scene we have just sketched—Lisabeta was sitting at her embroidery before the window, when, looking carelessly into the street, she saw an officer, in the uniform of the Engineers, standing motionless with his eyes fixed upon her. She lowered her head, and applied herself to her work more attentively than ever. Five minutes afterwards she looked mechanically into the street, and the officer was still in the same place. Not being in the habit of exchanging glances with young men who passed by her window, she remained with her eyes fixed on her work for nearly two hours, until she was told that lunch was ready. She got up to put her embroidery away, and, while doing so, looked into the street, and saw the officer still in the same place. This seemed to her very strange. After lunch she went to the window with a certain emotion, but the officer of Engineers was no longer in the street.

She thought no more of him. But two days afterwards, just as she was getting into the carriage with the Countess, she saw him once more, standing straight before the door. His face was half concealed by a fur collar, but his black eyes sparkled beneath his helmet. Lisabeta was afraid, without knowing why, and she trembled as she took her seat in the carriage.

On returning home, she rushed with a beating heart towards the window. The officer was in his habitual place, with his eyes fixed ardently upon her. She at once withdrew, burning at the same time with curiosity, and moved by a strange feeling, which she now experienced for the first time.

No day now passed but the young officer showed himself beneath the window. Before long a dumb acquaintance was established between them. Sitting at her work she felt his presence, and when she raised her head she looked at him for a long time every day. The young man seemed full of gratitude for these innocent favours.

She observed, with the deep and rapid perceptions of youth, that a sudden redness covered the officer's pale cheeks as soon as their eyes met. After about a week she would smile at seeing him for the first time.

When Tomski asked his grandmother's permission to present one of his friends, the heart of the poor young girl beat strongly, and when she heard that it was Naroumoff, she bitterly repented having compromised her secret by letting it out to a giddy young man like Paul.

Hermann was the son of a German settled in Russia, from whom he had inherited a small sum of money. Firmly resolved to preserve his independence, he had made it a principle not to touch his private income. He lived on his pay, and did not allow himself the slightest luxury. He was not very communicative; and his reserve rendered it difficult for his comrades to amuse themselves at his expense.

Under an assumed calm he concealed strong passions and a highly-imaginative disposition. But he was always master of himself, and kept himself free from the ordinary faults of young men. Thus, a gambler by temperament, he never touched a card, feeling, as he himself said, that his position did not allow him to "risk the necessary in view of the superfluous." Yet he would pass entire nights before a card-table, watching with feverish anxiety the rapid changes of the game. The anecdote of Count St. Germain's three cards had struck his imagination, and he did nothing but think of it all that night.

"If," he said to himself next day as he was walking along the streets of St. Petersburg, "if she would only tell me her secret—if she would only name the three winning cards! I must get presented to her, that I may pay my court and gain her confidence. Yes! And she is eighty-seven! She may die this week—to-morrow perhaps. But after all, is there a word of truth in the story? No! Economy, Temperance, Work; these are my three winning cards. With them I can double my capital; increase it tenfold. They alone can ensure my independence and prosperity."

Dreaming in this way as he walked along, his attention was attracted by a house built in an antiquated style of architecture. The street was full of carriages, which passed one by one before the old house, now brilliantly illuminated. As the people stepped out of the carriages Hermann saw now the little feet of a young woman, now the military boot of a general. Then came a clocked stocking, then a diplomatic pump. Fur-lined cloaks and coats passed in procession before a gigantic porter.

Hermann stopped. "Who lives here?" he said to a watchman in his box.

"The Countess Anna Fedorovna." It was Tomski's grandmother.

Hermann started. The story of the three cards came once more upon his imagination. He walked to and fro before the house, thinking of the woman to whom it belonged, of her wealth and her mysterious power. At last he returned to his den. But for some time he could not get to sleep ; and when at last sleep came upon him, he saw, dancing before his eyes, cards, a green table, and heaps of roubles and bank-notes. He saw himself doubling stake after stake, always winning, and then filling his pockets with piles of coin, and stuffing his pocket-book with countless bank-notes. When he awoke, he sighed to find that his treasures were but creations of a disordered fancy ; and, to drive such thoughts from him, he went out for a walk. But he had not gone far when he found himself once more before the house of the Countess. He seemed to have been attracted there by some irresistible force. He stopped, and looked up at the windows. There he saw a girl's head with beautiful black hair, leaning gracefully over a book or an embroidery-frame. The head was lifted, and he saw a fresh complexion and black eyes.

This moment decided his fate.

III

Lisabeta was just taking off her shawl and her bonnet when the Countess sent for her. She had had the horses put in again.

While two footmen were helping the old lady into the carriage, Lisabeta saw the young officer at her side. She felt him take her by the hand, lost her head, and found, when the young officer had walked away, that he had left a paper between her fingers. She hastily concealed it in her glove.

During the whole of the drive she neither saw nor heard. When they were in the carriage together the Countess was in the habit of questioning Lisabeta perpetually.

" Who is that man that bowed to us ? What is the name of this bridge ? What is there written on that signboard ? "

Lisabeta now gave the most absurd answers, and was accordingly scolded by the Countess.

" What is the matter with you, my child ? " she asked. " What are you thinking about ? Or do you really not hear me ? I speak distinctly enough, however, and I have not yet lost my head, have I ? "

Lisabeta was not listening. When she got back to the house

she ran to her room, locked the door, and took the scrap of paper from her glove. It was not sealed, and it was impossible, therefore, not to read it. The letter contained protestations of love. It was tender, respectful, and translated word for word from a German novel. But Lisabeta did not read German, and she was quite delighted. She was, however, much embarrassed. For the first time in her life she had a secret. Correspond with a young man! The idea of such a thing frightened her. How imprudent she had been! She had reproached herself, but knew not now what to do.

Cease to do her work at the window, and by persistent coldness try and disgust the young officer? Send him back his letter? Answer him in a firm, decided manner? What line of conduct was she to pursue? She had no friend, no one to advise her. She at last decided to send an answer. She sat down at her little table, took pen and paper, and began to think. More than once she wrote a sentence and then tore up the paper. What she had written seemed too stiff, or else it was wanting in reserve. At last, after much trouble, she succeeded in composing a few lines which seemed to meet the case. "I believe," she wrote, "that your intentions are those of an honourable man, and that you would not wish to offend me by any thoughtless conduct. But you must understand that our acquaintance cannot begin in this way. I return your letter, and trust that you will not give me cause to regret my imprudence."

Next day as soon as Hermann made his appearance, Lisabeta left her embroidery, and went into the drawing-room, opened the ventilator, and threw her letter into the street, making sure that the young officer would pick it up.

Hermann, in fact, at once saw it, and, picking it up, entered a confectioner's shop in order to read it. Finding nothing discouraging in it, he went home sufficiently pleased with the first step in his love adventure.

Some days afterwards, a young person with lively eyes called to see Miss Lisabeta, on the part of a milliner. Lisabeta wondered what she could want, and suspected, as she received her, some secret intention. She was much surprised, however, when she recognised, on the letter that was now handed to her, the writing of Hermann.

"You make a mistake," she said, "this letter is not for me."

"I beg your pardon," said the milliner, with a slight smile; "be kind enough to read it."

Lisabeta glanced at it. Hermann was asking for an appointment.

" Impossible ! " she cried, alarmed both at the boldness of the request and at the manner in which it was made. " This letter is not for me," she repeated ; and she tore it intò a hundred pieces.

" If the letter was not for you, why did you tear it up ? You should have given it me back, that I might take it to the person it was meant for."

" True," said Lisabeta, quite disconcerted. " But bring me no more letters, and tell the person who gave you this one that he ought to blush for his conduct."

Hermann, however, was not a man to give up what he had once undertaken. Every day Lisabeta received a fresh letter from him,—sent now in one way, now in another. They were no longer translated from the German. Hermann wrote under the influence of a commanding passion, and in a language which was his own. Lisabeta could not hold out against such torrents of eloquence. She received the letters, kept them, and at last answered them. Every day her answers were longer and more affectionate, until at last she threw out of the window a letter couched as follows :—

" This evening there is a ball at the Embassy. The Countess will be there. We shall remain until two in the morning. You may manage to see me alone. As soon as the Countess leaves home, that is to say towards eleven o'clock, the servants are sure to go out, and there will be no one left but the porter, who will be sure to be asleep in his box. Enter as soon as it strikes eleven, and go upstairs as fast as possible. If you find any one in the ante-chamber, ask whether the Countess is at home, and you will be told that she is out, and, in that case, you must resign yourself, and go away. In all probability, however, you will meet no one. The Countess's women are together in a distant room. When you are once in the ante-chamber, turn to the left, and walk straight on, until you reach the Countess's bedroom. There, behind a large screen, you will see two doors. The one on the right leads to a dark room. The one on the left leads to a corridor, at the end of which is a little winding staircase, which leads to my parlour."

At ten o'clock Hermann was already on duty before the Countess's door. It was a frightful night. The winds had been unloosed, and the snow was falling in large flakes ; the lamps gave an uncertain light ; the streets were deserted ; from time to time passed a sleigh, drawn by a wretched hack, on the look-out for a fare. Covered by a thick overcoat, Hermann felt neither the wind nor the snow. At last the Countess's carriage drew up. He saw two huge footmen come forward and take beneath the arms a dilapidated spectre, and place it on the cushions, well wrapped up in an enormous fur cloak. Immediately afterwards, in a cloak of lighter make, her head crowned with natural flowers, came Lisabeta, who sprang into the carriage like a dart. The door was closed, and the carriage rolled on softly over the snow.

The porter closed the street door, and soon the windows of the first floor became dark. Silence reigned throughout the house. Hermann walked backwards and forwards; then coming to a lamp he looked at his watch. It was twenty minutes to eleven. Leaning against the lamp-post, his eyes fixed on the long hand of his watch, he counted impatiently the minutes which had yet to pass. At eleven o'clock precisely Hermann walked up the steps, pushed open the street door, and went into the vestibule, which was well lighted. As it happened the porter was not there. With a firm and rapid step he rushed up the staircase and reached the ante-chamber. There, before a lamp, a footman was sleeping, stretched out in a dirty greasy dressing-gown. Hermann passed quickly before him and crossed the dining-room and the drawing-room, where there was no light. But the lamp of the ante-chamber helped him to see. At last he reached the Countess's bedroom. Before a screen covered with old icons [sacred pictures] a golden lamp was burning. Gilt arm-chairs, sofas of faded colours, furnished with soft cushions, were arranged symmetrically along the walls, which were hung with China silk. He saw two large portraits, painted by Madame le Brun. One represented a man of forty, stout and full coloured, dressed in a light green coat, with a decoration on his breast. The second portrait was that of an elegant young woman, with an aquiline nose, powdered hair rolled back on the temples, and with a rose over her ear. Everywhere might be seen shepherds and shepherdesses in Dresden china, with vases of all shapes, clocks by Leroy, work-baskets, fans, and all the thousand playthings for the use of ladies of fashion, discovered at the time of Montgolfier's balloons and Mesmer's animal magnetism.

Hermann passed behind the screen, which concealed a little iron bedstead. He saw the two doors; the one on the right leading to the dark room, the one on the left to the corridor. He opened the latter, saw the staircase which led to the poor little companion's parlour, and then, closing this door, went into the dark room.

The time passed slowly. Everything was quiet in the house. The drawing-room clock struck midnight, and again there was silence. Hermann was standing up, leaning against the stove, in which there was no fire. He was calm; but his heart beat with quick pulsations, like that of a man determined to brave all dangers he might have to meet, because he knows them to be inevitable. He heard one o'clock strike; then two; and soon afterwards the distant roll of a carriage. He now, in spite of himself, experienced some emotion. The carriage approached rapidly and stopped. There was at once a great noise of servants running about the staircases, and a confusion of voices. Suddenly the rooms were all lit up, and the Countess's three antiquated maids came at once into the bedroom. At last appeared the Countess herself.

The walking mummy sank into a large Voltaire armchair. Hermann looked through the crack in the door; he saw Lisabeta pass close to him, and heard her hurried step as she went up the little winding staircase. For a moment he felt something like remorse; but it soon passed off, and his heart was once more of stone.

The Countess began to undress before a looking-glass. Her head-dress of roses was taken off, and her powdered wig separated from her own hair, which was very short and quite white. Pins fell in showers around her. At last she was in her dressing-gown and her night-cap, and in this costume, more suitable to her age, was less hideous than before.

Like most old people, the Countess was tormented by sleeplessness. She had her armchair rolled towards one of the windows, and told her maids to leave her. The lights were put out, and the room was lighted only by the lamp which burned before the holy images. The Countess, sallow and wrinkled, balanced herself gently from right to left. In her dull eyes could be read an utter absence of thought; and as she moved from side to side, one might have said that she did so not by any action of the will, but through some secret mechanism.

Suddenly this death's-head assumed a new expression; the lips ceased to tremble, and the eyes became alive. A strange man had appeared before the Countess!

It was Hermann.

"Do not be alarmed, madam," said Hermann, in a low voice, but very distinctly. " For the love of Heaven, do not be alarmed. I do not wish to do you the slightest harm; on the contrary, I come to implore a favour of you."

The old woman looked at him in silence, as if she did not understand. Thinking she was deaf, he leaned towards her ear and repeated what he had said; but the Countess still remained silent.

" You can ensure the happiness of my whole life, and without its costing you a farthing. I know that you can name to me three cards——"

The Countess now understood what he required.

" It was a joke," she interrupted. " I swear to you it was only a joke."

" No, madam," replied Hermann in an angry tone. " Remember Tchaplitzki, and how you enabled him to win."

The Countess was agitated. For a moment her features expressed strong emotion; but they soon resumed their former dulness.

" Cannot you name to me," said Hermann, " three winning cards?"

The Countess remained silent. " Why keep this secret for your great-grandchildren?" he continued. " They are rich enough without; they do not know the value of money. Of what profit would your three cards be to them? They are debauchees. The man who cannot keep his inheritance will die in want, though he had the science of demons at his command. I am a steady man. I know the value of money. Your three cards will not be lost upon me. Come!"

He stopped tremblingly, awaiting a reply. The Countess did not utter a word. Hermann went upon his knees.

" If your heart has ever known the passion of love; if you can remember its sweet ecstasies; if you have ever been touched by the cry of a new-born babe; if any human feeling has ever caused your heart to beat, I entreat you by the love of a husband, a lover, a mother, by all that is sacred in life, not to reject my prayer. Tell me your secret! Reflect! You are old; you have not long to live! Remember that the happiness of a man is in your hands; that not only myself, but my children and my grandchildren will bless your memory as a saint."

The old Countess answered not a word.

Hermann rose, and drew a pistol from his pocket.

" Hag!" he exclaimed, " I will make you speak."

At the sight of the pistol the Countess for the second time showed agitation. Her head shook violently; she stretched out her hands as if to put the weapon aside. Then suddenly she fell back motionless.

" Come, don't be childish!" said Hermann. " I adjure you for the last time; will you name the three cards?"

The Countess did not answer. Hermann saw that she was dead!

IV

Lisabeta was sitting in her room, still in her ball dress, lost in the deepest meditation. On her return to the house, she had sent away her maid, and had gone upstairs to her room, trembling at the idea of finding Hermann there; desiring, indeed, *not* to find him. One glance showed her that he was not there, and she gave thanks to Providence that he had missed the appointment. She sat down pensively, without thinking of taking off her cloak, and allowed to pass through her memory all the circumstances of the intrigue which had begun such a short time back, and had already advanced so far. Scarcely three weeks had passed since she had first seen the young officer from her window, and already she had written to him, and he had succeeded in inducing her to make an appointment. She knew his name, and that was all. She had received a quantity of letters from him, but he had never spoken to her; she did not know the sound of his voice, and until that evening, strangely enough, she had never heard him spoken of.

But that very evening Tomski, fancying he had noticed that the young Princess Pauline, to whom he had been paying assiduous court, was flirting, contrary to her custom, with another man, had wished to revenge himself by making a show of indifference. With this noble object he had invited Lisabeta to take part in an interminable mazurka; but he teased her immensely about her partiality for Engineer officers, and pretending all the time to know much more than he really did, hazarded purely in fun a few guesses which were so happy that Lisabeta thought her secret must have been discovered.

" But who tells you all this?" she said with a smile.

" A friend of the very officer you know, a most original man."

" And who is this man that is so original?"

" His name is Hermann."

She answered nothing, but her hands and feet seemed to be of ice.

" Hermann is a hero of romance," continued Tomski. " He has the profile of Napoleon, and the soul of Mephistopheles. I believe he has at least three crimes on his conscience. . . . But how pale you are ! "

" I have a bad headache. But what did this Mr. Hermann tell you ? Is not that his name ? "

" Hermann is very much displeased with his friend, with the Engineer officer who has made your acquaintance. He says that in his place he would behave very differently. But I am quite sure that Hermann himself has designs upon you. At least, he seems to listen with remarkable interest to all that his friend tells him about you."

" And where has he seen me ? "

" Perhaps in church, perhaps in the street ; heaven knows where."

At this moment three ladies came forward according to the custom of the mazurka, and asked Tomski to choose between " forgetfulness and regret." [1]

And the conversation which had so painfully excited the curiosity of Lisabeta came to an end.

The lady who, in virtue of the infidelities permitted by the mazurka, had just been chosen by Tomski, was the Princess Pauline. During the rapid evolutions which the figure obliged them to make, there was a grand explanation between them, until at last he conducted her to a chair, and returned to his partner.

But Tomski could now think no more, either of Hermann or Lisabeta, and he tried in vain to resume the conversation. But the mazurka was coming to an end, and immediately afterwards the old Countess rose to go.

Tomski's mysterious phrases were nothing more than the usual platitudes of the mazurka, but they had made a deep impression upon the heart of the poor little companion. The portrait sketched by Tomski had struck her as very exact ; and with her romantic ideas, she saw in the rather ordinary countenance of her adorer something to fear and admire. She was now sitting down with her cloak off, with bare shoulders ; her head, crowned with flowers, falling forward from fatigue, when suddenly the door opened and Hermann entered. She shuddered.

" Where were you ? " she said, trembling all over.

[1] The figures and fashions of the mazurka are reproduced in the cotillon of Western Europe.—TRANSLATOR.

"In the Countess's bedroom. I have just left her," replied Hermann. "She is dead."

"Great heavens! What are you saying?"

"I am afraid," he said, "that I am the cause of her death."

Lisabeta looked at him in consternation, and remembered Tomski's words: "He has at least three crimes on his conscience."

Hermann sat down by the window, and told everything. The young girl listened with terror.

So those letters so full of passion, those burning expressions, this daring obstinate pursuit—all this had been inspired by anything but love! Money alone had inflamed the man's soul. She, who had nothing but a heart to offer, how could she make him happy? Poor child! she had been the blind instrument of a robber, of the murderer of her old benefactress. She wept bitterly in the agony of her repentance. Hermann watched her in silence; but neither the tears of the unhappy girl, nor her beauty, rendered more touching by her grief, could move his heart of iron. He had no remorse in thinking of the Countess's death. One sole thought distressed him—the irreparable loss of the secret which was to have made his fortune.

"You are a monster!" said Lisabeta, after a long silence.

"I did not mean to kill her," replied Hermann coldly. "My pistol was not loaded."

They remained for some time without speaking, without looking at one another. The day was breaking, and Lisabeta put out her candle. She wiped her eyes, drowned in tears, and raised them towards Hermann. He was standing close to the window, his arms crossed, with a frown on his forehead. In this attitude he reminded her involuntarily of the portrait of Napoleon. The resemblance overwhelmed her.

"How am I to get you away?" she said at last. "I thought you might go out by the back stairs. But it would be necessary to go through the Countess's bedroom, and I am too frightened."

"Tell me how to get to the staircase, and I will go alone."

She went to a drawer, took out a key, which she handed to Hermann, and gave him the necessary instructions. Hermann took her icy hand, kissed her on the forehead, and departed.

He went down the staircase and entered the Countess's bedroom. She was seated quite stiff in her armchair, but her features were in no way contracted. He stopped for a moment, and gazed into her face as if to make sure of the terrible reality. Then he entered the dark room, and, feeling behind the tapestry, found the little door which opened on to a staircase. As he went down it, strange ideas came into his head. "Going down this staircase," he said to himself, "some sixty years ago, at about this time, may have been seen some man in an embroidered coat with powdered wig, pressing to his breast a cocked hat: some gallant who has long been buried; and now the heart of his aged mistress has ceased to beat."

At the end of the staircase he found another door, which his key opened, and he found himself in the corridor which led to the street.

V

Three days after this fatal night, at nine o'clock in the morning, Hermann entered the convent where the last respects were to be paid to the mortal remains of the old Countess. He felt no remorse, though he could not deny to himself that he was the poor woman's assassin. Having no religion, he was, as usual in such cases, very superstitious; believing that the dead Countess might exercise a malignant influence on his life, he thought to appease her spirit by attending her funeral.

The church was full of people, and it was difficult to get in. The body had been placed on a rich catafalque, beneath a canopy of velvet. The Countess was reposing in an open coffin, her hands joined on her breast, with a dress of white satin, and head-dress of lace. Around the catafalque the family was assembled, the servants in black caftans with a knot of ribbons on the shoulder, exhibiting the colours of the Countess's coat-of-arms. Each of them held a wax candle in his hand. The relations, in deep mourning—children, grandchildren, and great-grandchildren—were all present; but none of them wept.

To have shed tears would have looked like affectation. The Countess was so old that her death could have taken no one by surprise, and she had long been looked upon as already out of the world. The funeral sermon was delivered by a celebrated preacher. In a few simple, touching phrases he painted the final departure of the just, who had passed long years of contrite preparation for a Christian end. The service concluded in the midst of respectful silence. Then the relations went towards the defunct to take a last farewell. After them, in a long procession, all who had been invited to the ceremony bowed, for the last time, to her who for so many years had been a scarecrow at their entertainments. Finally came the Countess's household; among them was remarked an old governess, of the same age as the deceased, supported by two women. She had not strength enough to kneel down, but tears flowed from her eyes, as she kissed the hand of her old mistress.

In his turn Hermann advanced towards the coffin. He knelt down for a moment on the flagstones, which were strewed with branches of yew. Then he rose, as pale as death, and walked up the steps of the catafalque. He bowed his head. But suddenly the dead woman seemed to be staring at him; and with a mocking look she opened and shut one eye. Hermann by a sudden movement started and fell backwards. Several persons hurried towards him. At the same moment, close to the church door, Lisabeta fainted.

Throughout the day, Hermann suffered from a strange indisposition. In a quiet restaurant, where he took his meals, he, contrary to his habit, drank a great deal of wine, with the object of stupefying himself. But the wine had no effect but to excite his imagination, and give fresh activity to the ideas with which he was preoccupied.

He went home earlier than usual; lay down with his clothes on upon the bed, and fell into a leaden sleep. When he woke up it was night, and the room was lighted up by the rays of the moon. He looked at his watch; it was a quarter to three. He could sleep no more. He sat up on the bed and thought of the old Countess. At this moment some one in the street passed the window, looked into the room, and then went on. Hermann scarcely noticed it; but in another minute he heard the door of the ante-chamber open. He thought that his orderly, drunk as usual, was returning from some nocturnal excursion; but the step was one to which he was not accustomed. Somebody seemed to be softly walking over the floor in slippers.

The door opened, and a woman, dressed entirely in white, entered the bedroom. Hermann thought it must be his old nurse, and he asked himself what she could want at that time of night.

But the woman in white, crossing the room with a rapid step, was now at the foot of his bed, and Hermann recognised the Countess.

"I come to you against my wish," she said in a firm voice. "I am forced to grant your prayer. Three, seven, ace will win, if played one after the other; but you must not play more than one card in twenty-four hours, and afterwards as long as you live you must never touch a card again. I forgive you my death, on condition of your marrying my companion, Lisabeta Ivanovna."

With these words she walked towards the door, and gliding with her slippers over the floor, disappeared. Hermann heard the door of the ante-chamber open, and soon afterwards saw a white figure pass along the street. It stopped for a moment before his window, as if to look at him.

Hermann remained for some time astounded. Then he got up and went into the next room. His orderly, drunk as usual, was asleep on the floor. He had much difficulty in waking him, and then could not obtain from him the least explanation. The door of the ante-chamber was locked.

Hermann went back to his bedroom, and wrote down all the details of his vision.

VI

Two fixed ideas can no more exist together in the moral world than in the physical two bodies can occupy the same place at the same time; and "three, seven, ace" soon drove away Hermann's recollection of the old Countess's last moments. "Three, seven, ace" were now in his head to the exclusion of everything else.

They followed him in his dreams, and appeared to him under strange forms. Threes seemed to be spread before him like magnolias, sevens took the form of Gothic doors, and aces became gigantic spiders.

His thoughts concentrated themselves on one single point. How was he to profit by the secret so dearly purchased? What if he applied for leave to travel? At Paris, he said to himself, he would find some gambling-house where, with his three cards, he could at once make his fortune.

Chance soon came to his assistance. There was at Moscow a society of rich gamblers, presided over by the celebrated Tchekalinski, who had passed all his life playing at cards, and had amassed millions. For while he lost silver only, he gained bank-notes. His magnificent house, his excellent kitchen, his cordial manners had brought him numerous friends and secured for him general esteem.

When he came to St. Petersburg, the young men of the capital filled his rooms, forsaking balls for his card-parties, and preferring the emotions of gambling to the fascinations of flirting. Hermann was taken to Tchekalinski by Naroumoff. They passed through a long suite of rooms, full of the most attentive, obsequious servants. The place was crowded. Generals and high officials were playing at whist ; young men were stretched out on the sofas, eating ices and smoking long pipes. In the principal room at the head of a long table, around which were assembled a score of players, the master of the house held a faro bank.

He was a man of about sixty, with a sweet and noble expression of face, and hair white as snow. On his full, florid countenance might be read good humour and benevolence. His eyes shone with a perpetual smile. Naroumoff introduced Hermann. Tchekalinski took him by the hand, told him that he was glad to see him, that no one stood on ceremony in his house ; and then went on dealing. The deal occupied some time, and stakes were made on more than thirty cards. Tchekalinski waited patiently to allow the winners time to double their stakes, paid what he had lost, listened politely to all observations, and, more politely still, put straight the corners of cards, when in a fit of absence some one had taken the liberty of turning them down. At last when the game was at an end, Tchekalinski collected the cards, shuffled them again, had them cut, and then dealt anew.

" Will you allow me to take a card ? " said Hermann, stretching out his arm above a fat man who occupied nearly the whole of one side of the table. Tchekalinski, with a gracious smile, bowed in consent. Naroumoff complimented Hermann, with a laugh, on the cessation of the austerity by which his conduct had hitherto been marked, and wished him all kinds of happiness on the occasion of his first appearance in the character of a gambler.

" There ! " said Hermann, after writing some figures on the back of his card.

" How much ? " asked the banker, half closing his eyes. " Excuse me, I cannot see."

" Forty-seven thousand roubles," said Hermann.

Every one's eyes were directed toward the new player.

" He has lost his head," thought Naroumoff.

" Allow me to point out to you," said Tchekalinski, with his eternal smile, " that you are playing rather high. We never put down here, as a first stake, more than a hundred and seventy-five roubles."

" Very well," said Hermann; " but do you accept my stake or not ? "

Tchekalinski bowed in token of acceptance. " I only wish to point out to you," he said, " that although I am perfectly sure of my friends,

I can only play against ready money. I am quite convinced that your word is as good as gold ; but to keep up the rules of the game, and to facilitate calculations, I should be obliged to you if you would put the money on your card."

Hermann took a bank-note from his pocket and handed it to Tchekalinski, who, after examining it with a glance, placed it on Hermann's card.

Then he began to deal. He turned up on the right a ten, and on the left a three.

" I win," said Hermann, exhibiting his three.

A murmur of astonishment ran through the assembly. The banker knitted his eyebrows, but speedily his face resumed its everlasting smile.

" Shall I settle at once ? " he asked.

" If you will be kind enough to do so," said Hermann.

Tchekalinski took a bundle of bank-notes from his pocket-book and paid. Hermann pocketed his winnings and left the table.

Naroumoff was lost in astonishment. Hermann drank a glass of lemonade and went home.

The next evening he returned to the house. Tchekalinski again held the bank. Hermann went to the table, and this time the players hastened to make room for him. Tchekalinski received him with a most gracious bow. Hermann waited, took a card, and staked on it his forty-seven thousand roubles, together with the like sum which he had gained the evening before.

Tchekalinski began to deal. He turned up on the right a knave, and on the left a seven.

Hermann exhibited a seven.

There was a general exclamation. Tchekalinski was evidently ill at ease, but he counted out the ninety-four thousand roubles to Hermann, who took them in the calmest manner, rose from the table, and went away.

The next evening, at the accustomed hour, he again appeared. Every one was expecting him. Generals and high officials had left their whist to watch this extraordinary play. The young officers had quitted their sofas, and even the servants of the house pressed round the table.

When Hermann took his seat, the other players ceased to stake, so impatient were they to see him have it out with the banker, who, still smiling, watched the approach of his antagonist and prepared to meet him. Each of them untied at the same time a pack of cards. Tchekalinski shuffled, and Hermann cut. Then the latter took up a card and covered it with a heap of bank-notes. It was like the preliminaries of a duel. A deep silence reigned through the room.

Tchekalinski took up the cards with trembling hands and dealt. On one side he put down a queen and on the other side an ace.

" Ace wins," said Hermann.

" No. Queen loses," said Tchekalinski.

Hermann looked. Instead of ace, he saw a queen of spades before him. He could not trust his eyes! And now as he gazed in fascination on the fatal card, he fancied that he saw the queen of spades open and then close her eye, while at the same time she gave a mocking smile. He felt a thrill of nameless horror. The queen of spades resembled the dead Countess!

Hermann is now at the Oboukhoff Asylum, room No. 17—a hopeless madman! He answers no questions which we put to him. Only he mumbles to himself without cessation, " Three, seven, ace; three, seven, *queen*!"

NICOLAI V. GOGOL
1809–1852

THE EVE OF SAINT JOHN

ALL his life Thomas Grigorovitch refused to tell the same story twice. It was an odd fancy of his, but he was never known to depart from it. If you insisted on hearing a story a second time, it was certain to become a new one in the retelling ; the old man's busy imagination would be ever inventing new facts and characters or transforming the originals until it was impossible to recognise them. One of his stories was once eagerly seized upon by a hungry journalist, on the prowl for scraps of any sort out of which to make fillings for the wretched little bundles of paper which these gentry are in the habit of giving out once a week or once a month. Thomas himself forgot all about the incident until one day the same young man, in his bright green cap, turned up again, this time bringing with him a small book which he opened and laid before us ; and the old man, taking up his spectacles, prepared to examine the pages. But the spectacles were out of commission ; they refused to stick upon his nose without the application of thread and wax which he was always forgetting to give them ; so he passed the book over to me. I know something of the arts of reading and writing, and have good eyesight ; so I started to read it to him.

" Wait ! " he interrupted, before I had read more than three or four pages. " Tell me what it is all about."

" What it is about ! " I exclaimed in amazement. " Why, it is your own story, Thomas ! "

" Who says it is my story ? " he demanded.

" Who says so ? Well, look here. Here it is in black and white : *Related by the verger of Dikanka.*"

" A plague on the man who said that," cried the old verger. " I never told him any of this stuff, the sneaking liar ! Listen to me, now, and I'll tell you the real story."

With that he began the following history.

. . . .

My grandfather—God rest his soul !—was a rare one to tell a story.

Folks would sit and listen to him, and never move while he was talking, though it should take all day to tell. He was none of your modern romancers, spinning a yarn like a beggar on the doorstep, till you get sick and tired of their lies. In those old days, before my mother died, we used to sit round the stove those dark nights in winter, she spinning and gently crooning a lullaby and rocking the cradle with her foot, while the frost glistened on the frozen window-panes and the little room was like an oven.

Grandfather was very very old ; for years he had never left the stove side, where he sat all day and night crouched over the heat ; and we children were never tired of sitting round him, huddled close together, while the spindle whirred and the lamp guttered and flared, and he told his wonderful stories. He had tales of all kinds, of heroes and adventures and battles, but those we loved best were his queer fairy tales, eerie stories of elves and witches and demons, which made our flesh creep and our hair stand on end. The fearsomeness of these stories used at times to impress us so strongly that everything for days afterward would seem strange and haunted. I well remember the impression I used to have of unearthly visitors slinking about the house, and how when I saw my own clothes hanging up I used to take them for the form of the foul fiend. Granddad's stories were indeed rather awful, but we always knew that every word of them was true.

The story which I am now going to tell you is one of the most extraordinary in his repertory. I know very well that many superior people would laugh at it; but, after all, do they not laugh at everything in heaven and earth, and call that wisdom ? Thank God, I have lived long enough to have learned the folly of incredulity. But let the old man speak for himself .

You would not have recognised this village if you had seen it as it was when I was a boy. It was then nothing more than a collection of wretched hovels. The fields were unfenced and there were no barns nor stables. Even the most prosperous lived in broken-down cottages, and the poor were glad of any kind of shelter. This was not altogether due to poverty, but at least in part came from nomadic instincts. The Cossack tradition of a wandering life was strong among us ; there was little respect for property, and, by reason of the wandering hordes, no one felt much security. No one, therefore, took the trouble to build a comfortable house.

What a strange figure the man made ! Was he, indeed, a man

or devil ? Whence did he come, and with what purpose ? You might meet him at any time prowling about the neighbourhood, often half-drunk, and then suddenly he would have disappeared and left no trace behind. He was a fellow of infinite humour ; all the Cossacks would crowd about him, and sing and laugh in merry carousal. He had ever a pleasant word for the girls and some pretty gaud to give them ; they were often unwilling to take his gifts, being doubtful perhaps of their origin. An ancient aunt of mine, whose tavern was specially favoured by this diabolical Basavriuk (for that was his name), used to say that nothing would persuade her to accept one of these presents with which he was so free. Yet it was difficult to refuse. The man frowned in such an ugly and uncanny manner when any of us crossed his will that we found it best to fall in with his every mood. Yet his gifts had unpleasant consequences ; a necklace of his beads round your neck would presently seem to strangle and burn your skin ; one of his rings would seem to bite your finger, and his ribbons twined in your hair would pull like the very devil. Moreover these fatal gifts were not to be got rid of ; you might throw them into the pond, but in some mysterious way they soon would be back with you again.

Next to the village church lived Father Athanasius, a man respected and beloved. He kept his eye on Basavriuk, and finding that this heathen neglected his Easter duties, reproved him boldly and laid penance upon him. The outlaw went near to murdering him. " You jolly well attend to your own business," he roared, " or I will do you in." What hope was there for this wretched fellow ? The good priest gave out that none of his flock should speak to Basavriuk, on pain of being considered an enemy of Christ and of the human race.

Peter the orphan (so called because no one had memory of his mother or father) was a labourer in the employment of a small farmer by name of Korzh. Some said that they had died of plague when the boy was two years old ; but old Aunt would not agree to this, and invented parents for him, though it is difficult to see what good that did to Peter. Her story was that his father had been taken prisoner by the Turks, had suffered incredible torments at their hands, and had at last escaped in disguise. The lads and girls of the village used to say that Peter would have made a fine figure if he had been well dressed. Unfortunately, however, he had nothing but an old grey suit full of holes as a Jew's pocket is of sovereigns. Now, Korzh had a daughter of incomparable beauty. Her cheeks were fresh as flowers of dawn, her eyebrows were like cords of black silk, her enticing little lips seemed suited to songs more beautiful than those of the nightingale, and her hair, soft as flax and raven-black, fell in the loveliest curls. Old as I am and worried by an aged wife, I would have given much to kiss her.

Then happened what always happens where youths and maidens are together. This pretty Pidorka and her Peter were ever whispering in twilight corners. Korzh, her father, was quite unsuspicious until one day he saw Peter kissing the girl with passionate fervour. The old man, who had just opened the door of his cottage, was astounded and horrified, as if he had received a blow on the head. As soon as he came to himself he took down his old hunting-crop from the wall, and was about to do justice upon Peter, when little Ivas, Pidorka's young brother, ran up and caught his father's knees, crying, " Oh, Daddy, don't hit Peter."

The old man relented and hung his whip again upon its nail, but, seizing Peter, threatened him with the direst punishment if he should be ever found about the cottage again. He concluded his address by striking the lad with his fists in the neck. The boy fled from his presence, and all their young love was blighted.

And now a report went about the village that a handsome soldier with splendid uniform and fierce moustache was a favoured visitor at the cottage where dwelled the pretty girl, and soon was talk of a marriage between the two. Pidorka, heartbroken, at last succeeded in sending a message to Peter by the hand of her little brother. " Beloved," she told him, " it is you alone whom I could have loved and worshipped all my life. To you only could I ever have belonged. But a cruel destiny has separated us for ever. Think not that I will be married to this soldier whom people name as my lover; they will carry me to my funeral instead of dancing at my wedding. Death, beloved, is now my choice, for I will never wed another man."

This message awoke Peter from the castle of dreams in which he had been building up a happy future for himself and Pidorka after successful adventures abroad should have made him rich. " Alas!" he cried, " an evil fate is upon us. There remains for me nothing but to die too. But who am I that I should complain of fate? Since it is the will of God to destroy me, I am content."

Early in the morning, when all the pious were at mass, my aunt was astonished to see Peter come into her tavern and order a great tankard of neat spirit, which he drank off at one gulp. But it was of no use; oblivion would not come to him. As he cast the tankard, in overwhelming gloom and despair, to the floor, he heard a deep voice behind him. It was Basavriuk, who thrust his hideous face with its fierce eyes and bristly hair close to his own. "Come, my friend, you have drunk deep enough of this bitter cup; is it not so? It is time for a new order of things. I can help you to what you desire; see, this is what you need, is it not?" and he rattled the coins in his huge leather purse with a cunning smile.

Peter looked at him, and a cold shudder ran suddenly down his back. The tempter shook out some of the coins into his hand and let the light gleam upon them. "Ha, ha," he laughed, "that is a fair sight; and a fair sound they make, too. A whole sack of this treasure shall be yours in return for one small condition."

"Done," cried Peter, recognising that this was indeed the devil himself. "They are mine. I will do anything you like." And the contract was sealed.

"Meet me at midnight in the glade of the Bear's Den. This is the Eve of Saint John Baptist, and the only night in the year when the fern blossoms. You are in the nick of time." And with that he was gone.

Peter waited with the utmost impatience for the end of the day, for sunset and the dark night. It was the longest day he had ever spent. At last the time came, and he made his way through the thick woods into the deep glade which bore the name of the Bear's Den. He found Basavriuk there waiting for him, who took him by the hand and led him through soft marshy ground where they had to walk carefully and with difficulty, clinging to the bushes, until they emerged upon a level stretch of open ground. The place was quite strange to Peter.

"See," said Basavriuk, pointing, "over there are three grassy mounds, and upon them myriad flowers of all kinds. You must not pick any of these flowers or evil will befall you; but the moment that you see the fern burst into bloom, pick its flower, and take no heed of anything that may be going on around you."

With the last words, Basavriuk disappeared, and Peter was alone. He walked across to the grassy mounds, but could see no flowers, only the rank gloomy steppe-grass growing everywhere. Then came a flash of lightning, and suddenly the ground before him was carpeted with a glowing mass of strange and beautiful flowers, and among them the plain green fern fronds. Peter stood staring at this marvellous wealth of beauty and colour, not quite certain that he was not dreaming. Then, as he was gazing at the homely fern-fronds, wondering whether Basavriuk had been laughing at him when he spoke of their blossoms, he observed upon the green a tiny crimson bud. It glowed and stirred as if alive, growing larger and larger every moment, and kindling as if with its own ardour. Then, radiant as a star, the swelling bud burst open, and the wonderful flower flamed in full glory, lighting up all around it. " This is the moment," Peter told himself, and stretched out his hand to pluck it. As he did so, he became aware of the sound of trampling feet all about him, and of hundreds of hoof-like hands trying to reach the flower. Remembering his instructions, he closed his eyes so as not to see them, and feverishly grasped at the fern stem. The flower was in his hand. Then everything was silent, and he saw nothing but Basavriuk, blue and ghastly as a spectre, seated upon a tree stump, and gazing open-mouthed and as if transfixed into the space before him. Suddenly through the gruesome stillness came a low whistle, freezing Peter's heart within him ; and then the wood became alive with the silvery voices of the flowers and the whisperings of the trees and grasses.

The whistle had stirred Basavriuk also into life. His eyes lighted up, and the colour came back to his face. " The old witch has got back," he muttered to himself ; and then to Peter, " Listen, Peter. In a few moments you will see before you a new kind of beauty. Take care to do whatever she tells you ; otherwise you will be utterly lost." Then, taking a stick, he pushed aside the branches of a bush beside him ; and there appeared a diminutive hut, which he hammered with his fist until it shook and shook again. Out of the hut leaped a huge black dog, which immediately after had become a fierce cat, and sprang at Basavriuk's eyes. " Come, come, old hag," said Basavriuk, swearing vilely at it, " you have no need to be in a temper."

As he spoke, the cat was gone, and a little hunched-up old woman, with wrinkled face and nut-cracker jaw, and of the most devilish aspect, stood in its place. " This is indeed a new sort of beauty," thought Peter, but he shivered with horror as she came near him and snatched the flower out of his hand. Taking water, she muttered incantations over it, while her mouth gave out jets of fire. Then, returning it to Peter, " Cast it from you," she commanded. As he obeyed, he was astounded to observe that it did not fall to the ground, but flew through the air, gliding gently away, until at last, at a great distance, it fell gradually and softly to earth. " There is the place," growled the old witch in a voice like a frog.

Basavriuk handed him a spade. " Go and dig there," he said, " and you will have riches beyond all that Korzh could ever imagine."

Peter took the tool and set to work in a businesslike manner. He had only turned up four spadefuls when the blade came in contact with something hard and resisting, and he could make out a little chest clamped with iron. He tried to lift it up, but it immediately sank deeper into the ground and out of his reach; and at the same time he heard a horrid hissing laugh at his ear. " Aha," said the old witch, " you must pay my price for the treasure. I must have human blood." She led up to him a young child, his face veiled in a white cloth, and signed to him to kill it. A mighty anger inflamed the heart of Peter, as he tore away the veil and discovered beneath it Pidorka's little brother Ivas; he grasped the knife she had given him, and sprang like a wild beast upon the old witch.

But Basavriuk was upon him, shouting, " You promised anything for your beautiful bride," and as the old witch stamped on the ground, flames shot forth all about him. He could see now all the treasure that lay buried in the earth. There, beneath his feet, reposed countless wealth, jewel-chests, and hoards of money, maddening stores beyond the power of man to count. He gazed on the intoxicating sight till his brain reeled, and suddenly seizing the knife in frenzy, he did the deed.

The horrible laughter of demons was all about him. The wood was full of gruesome and distorted forms. The old witch fell upon her victim. Peter fled headlong from the place, seeing red in everything, the trees, the sky, the air itself. At last he reached the wretched hut which served him as a dwelling, and, collapsing in a corner, fell into a heavy stupor of sleep.

When he awoke, three days later, all recollection of his adventure in the wood was obliterated from his memory. His foot touched something which jingled, and there beside him lay two great sacks of gold. A dim memory of having gone out to search for riches came back to him, and a vague sense of having been badly frightened; but for the rest, he remembered nothing at all.

The sacks of gold at once reached the heart of Korzh, and he discovered that Peter had always been to him as a beloved son, over whom he finally wept with emotion, and whom he welcomed with open arms as Pidorka's husband. The obnoxious soldier was sent about his business, and the wedding was arranged for an early day. Pidorka tried to tell her lover of the loss of her little brother, who had been stolen by gypsies, but so far did the devil's baneful influence extend, that Peter could not even remember the name or the features of little Ivas.

A wedding in those days was a grand affair. There was a great feast with music of all kinds, and then the young men and maidens, in their gorgeous attire, danced the old graceful and stately dances of the country. First the girls in their embroidered silk costumes, their high-heeled shoes, and their gaily-tied hair, danced their own graceful gliding dance; then the young men, in red and blue silk tunics and grotesque gold head-dress, each performed a dignified *pas seul*; and after this all the boys in their tall caps, light shirts, and gay silver belts, each with a short pipe stuck jauntily in his mouth, pranced about making everybody laugh by their pranks and jokes. Even Korzh himself felt the infection of youth in the light-hearted throng, and began to dance and sing with the rest. The fun became faster and more riotous; the young people took to dressing up as fairies and demons and all sorts of odd characters, getting ever less decorous and more hilarious. Even the old people could not remember a wedding so festive as this one.

After their marriage Pidorka and Peter lived in great style. Everything in their establishment was of the best, and there was enough and to spare of everything. There was a good deal of head-shaking over their way of living by the good folks of the neighbourhood. "No good ever yet came of ill-gotten wealth," they said to one another; "and how could Peter come honestly by so much money? It must have come from the Father of Evil himself." And in proof of their theory, they pointed out that Basavruik had never been seen since the time of Peter's good fortune.

There was only too sad witness to the perspicuity of these good people. Before he had been married one month, you could hardly have known Peter for the same man. He had become altogether silent and morose, sitting all day without moving, and apparently deep in thought, perplexed by the continual effort to remember something which always eluded his mind. Occasionally Pidorka would manage to draw him into life for a few moments, when he would talk and perhaps smile, forgetting his preoccupation ; but it was only a momentary relief ; the sight of his riches would suddenly bring back the misery, and crying, " Wait, I forget ; I must recollect," he would bury his face in his hands and sink once more into his gloomy reverie.

Pidorka tried every available remedy. She called in the help of a wise woman, and together they tried all sorts of spells for exorcising the source of the evil ; but in vain. And in this state of misery for both, the summer wore away. The harvest was gathered in ; and the flocks of wild ducks had sought their winter quarters in the home marshes ; the steppes had grown red, and the logs and faggots for the winter firing were being collected fast ; the ground was everywhere hardening, and touches of frost might be seen in the mornings. And the winter itself wore through, till the snow melted away and the frost disappeared ; but there was no change in Peter, except that he grew always more gloomy and more sullen. All day long he sat there, the bags of gold lying at his feet, always intent on remembering—remembering no one knew what. He became wild and dreadful to behold, with long unkempt hair and the fierce frightened glare of a wild beast ; and his anger grew to a mad rage because he could not remember.

It seemed that Peter was going mad. He would get up from his chair, and with fixedly staring eyes would make the wildest motions as of seizing something intangible, his lips moving rapidly all the time as if trying to form an unfamiliar word, but never making a sound. Then he would grow suddenly mad with rage, pulling out his hair and tearing at his hands and body like a maniac ; until, the spasm past, he would fall again into silence and sit brooding upon the memory which always escaped him, until another spasm of madness seized him, to pass off eventually in the same manner.

Life had become unbearable to Pidorka. At first a poignant anguish, it had become a dull dead misery worse than any suffering. No one would have recognised the beauty of Dikanka in this pale thin shadow with eyes faded by tears, who never smiled, and from whose face all hope and joy and sense was utterly obliterated. At last some one, pitying her wretchedness, advised her to seek the aid of the witch of the Bear's Den, who was said to be so clever that she could cure every illness that had ever been known. Pidorka in desperation decided to follow the advice, and at last induced the witch to come to her. As it happened it was on the Eve of Saint John. Peter, who had been lying, unseeing, on a couch, gradually aroused himself on her entrance and began to glare around him, trembling violently and in mortal terror. Suddenly he broke into an unearthly laugh, which smote Pidorka with a terrible fear. " Ha, ha," he shouted, " I remember now."

With that he seized a hatchet and giving it a great sweep round his head, flung it with tremendous force at the old witch. It missed its mark, but buried its head to the depth of four inches in the stout oaken door. The witch vanished, and in her place stood a child, its head veiled in a white cloth ; and then, the cloth falling off, Pidorka recognised him. " Ivas ! " she cried, and rushed to embrace him ; but before she could reach him the child's figure became blood-red all over, glowing with a terrible light. Pidorka, terrified, rushed out of the room, and before she could recover sufficiently to return, the door was made fast behind her so that she could not enter. She called in neighbours to her help, and at last between them they succeeded in battering in the door. By this time the house was full of smoke ; and in the middle of the room, at the spot where Peter had been standing, they found a little heap of ashes, still smouldering, and beside it the fatal sacks. The people fell on the sacks and tore them open. They contained nothing but broken earthenware. There was no treasure to be seen.

After these happenings, Pidorka, gathering together what property her father had left her, set out on a pilgrimage ; and before long, as is the usual way, she had become but a memory in the village. No one knew where she had gone. However, some years later, a soldier who came from Kief on a visit to Dikanka gave an account of a nun whom he had seen in a convent there, whom every one recognised as being certainly Pidorka. Her frame was worn to a shadow, and she spent her life in unceasing prayer, never speaking a word to any one. It was reported that she had come to the convent alone and on foot, and had brought with her a frame of precious stones for the holy picture of the Mother of God, of such marvellous worth and beauty that it dazzled all who looked at it.

THE CARRIAGE

NICOLAI V. GOGOL

THE little town of B—— became quite animated when the —— cavalry regiment came to be quartered there. Until then it had been horribly dull. When you happened to drive through it and looked out on the low greasy little houses that stared at the street in an incredibly sour manner, it was impossible to say what took place in your heart ; a feeling of despair such as you experience when you have lost heavily at cards, or when you have made some stupid remark—in a word, a most unpleasant feeling. The rain had washed some of the clay from the walls, so that, instead of being white, they were piebald. The roofs were, for the most part, made of cane, as is usual in our southern towns. The little front gardens had long been abolished by order of the police. Not a soul was to be met in the street, unless perhaps a cock happened to cross the bridge that felt as soft as a pillow from the thick layer of dust on it. This dust would turn to mud at the slightest rainfall. Then the streets of B—— would be full of those fat animals that the local police called " Frenchmen." Putting out their snouts from their troughs they raised such a grunting as to cause any one driving through to whip up his horses. However, one seldom met with any one driving through the town of B——. It was but rarely that some landowner, possessing eleven serfs, would appear over the bridge, dressed in a nankeen coat, in a vehicle that was a cross between a trap and a cart, and would peep out from among numerous sacks of flour, and pull up the bay mare after whom trotted a foal. Even the market square had a rather depressing appearance ; the tailor's house stood out cornerwise to the road in an absurd manner. On the opposite side of the road was some sort of two-storeyed building in stone that had been in the course of construction for fifteen years. Further on, there stood, quite by itself, a modern wooden fence painted grey but covered with dirt, which the chief of police had erected in keeping with the houses, in his youth, before he had taken to sleeping after dinner, and drinking a concoction of dried gooseberries at night. In other places the fences were entirely of wattle. In the middle of the square were tiny little shops; in them could be seen bundles of cracknels, a heap of soap, bitter almonds, buckshot, mercerized goods, and so on, while there was always a peasant woman in a red kerchief, and two merchant's clerks who always were to be found playing cards. But no sooner was the cavalry regiment quartered in B—— than everything was changed. The streets shone with gay colours and grew lively—in a word, took on quite another appearance. The low little houses would often see a handsome stately beplumed officer pass by on his way to a comrade to discuss the possibility of promotion or the merits of various tobaccos; or sometimes he would be paying calls in what may be called the regimental carriage, since it was used only by the regiment. Thus, one day the major would be seen driving in it, the next day it would be in the lieutenant's stables, and a week later the major's orderly would be seen greasing it with tallow. The wattle fences between the houses were covered with soldiers' caps airing in the sun; a grey coat would protrude somewhere on a gate; in the little streets you would meet soldiers with moustaches as stiff as a boot-brush. These moustaches were seen everywhere; the women had only to gather in the market-place with their jugs, when over their shoulders these moustaches were sure to be seen. The officers were a great addition to society which, up to that time, had consisted of the judge, who lived in the same house with the deacon's wife and the chief of police, a worthy man who slept absolutely the whole day—from dinner until the evening, and from the evening until dinner. Society grew larger and busier when the brigadier-general came to live in the town. The neighbouring landowners, whose existence one had barely suspected till then, came into the county town to see the gentlemen and officers, and sometimes to play cards, that had turned their heads already, muddled with their wives' commissions, the sowing and shooting. It is a pity I cannot remember what made the brigadier-general give his big dinner. The preparations for it were enormous; the sound of the chef's knives in the general's kitchen could be heard at the end of the town. Everything in the town was used for the dinner; the judge and his deaconess, for instance, could only eat buck-wheat cakes and corn-flour fruit jelly. The small courtyard belonging to the general's house was full of cabs and carriages. The company consisted of the officers and several local landowners. The most remarkable of the latter was Pifogor

Pifogorovitch Chertokutsky, who had driven over in a smart carriage. He was one of the principal gentry of the county of B——, and made most noise at elections. He had once served in a cavalry regiment and was one of those "important" ubiquitous officers. He was always to be seen at balls or reunions wherever his regiment happened to be stationed—the girls of the Tambovsk and Simirsk governments could testify to that. It is highly probable that he would have covered himself in glory—useful to himself—in other governments had he not been compelled to resign owing to what is commonly called an "ugly story"; either he had boxed the ears of some one older than himself, or that person had boxed his ears—I cannot remember which, at any rate the upshot of it was that he was requested to resign. However, this in no way made him lose his balance; he wore a high-waisted frock-coat, cut in military style, had spurs on his boots, and a moustache under his nose, since without this latter the gentry might have thought that he had been in the infantry, for which he had a profound contempt. He went to all the crowded fairs where the heart of Russia—consisting of mothers, daughters, children, an dportly landowners—came to make merry in traps, carriages, dog-carts, and such vehicles as one has never seen even in dreams. He could scent from afar where a cavalry regiment was quartered and would always come over to visit the officers, alighting nimbly before them from his elegant carriage, and soon getting acquainted with them. At past elections he had given a dinner to the gentry, at which he told them that if they elected him president he would place them in the very best position. Altogether, he conducted himself in a "noble style," as they say in the provinces. He married a very pretty girl, with whom he got a dowry of two hundred souls, besides several thousands in cash. The money was soon spent on a team of six horses—certainly excellent ones—gilt locks for the doors, a tame monkey for the house, and a French major-domo. The two hundred souls, together with twice as many of his own, were mortgaged in some sort of commercial transfer. In a word, he was what a squire should be—a tolerable squire, that is. Besides him there were several other squires at the general's dinner, but they do not call for remark. The rest of the company consisted of the officers of the regiment, and two staff officers, a colonel and a rather portly major. The general himself was stout and robust, in fact, a good chief as the officers said. He spoke in a somewhat heavy bass. The dinner was excellent; there was sturgeon and other kinds of fish, asparagus, quail, partridge, mushroom, fricassee and jelly ;—the chef had not had time for a hot meal since the day before, and four soldiers, knives in hand, had helped him the whole night. There was a number of bottles, long-necked ones containing champagne, and short-necked ones containing madeira. It was a beautiful summer day, the windows were wide open, there were plates of ice on the table, a cross conversation covered by the general's voice and drowned in champagne—everything was in keeping. After dinner, all rose feeling pleasantly heavy, and lighting their short- or long-stemmed pipes, went out of doors with cups of coffee in their hands.

"Now we can look at her," the general said.

"Will you be good enough, my dear," he said, turning to his aide, a rather sprightly youngster of pleasant appearance. "Tell them to have the bay mare brought here. You will soon see for yourselves." Here the general took a puff at his pipe and blew out the smoke. "She is not in proper condition yet! There are no decent stables in this miserable little town. A very—puff—puff—fine horse."

"And how long—puff—puff—have you had her, Your Excellency?"

"Puff, puff, puff, p—uff, not very long; it is only about two years since I took her from the stud."

"And was she broken in when you got her, or did Your Excellency have her broken in here?"

"Puff, puff, pu-pu-pu—puff — here." With these words the general disappeared amid clouds of smoke.

Meanwhile a soldier came out of the stables, there was a sound of hoofs, then another soldier appeared, with a long black moustache, clad in a white stable-coat and leading by the bridle a trembling, startled horse that, lifting its head, nearly lifted the little soldier and his moustache from the ground.

"Steady, steady, Agrafina Ivanovna!" he said, leading her up to the porch.

The mare was called Agrafina Ivanovna; strong and wild like a southern beauty. She knocked her hoofs against the wooden verandah and stopped suddenly.

The general, putting down his pipe, looked at Agrafina Ivanovna with an air of contentment. The colonel coming out of the verandah, took hold of her mouth; the major felt her legs, while the others clacked their tongues.

Chertokutsky came out of the verandah and walked round her.

The soldier, bending down and holding the reins, looked straight into the visitor's eyes as though he would have liked to have jumped into them.

" Very, very beautiful ! " Chertokutsky said.

" A graceful creature ! And may I ask Your Excellency how she goes ? "

" She has a good step, only—the devil knows why—that fool of a veterinary surgeon gave her a pill, and for two days now she keeps on sneezing."

" A beautiful creature ! And has Your Excellency a suitable carriage ? "

" A carriage ? . . . But this is a riding horse ! "

" I know, Your Excellency ; I meant have you a suitable carriage for other horses ? "

" I cannot say I have an over supply of carriages. I confess I have long wanted a modern calèche. I have written to my brother in St. Petersburg about it, and I do not know if he is sending me one or not."

" In my opinion, Your Excellency," the colonel remarked, " there is not a better calèche than the kind made in Vienna."

" You are right, puff, puff, puff."

" Your Excellency, I have a splendid calèche, of real Vienna make."

" Is it the one you came in ? "

" Oh no, that is an ordinary one I use for personal journeys ; but the other . . . is wonderful ; light as a feather, and when you get into it, you feel—if Your Excellency will permit my saying so—as though your nurse were rocking you in your cradle ! "

" Comfortable, no doubt."

" Very comfortable ; cushions and springs ; just like a picture."

" Very nice."

" And what a capacity too ! I have never seen one like it, Your Excellency. When I was in service, I kept ten bottles of rum and fifteen pounds of tobacco in the box, besides six uniforms, linen, and two long pipes ; and you could have put a whole ox in the pocket."

" Very nice."

" I paid four thousand for it, Your Excellency."

" To judge by the price, it must be a very good one. Did you buy it yourself ? "

"No, Your Excellency, I got it by accident. A friend of mine bought it, an excellent fellow, the chum of my boyhood, you would like him very much, Your Excellency; he and I have everything in common, what is his is as good as mine. I won it from him in a game of cards. Would you be good enough, Your Excellency, to do me the honour of dining with me to-morrow? You could see the calèche at the same time."

"I do not know what to say to that. Alone I . . . may I bring these gentlemen, my officers?"

"I shall be delighted. Gentlemen, I look upon it as a great honour to have the pleasure of seeing you in my house!"

The colonel, the major, and the other officers thanked him by a polite bow.

"It is my opinion, Your Excellency, that if you buy anything, it may as well be good, otherwise it is not worth while. When you do me the honour of coming to see me to-morrow, I will show you various implements I have introduced for agricultural purposes."

The general stared straight before him, sending out clouds of smoke.

Chertokutsky was very pleased that he had invited the officers; he began already to decide on the various pies and sauces he would have, and smiled amiably at the officers, who in their turn seemed to double their good disposition towards him, as could be seen in their eyes and their slight half-bows to him. Chertokutsky grew more at ease, and his voice was laden with pleasure.

"I shall have the pleasure, Your Excellency, of introducing you to the mistress of the house."

"It will give me great pleasure," the general said, stroking his moustache.

After this, Chertokutsky was anxious to go home quickly so as to prepare everything in good time for the next day's reception and dinner; he was about to take up his hat, but strangely enough, stayed on a little while longer. Meanwhile card-tables were placed about the room, and soon the whole company divided into fours and sat down to whist.

The candles were brought in. Chertokutsky could not, for a long time, decide whether to sit down and play or not. But as the officers began to press him, he felt it to be against the rules of convention to refuse, and sat down. Automatically a glass of punch appeared before him, which he drank off at once, unconsciously. After playing two rubbers he again found a glass of punch to hand which he again drank off unconsciously, saying beforehand:

"Gentlemen, it is time I was going home, quite time." But he sat down again to another rubber. Meanwhile the conversation in the various corners of the room was taking various directions. The whist players were rather silent, but those who did not play and sat on couches to one side, carried on conversations among themselves. In one corner the cavalry staff captain, with a cushion at his side and a pipe between his teeth, was talking about his love affairs in a free-and-easy way, completely holding the attention of those round him. One very portly squire, with short hands that looked like overgrown potatoes, listened with an unusually sweet expression, and only from time to time took the trouble to put one short hand behind his back to pull out his snuff-box. In another corner there was quite a heated discussion about squadron drill, and Chertokutsky, who at this time had twice played a knave instead of a queen, joined in the conversations and called out from his corner, "In what year?" or "What regiment?" without noticing that sometimes his questions had no connection with the matter under discussion. At last, a few minutes before supper, whist-playing was stopped, but continued in words, and it seemed that all heads were full of whist. Chertokutsky well recollected that he had won a great deal, but actually found nothing, and getting up from the table, stood for a long time like one who has lost a handkerchief. Meanwhile, supper was served. It goes without saying that there was no lack of wine, and Chertokutsky was almost compelled to fill his glass from time to time since there were bottles to the right and left of him.

The conversation at table became long and involved, but was conducted in a strange manner. A certain colonel who had served in the campaign of 1812 was telling them of a battle that had never taken place, and then, for some mysterious reason, he took the stopper from one of the decanters and stuck it in the fire. In a word, when the guests began to depart it was already three o'clock, and the coachmen had to carry some of them out in their arms like bundles of purchases, and Chertokutsky, notwithstanding his high birth, bowed so long and with such inflections of his head on taking his seat in the carriage that when he got home there were two burdocks in his moustache.

Every one in the house was asleep; the coachman could scarcely find the valet, who guided his master through the drawing-room and handed him over to the housemaid, after which Chertokutsky somehow or other got to his bedroom and lay down beside his pretty young wife, who was sleeping in a most graceful attitude clad in a nightdress as white as snow. Her husband's fall on the bed woke her. Stretching herself, she raised her lashes and blinking quickly three or four times, opened her eyes with a half-angry smile, but seeing that he took no notice of her, she turned over on the other side, and putting her soft cheek on her hand, went to sleep soon after he did.

It was at an hour that is not called *early* in the country when the young mistress awoke beside her snoring spouse. Recollecting that he had returned home at four in the morning, she did not want to wake him. She put on her bedroom slippers that her husband had ordered in St. Petersburg, and slipping on a white dressing-jacket that flowed round her like running water, she went into her dressing-room, washed in water as fresh as herself, and then walked up to the dressing-table. She found herself looking very pretty that day. This apparently important circumstance made her spend two extra hours before the mirror. At last she put on a pretty dress and went out into the garden for some fresh air. As though on purpose, the weather happened to be beautiful at the time, the kind of weather that only a southern summer day can boast of. The sun, almost at its zenith, poured down its burning rays, but it was cool walking under the thick shady avenues, and the flowers, warmed by the sun, trebled their scent. The pretty mistress quite forgot that it was twelve o'clock and that her husband was still asleep. Already there reached her the after-dinner snoring of the two coachmen asleep in the stables at the back of the garden. But she still sat on in the shady garden whence could be seen a view of the main road and gazed absently into the solitary plain, when suddenly her attention was attracted by distant clouds of dust. Looking hard, she soon distinguished several carriages. In front came an open, two-seated light calèche in which sat the general, his epaulettes sparkling in the sun, and beside him sat the colonel. Then followed another vehicle in which sat the general's aide and two other officers; behind that came the famous regimental carriage, that belonged for the moment to the portly major; behind the carriages came a four-seater bon voyage with four officers and a fifth on the box; behind that were seen three officers on beautiful bay horses amidst dark clouds.

"Are they coming to us, I wonder?" the mistress of the house thought. "Oh, heavens! they have turned at the bridge!" she cried, clapping her hands, and she ran over the flower-beds through the flowers, straight into her husband's bedroom. He was sleeping like a log.

"Get up, get up, get up quickly," she cried, pulling his hand.

"Yes," Chertokutsky said, stretching himself but not opening his eyes.

"Get up! do you hear! Guests are coming!"

"Guests? what guests?" Saying this, he made a noise like a calf when it seeks its mother's breast. "Mm . . ." he mumbled. "Come here, I want to kiss you, dear!"

"Get up, dear, for God's sake, get up quickly! The general and the officers are coming. Oh, heavens, you have burdocks in your moustache!"

"The general? Is he coming already? The devil! Why did no one wake me? And the dinner, what about the dinner? Is everything ready as it should be?"

"What dinner?"

"Didn't I tell you?"

"You? You came home at four in the morning, and in spite of all my questions would not tell me anything. I thought it a pity to wake you, dear, you had so little sleep. . . ." The last words were uttered in a soft, pleading voice.

Chertokutsky, rubbing his eyes, lay on the bed as though struck by lightning. At last he jumped out of bed.

"Oh, what an idiot I am!" he said, striking his forehead. "I invited them to dinner! What shall I do? Are they far away?"

"I don't know. . . . They should be here at any moment now."

"Darling . . . hide yourself! Who is there? You? What are you afraid of, you little fool? Some officers will be here in a moment, tell them that master is not at home, that he went away in the morning. . . . Do you hear? Tell the other servants too! Quickly!"

Saying this, he seized his dressing-gown and rushed away to hide himself in the coach-house, thinking that his position there would be without danger. But, standing in a corner, he realised that even here he could be seen. "That will be better," flashed through his head, and in a moment he stepped into the glittering calèche and shut the door behind him, and for greater safety put up the hood and sat huddled up in his dressing-gown and the rug.

Meanwhile the carriages arrived at the door. The general got out and shook himself, and after him came the colonel arranging the plumes on his hat with both hands. Then the portly major alighted, carrying his sword under his arm, then the slim lieutenants and the ensign alighted from the bon voyage, and finally the other officers got off their horses.

" Master is not at home," a footman announced, coming out of the porch.

" Not at home ! Perhaps he will be home to dinner ? "

" No, he went away for the day. He will be back about this hour to-morrow."

" Well ! " the general exclaimed ; " what does this mean ? "

" I believe it is a joke," the colonel said with a laugh.

" But how could he ? " the general continued with displeasure. " Confound it ! If he could not receive us, why did he invite us ? "

" I cannot understand, Your Excellency, how a man could behave like that," a young officer remarked.

" What ? " the general said—he always made use of this interrogation when addressing a subaltern.

" I merely wondered, Your Excellency, how a man could behave like that ! "

" Naturally. . . . If something had happened, he might have let us know, or not have asked us at all."

" There is nothing to do, Your Excellency, but to go back," the colonel said.

" Of course there is nothing else to be done. However, we can see his carriage without him. He probably did not take it with him. Hi ! vho is there ! Come here ! "

" What can I do for you, sir ? "

" Are you a stable man ? "

" Yes, Your Excellency."

" Show us the new carriage that your master acquired lately."

" Come into the coach-house, please."

The general and the officers went into the coach-house.

" Allow me, I will wheel it round ; it is rather dark here."

The general and the officers walked round the carriage and carefully examined the wheels and springs.

" Well, there is nothing remarkable about it," the general said, " a most ordinary carriage."

" A most ordinary carriage," the major said. " There is nothing remarkable about it."

" I don't think, Your Excellency, that it was worth four thousand roubles," one of the young officers remarked.

" What ? "

" I said, Your Excellency, that it was not worth four thousand roubles."

" Four thousand ! It is not worth two ! There is nothing to see in it, unless there is something extraordinary inside. Will you please open the flaps. . . ."

And before their eyes was Chertokutsky in his dressing-gown, huddled up in a most strange fashion. " Ah, you here ! " the astonished general exclaimed. With these words he banged the carriage door on Chertokutsky and went away, followed by his officers.

MICHAIL Y. LERMONTOFF
1814–1841

A FAIR SMUGGLER

TAMAN is the most wretched of all our maritime towns. I almost died of hunger there, besides being nearly drowned.

I arrived very late at night in a wretched *telega*. The coachman stopped his tired horses close to a stone building, which stands by itself at the entrance to the town. A Black Sea Cossack, who was on guard, heard the bells of my carriage, and cried out, with the sharp accent of a person suddenly waked up, " Who goes there ? "

Out came the sergeant and corporal. I told them I was an officer, travelling by order of the Crown, and that I wanted a billet somewhere.

The corporal took us into the town. All the houses we tried were already occupied. The weather was cold ; I had been three nights without sleep. I was very tired, and our useless inquiries ended by irritating me.

" My friend," I said to the corporal, " take me to some place where I can at least lie down, no matter where it is."

" I know a hut in the neighbourhood," replied the corporal, " where you might sleep ; but I am afraid it would scarcely suit your honour."

" Go on," I said, paying no attention to his observation.

After much walking through dirty little streets, we at last reached a sort of cabin on the edge of the sea.

The full moon cast its light on the thatched roof and the white walls of my proposed habitation. In the court, surrounded by a sort of palisade, I saw a hut, older and more broken down than the principal one. From this hut the ground sloped rapidly through the court down towards the sea, and I saw at my feet the foam of the troubled waters. The moon seemed to be contemplating the restless element, which was undergoing her influence. By the rays of the ruler of the night, I could make out, at a considerable distance from the shore, two ships, whose black sails stood out like spiders' webs against the dull tints of the sky. " This will do," I said to myself, " to-morrow morning I shall start for Ghelendchik."

A Cossack of the line was acting as my servant. I told him to take out my trunk and send away the postillion ; after which I called the master of the house. I could get no answer. I knocked, but there was still no reply. What could it mean ? I knocked again, and at last a boy of about fourteen showed himself.

" Where's the master of the house ? "

" There is none," returned the child, in the dialect of Little Russia.

" No master ! then where is the mistress ? "

" Gone into the village."

" Who will open the door then ? " I cried, at the same time kicking at it.

The door opened of itself, and out came a wave of damp steam.

I struck a match, and saw by its light a blind boy, standing motionless before me.

I must here say that I am strongly prejudiced against the blind, the deaf, the lame, the hunch-backed ; in short, against the deformed in general. I have remarked that there is always a singular correspondence between the physical formation of a man and his moral nature ; as though by the loss of a member the individual lost certain faculties of the soul.

I examined the child's face ; but what can one make of a physiognomy without eyes ? I looked at him for some time, with a feeling of compassion, when suddenly I saw on his lips a cunning smile, which produced upon me a very disagreeable impression. " Could this blind boy be not so blind as he appeared ? " I said to myself. Answering my own question I said that the boy was evidently suffering from cataract, and that the appearance of cataract cannot be simulated. Why, moreover, should he affect blindness ? Yet in spite of my argument I still remained vaguely suspicious.

" Is the mistress of the cabin your mother ? " I said to the boy.

" No."

" Who are you, then ? "

" A poor orphan," he replied.

" Has the mistress any children ? "

" She has one daughter, who has gone to sea with a Tartar."

" What Tartar ? "

" How do I know ? A Tartar of the Crimea, a boatman from Kertch."

I went into the hut. Two benches, a table, and a large wardrobe, placed near the stove, composed the whole of the furniture. No holy image against the wall—bad sign!

The sea-breeze came in through the broken panes of the window. I took a wax candle from my portmanteau, and after lighting it prepared to install myself. I placed on one side my sabre and my carbine, laid my pistols on the table, stretched myself out on a bench, and, wrapping myself up in my fur-lined coat, lay down.

My Cossack took possession of the other bench. Ten minutes afterwards he was fast asleep; I, however, was still awake, and could not drive from my mind the impression made upon me by the boy, with his two white eyes.

An hour passed. Through the window fell upon the floor the fantastic light of the moon.

Suddenly a shadow was cast, where before there had been bright light. I sprang up, and went to the window. A human figure passed once more, and then disappeared—heaven knows where. I could scarcely believe that it had escaped by the slope into the sea; yet there was no other issue.

Throwing on my overcoat, and taking my sabre, I went out of the cabin, and saw the blind boy before me. I concealed myself behind the wall, and he passed on confidently, but with a certain cautiousness. He was carrying something under his arm, and advanced slowly down the slope towards the sea. "This is the hour," I said to myself, "in which speech is restored to the dumb and sight to the blind."

I followed him at some distance, anxious not to lose sight of him.

During this time the moon became covered with clouds, and a black fog rose over the sea. It was just possible to distinguish in the darkness a lantern on the mast of a ship at anchor, close to the shore. The waves were rolling in, and threatened, if he continued to advance, to swallow up my blind adventurer. He was now so near the sea, that with another step he would be lost. But this was not the first of his nocturnal expeditions; so at least I concluded from the agility with which he now sprang from rock to rock, while the sea poured in beneath his feet. Suddenly he stopped as though he had heard some noise, sat down upon a rock, and placed his burden by his side. He was now joined by a white figure walking along the shore. I had concealed myself behind one of the rocks, and overheard the following conversation.

"The wind," said a woman's voice, "is very violent; Janko will not come."

" Janko," replied the blind boy, " Janko is not afraid of the wind."

" But the clouds get thicker and thicker."

" In the darkness it is easier to escape the coast-guard."

" And what if he gets drowned ? "

" You will have no more bright ribbons to wear on Sunday."

As I listened to this colloquy, I remarked that the blind boy, who had spoken to me in the Little Russian dialect, talked quite correctly the true Russian language.

" You see," he continued, clapping his hands, " I was right. Janko fears neither the sea, nor the wind, nor the fog, nor the coast-guard. Listen ! It is not the breaking of the waves I hear. No, it is the noise of his oars."

The woman got up, and, with an anxious look, tried to pierce the darkness. " You are wrong," she said, " I hear nothing."

I also tried to see whether there was not some sort of craft in the distance, but could distinguish nothing. A moment later, however, a black speck showed itself among the waves, now rising, now falling. At last I could make out the form of a boat dancing on the waters, and rapidly approaching the shore.

The man who was guiding it must have been a bold sailor to cross on such a night an arm of the sea some fourteen miles across, and must have had good reasons for braving so much danger. I watched the frail little craft which was now diving and plunging like a duck through the breakers. It seemed as though she must the next moment be dashed to pieces on the shore, when suddenly the skilful rower turned into a little bay, and there, in comparatively calm water, effected a landing.

The man was of middle height, and wore on his head a cap of black sheep-skin. He made a sign with his hand, when the two mysterious persons who had been talking together, joined him. Then the three united their forces to drag from the boat a burden which seemed to be so heavy, that I cannot even now understand how so slight a craft could have supported such a weight. They at last hoisted the cargo on their shoulders, then walked away and soon disappeared.

The best thing for me to do now was to return to my resting-place. But the strange scene I had witnessed had so struck me that I waited impatiently for daybreak.

My Cossack was much surprised when, on waking up, he found me fully dressed. I said nothing to him about my nocturnal excursion.

I remained for some little time looking through the window with admiration at the blue sky, studded with little clouds, and the distant shore, the Crimea, stretched along the horizon like a streak of violet, ending in a rock, above which could be seen the tower of a lighthouse. Then I went out, and walked to the fort of Chanagora to ask the commandant when I could go to Ghelendchik.

Unfortunately the commandant could give me no positive answer; the only vessels in port were stationary ones, and trading ships which had not yet taken in their cargo. "Perhaps," he said, "in three or four days a mail packet will come in, and then something can be arranged."

I went back in a very bad humour to my lodging. At the door stood the Cossack, who, coming towards me with rather a scared look, said inquiringly:

"Bad news?"

"Yes," I answered. "Heaven knows when we shall get away from here."

At these words the anxiety of the soldier seemed to increase. He came close to me, and murmured, in a low voice:

"This is not a place to stop at. I met just now a Black Sea Cossack of my acquaintance—we were serving in the same detachment last year. When I told him where we had put up: 'Bad place,' he said, 'bad people.' And what do you think of that blind boy? Did any one ever before see a blind person running about from one place to another; going to the bazaar, bringing in bread and water? Here they seem to think nothing of it."

"Has the mistress of the place come in?"

"This morning, while you were out, an old woman came with her daughter."

"What daughter? Her daughter is away."

"I don't know who it is, then. But look, there is the old woman sitting down in the cabin."

I went in. A good fire was shining in the stove, and a breakfast was being prepared, which, for such poor people, seemed to me rather a luxurious one. When I spoke to the old woman, she told me that she was stone deaf.

It was impossible, then, to talk with her. I turned to the blind boy, and, taking him by the ear, said:

"I say, you little wizard, where were you going last night with that parcel under your arm?"

He at once began to moan and cry, and then sobbed out :

" Where was I going last night ? I went nowhere. And with a parcel ! What parcel ? "

The old woman now proved that her ears, when she so desired it, were by no means closed.

" It is not true," she cried. " Why do you tease an unfortunate boy ? What do you take him for ? What harm has he done you ? "

I could stand the noise no longer. So I went out, determined somehow or other to find the solution of this riddle.

Wrapped up in my overcoat, I sat down on a bench before the door. Before me broke the waves of the sea, still agitated by the tempest of the night. Their monotonous noise seemed to resemble the confused murmurs of a town. As I listened I thought of bygone years—of the years I had passed in the north, of our bright, fresh capital ; and little by little I became absorbed in my recollections.

About an hour passed, perhaps more. Suddenly the cadences of a singing voice struck my ear. I listened, and heard a strange melody, now slow and sad, now rapid and lively. The sounds seemed to fall from the sky. I looked up, and on the roof of the cabin I saw a young girl, in a straight dress, with dishevelled hair, like a naiad. With one hand placed before her eyes to keep off the rays of the sun, she looked towards the distant horizon and still continued her song.

It seemed to me that this was the woman whose voice I had heard the night before on the seashore. I looked again towards the singer, but she had disappeared. A moment after she passed rapidly before me, singing another song and snapping her fingers. She went to the old woman and said something to her. The old woman seemed annoyed. The young girl burst into a laugh. Then, with a bound, she came close to me, suddenly stopped and looked at me fixedly, as though surprised to see me. Then turning away with an air of indifference, she walked quietly towards the shore.

But her manœuvres were not yet at an end. All the rest of the day I saw her at short intervals, always singing and dancing. Strange creature ! There was nothing in her physiognomy to denote insanity. On the contrary, her eyes were intelligent and penetrating. They exercised on me a certain magnetic influence, and seemed to expect a question. But whenever I was on the point of speaking she took to flight with a sly smile on her lips.

I had never seen such a woman before. She could scarcely be

called beautiful; but I have my own ideas on the subject of beauty. There was a thoroughbred look about her, and with women as with horses, there is nothing like breed. It can be recognised chiefly in the walk and in the shape of the hands and feet. The nose is also an important feature. In Russia regular noses are more rare than little feet. My siren must have been about eighteen years of age.

What charmed me in her was the extraordinary suppleness of her figure, the singular movements of her head, and her long, fair hair, hanging down in waves of gold on her neck, and her nose, which was perfectly formed.

In her sidelong glance there was something dark and wild; as there was something fascinating in the pure lines of her nose. The light-hearted singer recalled to me the Mignon of Goethe, that fantastic creation of the German mind. Between these two personages there was indeed a striking resemblance. The same sudden transitions from restless agitation to perfect calm; the same enigmatic words and the same songs.

Towards the evening I stopped my Undine at the door of the hut, and said to her:

"Tell me, my pretty one, what you were doing to-day on the roof?"

"I was seeing in what direction the wind blew."

"How did that concern you?"

"Whence blows the wind, thence comes happiness."

"And your singing was to bring you good fortune?"

"Where singing is heard, there is joy."

"But what should you say if your singing caused unhappiness?"

"If unhappiness arrives it must be borne. And from grief to joy the distance is not great."

"Who taught you these songs?"

"No one; I dream and I sing; those who understand me listen to me, and those who do not listen to me cannot understand me."

"What is your name?"

"Ask those who baptized me."

"And who baptized you?"

"I do not know."

"Ah! you are very mysterious; but I know something about you."

There was no sign of emotion on her face; he lips did not move.

" Last night," I continued, " you were on the seashore." Then I told her the scene I had witnessed. I thought this would have caused her to evince some symptom of anxiety, but it had no such effect.

" You assisted at a curious interview," she said to me with a laugh, " but you do not know much, and what you do know you had better keep under lock and key, as you would keep some precious treasure."

" But if," I continued, with a grave and almost menacing air, " I were to relate what I saw to the commandant ? "

At these words she darted away, singing, and disappeared like a frightened bird. I was wrong in addressing this threat to her. At the moment I did not understand all its gravity.

The night came. I told my Cossack to prepare the tea urn, lighted a wax candle, and sat down at the table, smoking my long pipe. I was drinking my tea when the door opened, and I heard the rustling of a dress. I rose hastily and recognised my siren.

She sat down silently before me, and fixed me with a look which made me tremble ; one of those magical looks which had troubled my life in earlier days. She seemed to expect me to speak to her, but some undefinable emotion deprived me of the faculty of speech. Her countenance was as pale as death. In this paleness I thought I could see the agitation of her heart. Her fingers struck mechanically on the table ; her body seemed to shudder ; her bosom rose violently and the moment afterwards seemed compressed.

This species of comedy tired me at last, and I was about to bring it to an end, in the most prosaic manner, by offering my fair visitor a cup of tea ; when suddenly she rose, and taking my head in her hands, gazed at me with all the appearance of passionate tenderness.

A cloud covered my eyes, and I wished in my turn to kiss her, but she escaped like a snake, murmuring as she did so, " To-night, when everything is quiet, meet me on the shore." Then she disappeared, upsetting as she did so my tea-urn and my solitary light.

" She is the very mischief ! " cried my Cossack, who had been looking out for his share of the tea.

He then lay down on his bench ; and gradually my agitation subsided.

" Listen," I said to him. " If you hear a pistol-shot, hurry down as fast as you can to the shore."

He rubbed his eyes, and replied mechanically, " Yes, sir."

I placed my pistol in my belt, and went out. The siren was waiting for me at the top of the path leading down to the sea, lightly clad in a stuff which clung to her waist like a scarf.

" Follow me," she said, taking me by the hand.

We walked down the rocky path in such a manner that I cannot understand how I failed to break my neck. Then we turned sharply to the right, as the blind boy had done the night before. The moon was not yet up. Two little stars, like the fires of lighthouses, relieved the darkness. The agitated waves lifted and let fall in regular cadence a solitary boat close to the shore.

" Get in," she said. I hesitated, for I confess that I have not the least taste for sentimental excursions on the sea. But it was impossible to refuse. She leapt into the barque, I followed her, and off we went.

" What does all this mean ? " I said, getting angry.

" It means," she replied, making me sit down on a bench, and putting her arms round my waist, " it means that I love you." Her burning cheek was close to mine, and I felt her hot breath on my face. Suddenly I heard something fall into the water. Instinctively my hand went to my belt. The pistol was no longer there !

A horrible suspicion seized me. The blood rushed to my brain. I looked at her. We were far from the shore and I could not swim. I tried to escape from her embrace, but she clung to me like a cat, and almost succeeded by a sudden jerk in throwing me out of the boat, which was already on one side. I contrived, however, to restore the equilibrium ; and then began, between my perfidious companion and myself, a desperate struggle, in which I employed all my strength, while feeling that the abominable creature was overcoming me by her agility.

" What do you mean ? " I said to her, squeezing her little hands so tightly that I heard her fingers crack ; but whatever pain I may have caused her she did not utter a word. Her reptile nature could not thus be overcome.

" You saw us," she cried at last. " You want to denounce us." Then by a rapid and violent effort she threw me down. Her body and mine were now bending over the side of the frail craft, and her hair was in the water. The moment was a critical one. I got up on my knees, took her with one hand by the hair, with the other by the throat, and when I had at last compelled her to unclutch my clothes, I threw her into the sea.

Twice her head reappeared above the foaming waves. Then I saw her no more.

In the bottom of the boat I found an old oar, with which, after much labour, I succeeded in getting to the shore. As I walked back to the hut by the path leading to the sea, I looked towards the place where the night before the blind boy had been awaiting the arrival of the sailor. The moon at this moment was shining in the sky, and I fancied I could discern on the seashore a white figure. Filled with curiosity, I concealed myself behind a sort of promontory, from which I could remark what was going on around me. What was my surprise, and I almost say my joy, when I saw that the white figure was my naiad? She was wringing the water out of her long, fair locks, and her wet dress clung to her body. A boat, which I could just see in the distance, was coming towards us. Out of it sprang the same boatman whom I had seen the night before, with the same Tartar cap. I now saw that his hair was cut in the Cossack fashion, and that from his girdle hung a large knife.

" Janko," cried the young girl, " all is lost."

Then they began to talk, but in so low a voice that I could not hear them.

" Where is the blind boy ? " said Janko at last, raising his voice.

" He will be here soon," was the answer.

At that very moment the blind boy appeared, carrying on his back a packet, which he placed in the barque.

" Listen," said Janko, " keep a good watch here ; the things you know are valuable. Tell "—(here a name was uttered which I could not catch) " that I am no longer in his service. Things have taken a bad turn. He will see me no more. The situation is so dangerous that I must get something to do elsewhere. He will not find such another very easily. You may add that, if he had rewarded more liberally the dangerous services rendered to him, Janko would not have left him in the lurch. If he wants to know where to find me—where the wind howls, where the sea foams, that is where I am at home."

After a moment's silence, Janko went on : " Say she accompanies me. She cannot remain here. Tell the old woman that she has done her time, and that she ought to be satisfied. We shall not see her again."

" And I ? " murmured the blind boy.

" I cannot be troubled about you."

The young girl leapt into the boat, and with her hand made a sign to her companion.

" Here," he said to the blind boy, " that will do to buy a gingerbread."

" Nothing more ? " replied the child.

" Yes, take this," and a piece of money fell upon the sands.

The blind boy did not pick it up.

Janko took his place in the boat. The blind boy remained sitting down on the seashore, and he seemed to be crying. Poor fellow ! his grief afflicted me. Why had fate thrown me in the midst of this peaceful circle of smugglers ? As a stone troubles the water, I had brought disorder into these lives, and like the stone, moreover, I had very nearly sunk.

When I got back to the cabin, my Cossack was so fast asleep that it would have been cruel to disturb him. I lighted the candle, and saw that my little box containing my valuables, my sabre with silver mountings, my Circassian dagger (given to me by a friend), had all been carried off. I now understood what the packet placed in the boat by the blind boy must have contained.

I woke up my Cossack with a blow, reproached him for his negligence, and fairly lost my temper. But my anger could not make me find what I had lost.

And how could I complain to the authorities ? Should not I have been laughed at if I had told them that I had been robbed by a blind boy, and almost drowned by a young girl ?

IVAN S. TURGENIEV
1818–1883

THE SINGERS

THE small village of Kolotovka once belonged to a lady known in the neighbourhood by the nickname of Skin-flint, in allusion to her keen business habits (her real name is lost in oblivion), but has of late years been the property of a German from Petersburg. The village lies on the slope of a barren hill, which is cut in half from top to bottom by a tremendous ravine. It is a yawning chasm, with shelving sides hollowed out by the action of rain and snow, and it winds along the very centre of the village street ; it separates the two sides of the unlucky hamlet far more than a river would do, for a river could, at least, be crossed by a bridge. A few gaunt willows creep timorously down its sandy sides ; at the very bottom, which is dry and yellow as copper, lie huge slabs of argillaceous rock. A cheerless position, there's no denying, yet all the surrounding inhabitants know the road to Kolotovka well ; they go there often, and are always glad to go.

At the very summit of the ravine, a few paces from the point where it starts as a narrow fissure in the earth, there stands a small square hut. It stands alone, apart from all the others. It is thatched, and has a chimney ; one window keeps watch like a sharp eye over the ravine, and on winter evenings when it is lighted from within, it is seen far away in the dim frosty fog, and its twinkling light is the guiding star of many a peasant on his road. A blue board is nailed up above the door ; this hut is a tavern, called the " Welcome Resort." Spirits are sold here probably no cheaper than the usual price, but it is far more frequented than any other establishment of the same sort in the neighbourhood. The explanation of this is to be found in the tavern-keeper, Nikolai Ivanitch.

Nikolai Ivanitch—once a slender, curly-headed and rosy-cheeked young fellow, now an excessively stout, grizzled man with a fat face, sly and good-natured little eyes, and a shiny forehead, with wrinkles like lines drawn all over it—has lived for more than twenty years in Kolotovka. Nikolai Ivanitch is a shrewd, acute fellow, like the majority of tavern-keepers. Though he makes no conspicuous effort to please or to talk to people, he has the art of attracting and keeping customers, who find it particularly pleasant to sit at his bar under the placid and genial, though alert eye, of the phlegmatic host. He has a great deal of common sense; he thoroughly understands the landowner's conditions of life, the peasant's, and the tradesman's. He could give sensible advice on difficult points, but, like a cautious man and an egoist, prefers to stand aloof, and at most—and that only in the case of his favourite customers—by remote hints, dropped, as it were, unintentionally, to lead them into the true way. He is an authority on everything that is of interest or importance to a Russian; on horses and cattle, on timber, bricks, and crockery, on woollen stuffs and on leather, on songs and dances. When he has no customers he is usually sitting like a sack on the ground before the door of his hut, his thin legs tucked under him, exchanging a friendly greeting with every passer-by. He has seen a great deal in his time; many a score of petty landowners, who used to come to him for spirits, he has seen pass away before him; he knows everything that is done for eighty miles round, and never gossips, never gives a sign of knowing what is unsuspected by the most keen-sighted police-officer. He keeps his own counsel, laughs, and makes his glasses ring. His neighbours respect him; the civilian general Shtcherpetenko, the landowner highest in rank in the district, gives him a condescending nod whenever he drives past his little house. Nikolai Ivanitch is a man of influence; he made a notorious horse-stealer return a horse he had taken from the stable of one of his friends; he brought the peasants of a neighbouring village to their senses when they refused to accept a new overseer, and so on. It must not be imagined, though, that he does this from love of justice, from devotion to his neighbour—no! he simply tries to prevent anything that might, in any way, interfere with his ease and comfort. Nikolai Ivanitch is married, and has children. His wife, a smart, sharp-nosed, and keen-eyed woman of the tradesman class, has grown somewhat stout of late years, like her husband. He relies on her in everything, and she keeps the key of the cash-box. Drunken brawlers are afraid of her; she does not like them; they bring little profit and make a great deal of noise: those who are taciturn and surly in their cups are more to her taste. Nikolai Ivanitch's children are still small; the first four all died, but those that are left take after their parents: it is a pleasure to look at their intelligent, healthy little faces.

It was an insufferably hot day in July when, slowly dragging my feet along, I went up alongside the Kolotovka ravine with my dog towards the Welcome Resort. The sun blazed, as it were, fiercely in the sky, baking the parched earth relentlessly ; the air was thick with stifling dust. Glossy crows and ravens with gaping beaks looked plaintively at the passers-by, as though asking for sympathy ; only the sparrows did not droop, but, pluming their feathers, twittered more vigorously than ever as they quarrelled among the hedges, or flew up all together from the dusty road, and hovered in grey clouds over the green hempfields. I was tormented by thirst. There was no water near : in Kolotovka, as in many other villages of the steppes, the peasants, having no spring or well, drink a sort of thin mud out of the pond. . . . For no one could call that repulsive beverage water. I wanted to ask for a glass of beer or kvas at Nikolai Ivanitch's.

It must be confessed that at no time of the year does Kolotovka present a very cheering spectacle ; but it has a particularly depressing effect when the relentless rays of a dazzling July sun pour down full upon the brown, tumble-down roofs of the houses and the deep ravine, and the parched, dusty common over which the thin, long-legged hens are straying hopelessly, and the remains of the old manor-house, now a hollow, grey framework of aspenwood, with holes instead of windows, overgrown with nettles, wormwood, and rank grass, and the pond black, as though charred and covered with goose feathers, with its edge of half-dried mud, and its broken-down dyke, near which, on the finely trodden, ash-like earth, sheep, breathless and gasping with the heat, huddle dejectedly together, their heads drooping with weary patience, as though waiting for this insufferable heat to pass at last. With weary steps I drew near Nikolai Ivanitch's dwelling, arousing in the village children the usual wonder manifested in a concentrated, meaningless stare, and in the dogs an indignation expressed in such hoarse and furious barking that it seemed as if it were tearing their very entrails, and left them breathless and choking, when suddenly in the tavern doorway there appeared a tall peasant without a cap, in a frieze cloak, girt about below his waist with a blue handkerchief. He looked like a house-serf ; thick grey hair stood up in disorder above his withered and wrinkled face. He was calling to some one hurriedly, waving his arms, which obviously were not quite under his control. It could be seen that he had been drinking already.

"Come, come along!" he stammered, raising his shaggy eyebrows with an effort. "Come, Blinkard, come along! Ah, brother, how you creep along, 'pon my word! It's too bad, brother. They're waiting for you within, and here you crawl along. . . . Come."

"Well, I'm coming, I'm coming!" called a jarring voice, and from behind a hut a little, short, fat, lame man came into sight. He wore a rather tidy cloth coat, pulled half on, and a high pointed cap right over his brows, which gave his round plump face a sly and comic expression. His little yellow eyes moved restlessly about, his thin lips wore a continual forced smile, while his sharp, long nose peered forward saucily in front like a rudder. "I'm coming, my dear fellow." He went hobbling towards the tavern. "What are you calling me for? . . . Who's waiting for me?"

"What am I calling you for?" repeated the man in the frieze coat reproachfully. "You're a queer fish, Blinkard: we call you to come to the tavern, and you ask what for? Here are honest folks all waiting for you: Yashka the Turk, and the Wild Master, and the booth-keeper from Zhizdry. Yashka's got a bet on with the booth-keeper: the stake's a pot of beer—for the one that does best, sings the best, I mean . . . do you see?"

"Is Yashka going to sing?" said the man addressed as Blinkard, with lively interest. "But isn't it your humbug, Gabbler?"

"I'm not humbugging," answered the Gabbler, with dignity; "it's you are crazy. I should think he would sing since he's got a bet on it, you precious innocent, you noodle, Blinkard!"

"Well, come in, simpleton!" retorted the Blinkard.

"Then give us a kiss at least, lovey," stammered the Gabbler, opening wide his arms.

"Get out, you great softy!" responded the Blinkard contemptuously, giving him a poke with his elbow, and both, stooping, entered the low doorway.

The conversation I had overheard roused my curiosity exceedingly. More than once rumours had reached me of Yashka the Turk as the best singer in the vicinity, and here was an opportunity all at once of hearing him in competition with another master of the art. I quickened my steps and went into the house.

Few of my readers have probably had an opportunity of getting a good view of any village taverns, but we sportsmen go everywhere. They are constructed on an exceedingly simple plan. They usually consist of a dark outer-shed, and an inner room with a chimney, divided in two by a partition, behind which none of the customers have a right to go. In this partition there is a wide opening cut above a broad oak table. At this table or bar the spirits are served. Sealed-up bottles of various sizes stand on the shelves, right opposite the opening. In the front part of the room, devoted to customers, there are benches, two or three empty barrels, and a corner table. Village taverns are for the most part rather dark, and you hardly ever see on their wainscotted walls any of the glaring cheap prints which few huts are without.

When I went into the Welcome Resort, a fairly large party were already assembled there.

In his usual place behind the bar, almost filling up the entire opening in the partition, stood Nikolai Ivanitch in a striped print shirt; with a lazy smile on his full face, he poured out with his plump white hand two glasses of spirits for the Blinkard and the Gabbler as they came in; behind him, in a corner near the window, could be seen his sharp-eyed wife. In the middle of the room was standing Yakov the Turk, a thin, graceful fellow of three-and-twenty, dressed in a long skirted coat of blue nankin. He looked a smart factory hand, and could not, to judge by his appearance, boast of very good health. His hollow cheeks, his large, restless grey eyes, his straight nose, with its delicate mobile nostrils, his pale brown curls brushed back over the sloping white brow, his full but beautiful, expressive lips, and his whole face betrayed a passionate and sensitive nature. He was in a state of great excitement; he blinked, his breathing was hurried, his hands shook, as though in fever, and he was really in a fever—that sudden fever of excitement which is so well known to all who have to speak and sing before an audience. Near him stood a man of about forty, with broad shoulders and broad jaws, with a low forehead, narrow Tartar eyes, a short flat nose, a square chin, and shining black hair coarse as bristles. The expression of his face—a swarthy face, with a sort of leaden hue in it—and especially of his pale lips, might almost have been called savage, if it had not been so still and dreamy. He hardly stirred a muscle; he only looked slowly about him like a bull under the yoke. He was dressed in a sort of surtout, not over new, with smooth brass buttons; an old black silk handkerchief was twisted round his immense neck. He was called the Wild Master. Right opposite him, on a bench under the holy pictures, was sitting Yashka's rival, the booth-keeper from Zhizdry; he was a short, stoutly-built man about thirty, pock-marked, and curly-headed, with a blunt, turn-up nose, lively brown eyes, and a scanty beard. He looked keenly about him, and, sitting with his hands under him, he kept carelessly swinging his legs and tapping with his feet, which were encased in stylish top-boots with a coloured edging. He wore a new thin coat of grey cloth, with a plush collar, in sharp contrast with the crimson shirt below, buttoned close across the chest. In the opposite corner, to the right of the door, a peasant sat at the table in a narrow, shabby smock-frock, with a huge rent on the shoulder. The sunlight fell in a narrow, yellowish streak through the dusty panes of the two small windows, but it seemed as if it struggled in vain with the habitual darkness of the room; all the objects in it were dimly, as it were patchily, lighted up. On the other hand, it was almost cool in the room, and the sense of stifling heat dropped off me like a weary load directly I crossed the threshold.

My entrance, I could see, was at first somewhat disconcerting to Nikolai Ivanitch's customers; but observing that he greeted me as a friend, they were reassured, and took no more notice of me. I asked for some beer and sat down in the corner, near the peasant in the ragged smock.

"Well, well," piped the Gabbler, suddenly draining a glass of spirits at one gulp, and accompanying his exclamation with the strange gesticulations, without which he seemed unable to utter a single word; "what are we waiting for? If we're going to begin, then begin. Hey, Yashka?" (familiar for Yakov).

"Begin, begin," chimed in Nikolai Ivanitch approvingly.

"Let's begin, by all means," observed the booth-keeper coolly, with a self-confident smile; "I'm ready."

"And I'm ready," Yakov pronounced in a voice thrilled with excitement.

"Well, begin, lads," whined the Blinkard. But, in spite of the unanimously expressed desire, neither began; the booth-keeper did not even get up from the bench—they all seemed to be waiting for something.

"Begin!" said the Wild Master sharply and sullenly. Yashka started. The booth-keeper pulled down his girdle and cleared his throat.

"But who's to begin?" he inquired in a slightly changed voice of the Wild Master, who still stood motionless in the middle of the room, his stalwart legs wide apart and his powerful arms thrust up to the elbow into his breeches pockets.

"You, you, booth-keeper," stammered the Gabbler; "you, to be sure, brother."

The Wild Master looked at him from under his brows. The Gabbler gave a faint squeak, in confusion looked away at the ceiling, twitched his shoulder, and said no more.

"Cast lots," the Wild Master pronounced emphatically; "and the pot on the table."

Nikolai Ivanitch bent down, and with a gasp picked up the pot of beer from the floor and set it on the table.

The Wild Master glanced at Yakov, and said "Come!"

Yakov fumbled in his pockets, took out a halfpenny, and marked it with his teeth. The booth-keeper pulled from under the skirts of his long coat a new leather purse, deliberately untied the string, and shaking out a quantity of small change into his hand, picked out a new halfpenny. The Gabbler held out his dirty cap, with its broken peak hanging loose; Yakov dropped his halfpenny in, and the booth-keeper his.

"You must pick out one," said the Wild Master, turning to the Blinkard.

The Blinkard smiled complacently, took the cap in both hands, and began shaking it.

For an instant a profound silence reigned; the halfpennies clinked faintly, jingling against each other. I looked round attentively; every face wore an expression of intense expectation; the Wild Master himself showed signs of uneasiness; my neighbour, even, the peasant in the tattered smock, craned his neck inquisitively. The Blinkard put his hand into the cap and took out the booth-keeper's halfpenny; every one drew a long breath. Yakov flushed, and the booth-keeper passed his hand over his hair.

"There, I said you'd begin," cried the Gabbler; "didn't I say so?"

"There, there, don't cluck," remarked the Wild Master contemptuously. "Begin," he went on, with a nod to the booth-keeper.

"What song am I to sing?" asked the booth-keeper, beginning to be nervous.

"What you choose," answered the Blinkard; "sing what you think best."

"What you choose, to be sure," Nikolai Ivanitch chimed in, slowly smoothing his hand on his breast, " you're quite at liberty about that. Sing what you like; only sing well; and we'll give a fair decision afterwards."

" A fair decision, of course," put in the Gabbler, licking the edge of his empty glass.

" Let me clear my throat a bit, mates," said the booth-keeper, fingering the collar of his coat.

" Come, come, no nonsense—begin ! " protested the Wild Master, and he looked down.

The booth-keeper thought a minute, shook his head, and stepped forward. Yakov's eyes were riveted upon him.

But before I enter upon a description of the contest itself, I think it will not be amiss to say a few words about each of the personages taking part in my story. The lives of some of them were known to me already when I met them in the Welcome Resort; I collected some facts about the others later on.

Let us begin with the Gabbler. This man's real name was Evgraf Ivanovitch; but no one in the whole neighbourhood knew him as anything but the Gabbler, and he himself referred to himself by that nickname; so well did it fit him. Indeed, nothing could have been more appropriate to his insignificant, ever-restless features. He was a dissipated, unmarried house-serf, whose own masters had long ago got rid of him, and who, without any employment, without earning a halfpenny, found means to get drunk every day at other people's expense. He had a great number of acquaintances who treated him to drinks of spirits and tea, though they could not have said why they did so themselves; for, far from being entertaining in company, he bored every one with his meaningless chatter, his insufferable familiarity, his spasmodic gestures and incessant, unnatural laugh. He could neither sing nor dance; he had never said a clever, or even a sensible thing in his life; he chattered away, telling lies about everything—a regular Gabbler! And yet not a single drinking party for thirty miles around took place without his lank figure turning up among the guests; so that they were used to him by now, and put up with his presence as a necessary evil. They all, it is true, treated him with contempt; but the Wild Master was the only one who knew how to keep his foolish sallies in check.

The Blinkard was not in the least like the Gabbler. His nickname, too, suited him, though he was no more given to blinking than other people; it is a well-known fact, that the Russian peasants have a talent for finding good nicknames. In spite of my endeavours to get more detailed information about this man's past, many passages in his life have remained spots of darkness to me, and probably to many other people; episodes, buried, as the bookmen say, in the darkness of oblivion. I could only find out that he was once a coachman in the service of an old childless lady; that he had run away with three horses he was in charge of; had been lost for a whole year, and no doubt, convinced by experience of the drawbacks and hardships of a wandering life, he had gone back, a cripple, and flung himself at his mistress's feet. He succeeded in a few years in smoothing over his offence by his exemplary conduct, and, gradually getting higher in her favour, at last gained her complete confidence, was made a bailiff, and on his mistress's death, turned out—in what way was never known—to have received his freedom. He got admitted into the class of tradesmen; rented patches of market garden from the neighbours; grew rich, and now was living in ease and comfort. He was a man of experience, who knew on which side his bread was buttered; was more actuated by prudence than by either good or ill-nature; had knocked about, understood men, and knew how to turn them to his own advantage. He was cautious, and at the same time enterprising, like a fox; though he was as fond of gossip as an old woman, he never let out his own affairs, while he made every one else talk freely of theirs. He did not affect to be a simpleton, though, as so many crafty men of his sort do; indeed it would have been difficult for him to take any one in, in that way; I have never seen a sharper, keener pair of eyes than his tiny cunning little "peepers," as they call them in Orel. They were never simply looking about; they were always looking one up and down and through and through. The Blinkard would sometimes ponder for weeks together over some apparently simple undertaking, and again he would suddenly decide on a desperately bold line of action, which one would fancy would bring him to ruin. . . . But it would be sure to turn out all right; everything would go smoothly. He was lucky, and believed in his own luck, and believed in omens. He was exceedingly superstitious in general. He was not liked, because he would have nothing much to do with any one, but he was respected. His whole family consisted of one little son, whom he idolised, and who, brought up by such a father, is likely to get on in the world. "Little Blinkard'll be his father over again," is said of him already in undertones by the old men, as they sit on their mud walls gossiping on summer evenings, and every one knows what that means ; there is no need to say more.

As to Yakov the Turk and the booth-keeper, there is no need to say much about them. Yakov, called the Turk because he actually was descended from a Turkish woman, a prisoner from the war, was by nature an artist in every sense of the word, and by calling, a ladler in a paper factory belonging to a merchant. As for the booth-keeper, his career, I must own, I know nothing of ; he struck me as being a smart townsman of the tradesman class, ready to turn his hand to anything. But the Wild Master calls for a more detailed account.

The first impression the sight of this man produced on you was a sense of coarse, heavy, irresistible power. He was clumsily built, a " shambler," as they say about us, but there was an air of triumphant vigour about him, and—strange to say—his bear-like figure was not without a certain grace of its own, proceeding, perhaps, from his absolutely placid confidence in his own strength. It was hard to decide at first to what class this Hercules belonged : he did not look like a house-serf, nor a tradesman, nor an impoverished clerk out of work, nor a small ruined landowner, such as takes to being a huntsman or a fighting man ; he was, in fact, quite individual. No one knew where he came from or what brought him into our district ; it was said that he came of free peasant-proprietor stock, and had once been in the Government service somewhere, but nothing positive was known about this ; and indeed there was no one from whom one could learn—certainly not from him ; he was the most silent and morose of men. So much so that no one knew for certain what he lived on ; he followed no trade, visited no one, associated with scarcely any one ; yet he had money to spend ; little enough, it is true, still he had some. In his behaviour he was not exactly retiring—retiring was not a word that could be applied to him : he lived as though he noticed no one about him, and cared for no one. The Wild Master (that was the nickname they had given him ; his real name was Perevlyesov) enjoyed an immense influence in the whole district ; he was obeyed with eager promptitude, though he had no kind of right to give orders to any one, and did not himself evince the slightest pretension to authority over the people with whom he came into casual contact. He spoke—they obeyed : strength always has an influence of its own. He scarcely drank at all, had nothing to do with women, and was passionately fond of singing.

There was much that was mysterious about this man; it seemed as though vast forces sullenly reposed within him, knowing, as it were, that once roused, once bursting free, they were bound to crush him and everything they came in contact with; and I am greatly mistaken if, in this man's life, there had not been some such outbreak; if it was not owing to the lessons of experience, to a narrow escape from ruin, that he now kept himself so tightly in hand. What especially struck me in him was the combination of a sort of inborn natural ferocity, with an equally inborn generosity—a combination I have never met in any other man.

And so the booth-keeper stepped forward, and, half shutting his eyes, began singing in high falsetto. He had a fairly sweet and pleasant voice, though rather hoarse: he played with his voice like a woodlark, twisting and turning it in incessant roulades and trills up and down the scale, continually returning to the highest notes, which he held and prolonged with special care. Then he would break off, and again suddenly take up the first motive with a sort of go-ahead daring. His modulations were at times rather bold, at times rather comical; they would have given a connoisseur great satisfaction, and have made a German furiously indignant. He was a Russian *tenore di grazia, ténor léger*. He sang a song to a lively dance-tune, the words of which, all that I could catch through the endless maze of variations, ejaculations, and repetitions, were as follows:

A tiny patch of land, young lass,
I'll plough for thee,
And tiny crimson flowers, young lass,
I'll sow for thee.

He sang; all listened to him with great attention. He seemed to feel that he had to do with really musical people, and therefore was exerting himself to do his best. And they really are musical in our part of the country; the village of Sergievskoe on the Orel high road is deservedly noted throughout Russia for its harmonious chorus-singing. The booth-keeper sang for a long while without evoking much enthusiasm in his audience; he lacked the support of a chorus; but at last, after one particularly bold flourish, which set even the Wild Master smiling, the Gabbler could not refrain from a shout of delight. Every one was roused. The Gabbler and the Blinkard began joining in in an undertone, and exclaiming: "Bravely done! . . . Take it, you rogue! . . . Sing it out, you serpent! Hold it! That shake again, you dog you! . . . May Herod confound your soul!" and so on. Nikolai Ivanitch behind the bar was nodding his head from side to side approvingly. The Gabbler at last was swinging his legs, tapping with his feet and twitching his shoulder, while Yashka's eyes fairly glowed like coal, and he trembled all over like a leaf, and smiled nervously. The Wild Master alone did not change countenance, and stood motionless as before; but his eyes, fastened on the booth-keeper, looked somewhat softened, though the expression of his lips was still scornful. Emboldened by the signs of general approbation, the booth-keeper went off in a whirl of flourishes, and began to round off such trills, to turn such shakes off his tongue, and to make such furious play with his throat, that when at last, pale, exhausted, and bathed in hot perspiration, he uttered the last dying note, his whole body flung back, a general united shout greeted him in a violent outburst. The Gabbler threw himself on his neck and began strangling him in his long, bony arms; a flush came out on Nikolai Ivanitch's oily face, and he seemed to have grown younger; Yashka shouted like mad, "Capital, capital!"—even my neighbour, the peasant in the torn smock, could not restrain himself, and with a blow of his fist on the table he cried, "Aha! well done, bless my soul, well done!" And he spat on one side with an air of decision.

"Well, brother, you've given us a treat!" bawled the Gabbler, not releasing the exhausted booth-keeper from his embraces; "you've given us a treat, there's no denying! You've won, brother, you've won! I congratulate you—the quart's yours! Yashka's miles behind you . . . I tell you: miles . . . take my word for it." (And again he hugged the booth-keeper to his breast.)

"There, let him alone, let him alone; there's no being rid of you" . . . said the Blinkard with vexation; "let him sit down on the bench; he's tired, see . . . You're a ninny, brother, a perfect ninny! What are you sticking to him like a wet leaf for? . . ."

"Well, then, let him sit down, and I'll drink to his health," said the Gabbler, and he went up to the bar. "At your expense, brother," he added, addressing the booth-keeper.

The latter nodded, sat down on the bench, pulled a piece of cloth out of his cap, and began wiping his face, while the Gabbler, with greedy haste, emptied his glass, and, with a grunt, assumed, after the manner of confirmed drinkers, an expression of careworn melancholy.

"You sing beautifully, brother, beautifully," Nikolai Ivanitch observed caressingly. " And now it's your turn, Yashka; mind, now, don't be afraid. We shall see who's who; we shall see. The booth-keeper sings beautifully, though; 'pon my soul, he does."

" Very beautifully," observed Nikolai Ivanitch's wife, and she looked with a smile at Yakov.

" Beautifully, ha!" repeated my neighbour in an undertone.

" Ah, a wild man of the woods!" the Gabbler vociferated suddenly, and going up to the peasant with the rent on his shoulder, he pointed at him with his finger, while he pranced about and went off into an insulting guffaw. " Ha! ha! get along! wild man of the woods! Here's a ragamuffin from Woodland village! What brought you here?" he bawled amidst laughter.

The poor peasant was abashed, and was just about to get up and make off as fast as he could, when suddenly the Wild Master's iron voice was heard:

" What does the insufferable brute mean?" he articulated, grinding his teeth.

" I wasn't doing nothing," muttered the Gabbler. " I didn't . . . I only . . ."

" There, all right, shut up!" retorted the Wild Master. " Yakov, begin!"

Yakov took himself by his throat:

" Well, really, brothers, . . . something. . . . H'm, I don't know, on my word, what . . ."

" Come, that's enough; don't be timid. For shame! . . . why go back? . . . Sing the best you can, by God's gift."

And the Wild Master looked down expectant. Yakov was silent for a minute; he glanced round, and covered his face with his hand. All had their eyes simply fastened upon him, especially the booth-keeper, on whose face a faint, involuntary uneasiness could be seen through his habitual expression of self-confidence and the triumph of his success. He leant back against the wall, and again put both hands under him, but did not swing his legs as before. When at last Yakov uncovered his face it was pale as a dead man's; his eyes gleamed faintly under their drooping lashes. He gave a deep sigh, and began to sing. . . . The first sound of his voice was faint and unequal, and seemed not to come from his chest, but to be wafted from somewhere afar off, as though it had floated by chance into the room. A strange effect was produced on all of us by this trembling, resonant note; we glanced at one another, and Nikolai Ivanitch's wife seemed to draw herself up. This first note was followed by another, bolder and prolonged, but still obviously quivering, like a harp-string when suddenly struck by a stray finger it throbs in a last, swiftly-dying tremble ; the second was followed by a third, and, gradually gaining fire and breadth, the strains swelled into a pathetic melody. " Not one little path ran into the field," he sang, and sweet and mournful it was in our ears. I have seldom, I must confess, heard a voice like it ; it was slightly hoarse, and not perfectly true ; there was even something morbid about it at first ; but it had genuine depth of passion, and youth and sweetness and a sort of fascinating, careless, pathetic melancholy. A spirit of truth and fire, a Russian spirit, was sounding and breathing in that voice, and it seemed to go straight to your heart, to go straight to all that was Russian in it. The song swelled and flowed. Yakov was clearly carried away by enthusiasm ; he was not timid now ; he surrendered himself wholly to the rapture of his art ; his voice no longer trembled ; it quivered, but with the scarce perceptible inward quiver of passion, which pierces like an arrow to the very soul of the listeners ; and he steadily gained strength and firmness and breadth. I remember I once saw at sunset on a flat sandy shore, when the tide was low and the sea's roar came weighty and menacing from the distance, a great white sea-gull ; it sat motionless, its silky bosom facing the crimson glow of the setting sun, and only now and then opening wide its great wings to greet the well-known sea, to greet the sinking lurid sun : I recalled it, as I heard Yakov. He sang, utterly forgetful of his rival and all of us ; he seemed supported, as a bold swimmer by the waves, by our silent, passionate sympathy. He sang, and in every sound of his voice one seemed to feel something dear and akin to us, something of breadth and space, as though the familiar steppes were unfolding before our eyes and stretching away into endless distance. I felt the tears gathering in my bosom and rising to my eyes ; suddenly I was struck by dull, smothered sobs. . . . I looked round—the inn-keeper's wife was weeping, her bosom pressed close to the window. Yakov threw a quick glance at her, and he sang more sweetly, more melodiously than ever ; Nikolai Ivanitch looked down ; the Blinkard turned away ; the Gabbler, quite touched, stood, his gaping mouth stupidly open ; the humble peasant was sobbing softly in the corner, and shaking his head with a plaintive murmur ; and on the iron visage of the Wild Master, from under his overhanging brows there slowly rolled a heavy tear; the booth-keeper raised his clenched fist to his brow, and did not stir. . . . I don't know how the general emotion would have ended, if Yakov had not suddenly come to a full stop on a high, exceptionally shrill note—as though his voice had broken. No one called out, or even stirred; every one seemed to be waiting to see whether he was not going to sing more; but he opened his eyes as though wondering at our silence, looked round at all of us with a face of inquiry, and saw that the victory was his. . . .

"Yashka," said the Wild Master, laying his hand on his shoulder, and he could say no more.

We all stood, as it were, petrified. The booth-keeper softly rose and went up to Yakov.

"You . . . yours . . . you've won," he articulated at last with an effort, and rushed out of the room. His rapid, decided action, as it were, broke the spell; we all suddenly fell into noisy, delighted talk. The Gabbler bounded up and down, stammered and brandished his arms like mill-sails; the Blinkard limped up to Yakov and began kissing him; Nikolai Ivanitch got up and solemnly announced that he would add a second pot of beer from himself. The Wild Master laughed a sort of kind, simple laugh, which I should never have expected to see on his face; the humble peasant as he wiped his eyes, cheeks, nose, and beard on his sleeves, kept repeating in his corner, "Ah, beautiful it was, by God! blast me for the son of a dog, but it was fine!" while Nikolai Ivanitch's wife, her face red with weeping, got up quickly and went away. Yakov was enjoying his triumph like a child; his whole face was transformed, his eyes especially fairly glowed with happiness. They dragged him to the bar; he beckoned the weeping peasant up to it, and sent the innkeeper's little son to look after the booth-keeper, who was not found, however; and the festivities began. "You'll sing to us again; you're going to sing to us till evening," the Gabbler declared, flourishing his hands in the air.

I took one more look at Yakov and went out. I did not want to stay—I was afraid of spoiling the impression I had received. But the heat was as insupportable as before. It seemed hanging in a thick, heavy layer right over the earth; over the dark blue sky, tiny bright fires seemed whisking through the finest, almost black dust. Everything was still; and there was something hopeless and oppressive in this profound hush of exhausted nature. I made my way to a hay-loft, and lay down on the fresh-cut, but already almost dry grass. For a long while I could not go to sleep ; for a long while Yakov's irresistible voice was ringing in my ears. . . . At last the heat and fatigue regained their sway, however, and I fell into a dead sleep. When I waked up, everything was in darkness ; the hay scattered around smelt strong and was slightly damp ; through the slender rafters of the half-open roof pale stars were faintly twinkling. I went out. The glow of sunset had long died away, and its last trace showed in a faint light on the horizon ; but above the freshness of the night there was still a feeling of heat in the atmosphere, lately baked through by the sun, and the breast still craved for a draught of cool air. There was no wind, nor were there any clouds ; the sky all round was clear, and transparently dark, softly glimmering with innumerable, but scarcely visible stars. There were lights twinkling about the village ; from the flaring tavern close by rose a confused, discordant din, amid which I fancied I recognised the voice of Yakov. Violent laughter came from there in an outburst at times. I went up to the little window and pressed my face against the pane. I saw a cheerless, though varied and animated scene ; all were drunk—all from Yakov upwards. With breast bared, he sat on a bench, and singing in a thick voice a street song to a dance-tune, he lazily fingered and strummed on the strings of a guitar. His moist hair hung in tufts over his fearfully pale face. In the middle of the room, the Gabbler, completely " screwed " and without his coat, was hopping about in a dance before the peasant in the grey smock ; the peasant, on his side, was with difficulty stamping and scraping with his feet, and grinning meaninglessly over his dishevelled beard ; he waved one hand from time to time, as much as to say, " Here goes ! " Nothing could be more ludicrous than his face ; however much he twitched up his eyebrows, his heavy lids would hardly rise, but seemed lying upon his scarcely visible, dim, and mawkish eyes. He was in that amiable frame of mind of a perfectly intoxicated man, when every passer-by, directly he looks him in the face, is sure to say, " Bless you, brother, bless you ! " The Blinkard, as red as a lobster, and his nostrils dilated wide, was laughing malignantly in a corner ; only Nikolai Ivanitch, as befits a good tavern-keeper, preserved his composure unchanged. The room was thronged with many new faces ; but the Wild Master I did not see in it.

I turned away with rapid steps and began descending the hill on which Kolotovka lies. At the foot of this hill stretches a wide plain ; plunged in the misty waves of the evening haze, it seemed more immense, and was, as it were, merged in the darkening sky. I walked with long strides along the road by the ravine, when all at once from somewhere far away in the plain came a boy's clear voice : " Antropka ! Antropka-a-a ! . . ." He shouted in obstinate and tearful desperation, with long, long drawing out of the last syllable.

He was silent for a few instants, and started shouting again. His voice rang out clear in the still, lightly slumbering air. Thirty times at least he had called the name, Antropka. When suddenly, from the farthest end of the plain, as though from another world, there floated a scarcely audible reply :

" Wha-a-t ? "

The boy's voice shouted back at once with gleeful exasperation :

" Come here, devil ! woo-od imp ! "

" What fo-or ? " replied the other, after a long interval.

" Because dad wants to thrash you ! " the first voice shouted back hurriedly.

The second voice did not call back again, and the boy fell to shouting Antropka once more. His cries, fainter and less and less frequent, still floated up to my ears, when it had grown completely dark, and I had turned the corner of the wood which skirts my village and lies over three miles from Kolotovka. . . . " Antropka-a-a ! " was still audible in the air, filled with the shadows of night.

VISIONS—A PHANTASY

IVAN S. TURGENIEV

FOR a long time I tried in vain to sleep, and kept tossing from side to side. "The devil take all this nonsense of tipping tables," I said to myself, "it certainly shakes the nerves." At length, however, drowsiness began to get the upper hand.

Suddenly it seemed to me that a harp-string twanged feebly in my chamber. I lifted my head. The moon was low in the sky and shone full in my face; its light lay like a chalk-mark on the carpet. The strange sound was distinctly repeated. I raised myself on my elbow, my heart beat forcibly. A minute passed so—another—then in the distance a cock crowed and a second answered him from yet further.

My head fell back on the pillow. "It comes even to that," I thought, "my ears are fairly ringing."

In a moment more I was asleep, or seemed to myself to be sleeping. I had a singular dream. I thought that I was in my chamber in my own bed, wide awake. Suddenly I hear the noise again. I turn. The moonbeam on the floor begins to waver, to rise, to take shape, stands motionless before me like the white figure of a woman, transparent as mist.

"Who are you?" I ask, trying to retain my composure.

A voice resembling the soughing of the wind among the tree-tops answers me. "It is I—I—I. I am come for you."

"For me? But who are you?"

"Come at nightfall to the old oak-tree at the edge of the wood. I will be there."

I wish to see more closely the features of this mysterious being; an involuntary cold shudder runs through me. I find myself not lying, but in a sitting posture on my bed, and where the appearance of the figure was there is a long pale moon-streak on the floor.

I do not know how the next day passed. I tried, I remember, to read and to work a little, but could accomplish nothing. Night fell; my heart beat as if I had been expecting some one. I went to bed and turned my face to the wall.

" Why did you not come ? " The whisper was plainly audible in the chamber.

Hastily I turned my head.

There was the form again, the mysterious being with fixed eyes in its rigid countenance and an expression of woe.

" Come ! " I heard faintly.

" I will come," I answered with uncontrollable terror. The shape wavered, sank into itself like a puff of smoke, and once more it was only the wan moonlight that lay on the smooth floor.

I passed the day in excitement. At tea I nearly emptied a bottle of wine, and for a moment stood hesitating at the open door, but almost immediately turned back and threw myself upon my couch. The blood rushed at fever-speed through my veins.

Again I heard the tones. I shrank, but would not look up. Then suddenly I felt myself tightly clasped by something, and a whisper in my very ear, " Come, come, come ! " Trembling with fright I stammered, " I will come," and raised myself upright.

The woman's form was bending over the head of my bed. It smiled slightly, and faded, but not before I had been able to distinguish the features. It seemed to me that I had seen them before ; but where—when ? It was late when I rose, and I spent almost the whole day in the fresh air, went to the old oak-tree at the edge of the wood and regarded it thoroughly. Toward evening I seated myself beside the open window in my study. My housekeeper brought me a cup of tea, but I was unable to taste it. All sorts of thoughts besieged me, and I asked myself seriously whether I was not on the road to madness.

It was just after sunset, and not only the sky but the whole atmosphere was suddenly suffused with a supernatural purple light ; leaves and weeds, smooth as if freshly varnished, were alike motionless, there was something singular, almost mysterious, in this absolute quiet, this dazzling sharpness of outline, this combination of intense glow with the stillness of death itself. A large grey bird flew noiselessly toward me and settled itself upon the balustrade of my balcony. I looked at it and it looked at me, its head sideways, with its round, dusky eye.

" Are you sent to remind me ? " I thought.

The bird spread its wings and flew away as silently as it had come. I remained at the window for some time longer absorbed in thought.

I seemed to be under a spell, a gentle but irresistible power controlled me, as the boat is swept on by the current long before the cataract is in sight.

When I regained possession of myself the glow was gone from the sky, which had grown dark, and the enchanted stillness had ceased. A light breeze had sprung up, the moon rode bright and brighter through the blue expanse, and in her cold light the trees shimmered, half dusk half silver. My old servant entered with a lamp, but the draught from the window extinguished the flame. I waited no longer, thrust my hat on my head and hurried to the old oak-tree at the edge of the wood.

Years ago this oak had been struck by lightning; its top was shivered and entirely blasted, but the trunk had still vigour for coming centuries. As I approached, a filmy cloud drew over the moon; blackest shadow lay under the broad branches. At first I was not conscious of anything unusual, but as I glanced to one side my heart throbbed—a white form was standing motionless by a tall sapling between me and the tree. My hair stood on end, but I plucked up courage and walked steadily on.

Yes, it was she, my nightly visitant. As I drew near, the moon shone out in full splendour. The figure seemed woven, as it were, out of a half-transparent milky cloud; through the face I could see a twig that stirred with the wind, only the hair and the eyes were of a somewhat darker colouring, and on one finger of the folded hands I saw the faint glimmer of a narrow ring. I remained standing before it and attempted to speak to it, but my voice died in my throat; although I was not sensible of fear. Its glance was full upon me, the expression was neither of grief nor of gladness, but a rigid, unlife-like attention. I waited to be addressed, but it kept immovable and silent, with its death-like stare fixed on me. Again I felt my self-possession failing.

"I am come," I said at last with a mighty effort. My voice was hollow and unnatural.

"I love you," returned a whisper.

"You love me?" I asked in amazement.

"Give yourself to me," was answered, still in the same tone.

"Give myself to you? You are only a ghost. You have no bodily existence." A peculiar excitement had taken possession of me. "What are you? Smoke—air—vapour? Give myself up to you? First answer me—who are you? Have you lived on earth? And whence do you now come?"

"Give yourself to me. I will do you no ill. Say but two words: 'Take me.'"

I looked at it attentively. "What is it talking about?" I thought. "What does it all mean? How can it take me? Shall I venture?"

"Very good," I answered so that it should hear, with unexpected loudness, indeed, as if some one had hit me from behind, "Take me!"

I had hardly pronounced the syllables when the form bent forward with a smile, so that the features trembled for a moment, and slowly extended its arms. I would fain have drawn back, but found it already out of my power. It twined about me, my body was caught up a yard from the ground, and gently, and not too rapidly, I floated over the still and dewy grass.

My head swam. Involuntarily I closed my eyes, only to open them, however, the next moment. We were still floating upward. But the wood was no longer to be seen. Under us lay a wide plain, flecked here and there with shadow. With horror I realised that we had gained a fearful height.

"I am lost. I am in the devil's clutches," was the thought that shot lightning-like through my brain. Till this moment the idea of demoniacal interference in my undertaking had not occurred to me. We were borne constantly farther, and took our flight higher and higher, as it appeared.

"Where are you taking me?" burst from me at length.

"Wherever you will," answered my guide. It clung closer and closer to me, its face almost touching my own. Yet I could not feel the contact.

"Take me back to the earth. This height makes me giddy."

"Good; only shut your eyes and hold your breath."

I followed this counsel and found myself sinking like a stone, the wind fairly whistling through my hair. When I recovered myself we were hovering just above the ground, so that we stirred the tops of the grass blades.

"Put me down," I said, "on my feet, I have had enough of flying. I am no bird."

"I believed it would be pleasant to you. We have no other power."

"We? Who are you, then?"

No answer.

" Can't you tell me anything ? "

A woeful tone, like that which had wakened me the first night, trembled at my ear. All this while we had been moving almost imperceptibly through the damp night air.

" Set me down," I repeated. My guide moved quietly aside, and I stood upon my feet. It remained before me again with folded hands. I had regained my composure, and looked closely in its face. There was the same expression of melancholy not human.

" Where are we ? " I inquired, for I did not recognise my surroundings.

" You are not far from home, but in a moment you may be there."

" What ? Must I trust myself to you again ? "

" I have done you no harm and will let none come to you. We can fly till dawn, not later. I can take you wherever you may desire—to the ends of the earth. Resign yourself to me ; say once more, ' Take me.' "

" Then—' take me.' "

Again she clasped me. I was lifted from the ground and we floated in air.

" Whither ? " she asked me.

" On, straight on."

" But here are trees."

" Rise above them—only gingerly."

We soared upward, and took once more an onward course. Instead of grass, the tops of the trees waved under our feet. The wood, seen from above, presented a singular appearance, with its moon-lighted, prickly back. It was like some monstrous sleeping creature, and the low, steady rustling of the leaves, like measured breath, carried the resemblance yet farther. Now and then we passed above a little clearing, along whose edge a charmingly indented line of shadow lay. Occasionally we heard below us the plaintive cry of a hare, nearer, the hoot of owls rang dolefully ; the air was full of wild and piny smells ; on all sides the moonlight lay absolute and cold, and high above our heads shone the Pleiades.

Speedily we left the wood behind us, and debouched upon a plain through which some stream ran like a ribbon of mist. We flew along its banks over bushes that were still and heavy with dampness. Here the little waves swelled blue on the river, there they rose dark and threatening. Sometimes a fine faint fragrance rose in a wonderful fashion, as if the water were taking life and soul; it was where the water-lilies unfolded their white petals in a maidenly splendour, conscious that no hand could reach them. The whim seized me to gather one of these, and behold me already at the surface of the stream. There was an unpleasant sensation of moisture in my face as I broke the tough stem of a great flower.

We flew from shore to shore like the jack-o'-lanthorns which we saw glittering about us, and which we seemed to chase. At times we hit upon whole families of wild ducks squatting in a circle in a hollow of the reeds, but they did not stir; it was a chance if one or another would withdraw its head from its wing, look about it, and hasten to bury its beak again in the soft down, or make a cackling accompanied by a shake of the whole body. We roused a heron; he emerged from a clump of willows, stretched his legs, spread his clumsy wings, and flapped heavily away. Nowhere did a fish leap in the water, apparently they also slept. I had by this time become accustomed to the sensation of flying, and even began to find it agreeable: every one who has dreamed of flying will understand this. I began to scrutinise the wonderful being who bore me, and whom I had to thank for these incredible experiences.

It had the appearance of a woman with delicate, not Russian, features. Greyish-white, nearly transparent, with scarcely perceptible shading, it reminded me of an alabaster vase, and once more seemed suddenly, strangely familiar to me.

"May I talk to you?" I asked it.

"Speak."

"I see a ring on your finger. You have lived on earth, then, have been married?"

I stopped, but there was no answer.

"What is your name, or rather what was your name?"

"You may call me Ellis."

"Ellis! That is an English name. Are you an Englishwoman? Have you known me before?"

"No."

"Why have you appeared to me then?"

"I love you."

"Well—does this satisfy you?"

"Yes; we are flying and circling together in pure space."

"Ellis!" I cried, "can it be that you are a lost soul?"

My companion's head sank. " I do not understand," she whispered.

" I conjure you in the name of God "—I began.

" What are you saying ? " she asked, bewildered. And I fancied that the arm that surrounded me like a chill girdle, trembled slightly.

" Do not fear, my beloved," Ellis said, " do not fear." Her face turned to mine and approached it closely, and I felt a curious sensation on my lips, like the prick of a fine needle.

. . . .

I looked down. We had again ascended to a tremendous height, and were flying over a large city unknown to me, which was built on the side of a high hill. Church spires rose here and there from the dark mass of roofs and gardens, a bridge arched the river-bend, everything lay in the deepest stillness, bound in sleep. Domes and crosses glimmered faintly in the peaceful light ; a grey-white road ran still and straight as an arrow from one end of the city and vanished still and straight in the dim distance among the monotonous fields.

" What is this city ? " I asked.

" ——sow."

" ——sow is in the ——schen province, is it not ? "

" Yes."

" Then we are a long way from home ? "

" For us distance is not."

" Truly ? " A sudden recklessness awoke in me. " Take me to South America then."

" To America—there I cannot. There it is day."

" So, we are birds o' night, then, both of us. Well, wherever you can, only let it be far—far."

" Shut your eyes and hold your breath," was Ellis's response, and we began to move with the swiftness of a hurricane. With stunning violence the wind rushed past my ears.

We stopped, but the rushing sound did not cease. On the contrary, it increased to a frightful roar, like a thunder peal.

" Now you can open your eyes," Ellis said.

I obeyed. Good Heavens, where am I ?

Above the heavy clouds are hurrying across the sky like a herd of angry beasts, and below is another monster, the sea, in wildest rage. White foam is spouting and seething madly, waves tower mountain-high and dash themselves with hoarse fury against a gigantic, pitch-black reef. Everywhere the howling of the tempest, the icy breath of the revolted elements, the hollow roar of the breakers, through which at times I caught something like loud lamentations, distant cannon and the peal of bells ; ear-splitting grate and crunch of the chalk cliffs, the sudden cry of an unseen gull, and against the grey horizon the outline of a reeling vessel—everywhere confusion, horror, and death. My head swam, my heart stopped ; I closed my eyes anew.

" What is that and where are we ? "

" Off the southerly coast of the Isle of Wight, before the Blackgang Rock, where so many vessels are lost," replied Ellis, this time with great distinctness of tone, and, as I fancied, a shade of joyous excitement.

" Take me away—away from here—home."

I shrank into myself and pressed my hands over my eyes. I could feel that we were moving more swiftly than before ; already the wind ceased to howl and shriek, it blew evenly in my face, but so strongly that I could hardly breathe.

" Take your foothold," I heard Ellis say.

I made a mighty effort to regain my full consciousness and the mastery of myself. I felt the ground beneath my feet, but could hear no more than if everything about me lay dead ; only on my own temples the veins throbbed violently, unevenly, and with a little inward ringing ; I was still half fainting. But I stood up and opened my eyes.

We were on the bank of my own pond. Straight before me I could see through the slender willow leaves the glassy surface of the water, dappled here and there with mist. On the right was a ryefield in tremulous motion, on the left rose steady and dewy-wet the trees of my garden. The morning had already breathed on them. In the empty grey sky a pair of narrow clouds hung like smoke-wreaths ; they were russet, the first faint hint of dawn had reached them, the eye could not distinguish as yet any spot on the wide horizon where the daylight should break. The stars were gone, there was no stir yet in the magical half-light, everything drew consciously to its awakening.

" Morning, morning is here ! " Ellis murmured in my ear. " Farewell till to-morrow."

I turned to her. She rose, lightly swaying, from the ground, and lifted both arms above her head. Head, arms, and shoulders were suddenly suffused with a warm, rosy flesh tint, the fire of life glowed in the shadowy eyes, a smile of secret joy played over the scarlet lips, it was a charming woman all at once who stood before me. But almost instantly she sank back as if exhausted, and melted away like mist.

I stood motionless.

When things about me had reassumed the aspects of ordinary life, I looked round, and it seemed to me as if the rosy glow that had irradiated the form of my shadowy companion had not faded, but still permeated the air and surrounded me on every side. It was the Dawn. An irresistible languor crept over me, and I went to the house.

As I was passing the hennery my ear caught the first morning gabble of the young geese (of all winged creatures these are the earliest to stir), and I saw the jackdaws perched on the ridge-pole busily preening their feathers against the milky-coloured sky. From time to time they all flew off simultaneously, and after a short flight settled again silently in their old places. From the wood at hand sounded twice or thrice the shrill cry of the mountain cock that had alighted in the dewy grass to seek for berries there. With a slight chilliness in my limbs I reached my own bed and sank at once into a profound sleep.

On the following night as I neared the oak-tree, Ellis glided to meet me as toward a familiar friend. Nor did I experience the horror of yesterday in her presence, indeed I was almost glad to see her ; I did not even speculate on what might happen, but only desired to be taken to some great distance and to some interesting places.

Ellis placed her arm about me and our flight began.

. . . .

Our flight was less rapid than usual, and I could follow with my eye the unfamiliar aspect of the familiar ground as it unrolled like an endless panorama before me. Woods, bushes, fields, ravines, streams, occasionally villages and churches ; then fields, woods, bushes, and ravines again. I had a feeling of sadness and also of indifference, almost of ennui ; but not in the least because it was Russia over which we were taking our flight. No ; the earth in and for itself ; this flat plain that spread beneath me, the whole planet with its short-lived, helpless races, oppressed with poverty, sickness, and care, chained to a clod of dust ; this rough and brittle crust, this sediment upon our planet's fiery core on which a mould is grown that we call by the high-sounding title of the vegetable world ; these men-flies, a hundred times less useful than the flies themselves, with their dwellings of clay and the fugitive trace of their little monotonous lives, their eternal strife against the inevitable and the immutable—how it shocked me!

My heart beat heavily in my bosom; the desire to contemplate any longer these unmeaning pictures had entirely left me. Yes, it was ennui that I felt, but something sharper than ennui as well. Not once did I feel pity for my fellow-men; every other thought was swallowed up in one that I hardly dare to name; it was loathing, and the profoundest, deepest loathing of all was—for myself.

"O cease," breathed Ellis, "cease your thoughts, else it would be impossible for me to carry you. You are too heavy."

"Home!" I cried to her with the tone in which I had summoned my driver once when at four o'clock in the morning I took leave of the friends at Moscow with whom I had been discussing Russia's future. "Home!" I repeated and closed my eyes.

It was not long till I opened them. Ellis began to nestle against me in a singular way; she nearly stifled me. I turned my eyes upon her and the blood curdled in my veins. Every one will understand me who has ever chanced to catch an expression of extreme terror on a stranger's face without any suspicion of its cause. A transport of horror drew and distorted Ellis's pallid, almost blotted-out features. Never had I seen the like on mortal face; here was a bodiless, nebulous ghost, a shadow, and such rigidity of fear!

"Ellis! What is the matter with you?" I asked at last.

"He! It is he!" With difficulty she brought the words forth.

"He? Who is he?"

"Do not name him, do not name him," Ellis stammered in haste. "We must seek some refuge, else it is all at an end, and for ever. Look! There!"

I turned my head to the side where her shuddering finger was pointing, and was conscious of Something—something that was indeed awful to look upon.

This something was the more frightful that it had no decided form. A clumsy, horrible, dark-yellow thing, spotted like a lizard's belly, neither cloud nor smoke, was crawling snake-like over the earth. Its motion was measured, broad-sweeping from above to below and from below to above, like the ill-omened flight of a bird of prey that seeks its booty; from time to time it swooped upon the earth in an indescribable, hideous way; so the spider pounces upon the entrapped fly.

Who or what art thou, gruesome Shape? Under its influence—I saw and felt this—everything shrivelled and grew rigid. A foul, pestilential chill spread upward. I felt myself fainting; my sight grew dim, my hair stood on end. It was a Power that was approaching; a power that knows no obstacle, that subjects everything to itself; that, blind and formless and senseless, sees everything, knows everything, controls everything; like a vulture selects its prey, like a snake crushes it and licks it with its deadly tongue.

"Ellis, Ellis," I shrieked like a madman, "That is Death! The very, living Death himself!"

The lamentable sound that I had heard before escaped Ellis's lips, only this time it was far more like a mortal cry of despair; and we flew on. Our flight was singularly and frightfully unsteady; Ellis turned over and over in the air, plunged first in one direction then in the other, like a partridge that, wounded unto death, still endeavours to distract the dog from her brood. But in the meanwhile long feelers, like extended arms, had disengaged themselves from the lump, and were stretching out after us with groping movements. And then of a sudden it rose into the gigantic shape of a shrouded figure on a pale horse. It grew, filling the heavens themselves. More agitated, more desperate became Ellis's flight. "He has seen me—it is all over—I am lost," I caught in broken whispers. "O miserable that I am! The opportunity so close! Life within my grasp! and now—nothingness—nothingness!"

I could bear it no longer. Consciousness left me.

When I came to myself I was lying on my back in the grass, and I felt through my body a dull ache as if after a heavy fall. Morning flickered in the sky. I could clearly distinguish my surroundings. Not far off there was a willow-fringed road that ran beside a birch wood. The region seemed familiar. I began to recall what had happened to me, and could not repress a shudder as I remembered the last awful spectacle.

"But what can have terrified Ellis?" I thought. "Can she be subject to his power? Is she not immortal? How is it possible that she can be doomed to annihilation?"

A low moan sounded not far away. I hastily turned my head in that direction, and there, two paces from me, lay the motionless form of a young woman in a white garment, with thick, unbound hair, and shoulders bared. One arm was over her head, the other had fallen across her bosom, the eyelids were closed, and the tightly-compressed lips were stained slightly with a reddish froth.

Could it be Ellis ? But Ellis was a ghost, and it was a real woman whom I saw. I crawled over to her and bent above her. " Ellis, is it you ? " I cried. The eyelids quivered, slowly uplifted ; dark, expressive eyes fixed themselves earnestly on my face, and in the next instant a warm, moist, fragrant mouth was pressed to mine, slender, strong arms clasped themselves round my neck, a hot breast swelled against my own. " Farewell ! farewell ! " the dying voice said, and everything disappeared.

I staggered to my feet like a drunken man, passed my hand across my forehead, and looked about me. I found myself on the ——schen road, two versts from my country-seat. Before I reached home the sun had risen.

For some nights following this I waited, let me confess it, not altogether without fear, for the return of my companion, but she came no more. One evening, indeed, I stationed myself at the old place, at the old hour, but nothing unusual occurred. After all, I could not regret the end of so singular an intimacy. I pondered much and earnestly upon this inexplicable, incomprehensible experience, and had to come to the conclusion that not only positive science is in no condition to handle it, but that it is out of the range of legends and fairy tales even. Indeed, what was Ellis ? A ghost, a wandering soul, an evil spirit, a sylph, a vampire, finally ? At times the fancy possessed me that Ellis was in truth a woman whom I had known ; and I ransacked my memory to find where I might have seen her before. Hold ! a moment more and I have it !

But it never came. Everything grew confused like a dream. Yes, I have thought much and, as is very often the case, have arrived at no conclusion. I could not bring myself to ask the advice or the opinion of others, for fear of being taken for a madman. At last I gave up all my gropings ; to tell the truth, I had other things to think of. First, the emancipation of the serfs and the equal distribution of lands, etc., intervened ; then the condition of my health, that has received a shock ; I have a pain in my chest, cough much, and suffer from sleeplessness. I am visibly growing thin. I am as yellow as a mummy. The doctor assures me that I suffer from consumption of the blood, calls my complaint by a Greek name, " *anémie,* " and declares that I must go to Gastein.

THE RENDEZVOUS

Ivan S. Turgeniev

I WAS sitting in a birch grove in autumn, near the middle of September. It had been drizzling ever since morning; occasionally the sun shone warmly; the weather was changeable. Now the sky was overcast with watery white clouds; now it suddenly cleared up for an instant, and then the bright, soft azure, like a beautiful eye, appeared from beyond the dispersed clouds. I was sitting looking about me and listening. The leaves were slightly rustling over my head; and by their very rustle one could tell what season of the year it was. It was not the gay, laughing palpitation of spring; not a soft whispering, nor the lingering chatter of summer, nor the timid and cold lisping of late autumn, but a barely audible, drowsy prattle. A faint breeze was whisking over the tree-tops. The interior of the grove, moist from the rain, was ever changing, as the sun shone or hid beyond the clouds; now the wood was all illumined as if everything in it had burst into a smile; the trunks of the birch trees suddenly assumed the soft reflection of white silk; the small leaves which lay scattered on the ground all at once became variegated and flashed up like red gold; and the comely stalks of the tall, branchy ferns, already tinted to their autumn hue, resembling the colour of over-ripe grapes, appeared here and there tangling and crossing one another. Now again everything suddenly turned blue; the bright colours died out instantly, the birch trees stood all white, lustreless, like snow which has not yet been touched by the cold rays of the winter sun; and stealthily, furtively, a drizzling rain began to sprinkle and whisper over the forest. The leaves on the birches were almost all green yet, though they had turned somewhat pale; only here and there stood a solitary young little birch, all red or all golden, and you should have seen how brightly these birches flashed in the sun when its rays suddenly appeared, gliding and flashing through the dense net of the thin branches which had just been washed by the sparkling rain. Not a single bird was heard; all had found shelter, and were silent; only rarely the mocking voice of the robin sang out like a little steel bell.

Before stopping in this birch wood I passed with my dog through a poplar grove. I confess I am not very fond of the poplar tree with its pale lilac-coloured trunk and its greyish-green, metallic leaves, which it lifts high and spreads in the air like a trembling fan ; I do not like the constant shaking of its round, untidy leaves, which are so awkwardly attached to long stems. The poplar is beautiful only on certain summer evenings, when, rising high amid the low copse, it stands against the red rays of the setting sun, shining and trembling, bathed from root to top in uniform yellowish purple ; or when, on a clear windy day, it rocks noisily, waving against the blue sky, and each leaf seems eager to tear itself away, to fly and hurry off into the distance. But in general I do not like this tree, and, therefore, not stopping to rest in the poplar grove, I made my way to the birch wood, and seated myself under a tree whose branches started near the ground, and thus could protect me from the rain. Having admired the surrounding view, I fell asleep ; I slept that tranquil, sweet sleep which is known only to sportsmen.

I cannot say how long I slept, but when I opened my eyes the entire hollow of the forest was filled with sunshine, and everywhere the bright blue sky was flashing through the cheerfully whispering leaves ; the clouds disappeared, driven asunder by the wind which had begun to play ; the weather was clear now, and one felt in the air that peculiar, dry freshness which, filling the heart with vigour, almost always predicts a quiet, clear night after a rainy day. I was about to rise and try my luck at shooting again, when my eyes suddenly fell on a motionless human figure. I gazed at it steadily ; it was a young peasant girl. She was sitting some twenty feet away from me, her head bowed pensively and her hands dropped on her knees ; in one hand, which was half open, lay a heavy bunch of field flowers, and every time she breathed the flowers were softly gliding over her checkered skirt. A clear white blouse, buttoned at the neck and the wrists, fell in short, soft folds about her waist ; large yellow beads were hanging down from her neck on her breast in two rows. She was not at all bad-looking. Her heavy fair hair, of a beautiful brown, parted in two neatly combed half-circles from under a narrow, dark-red head-band, which came down almost to her ivory-white forehead ; the rest of her face was slightly tanned, with the golden sunburn peculiar to a tender skin. I could not see her eyes, for she did not lift them ; but I saw her thin, high eyebrows, her long lashes ; these were moist, and on her cheek gleamed a tear-drop, which had stopped near her somewhat pale lips. Her little head was very charming; even her somewhat thick round nose did not spoil it. I liked especially the expression of her face; it was so simple and gentle, so sad, and so full of childish perplexity at her own sadness. She was apparently waiting for some one.

Something cracked faintly in the woods. Immediately she raised her head and looked round; her eyes flashed quickly before me in the transparent shade; they were large, bright, and shy like a deer's. She listened for a few seconds, not moving her wide-open eyes from the spot whence the faint sound had come; she heaved a sigh, turned her head slowly, bent down still lower and began to examine the flowers. Her eyelids turned red, her lips quivered bitterly, and a new tear-drop rolled down from under her heavy eyelashes, stopping and sparkling on her cheek. Thus quite a long while passed; the poor girl did not stir; only occasionally she moved her hands and listened, listened all the time. Something cracked once more in the forest; she started. This time the noise did not stop, it was becoming more distinct, it was nearing. At last firm footsteps were heard. She straightened herself, and it seemed as if she lost her courage, for her eyes began to quiver. The figure of a man appeared through the undergrowth. She looked steadily, suddenly flushed, and smiling joyously and happily, seemed about to rise, but she immediately cast down her head again, turned pale, confused; and then she lifted her quivering, almost prayerful eyes to the man as he paused beside her.

I looked at him from my hiding-place with curiosity. I confess he did not produce a pleasant impression. He was, by all appearance, the spoiled valet of some rich young man. His clothes betokened a claim to taste and smart carelessness. He wore a short overcoat of bronze colour, which evidently belonged to his master, and which was buttoned up to the very top; he had on a pink necktie with lilac-coloured edges; and his black velvet cap, trimmed with gold stripes, was pulled over his eyebrows. The round collar of his white shirt propped his ears up and cut his cheeks mercilessly, and the starched cuffs covered his hands up to his red, crooked fingers, which were ornamented with silver and gold rings, set with forget-me-nots of turquoise. His red, fresh, impudent face belonged to those which, as far as I have observed, are almost always repulsive to men, but, unfortunately, are often admired by women. Apparently trying to give an expression of contempt and of weariness to his coarse features, he was ever closing his small, milky-grey eyes, knitting his brows, lowering the corners of his lips, yawning, and, with careless, although not too clever ease, now adjusting his reddish, smartly twisted curls, now fingering the yellow hair which bristled upon his thick upper lip. In a word, he was making an insufferable display of himself. He began to do this as soon as he noticed the young peasant girl who was awaiting him. He advanced to her slowly, with long strides, then stood for a while, shrugged his shoulders, thrust both hands into the pockets of his coat, and, casting a quick and indifferent glance at the poor girl, sank down on the ground.

"Well ?" he began, continuing to look aside, shaking his foot and yawning. "Have you waited long ?"

The girl could not answer him at once. "Long, Victor Alexandrich," she said at last, in a scarcely audible voice.

"Ah !" He removed his cap, majestically passed his hand over the thick, curly hair whose roots started almost at his eyebrows, and, looking round with dignity, covered his precious head again cautiously. "And I almost forgot all about it. Besides, you see, it's raining." He yawned again. "I have a lot of work to do ; you can't look after everything, and he is in a bad temper. We are leaving to-morrow——"

"To-morrow ?" said the girl, and fixed a frightened look upon him.

"To-morrow. Come, come, come, please," he replied quickly, vexed, noticing that she shook, and bowed her head in silence. "Please, Akulina, don't cry. You know I can't bear it" (and he twitched his flat nose). "If you don't stop, I'll leave you at once. What nonsense—to whimper !"

"Well, I won't, I won't," said Akulina hastily, swallowing the tears with an effort. "So you're going away to-morrow ?" she added, after a brief silence. "When will it please God that I shall meet you again, Victor Alexandrich ?"

"We'll meet, we'll meet again. If it isn't next year, it'll be later. My master, it seems, wants to enter the service in Petersburg," he went on, pronouncing the words carelessly and somewhat indistinctly. "And it may be that we'll go abroad."

"You will forget me, Victor Alexandrich," said Akulina sadly.

"No—why should I ? I'll not forget you, only you had better be sensible ; don't make a fool of yourself ; obey your father. And

I'll not forget you. Oh, no ; oh, no." And he stretched himself calmly and yawned again.

" Do not forget me, Victor Alexandrich," she resumed in a beseeching voice. " I have loved you so much, it seems—all, it seems, for you. You tell me to obey Father, Victor Alexandrich. How am I to obey my father ? "

" How's that ? " He pronounced these words as if from the stomach, lying on his back and holding his hands under his head.

" Why, Victor Alexandrich—you know very well ! "

She fell silent. Victor fingered his steel watch-chain.

" Akulina, you are not a foolish girl," he said at last, " so don't talk nonsense. It's for your own good, do you understand me ? Of course, you are not foolish, you're not altogether a peasant, so to say, and your mother wasn't always a peasant either. Still, you are without education. Therefore you must obey when you are told to."

" But it's terrible, Victor Alexandrich."

" Oh, what nonsense, my dear ! What is she afraid of ! What is that you have there," he added, moving closer to her, " flowers ? "

" Flowers," replied Akulina sadly. " I have picked some field tansies," she went on, with some animation. " They're good for the calves. And here I have some marigolds—for scrofula. Here, look, what a pretty flower ! I haven't seen such a pretty flower in all my life. Here are forget-me-nots, and—these I have picked for you," she added, taking from under the tansies a small bunch of cornflowers, tied around with a thin blade of grass. " Do you want them ? "

Victor stretched out his hand lazily, took the flowers, smelled them carelessly, and began to turn them around in his fingers, looking up with thoughtful importance. Akulina gazed at him. There was so much tender devotion, reverent obedience and love in her pensive eyes. She feared him, and yet she dared not cry, and inwardly she bade him farewell, and admired him for the last time ; and he lay there, stretched out like a sultan, and endured her admiration with magnanimous patience and condescension. I confess I was filled with indignation as I looked at his red face, which betrayed satisfied selfishness through his feigned contempt and indifference. Akulina was so beautiful at this moment ! All her soul opened before him trustingly and passionately ; it reached out to him, caressed him, and he—— He dropped the cornflowers on the grass, took out from the side-pocket of his coat a round glass in a bronze frame and began to force it into his eye ;

but no matter how hard he tried to hold it with his knitted brow, his raised cheek, and even with his nose, the glass dropped out and fell into his hands.

"What's this ?" asked Akulina at last, with surprise.

"An eyeglass," he replied importantly.

"What is it for ?"

"To see better."

"Let me see it."

Victor frowned, but gave her the glass. "Look out; don't break it."

"Don't be afraid, I'll not break it." She lifted it timidly to her eye. "I can't see anything," she said naïvely.

"Shut your eye," he retorted in the tone of a dissatisfied teacher. She closed the eye before which she held the glass.

"Not that eye, not that one, stupid ! The other one !" exclaimed Victor ; and, not allowing her to correct her mistake, he took the glass away from her. Akulina blushed, laughed slightly, and turned away.

"It seems it's not for me." "Of course not !"

The poor girl maintained silence, and heaved a deep sigh.

"Oh, Victor Alexandrich, how shall I get along without you ?" she said suddenly.

Victor wiped the eyeglass and put it back into his pocket.

"Yes, yes," he said at last. "At first it will really be hard for you." He tapped her on the shoulder condescendingly ; she quietly took his hand from her shoulder and kissed it. "Well, yes, yes, you are indeed a good girl," he went on, with a self-satisfied smile ; "but it can't be helped ! Consider it yourself ! My master and I can't stay here, can we ? Winter is near, and to pass the winter in the country is simply impossible—you know it yourself. It's a different thing in Petersburg ! There are such wonders over there that you could not imagine even in your dreams, you silly ! What houses, what streets, and society, education—it's something wonderful !" Akulina listened to him with close attention, slightly opening her lips like a child. "However," he added, wriggling on the ground, "why do I say all this to you ? You can't understand it anyway !"

"Why not, Victor Alexandrich ? I understood, I understood everything."

"Just think of her !"

Akulina cast down her eyes. "You never spoke to me like this before, Victor Alexandrich," she said, without lifting her eyes.

"Before? Before! Just think of her! Before!" he remarked, indignantly. Both grew silent.

"However, it's time for me to go," said Victor, and leaned on his elbow, about to rise.

"Wait a little," said Akulina in an imploring voice.

"What for? I have already said to you, Good-bye!"

"Wait," repeated Akulina.

Victor again stretched himself on the ground and began to whistle. Akulina kept looking at him steadfastly. I could see that she was growing agitated; her lips twitched, her pale cheeks were reddening.

"Victor Alexandrich," she said at last in a broken voice, "it's a sin in you, it's a sin, Victor Alexandrich, by God!"

"What's a sin?" he asked, knitting his brows. He raised his head and turned to her.

"It's a sin, Victor Alexandrich. If you would only say a good word to me before leaving; if you would only say one word to me, miserable little orphan that I am——"

"But what should I say to you?"

"I don't know. You know that better than I do, Victor Alexandrich. Here you are going away—if you would only say one word—— What have I done to deserve this?"

"How strange you are! What can I say?"

"If only one word——"

"There, she's always at the same thing," he muttered with vexation, and got up. "Don't be angry, Victor Alexandrich," she added hastily, unable to repress her tears.

"I'm not angry—only you are foolish. What do you want? I can't marry you! I can't, can I? Well, then, what do you want? What?" He stared at her, as if awaiting an answer, and opened his fingers wide.

"I want nothing—nothing," she replied, stammering, not daring to outstretch her trembling hands to him, "but only—at least one word, at parting!"

And the tears began to stream from her eyes.

"Well, there you are, she's started crying," said Victor indifferently, pulling the cap over his eyes.

"I don't want anything," she went on, sobbing and covering her face with her hands; "but how shall I feel now at home, how shall I feel? And what will become of me, what will become of me, wretched one that I am? They'll marry the poor little orphan to a man she does not like. My poor little head!"

"Oh, go on, go on!" muttered Victor in a low voice, stirring restlessly.

"If you only said one word, just one: 'Akulina—I——'"

Sudden heartrending sobs interrupted her. She fell with her face upon the grass and cried bitterly, bitterly. All her body shook convulsively. The long-suppressed sorrow at last burst forth in a stream of tears. Victor stood a while near her, then shrugged his shoulders, turned around and walked off with long strides.

A few moments went by. She became silent, lifted her head, looked around and clasped her hands; she was about to run after him, but her feet failed her; she fell down on her knees. I could not endure it any longer and rushed over to her; but before she had time to look at me, she suddenly seemed to have regained her strength, and with a faint cry she rose and disappeared behind the trees, leaving the scattered flowers on the ground.

I stood a while, picked up the bunch of cornflowers, and walked out of the wood to the open. The sun was low in the pale, clear sky; its rays seemed to have faded and turned cold; they did not shine now, they spread in an even, almost watery, light. There was only a half-hour left until nightfall, and twilight was setting in. A violent wind was blowing fast toward me across the yellow, dried-up stubble-field; the small withered leaves were carried quickly past me across the road; the side of the wood which stood like a wall by the field trembled and flashed clearly, but not brightly; everywhere on the reddish grass, and on the bracken, innumerable autumn cobwebs flashed and trembled. I stopped. I began to feel sad; it seemed as if a dismal fear of approaching winter was stealing through the gay, fresh smile of fading nature. High above me, a cautious raven flew by heavily, sharply cutting the air with his wings; then he turned his head, looked at me sidelong, and croaking abruptly, disappeared beyond the forest; a large flock of pigeons rushed past me from a barn, and suddenly whirling about in a column, they came down and set themselves busily to search the field—a sign of autumn! Some one drove past beyond the bare hillock, making much noise with an empty waggon.

I returned home, but the image of poor Akulina did not leave my mind for a long time, and the cornflowers, long withered, are in my possession at this day.

FIODOR N. DOSTOYEVSKY
1822–1881

THE HONEST THIEF

ONE morning as I was just starting for work, Agraphina, my cook, laundress, and maid-of-all-work, entered into conversation with me to my great astonishment. Up to that time she had been such a silent, simple woman, that, except for two words daily as to what she was to cook for dinner, she hadn't spoken in six years. At least I had heard nothing further from her.

" I came to you, sir," she began suddenly, " you should let the small room."

" What small room ? "

" The one by the kitchen, of course."

" Why ? "

" Why ? Because people take lodgers, of course."

" And who will hire it ? "

" Who will hire it ? Why, of course, a lodger."

" But, my good woman, it's too narrow to place even a bed there. Who will live in it ? "

" Why live there ? Just sleep there and live by the window."

" What window ? "

" You know as well as I do ! The one in the hall. He can sit here and do whatever work he has. He can even sit on a chair there. He has a chair, and a table—everything."

" Who is he ? "

" Oh, an excellent, experienced man. I will cook for him, and will only charge three roubles a month for board and lodging. . . ."

After long efforts I succeeded in finding out that some elderly man had induced or somehow got round Agraphina to take him in the kitchen as a lodger. Then she took it upon her to decide how it was to be done ; otherwise, I know she would have given me no peace. Whenever she disapproved of something she at once became pensive, lapsed into deep melancholy, and continued so for two or three weeks. During this period she spoiled the food, neglected the washing, did not clean the floors, in a word, life was made unpleasant for me. I often remarked that these silent women are incapable of reasoning and remain obsessed with their own ideas. But whenever in some strange manner something like an idea or an enterprise had taken form in her feeble mind, to thwart or to refuse her was morally to kill her for a time, and as I liked my own peace of mind, I agreed at once.

" Has he, at any rate, a passport or something ? "

" How d'you mean ? Of course there is. An excellent man ; promised to pay three roubles a month."

The next day the new lodger appeared in my modest bachelor quarters ; but I did not grieve over it, rather I felt glad. I always lead the solitary life of a recluse. I have hardly any acquaintances and go out rarely. After ten years of solitary life, I am naturally used to loneliness, but ten, fifteen, or even more years of such solitude, with such a woman as Agraphina, in a bare flat, appeared an unalluring prospect ! So under the circumstances another man was indeed a blessing from heaven.

Agraphina spoke the truth : my lodger was a retired soldier, which I saw at the first glance without looking at his passport. They are easy to recognise. Eustace Ivanitch, my lodger, came of a well-to-do family. We settled down well together, but what was better was that he had many interesting stories of his life which he told well. In the dull monotony of my existence such a raconteur was a treasure-trove. He made a considerable impression on me, but now follows the incident which brings about this story.

One day I was alone in the flat : and Eustace and Agraphina had gone out on business. Suddenly I heard something which seemed to me strange in the next room ; I went in ; there, indeed, in the hall stood a strange man, small in stature and wearing a smock without a coat in spite of the bitter autumn weather.

" What do you want ? "

" Inspector Alexandrov : does he live here ? "

" No, my friend ; good-bye."

" The concierge said he lived here," said my visitor, retreating cautiously to the door.

" Get away, take yourself off."

Next day after dinner, when Eustace Ivanitch was trying a coat on me which he was altering, some one again came into the hall. I opened the door.

The gentleman of yesterday, under my very eyes, calmly took my short winter coat from the peg, folded it under his arm and rushed from the flat. Agraphina looked at him, her mouth wide open with astonishment, and did nothing to rescue the coat. Eustace Ivanitch dashed after the thief and returned ten minutes later completely out of breath and empty-handed. The man had absolutely escaped.

" Well, Eustace Ivanitch, no success? Lucky he left the great-coat or we should have been in a nice mess, the rascal!"

But all this so upset Eustace Ivanitch that I quite forgot the theft in watching him. He couldn't get over it. He constantly threw down his work and related again and again how it all happened, how the man stood two paces off and took the coat under our very eyes in a most incomprehensible manner. Then he started work again, only to throw it down, and finally I saw him go off to tell the concierge about it and reproach him for such a thing happening in his house. Then he returned and started blaming Agraphina. Then again sat down to work and muttered to himself all the time about the theft. In a word, though he could work, Eustace Ivanitch was a most pertinacious busybody.

" He made a fool of us, Eustace Ivanitch," said I that evening, as I handed him a glass of tea, feeling so bored that I wished him to relate the story again, which, from constant repetition and the deep sincerity of the narrator, had begun to grow very comic.

" Fooled us, sir! Yes, it was a great pity, and in my opinion there is no worse crime in the world than theft. One works in vain, for another steals the result of your work, the labour of years. . . . Horrible! One hardly wants to talk of it. What d'you think of it, sir . . . isn't it pitiable?"

" Yes, it's true, Eustace Ivanitch; better to burn the thing than let the thief have it."

" Yes, as you say, but of course all thieves are not alike. It was once my strange lot to meet an honest thief."

" What, an honest one? What thief can be honest?"

" It's true, sir! The honest thief is not a thief. I only wished to say that the man seemed honest and stole. It was really rather sad."

" And how did it happen?"

" Yes, sir, it was about two years ago. I had been out of a place almost a year, and before I had secured one I fell in with an absolutely broken man. We met in an eating-house. He was a drunkard, a vagabond, a parasite, had held a position somewhere but had lost it long ago through drink. God knows what clothes he wore! Sometimes you wondered if he had a shirt beneath his great-coat; everything he laid hands on he drank. He wasn't a brawler ; very gentle and kindly in character, but you soon saw how he craved for drink. Well, I foregathered with him, or rather he attached himself to me. And what a man he was ! Like a dog, you go there—he follows ; only once had I seen such a helpless creature ! At first I allowed him to spend the night—why, I don't know ; his passport was in order and the man himself all right. The next day I again let him stop the night, and the third day he came again, spent the whole day sitting in the window and stopped the night. Well, thought I, he's attached himself to me, and if I, a poor man, give him food and drink and a night's lodging, it's a millstone round my neck. Previously he had attached himself to some official in the same way. The two drank together, but the official overdrank and died. He was called Emil, Emil Ileetch. I thought and thought : what am I to do with him ? Send him away—I haven't the heart to, he's such a miserable, broken man. And he's so silent ; never asks for anything, just sits and looks at you with dog-like eyes. This is what drunkenness makes a man, I thought to myself : how shall I say to him, 'Be off with you, Emil, you've no business here, you can't force yourself on anybody ; soon there will be nothing to eat, how can I keep and feed you ?' I sit and think, what will he do when I say this to him ? And I see how long he would look at me when he heard without understanding my words, how, bent and ragged, he would get up at length with his bundle in which he carried God knows what, how he would arrange his overcoat to look all right and not show the holes—for he was well brought up ; how he would open the door and go out, till I felt I could not cast him adrift. God knows I might have been such a one myself. Wait, thought I, you won't have much longer to stay with me. Soon I'm going, then you won't find me again.

"Well, sir, we parted. When the late Alexander Philimovitch (God rest his soul) was alive, he said to me, 'We are very pleased with your work ; when we return from the country we will engage you again.' So I went to them again. He was a kind gentleman, but died the same year. So, gathering my scanty belongings, I left his house and hired a room from an old woman, her only spare one ; so, thought I, good-bye to Emil. But what do you think, sir ? Returning towards evening (I had been to see a friend), the first person I saw in my room was Emil in his old great-coat, his bundle by his side, sitting on my trunk, waiting for me . . . yes, and reading a book of Church services, which he had borrowed from the old woman to pass the time. He had found me! My hands dropped: 'Well,' thought I, 'there's nothing to be done, why didn't I send him away at first?' I went straight up and asked: 'Have you brought your passport, Emil?'

"I sat down and began to think; what was I to do with this man in my room? He must eat, though a drunkard does not eat much. I felt certain he would go off on drinking bouts, yet I knew I should feel sorry if he left me. So I decided to be his benefactor. I will keep him, thought I, from evil and disaster, so I said: 'Stop here, Emil, but you must do as I tell you.'

"I thought to myself I will teach you to do some work—not all at once, but by degrees. I may find some ability in you, because for any work only human ability is needed. I looked quietly at him, and saw before me a man in the lowest depths. I began to encourage him with kind words: 'Look to yourself, Emil,' I said, 'and see if you can't do more for yourself. Enough of this life! Look at your clothes, your overcoat is only fit for use as netting; it's not right! It's time to learn honour.'

"Emil sat and listened to me for a long time with downcast eyes and incapable of speech. Then he sighed heavily. 'Why do you sigh?' I asked. 'Oh, nothing, Eustace Ivanitch, don't be disturbed. To-day two peasant women were quarrelling in the street and one upset the other's basket of berries.'

"'Well, what of it?'

"'And the other knocked over the first one's basket of berries on purpose, and kicked it with her foot.'

"'Well, what of it, Emil Ileetch?'

"'Oh, nothing, Eustace Ivanitch, it just happened.'

"'Nothing, it just happened!' Oh, thought I, my poor Emil, you've been over-drinking.

"'And then a gentleman dropped a bank note in the Sadovaya. A peasant saw it and said: "Mine!" but another saw it and said, "No, mine! I saw it first"—so they started to fight, but a policeman came up, picked up the note, gave it to the gentleman, and threatened to arrest both the peasants.'

"'Well, what of it? What is there important in it?'

"'Oh, nothing. The crowd laughed, Eustace Ivanitch.'

"'Oh, Emil! What do the crowd matter? You have sold your soul for a copper, I tell you.'

"'How, Eustace Ivanitch?'

"'Take some work, for the hundredth time, I say, take pity on yourself and work.'

"'What shall I do? No one will take me.'

"'For the reason that you were dismissed, Emil, because you are a drunkard!'

"He was just cunning. He would listen to me till it bored him, then slink away. Drink all day and return home drunk. Who gave him the drink, or from where he got the money, God only knows. I at least was not guilty.

"'No, Emil,' I said to him, 'I can stand it no longer. Enough of this, d'you hear, enough! Next time you come back drunk I will turn you out to sleep on the stairs.'

"After hearing this Emil stopped two days at home, but slipped away on the third. I waited and waited, still he did not come back. I began to be alarmed. What had I done to him? Had I frightened him? Whither he had gone, God knew. Night came, no Emil. In the morning I went out to the hall and saw him lying there. He lay there, his head on the step, absolutely stiff with cold.

"'What's the matter with you, Emil? What are you doing there?'

"'You were angry with me the other day and threatened to put me out on the stairs, so I was afraid to come in and lay here.'

"Then wrath and pity seized me. 'Why don't you do some work instead of lying on the stairs?'

"'But what work can I do, Eustace Ivanitch?'

"'You miserable wretch,' said I angrily, 'learn tailoring. Look at your coat! It's nothing to you that it's all in rags, so you wear it out on the stairs! Take a needle and try to mend it, you good-for-nothing drunkard!'

"Well, sir, he took a needle; I had spoken in derision, but he was frightened. He took off his coat, took some thread and tried to thread the needle, but in vain; his hands trembled, his eyes grew red, and at length he put it down and looked at me. . . .

"'Let me help you, Emil,' said I. 'I spoke scornfully to try and rouse your shame. Give up your weakness, and let's have no more nights on the stairs.'

"'But what am I to do? I know I'm a drunkard and good for nothing! . . . To you my be— benefactor my heart is everlastingly! . . .

"Suddenly his blue lips trembled as tears rolled down his white cheeks to his unshaved chin in a torrent. How they flowed! It was as if a knife had pierced my heart.

"'Oh, you sensitive man! Who would have known it, who would have guessed it of you?'

"Well, sir, there is yet much more to tell. Events so miserable and sordid that you would despise them utterly, but I would give much if they had not happened. I had a pair of breeches of excellent material which I had made for a certain landowner, who, however, said they were too narrow and left them on my hands. I considered them valuable. In the market they would have fetched five roubles—much to a poor man. At that time Emil was passing through a severe, trying period. I watched him, a whole day he drank nothing, then a second, a third day, nothing passed his lips and he sat silent and disconsolate. Thought I, 'Either you have not wherewithal to buy it, or maybe you have turned over a new leaf.' This was the state of affairs when a big holiday came. I went out to vespers; came back—found Emil in the window, drunk and staggering. Alas! thought I, what a man, and went to my trunk for something or other. Looked in—no breeches! . . . I searched everywhere but could not find them. I rushed off to the old landlady and blamed her, for it was no use talking to a drunken man. 'No,' said the old woman, 'what do I want with your breeches?' 'I don't know,' said I, 'but who has been here?' 'No one has been here,' she answered, 'Emil Ileetch went out, but came in and is sitting up there. Ask him.' 'You didn't take those breeches for any reason, Emil, did you?' said I, 'you remember the ones I made for the landowner.' 'No, Eustace Ivanitch,' answered he, 'I didn't take them.'

"What a state of affairs! Again I looked everywhere—no breeches! And Emil sat and swayed. I sat on the trunk straight opposite him, and at length caught his eye.

"'No,' said he, 'you may think I took them but I didn't.'

"'Where can they have got to, Emil?'

"'No, Eustace Ivanitch, I haven't seen them at all.'

"I listened to him unheeding, crossed to the window, sat down and began to work at a waistcoat I was altering for some official in the house. I felt sick at heart and ready to let things slide, till Emil felt the anger that possessed me. Thus does a man who has participated in an evil act feel the approach of misfortune, as birds feel the oncoming storm.

" 'Eustace Ivanitch,' began Emil, and his voice trembled, 'to-day Anton Prokovitch, who married the other day . . .'

" I looked at him till he understood my thoughts. Getting up he walked to the bed and started shuffling round it. I waited while he kept on saying to himself: 'No, no, where can they have got to?' I waited to see what would happen and saw him crawl under the bed. I could restrain myself no longer.

" 'What are you doing, crawling under there, Emil?'

" 'I was looking for the breeches. Perhaps they have fallen down somewhere.'

" 'You poor fool,' said I, 'what good d'you expect to do crawling about on your knees?'

" 'Well, why not, Eustace Ivanitch? I thought it would be well to look for them.'

" 'H'm, listen,' said I. 'What?' answered Emil.

" 'Wasn't it you,' said I, 'who stole them from me like a thief and a rascal?'—for thus only could I account for his strange conduct.

" 'No, Eustace Ivanitch . . .' All this time he stopped under the bed. At length he crawled out. I looked at him—he was as white as a sheet. He went to the window and sat opposite to me for about ten minutes. 'No,' said he as he suddenly rose and approached me, and I see him now, white and guilty-faced, 'No, I never took them.'

" He was trembling all over and his fingers clutched his breast convulsively, his voice shook, so that I myself grew frightened and went to the window.

" 'Well, Emil,' I said, 'as you wish, and forgive me if in my stupidity I accuse you unjustly. And let the breeches be; we shall live in spite of the loss; we have hands, thank God, and will not sink to theft and steal from another poor man. We will earn our bread . . .!'

" Emil stood and listened to me, then sat down. There he sat the whole evening without stirring, and when I fell asleep he was still there. When I woke up in the morning he was lying on the bare floor, wrapped in his coat. Well, sir, I never liked him since then, and during those first few days hated him. It was as if my own son had robbed me and caused me grievous harm. And Emil drank without a stop for two weeks till he was sodden with drink. He went out early and came back late, and for two weeks I never heard a word from him. Perhaps conscience pricked him, or he hoped to escape from himself. At length the orgy ended, all his money was finished, and again he sat at the window. For three days I remember he sat in silence. I looked at him ; he was crying. The tears came copiously like a fountain, and it's a sad thing to see a grown man cry, especially an old man like Emil.

" ' What's the matter, Emil ? ' I said.

" And he trembled all over. It was the first time I had spoken to him. ' Nothing . . . Eustace Ivanitch.'

" ' But good heavens, Emil, why are you sitting like that ? ' He aroused my pity.

" ' I don't know, I wish to get some work, Eustace Ivanitch.'

" ' What kind of work, Emil ? '

" ' Oh, any kind. Perhaps I shall find a position like I held before : I have already been to ask for one. I don't wish to abuse your kindness further ; if only I can get a place I will repay you in full.'

" ' Enough of that, Emil ! Let's live on as before.'

" ' No, Eustace Ivanitch, perhaps you still think . . . but I never took those breeches. . . .'

" ' Oh, well, my dear Emil, do as you please.'

" ' No, Eustace Ivanitch, I certainly can't live on here any longer.'

" ' But what's the matter with you ? ' said I. ' Who's driving you away ? '

" ' No,' answered Emil, ' it isn't right I should stay, I had much better go.' And, indeed, he rose and put on his coat.

" ' But what are you doing, Emil ? Listen to reason. Where are you going ? '

" ' Good-bye, Eustace Ivanitch, don't keep me back—I'm going. You have changed towards me.'

" ' How have I changed ? You will be lost alone, Emil, like a small ignorant child.'

" ' No, Eustace Ivanitch. When you go out now you lock your trunk, and I notice it and it grieves me . . . better let me go and forgive me for bringing trouble on you.'

" What was I to do ? The man went out. All day I expected him to return at evening—but no. Another day—no ; a third—no. I got frightened and anxious ; neither drank, ate, nor slept. The man had disarmed me entirely ! Next day I started off and searched all the cabarets,—but in vain, he had vanished. ' Have you succumbed already ? ' thought I. ' Perhaps the end came in a drunken fit and you are lying out somewhere like a rotted log.' Half dead, half living, I returned home. The next day I again searched in vain and blamed myself bitterly for allowing the poor helpless fellow to leave me. The fifth day (it was a holiday) the door creaked. I looked up and saw Emil enter, pinched and blue, his hair plastered with mud as if he had slept in the streets, while he had grown thin out of all knowledge. He took off his coat and sat down opposite me on the trunk. I rejoiced after my anguish at his loss. Naturally it was sad to see a man in his state. I began to soothe and comfort him.

" 'Well, Emil,' said I, 'glad to see you back. You were so late I almost went round the cabarets to look for you. Have you had anything to eat?'

" 'Yes, thanks, Eustace Ivanitch.'

" 'Enough to eat? Here is some of yesterday's supper left, some veal and a piece of bread. Eat it, it won't do you any harm.'

" I helped him, and saw he had not eaten for three days, so great was his appetite. It meant that hunger had driven him to me, and my thoughts hardened towards him. To finish his meal I brought some vodka.

" 'Well, Emil,' I said, 'let's drink to the holiday. D'you want some? It's excellent.'

" He stretched out his hand and seized it greedily, then stopped. I waited and watched. He lifted it to his mouth, spilling some over his sleeve; but it never reached his mouth, for he put it down on the table untasted.

" 'What's the matter, Emil?'

" 'No, thanks, Eustace Ivanitch, I don't want to drink any more.'

" 'Have you made up your mind to give it up, or is it just for to-day?'

" He was silent and his head dropped on to his hand as I watched. 'You're not ill, are you, Emil?'

" 'I'm not feeling very well.'

" I took him and placed him on the bed. How thin he had grown: his head burned and he shook with fever. I sat by his side all day: towards night he grew worse. I offered him some light food, saying, 'Try and eat or you will be worse.' He shook his head: 'No,' says he, 'I won't dine to-day.'

" The next morning I went for the doctor. Doctor Kostopravov, whom I knew, lived near by. I met him when working for the Bosomiagins, where he attended me. 'He's in a bad way,' said the doctor, and gave me some powders for him, but I didn't give the powders as I had no confidence in them. So the day passed.

" The end came as he lay opposite me ; I was sitting in the window working, and the old landlady was lighting the stove. All were silent. I was grieving for him as for a son. I knew he was looking at me and had been trying to say something since morning, but did not dare. At length I looked at him and saw his eyes fixed on me with a look of unutterable anguish, but he looked quickly away when he met my gaze. ' Eustace Ivanitch.'

" ' What is it, Emil ? '

" ' How much is my coat worth in the market ? '

" ' Well,' I said, ' I don't know, perhaps three roubles.' Though I knew full well they would only laugh at any one who tried to sell such useless rags, but I just said it to comfort him.

" ' And I too thought they would give three roubles for it. It is a cloth coat. Are you sure they'd give three roubles ? '

" ' I don't know, Emil, if you take it you must start by asking for three.'

" He was silent for a little : then spoke again.

" ' Eustace Ivanitch ! '

" ' What is it, Emil ? '

" ' Sell my great-coat when I die, don't bury me in it. It has some value and will do for you perhaps.'

" My heart was full of pity as I saw death approaching rapidly. Again we were silent and so an hour passed. He watched me the whole time till I looked at him and then his eyes always looked away.

" ' Would you like some water, Emil ? ' I said.

" ' Yes, please, Eustace Ivanitch.' He took it and drank eagerly.

' ' Is there anything else you want ? '

" ' No, Eustace Ivanitch ; I want nothing ; but . . .'

" What ? '

" ' Those . . .'

" ' What, Emil ? '

" ' Those breeches . . . I took them from you . . . when . . .'

" ' Well, God forgive you, Emil, rest in peace. . . .'

" The tears ran down my cheeks as I turned away.

" ' Eustace Ivanitch. . . .'

" He was trying to speak, raising himself up as his lips moved. His face grew red suddenly as he looked at me, then in a flash he turned ghastly pale, his head fell back, he sighed once and gave his soul to his Maker."

NICOLAI SCHEDRIN
1826–1889

TWO LITTLE MOUJIKS

IT is midnight. A vast, gloomy hall, lighted only by a flickering tallow candle; two little boys, aged eight and eleven years, are sitting on the floor leaning against an oblong table. Death-like silence reigns; man and beast are both asleep. The little serfs alone dare not close their eyes before the return of their mistress, who is out visiting and detained late.

Midnight! The hour of ghosts, and that hall is so immense! Such dark corners! The children look at each other. The elder tries hard to assume an air of easy courage, while the little fellow of eight dries his wet blue eyes on his ragged sleeve. The solitary candle is wasting rapidly away. From time to time pale shadows flit across the frost-covered window-pane; the shutters creak and groan dismally. Outside great flakes of snow are whirled about by a furious wind.

The trembling children press closer to one another. In that white, spectral gleam they seem to trace the phantom of a soul in pain. In the "hou-hou-hou" of the winter wind they hear a cry from the unseen world.

The elder boy is named Vania; the little one Mischa. The latter is a slight, pale child, with blond hair and great blue eyes which glance timidly around the hall; when they rest upon the gloomy corners he turns paler still. Vania is a sturdy, black-eyed fellow, who would fain persuade little Mischa that he is not afraid—not in the least; "for I saw a ghost one day, a real ghost, and did not cry out, nor even feel frightened. Indeed, Mischa, I am not afraid," he repeated, starting nevertheless at the slightest sound. "I am only low-spirited, and I don't feel nearly so much so when you are with me."

"But then if we should be burned," murmured poor little Mischa.

"Burned! Oh, that is impossible!"—with such an assured air that Mischa is completely soothed.

"Tell me, Vania," said Mischa, after a pause, "does the touch of a sharp, cold knife hurt much?"

"It hurts a little, for the first moment, and then you don't feel it at all," replied Vania sententiously, stroking Mischa's blond curls with a reassuring touch.

" But, oh, don't you remember when the cook, Mihei, cut his throat ? ' I am going to cut my throat,' he cried, and when he drew the knife across—oh, how the blood ran ! "

" Oh, Mihei—never mind Mihei—he was an imbecile, for he did not die. He was cured by the doctors, and much good it did him, for he was beaten all the same. But we will manage better : when we cut our throats it shall be well done—they shall not cure us to be beaten again."

" And the knives—are they ready, Vania ? "

" Ready ? I have had them sharp and shining for three days. Are you going to draw back at the last minute, little coward that you are ? "

Mischa did not answer, but drew a long, sobbing breath and fixed his scared blue eyes on the wasting candle.

" Shall I snuff it, Vania, for—for the last time ? " he asked in a trembling voice.

" What is the use ? Let it alone, and pay strict attention to what I am saying. If we do what we have sworn to do *now,* we shall go straight to heaven because we are little children and have not lived long enough to sin much ; but Katerina Afanasievna will be punished for having driven us to it, and she will go to hell."

" And Ivan Vasilich—will he go there too ? "

" Perhaps the good God may pardon him, for he would not be so wicked if left to himself."

" Then Katerina will be punished for her sins ? "

" Oh, that she will, my little comrade," cried Vania exultingly. " They will hang her on a great iron hook and beat her with a knout until the blood flows ; they will make her walk with naked feet over red-hot bricks ; perhaps they will make her lick them, as she made poor Sienka a few days ago. Oh, yes, she will be beaten and tormented until it makes one's blood run cold to think of it."

" But how can she endure it ? " murmured soft-hearted little Mischa, with awe-struck pity.

" They'll make her endure it. Down there, little brother, they pay no attention to cries and complaints ; and whether you can bear it or not, you have to suffer all the same."

The dog in the outer court uttered a long, mournful howl.

"Oh! Tresor has scented a ghost!" exclaimed Mischa, turning pale.

"Nonsense! And suppose he has—are you not ashamed to be such a coward?"

"No, Vania, I am not a coward; but why does this dog always scent ghosts?"

"Ah, that is because a dog is friendly to man. Now, a horse has no idea about such things; but a dog understands—that is why he barks when a ghost is near."

"Vania," interrupted Mischa, "suppose we were to drown ourselves instead."

"How silly you are! Is this summer-time?"

"It is true, the water is cold—so cold—perhaps if we plunged in we could not bear it."

"Drown ourselves indeed! First, we would have to break the ice, and then no doubt you would try to get out, little coward. Then, too, what suffering! While the knife is quite another matter. Draw it firmly across your throat, and it is done. Only, your hand must not tremble."

"And shall we never be beaten any more?" queried little Mischa.

"No, no! Nobody will ever beat us again. The angels will take our souls, and carry them straight to the feet of our Father in heaven."

"And what will our Father say?"

"Our Father will say: 'My little serfs, why have you not waited patiently for the end? Why have you taken your lives?' And we will answer: 'Dear Lord, it was so hard to live,' and we will tell Him all—how Katerina has beaten us again and again, till the blood flowed—beaten us and tortured us."

Mischa listened eagerly; the agony that filled his little heart to bursting found vent in a flood of burning tears. Vania tried to comfort him.

"We will play her one last trick to-morrow. She expects a crowd of fine people to dinner, and I have hidden away every knife, so she cannot find one for her grand company to eat with."

But Mischa continued to weep. Vania snuffed the candle, and looked out of the window.

"What a wind, what a wind!" And then he began to hum the song, "O Night! O Sombre Night!" But Mischa sobbed louder when he heard the familiar strain.

"What a cry-baby you are!" exclaimed Vania impatiently.

The striking of the clock broke the silence. Mischa dried his eyes and said timidly:

" Mistress will be here in a moment."

" Yes, you may be sure she will, but how pleasant it would be if we could go to sleep now!'

" No, no! For the love of Christ, Vania, I implore you, don't go to sleep."

" You are afraid?"

" Yes—y-e-s—I am afraid," stammered poor little Mischa.

" Idiot! how many times must I tell you there is nothing to be afraid of in this hall? If you wish I will go about and search"—but he took good care not to stir. There was a deep silence—one of those hushed pauses, when great waves of sadness seem to sweep over the soul. The boys gazed silently at the dying flame of the wasting candle. The dog howled again.

" Cursed dog," said Mischa.

" Where is Olia now?" demanded Vania suddenly.

Olia was Mischa's sister, a girl of eighteen who had disappeared six months ago, and no one knew what had become of her, though there had been much whispering and many conjectures in the household. Some said that she had fled to escape the daily martyrdom of her life, others that she had disappeared to hide her shame. All that was known was that one day she went to the river to wash some linen, and had never been seen again. The linen was found on the river-bank. Two days before she disappeared they had cut her hair off close to her head, as is customary when a young girl had gone astray. Olia had struggled desperately while it was being done. The mistress affirmed that the wicked Olia had drowned herself, not to escape ill treatment, but to hide her ill-conduct. Still a mystery hung over her fate. During the inquest the boldest among the household witnesses declared that Olia's daily life was a hard one, but the judge did not believe a word they said.

" You are summoned to speak the truth and not to lie," he admonished them, and thereupon he summoned Katerina herself. She declared that not only were her serfs well treated, but that they were even fed on meat. She brought forward witnesses who confirmed her statements. The judge hesitated, reflected, and made the following note: " The aristocrats of District R—— not only treat their serfs with great kindness, but actually feed them on meat."

" Why have you told such falsehoods ? " he then said, turning to the first witnesses. But they stood pale and mute, biting their lips until the blood came. Katerina noticed this, and, overcome by such audacity, she thought proper to faint on the spot. The court rendered the following verdict :

" Disappeared on the morning of June twenty-fourth, from the Polianok estate, a girl, Olga Nilandrova, belonging to Ivan Vasilich, retired captain of cavalry ; said girl was tall, fair, with flaxen hair, cut close, clear complexion, blue eyes, well-shaped nose and mouth, a tiny black mole on the left cheek. The military in the district to which the said girl belongs are ordered to deliver her to the court of District R——, to be held at the disposal of her owners."

And thus the affair was legally brought to an end. Katerina was more cautious for a while, but in a month or two resumed her former amusements. Was she looked upon as a wicked, hard-hearted woman ? No, indeed. Everybody visited her, and her salon was thronged every day. To be sure, everybody knew she was fond of amusing herself by punishing her serfs in many original, eccentric ways, but nobody judged her severely for that. Indeed, she was really extremely popular among her own circle for her gaiety, and her fascinating and gracious manners to her friends, whom she entertained charmingly.

One day she found a small beetle in the soup. She summoned her cook and with great coolness ordered him to swallow it, and none of the company was at all shocked.

Another time she said : " Sienka, go and lick the stove," and Sienka dared not disobey. She came back with a blistered tongue, her face crimson with pain, her hair scorched, and great tears rolling down her face.

" Idiot ! What a fuss she makes," said one. " What a fool," said another, and all burst into peals of laughter. It was only the manner of the day, the fashionable way of entertaining one's guests.

The thought of his sister Olia weighed heavily on Mischa's childish heart. It had bowed his little form and blanched his cheek. Great tears now rose to his eyes as Vania continued :

" Olia has come back ; she appeared to the mistress the other day."

" It is false," cried Mischa.

" It is true—she did come back. Matrena told us that the mistress rushed out of her room whiter than a sheet."

"It is false! Olia lives—she did not drown herself," sobbed Mischa.

"Oh, as to that, Mischa, she did drown herself as sure as two and two make four."

"It is false! It is false!" moaned Mischa.

"You baby! Why should you make such a noise about it? Are we not going to die in a few hours?"

Mischa was silenced. How many memories came back to him! He saw Olia as she used to come toward him, tapping his cheek and saying in her sweet, caressing voice: "Dear little simpleton." Or as she used to smile when bringing a new blouse she had just finished for him, and saying, "May you be happy while you wear it, little brother." And then he recalled the day when, her face disfigured with weeping, her beautiful hair cut short, she had rushed from the mistress's room—and that voice imploring mercy! He heard them still, those prayers interrupted by sobs: "Oh, spare me! Spare me! I'll never, never do it again. Oh, do not cut my hair, for Christ's sake!" And her one thrilling cry of agony and shame as the long, beautiful blond braids fell beneath the scissors! And in Mischa's anguish the scene came back with such piercing reality that he thought he saw Olia—that her spirit had indeed come back to torment the mistress, and even that she was there, close to him. He seemed to hear her voice murmuring: "Dear little brother."

"Oh, Olia is here! Vania, do you not see her—hear her?" he cried in terror.

"Now it is you who are telling falsehoods," said Vania, glancing around with a scared look on his brown face.

"I swear to you that she is here," insisted Mischa.

"I tell you she is not. Why should Olia come back to trouble us? Ghosts only come back to torment people. What harm can she wish us? She was good. Olia was a good girl."

"Yes, yes, my Olia was good," repeated Mischa mechanically.

"Wait, I will look in all the corners," said Vania, as if to reassure his companion, but not sorry to be able to reassure himself. He looked under the table, peered into the corners, and half opened the door leading into the corridor. Nothing was to be seen.

"There, Mischa, you see there is nothing."

"Olia was good," repeated Mischa, like a melancholy echo.

"Yes," said Vania, "and that was why we loved her so. You know that Stepka loved her dearly and wished to marry her, so they put him in prison. When Olia drowned herself, he said to the mistress: 'Put me in the army. I would rather serve as a soldier than serve you.' And the mistress answered: 'No, Stepka, you shall not go in the army, but you may go and be a herdsman, and take care of the flocks in the pasture.' And he had to go."

"Tell me, Vania, does one suffer much when one is a soldier?"

"I don't know. It cannot be worse than this. Oh, Mischa, what a life ours is!" And he shuddered.

"Now, Mischa, let us go and walk once more through all the rooms."

"Yes," Mischa whispered, "it is for the last time."

Vania took the lead. "Here is the great hall," said he.

"Here is the great hall," echoed Mischa.

"Ah, well, little brother, make a bow to each of the four corners."

Mischa bowed four times, Vania did the same. They went through all the rooms, bowing to the four corners of each, and finally reached their sleeping-room. Here Vania spat upon the floor; Mischa did the same.

"Now, Mischa, suppose we make an illumination."

"Yes, let us make an illumination," and his blue eyes beamed for a moment while something like a childish smile lighted up the pallid face of the poor little serf. They lighted all the candles. Mischa played the host, Vania the guest. But they had scarcely time to settle themselves on the velvet divans when the bell rang violently. Host and guest turned pale, made a hurried leap from the divans and began to put out the lights. A second time the bell was rung furiously, as if by an angry hand. At last the lights were all extinguished. They rushed through the vestibule, but they could hear outside of the door the terrible voice of the mistress.

"What are you doing, good-for-nothing little wretches? How dare you keep me waiting, you devil's brats!"

"Do not agitate yourself, my love," came her husband's voice. "Perhaps our brother Nicanor has come."

At this moment Vania opened the door.

"Has our brother Nicanor arrived?" demanded the mistress in a terrible voice.

"No, madam; nobody has arrived," answered Vania.

"Who then, has dared to light all the candles?"

"Nobody, madam."

A violent blow interrupted Vania and sent him rolling over on the floor.

" Who lighted the candles ? " again demanded the mistress, seizing hold of little Mischa.

" Nobody, madam," he stammered.

" You shall not torment us long," shrieked Vania in a frenzy that made him forget all fear, as he threw himself on the mistress and began to tear her face with his nails. Madam fainted away, and Vania fought with such blind fury that it was no easy task to conquer him. He was beside himself with rage and excitement, but finally he was dragged into the kitchen, where he did not shed a tear, but uttered wild cries like a wounded animal brought to bay.

Strange to say, the mistress gave no orders to punish the little moujiks that night. Vania slept from exhaustion after the crisis was passed. Poor little Mischa nestled close to him, but never closed his eyes. He shuddered to think what tortures might await them on the morrow. Again he saw Olia's face and heard her voice. But she no longer wore her woollen dress ; a transparent white robe seemed to envelop her form, and she wore a shining crown on her flaxen hair. Toward three o'clock he fell asleep, and at four Vania awoke him, whispering : " It is time."

Mischa rose and dressed himself mechanically, without understanding what he did or where he was going. They crossed the hall, and stood without in the chill morning air. Vania carried a pair of scissors. He tore off his blouse and cut it in pieces, then cut his boots to shreds, and stood barefooted.

" They shall never be of any use to her," he muttered.

Mischa watched him, and it dawned upon his childish soul that they were indeed bidding adieu to life. He began to sob bitterly.

" Go back to bed, cry-baby," said Vania between his teeth.

" No, no, Vania, I will never leave you."

" Ah, then, why do you cry ? Have you forgotten last night ? "

They crossed the courtyard. The dog bounded toward them, barking a joyous welcome, but Vania showed him the whip, which made him go growling back to his kennel. The morning was damp and cold, and Vania shivered in his shirt. They sprang through the hedge ; the fields were deserted—a profound silence reigned around them. Before them yawned a deep ditch. There the blow was to be struck.

Vania sprang in first. Mischa followed, the dumb, imperious instinct of life growing stronger at every step he made. But would he dare to speak ? Vania frightened him, but perhaps at this moment Vania, too, might feel one pang of regret for life ; perhaps the same irresistible instinct was making itself felt in his soul, too. Although he was shivering with cold his brain seemed on fire.

Vania walked straight on, sharpening one knife against the other. The awful sound seemed to make Mischa's heart stand still, but he followed, submissive, blind, stupefied.

At daybreak the herdsman, buried in profound slumber, was rudely awakened by two passing moujiks, who told him they heard mournful cries for help proceeding from the ditch. " Batiouschki, help ! Batiouschki, help ! " resounded mournfully over the deserted field. They hurried to the ditch and found the two children—one half naked and both covered with blood. Vania lay still, cold and lifeless. His hand had not faltered, but had struck home firmly, surely. Mischa was still breathing ; his little, trembling hand had indeed struck, but ineffectually. The instinct of life had spoken, and at the last moment had prevailed.

THE SELF-SACRIFICING RABBIT

NICOLAI SCHEDRIN

ONE day a rabbit incurred the displeasure of a wolf. You see, he was running along not far from the wolf's lair, and the wolf saw him, and called out: " Little bunny! Stop a minute, dear!" But the rabbit, instead of stopping, ran on faster than ever. So the wolf, with just three bounds, caught him, and said:

" Because you did not stop when I first spoke, this is the sentence I pronounce: I condemn you to death by dismemberment. But, as I have dined to-day, and my wife has dined, and we have stored up food enough to last us five days, you sit down under this bush and wait your turn. Then perhaps—ha! ha! ha!—I will pardon you!"

So the rabbit sat on his haunches under the bush, and never moved. He thought of only one thing—how many days, how many hours would pass before he must die. He looked towards the lair, and saw the glittering eyes of the wolf watching him. And sometimes it was still worse; the wolf and his wife would come out into the field, and stroll up and down close by him. They would look at him, and the wolf would say something to his wife in wolf language; then they would burst out laughing, " Ha! ha! ha! . . ." And all the little wolf-cubs would come with them, and run up to him in play, rub their heads against him, gnash their teeth. . . . And the poor rabbit's heart fluttered and bounded.

Never had he loved life so well as now. He was a highly respectable rabbit, and had chosen for a bride the daughter of a widowed lady-rabbit. At the moment when the wolf caught him by the neck, he was just running to his betrothed.

And now she, his betrothed, would wait, and think, " My squint-eyed one has forsaken me!" Or perhaps—perhaps she has waited—waited . . . and loved another, . . . and . . . or it may be . . . she, too, . . . playing, poor child, among the bushes, caught by a wolf! . . .

Tears almost choked the poor fellow at this thought. " And this is the end of all my warrens in the air! I, that was about to marry, had bought the samovár already, looked forward to the time when I should drink tea with sugar in it with my young wife,—and now, instead, what has befallen me! . . . How many hours now till death?" . . .

One night he fell asleep where he sat. He dreamed that the wolf had appointed him his special commissioner, and while he was absent, performing his duties, the wolf paid visits to his lady-rabbit. . . . Suddenly he felt some one touching his side; he awoke, and saw the brother of his betrothed.

"Your bride is dying," said he. "She heard of your misfortune, and sank at once under the blow. Her one thought now is, 'Must I die thus, and not say farewell to my beloved?'"

At these words the condemned one felt as though his heart would burst. Oh, why! How had he deserved his bitter fate? He had lived honestly, he had never stirred up revolutions, had never gone about with firearms, he had attended to his business—and must he die for that? Death! Oh, think what that word means! And not he alone must die, but she too, his little grey maiden-rabbit, whose only crime was that she had loved him, her squint-eyed one, with all her heart! Oh, if he could, how he would fly to her, his little grey love, how he would clasp his fore-paws behind her ears, and caress her, and stroke her little head!

"Let us escape," said the messenger.

At these words the condemned one was for a moment as if transformed. He shrank up altogether, and laid his ears along his back. He was just ready to spring, and leave not a trace behind. But at that moment he glanced at the wolf's lair. The rabbit heart throbbed with anguish.

"I can't," he said; "the wolf has not given me permission."

All this time the wolf was looking on and listening, and whispering softly in wolf language with the she-wolf. No doubt they were praising the rabbit's noble-mindedness.

"Let us escape," said the messenger once more.

"I can't," repeated the condemned.

"What treason are you muttering there?" suddenly snarled the wolf.

The rabbits stood as petrified. Now the messenger was lost too. To incite a prisoner to flight—is that permitted? Ah! the little grey maiden-rabbit will lose both lover and brother; the wolf and the she-wolf will tear them both in pieces.

When the rabbits came to their senses, the wolf and the she-wolf were gnashing their teeth before them, and in the darkness their eyes shone like lamps.

" Your Excellency, it was nothing ; we were just talking ; . . . a neighbour came to visit me," stammered the condemned, half-dead with terror.

" Nothing ! I dare say ! I know you ! Butter won't melt in your mouths ! Speak the truth. What is it all about ? "

" It's this way, your Excellency," interposed the bride's brother. " My sister, his betrothed, is dying, and asks, may he not come to say farewell to her ? "

" H'm ! It's right that a bride should love her betrothed," said the she-wolf. " That means that they will have a lot of little ones, and there will be more food for wolves. The wolf and I love each other, and we have a lot of cubs. Ever so many are grown up, and now we have four little ones. Wolf ! wolf ! shall we let him go to take leave of his betrothed ? "

" But we were to have eaten him the day after to-morrow——"

" I will come back, your Excellency. I'll go like a flash ; I—indeed. . . . Oh, as God is holy, I'll come back ! " hurriedly exclaimed the condemned. And, in order to convince the wolf that he *could* move like a flash, he sprang up with such agility that even the wolf looked at him admiringly, and thought—

" Ah ! if only my soldiers were like that."

And the she-wolf became quite sad, and said :

" See that, now ! A rabbit, and how he loves his she-rabbit."

There was nothing for it ; the wolf consented to let the rabbit go on *parole* with the stipulation that he should return exactly at the appointed time. And he kept the bride's brother as hostage.

" If you are not back the day after to-morrow by six in the morning," he said, " I'll eat him instead of you ; then if you come I'll eat you too ; perhaps, though, I'll—ha ! ha !—pardon you ! "

The squint-eyed one darted off like the arrow from the bow. The very earth quivered as he ran. If a mountain barred his way, he simply dashed at it ; if a river, he never stopped to look for a ford, but swam straight across ; if a marsh, he sprang from tuft to tuft of grass. Not easy work ! To get right across country, and go to the bath, and be married (" I will certainly be married ! " he kept repeating to himself), and get back in time for the wolf's breakfast. . . .

Even the birds wondered at his swiftness, and remarked :

" Yes, the *Moscow Gazette* says that rabbits have no souls, only a kind of vapour, and there it goes."

At last he arrived. Tongue cannot speak, neither can pen write the rapture of that meeting. The little grey maiden-rabbit forgot her sickness at the sight of her beloved. She stood up on her hind paws, put a drum upon her head, and with her fore-paws beat out the " Cavalier March " ; she had been practising it as a surprise for her betrothed. And the widowed lady-rabbit completely lost her head with joy ; she thought no place good enough for her future son-in-law to sit in, no food good enough to give him. Then the aunts and cousins and neighbours came running from all sides, overjoyed to see the bridegroom, and perhaps, too, to taste the good cheer.

The bridegroom alone was not like himself. While still embracing his betrothed, he suddenly exclaimed :

" I must go to the bath, and then be married at once."

" Why should you be in such a hurry ? " asked the mother rabbit, smiling.

" I must go back. The wolf only gave me leave of absence for one day."

Then he told them all, and his bitter tears flowed as he spoke. It was hard to go, and yet he must not stay. He had given his word, and to a rabbit his word is law. And all the aunts and cousins declared with one voice : " Thou speakest truth, O squint-eyed one. Once given, the spoken word is holy. Never in all our tribe was it known that a rabbit was false to his word ! "

A tale is soon told, but a rabbit's life flies faster still. In the morning they greeted the squint-eyed one, and before evening came he parted from his young wife.

" Assuredly the wolf will eat me," he said. " Therefore be thou faithful to me. And if children shall be born to thee, educate them strictly ; best of all, apprentice them in a circus ; there they will be taught not only to beat the drum, but also to shoot peas from a pop-gun."

Then suddenly, as though lost in thought, he added, remembering the wolf :

" It may be, though, that the wolf will—ha ! ha !—pardon me ! "

And that was the last of him they saw.

. . . .

Meantime, while the squint-eyed one was making merry and getting married, great misfortunes were happening in the tract of country which divided him from the wolf's lair. In one place heavy rains had fallen, so that the river, which the rabbit swam across so easily the day before, overflowed and inundated ten versts of ground. In another place King Aaron declared war against King Nikita, and a battle was pitched right in the rabbit's path. In a third place the cholera appeared, so that quarantine was established for a hundred versts round. And, besides all that, wolves, foxes, owls—they seemed to lie in wait at every step.

The squint-eyed one was prudent; he had so calculated his time as to leave himself three hours extra; but when one hindrance after another beset him his heart sank. He ran without stopping all the evening, half the night; the stones cut his feet, the fur on his sides hung in ragged tufts, torn by the thorny branches, a mist covered his eyes, blood and foam fell from his mouth,—and still he had so far to go! And his friend, the hostage, haunted him constantly, as though alive before him. Now he stands like a sentinel in front of the wolf's lair, thinking: "In so many hours my dear brother-in-law will return to deliver me." . . . When the rabbit thought of that, he darted on yet faster. Mountains, valleys, forests, marshes—it was all the same to him. Often he felt as though his heart would break; then he would crush it down, by sheer force of will, that fruitless emotion might not distract him from his great aim. He had no time now for sorrow or tears: he must think of nothing but how to tear his friend from the wolf's jaws.

And now the day began to break. The owls and bats slipped into their hiding-places; the air became chilly. Suddenly all grew silent, like death. And still the squint-eyed one fled on and on, with the one thought ever in his heart: "Shall I come too late to save my friend?"

The east grew red; first on the far horizon the clouds were faintly tipped with fire; then it spread and spread, and suddenly—a flame. The dew flashed on the grass, the birds awoke, the ants and worms and beetles began to move, a light smoke rose from somewhere; through the rye and oats a whisper seemed to pass—clearer, clearer. . . . But the squint-eyed one saw nothing, heard nothing, only murmured to himself again and again: "I have destroyed my friend,—destroyed my friend!"

At last, a hill! Beyond that was a marsh, and in the marsh the wolf's lair. . . . Too late, O squint-eyed one, too late! . . .

With one last effort he put forth all his remaining strength, and bounded to the top of the hill. But he could go no farther; he was sinking from exhaustion. And must he fail now? . . .

The wolf's lair lay before him as on a map. Somewhere far off six o'clock struck from a church steeple, and every stroke of the bell beat like a hammer on the heart of the agonised creature. At the last stroke the wolf rose from his lair, stretched himself, and wagged his tail for pleasure. Then he went up to the hostage, seized him in his fore-paws, and stuck the claws into his body, in order to tear him in two halves, one for himself, the other for his wife. And the wolf-cubs surrounded their father and mother, gnashing their teeth and looking on. . . .

"I am here!—Here!" shrieked the squint-eyed one, like a hundred thousand rabbits at once; and he flung himself down from the hill into the marsh.

And the wolf praised him.

"I see," he said, "that a rabbit's word can be trusted. And now, my little dears, this is my command: Sit, both of you, under this bush, and wait till I am ready, and afterwards I will . . . ha! ha! . . . pardon you!"

COUNT LEO N. TOLSTOY
1828–1910

HOW MUCH LAND DOES A MAN NEED?

THE two sisters met in the country. The elder, a shopkeeper's wife, had come down to the peasant home of the younger. They talked endlessly over their tea. The elder sister had a very good idea of herself. Town life was better than country; she lived in some style; her children were well dressed; there was always enough to eat and drink, and in the evening you could go to the theatre.

The younger girl was not at all pleased at this. She thought that life in the country was better than in the town. She said, "I should not like to be in your place. Our life is stupid enough, but it is without trouble. You people have plenty of swank; but though you get on well, you may be ruined at any moment. Haven't you heard the proverb, 'Income and Loss are brothers'? You are well enough off to-day, but to-morrow you may be begging your bread at my door. Country life is in every way better; of course we are not rich, but we always have enough."

"You call that enough?" cried the town sister, contemptuously. "The beasts have enough to eat, and you live just as they do. There is no trace of refinement or comfort in your lives; and however hard your husband may work, he can never make things any different; you will die like the lower animals, even as you live."

"Well," answered the younger, "granted all that, we are content that it should be so. For, on the other hand, we have security in our lives. We need not toady to any man. But you town people are surrounded with insecurity and all sorts of dangers; you never know when the Evil One may entice away your husband to gambling or drink or even to worse vices; and then there is an end to all your money and all your comfort. You know I speak the truth."

Her husband, who was lying near the fire, had been listening to his wife's defence of peasant life. "It is all gospel truth," he thought approvingly. "I have been too hard at work all my life on my bit of earth for any such dangerous rubbish to find its way into my head. The only wickedness here is that it's so devilish hard to get a bit of land. Just give me a tidy piece of ground, and I should have no fear of any one, not even of Old Nick himself."

When the two wives had finished their tea and their chatter, and had cleared away the tea-cups, they went to bed. Then the Devil, who had been listening all the time from the corner behind the stove, gave himself a quiet hug of satisfaction at the peasant's vain boast against him. "So, so! If he had a nice bit of land he would not fear Old Nick himself!" thought the malicious fiend. "We'll soon see about that! You shall have the land all right, and Old Nick will have both you and your land, my friend."

Near by Pakhom's cottage lived a lady who owned some hundred odd acres of land. Until recently she had been a good and easy mistress, and had kept a friendly understanding with the peasants on her land; but she had lately appointed an ex-soldier as her bailiff, and the peasants had a bad time of it under him. Pakhom began to find trouble and misery on every hand; in spite of all his care, his horses would get into the standing oats; then his cow would break through the fence into a garden; and another time his calf would trespass in the lady's fields. Every time an offence of this sort occurred, Pakhom was heavily fined by the new bailiff; and it was of little avail that he scolded and punished his own servants, or tore out his hair in his anger. All summer his offences accumulated, so that he was glad when winter came, and he had to bring in his cattle to the yard. Stall feeding was hard enough, indeed, but at any rate there could be no more fines during the winter.

Before winter was over, however, a new terror came upon the peasants, which made all their hearts quail. It was whispered abroad that their lady was going to sell her land, and that the hated ex-soldier was to purchase it. "Alas," they told one another, "if he should get the land, our miseries will be greater than we can bear; he will inflict more grievous fines than ever upon us. What shall we do? For we cannot live but by the land!"

At last the peasants went in a body to their lady, and implored her not to let the bailiff have the land, but to sell it to them, promising to pay as much and more for it than he would have paid. She acceded to their request; and the peasants held a great meeting of their common council to decide on the best way to proceed in the matter of buying the land. Many meetings were held, and yet nothing could be agreed upon, and no progress at all was made. In the end it was arranged that each peasant should buy his own separate bit of land, as much or as little as he could afford. Their lady fell in with this arrangement, and Pakhom heard before long that twenty acres had been purchased by his next-door neighbour, who had only had to find half the amount in ready money and was to pay the remainder within a year. This kindled Pakhom's heart to envy, and he thought within himself, " Here are all our neighbours buying up the land, and presently I shall find myself cut off and left with nothing ! "

He talked the matter over with his wife. " Every one is buying up land now," he said, " and we ought to get a bit for ourselves. If we can't raise the price of ten acres, we are done, for the bailiff will have no mercy on us ; we shall be beggared with his fines."

They spent a lot of time planning how it was to be done. All their savings amounted to £10 ; and when they had sold the horse and most of the bees, and had hired out their son as a labourer, they managed to bring the total sum up to one-half of the purchase money. Pakhom managed to conclude an arrangement with the lady of the manor for a piece of fifteen acres, which he chose on account of a little wood included in it which he had long coveted. He walked into the neighbouring town and had the contract executed, paying down half the money and undertaking to complete the payment within two years ; and so he got his land.

Pakhom then got his brother-in-law to lend him money for seed, and soon the land was tilled and sown. Fortune favoured him, and before the year was out he had paid off all he owed both to the lady of the manor and to his brother-in-law, and felt himself indeed a landowner. The earth that he worked so vigorously was his own bit of earth ; the crops that he reaped, the hay, the stacks of firewood, the pasture for his beasts, were all his very own, and his heart swelled as he walked about over his possessions. He never tired of the joy of possession ; never were such cornfields, such green grass, such wonderful flowery meadows. Nothing on the land was the same as before ; the pride of ownership had transformed it into a veritable Eden.

Life had become very delightful to Pakhom, and for some time all was as merry as a song. Then a small cloud came up on the horizon, for the peasants began to let their animals trespasss on his meadows and over his corn. Pakhom at first remonstrated, driving the cows out of the fields and the horses from amid the corn ; and even when they took no notice, it was not for some time that he could bring himself to appeal to the law against them. But at last he lost patience, and in a burst of anger, prosecuted first one of them and then others, though his heart and his own experience told him that the peasants were driven to such courses by sheer poverty and misery and by no ill-will. " Still, I cannot afford always to let it pass," he told himself. " If this goes on I shall be brought to the workhouse myself. I must teach them that this has to stop."

When Pakhom took to prosecuting the peasants, among whom he had lived so many years as an equal, they felt very sore about it, and soon began to work him ill out of real spite. His cherished wood was invaded one night, and all the young saplings were wantonly barked. And Pakhom, walking amid the desolation, and seeing the torn bark lying all around and the gaunt bare trunks gleaming white throughout the copse, grew pale with anger and with desire for vengeance on his enemies. Sheer malice had prompted such ruthless destruction, which could not content itself with cutting down a few trees, but must wantonly ruin the whole lot.

" If I could only get hold of the miscreant," he growled between his teeth, " he should pay dearly for this." Then he cast about in his mind, trying to fix the blame. " Simeon ! " he thought at last, " it was certainly Simeon," and went off at once to Simeon's farm to have it out with him.

Simeon denied all his charges, and bitter recriminations ensued. The quarrel, however, strengthened Pakhom's suspicions into certainty, and he took out a summons against Simeon. There was a lengthy process in the Court, which finally decided that there was no real evidence against the peasants, and dismissed the case. Pakhom, whose anger at the decision became uncontrollable, vented it upon the magistrates, crying out, " You are upholders of criminals and thieves ; if you were honest men yourselves you would not be afraid to punish the vagabonds." So the magistrates, as well as the peasants, became his enemies.

The village council soon became too hot to hold him ; and at home he had more room than company, for all left him alone. Then a report began to get abroad that the villagers were going away in search of fresh land ; and Pakhom thought to himself, " All the better for those who stay. I need not go away, for I shall be able to get hold of the land of those who go, and so make my estate complete; I am dreadfully cramped for room as it is."

One day a stranger, a peasant who was passing through the village, called at the house, and Pakhom, who happened to be at home, welcomed him, gave him a meal and a bed, and they had a long talk.

"Well, friend, and where are you going?" asked Pakhom.

The peasant told him that his home was in the district of the lower Volga, and that work was to be had there in plenty. So they fell to talking of these parts, and the peasant related how the land was being settled there. His own family, he said, had gone thither, had put down their names on the local land-roll, and had ten acres allotted to them. "The land is so fertile that barley grows higher than the horses' heads, and the ears are so thick that it only takes a few handfuls to make a small stack. I know one peasant who was as poor as Job when he went there, and he was given a plot of fifty acres. Well, last year one wheat-field alone brought him in £100."

Pakhom's excitement mounted to fever heat as he listened. Why should he stay here, where he only became poorer the harder he worked, when in this new place he might easily live so well? "I will sell my land and stock," he said, "and with the money I raise I will take up a large piece of land there, and go in for farming on a really big scale. It is a shame to stay in such a hole-and-corner place as this. I must go and see your place, first, however, to see for certain that all is as you say."

When summer came, Pakhom made his journey. He went by steamer down the Volga to Samara, and then walked the remaining forty miles to the specified place. Here he found everything just as it had been described to him, and all the peasants living on the fat of the land. Every fresh settler who came to the district was given ten acres of land free, and might buy as much as he wished of the very best land at six shillings an acre. Pakhom, after a full investigation, went back home in the autumn, sold his land, his house and buildings and all that he possessed, and had his name removed from the village roll. Then, when spring came, he and his family migrated to their new home.

Pakhom and his family settled in the largest village of the new district, and were inscribed upon its roll. He entertained all the most important people of the village, showed them his credentials, was accepted as a member of the community, and received fifty acres of land in various fields, being the portion allowed for five persons, together with the right of pasture on the common land. Pakhom then built a house and bought a lot of cattle ; he had more than twice the amount of land he had had in the old place, and much better land ; so that he lived now on a scale many times beyond his former style of life. There was any amount of meadow and arable land, and no limit to the number of cattle it was possible to rear.

Just at first, while his mind was filled with the new house he was building and with all the stock he was buying, Pakhom was altogether happy and satisfied ; but it was not long before he began to feel that here too he was cramped and limited. He had conceived an ambition to grow Turkish wheat like some of his neighbours ; but the land suited to this particular crop was very small in extent, and there was great competition for it. Most of the wheat had to be sown alternately with grass and fallow ; a lot of the land was of too light soil for any crops but rye ; and though every one wanted to get heavy soil and to grow wheat, there were only a very few who succeeded. Hence it was not long before jealousy and ill-feeling were produced, and quarrels broke out. The rich peasants held tenaciously to all that they had managed to get, and the poorer ones soon had to sell more and more of theirs to pay the taxes. Pakhom had sowed his land with wheat the first year, and had secured a fine crop ; so that the next year nothing would satisfy him but to sow wheat again ; but he was not able to secure more than a very little wheat land, and that of poor quality. He went, therefore, to a large farmer and rented more land ; and this year he sowed wheat on a large scale ; and once more he reaped a splendid crop. But there was still a fly in the ointment ; the field was fifteen miles away, and as Pakhom went backwards and forwards between his house and his wheat, he was struck with envy of the peasant proprietors whose estates he passed on the way, and who all looked so prosperous. " That's the life for me," he told himself ; " I should have all I could wish if only I could buy a holding and build my own farm on it." From that time his one idea was how to compass the complete purchase of a holding.

Five years passed away, years of great prosperity for Pakhom. He rented more and more land, and grew ever larger and larger crops of wheat ; his wheat was excellent and the money began to roll in. Pakhom would now have felt that life was good indeed, had it not been for the bother of having to rent land every year, and the waste of time which the transaction involved. Whenever there was an extra good bit of land to be had, all the peasants would rush to get some of it; and if he wanted to get a piece it was necessary to be on the spot at the earliest moment, or there would be none left. One year Pakhom rented a great section of the common land, and had already ploughed it up, when the peasants, highly incensed, appealed to the law against him, and the land had to be restored. So Pakhom felt thwarted on every hand, because he had not land which was all his own property.

The problem of how to acquire land of his own occupied his mind night and day. He happened one day to meet a peasant who was faced with ruin, and had to sell his land for anything he could get for it. Pakhom at once determined to get it at a bargain, and after a lot of haggling, at last arranged to buy the whole of it, five hundred acres, for £100, one-half of which amount he agreed to pay down in cash. But as they were on the point of clinching the bargain, a trader who was passing stopped to ask a feed for his horses. Pakhom gave him tea, and was soon engaged in earnest conversation with him. He learned that the merchant had just purchased a huge estate of 5000 acres from the Bashkirs, from whose country he was now making his way home, and that the whole estate had only cost him £100. Pakhom, fired with envy, induced him to tell the whole story of how the bargain was made.

"All you need do, is to get round the chiefs," said the trader. "I got my way by means of a present of ten pounds' worth of raiment and carpets and a chest of tea, and by treating all the notables with wine. They let me have the land, which lies alongside the river, and on the grassy steppes, for fivepence an acre."

Pakhom was greedy for information.

"The country of the Bashkirs," the merchant told him, "is of such vast extent that one could not possibly traverse the whole of it in a year, travelling all the time. The people are like children, quite simple and unsophisticated, and I should not wonder if you could get them to give you some of their land for nothing."

"If this is all true," thought Pakhom to himself, "I should be a fool to pay £100 for five hundred acres, and involve myself in debt too, when I could get all I want for the same sum."

Having learned carefully the way to the Bashkir country, Pakhom prepared to set out at once. He left his wife in charge of the farm, taking with him one of his farm servants. They went first to the nearest town, and there purchased all the presents that the merchant had suggested, such as clothes, tea, wine, and other things. Over five hundred miles they travelled, and came at last to the country of the nomad tribe of Bashkirs, who lived on the steppe beside a great river, and had their homes in tent-like caravans. He found that the merchant had described them and their country correctly. These simple people made no effort to grow corn, and never ate bread ; but moved across the steppe with their vast herds of cattle and horses, the foals being fastened to the backs of the vans. Twice a day they rounded up the mares and milked them, and from the milk koumiss and cheese were made, but the cheese was different from any which Pakhom knew at home. These merry, hospitable people ate their mutton, drank tea and koumiss, and made every day a festival with music and gaiety. Strong, lithe and free-hearted, they welcomed every stranger, and the moment Pakhom appeared he was surrounded by a chattering throng, who could not speak a word of Russian, but whose kindly feelings were evident. As luck would have it, there was a man among them able to act as interpreter, and Pakhom soon made known his desire to purchase land from them. The Bashkirs were immensely pleased with Pakhom and his mission, led him away into the grandest of their vans, made him a comfortable seat with carpets and pillows, and gave him tea and koumiss to drink. A sheep was slain and cooked, and all did their best to feast him and make him welcome. Pakhom fetched out the presents he had brought with him, and gave them away among the men, who were more than ever pleased with him. They talked incessantly, and the interpreter told Pakhom the meaning of their eager chatter.

" The people are greatly taken with you," he said, " and as their custom is, they wish to give you whatever you may choose, in return for the presents you have made. Tell us, then, what is it that you most desire ? "

" What I long for most of all," Pakhom answered, " is to possess a piece of your land. In our part, there is but little land to be had, and what there is is dreadfully poor, but you have any amount of land, and of such quality as I never saw before ! "

The Bashkirs, on learning what Pakhom had said, held a long discussion among themselves ; and though Pakhom could not of course understand a word, he could tell that something had amused them, by the way in which they all laughed. When they stopped speaking, and the interpreter explained their decision to Pakhom, they all sat looking at him while he listened.

" The people have decided," the interpreter said, " that since you have been so good to them, they are ready to let you have all the land you want; you have only to point out to them which is the land you would like, and you shall have it."

Pakhom saw, however, that an argument was taking place among the Bashkirs, and asked what was the matter. " There is a difference of opinion," the interpreter answered; " some of them think that the Chief must be consulted before anything can be settled about the land; the rest think that it can all be settled just as well without him."

While the discussion was still going on, a fine, tall man wearing a head-dress of fox-skin strode into their midst, at sight of whom talking ceased and all at once stood up respectfully.

" It is the Chief himself," explained the interpreter.

Pakhom opened his bundle and presented the Chief with a fine robe and five pounds of tea. These gifts were graciously received, and when the Chief had seated himself the Bashkirs reported all they knew about Pakhom. The great man listened with an occasional smile. Then, speaking in Russian, he said, " Very well, you are welcome to your choice of land. There is enough for all of us."

Pakhom was amazed and delighted, but a little suspicious. He was afraid that they might offer the land to-day, and to-morrow go back on their word.

" Thank you very much," he said. " Your land is indeed unlimited, and my wants are small. Yet it would be well that we should agree definitely with regard to my holding. Let us survey it accurately, so that I may have an unquestionable title to it. Only God knows how long any one of us may live; and though yourselves are to be trusted, you cannot answer for your sons."

Again that quizzical smile on the Chief's features. " Very good," he said; " let us make the matter absolutely certain."

" I was told," said Pakhom, " by a trader who came from here that you made a formal agreement about his land, and I ask no more for myself."

"Quite right," the Chief replied. "Here is one who can write, and we can go to the town and have the contract duly signed."

"What is your price?" Pakhom inquired.

"We ask always the same figure—£100 per day."

"But how can you sell it *by the day*? How can you measure land that way?"

"The matter is simple enough," was the reply. "We sell for £100 as much land as you can run round in one day."

The purchaser was astonished. "One can run round a great deal of land in one day!"

Again that queer smile. "All that you can compass will be yours. But you must understand that if you fail to return before sunset to your starting-point, you get no land and you lose your money."

"How do you propose to measure my course?"

"We ourselves will remain at the place whence you set out. You will pursue your course, followed by mounted men who will set up posts at each place you indicate; and then a furrow will be ploughed from each post to the next. You choose your own course, but you must return before sunset to your starting-point. All that your circle includes will then be your own property."

This proposal was readily agreed to, and the adventure was fixed for dawn on the following day. Then followed a pleasant evening of conversation and the drinking of koumiss and of tea. A comfortable bed was prepared for Pakhom, and the Bashkirs left him to his slumbers, promising to meet at earliest dawn.

But sleep deserted the delighted purchaser. "What wonderful fortune!" he said to himself. "It will make a vast estate. The days are now the longest of the year, and to-morrow I can easily do fifty miles. A circuit of that length will include 10,000 acres. I shall be a wealthy man. With two teams of oxen and a couple of men I will plough up the choicest parts, and feed cattle on the rest." Not until it was nearly dawn did Pakhom fall into an uneasy sleep, haunted by a strange dream.

He seemed to be lying where he was in the van, and to hear a mocking laughter outside. He dreamed that he descended from the van, and found the Bashkir Chief sitting on the ground and shouting with uncontrollable laughter. "What amuses you so much?" he asked; and then, behold, it was not the Chief at all, but the trader who had stayed with him a few days before and had told him about the land. " Hullo," he inquired, " how long have you been down here ? " But now it was no longer the trader, but the peasant from the Volga who had told him of his last venture. But now, again, it was not the peasant after all, but the Devil himself, with his horns and hoofs, laughing horribly at some object at which he was looking. And Pakhom crept nearer, and gazing, saw a dead man lying on the ground in shirt and trousers. The feet of the corpse were bare and its upturned face as white as a sheet. Looking more closely, Pakhom saw in his dream that the dead man was no other than himself. He awoke with a horrid cry ; and after considering the absurdity of this nightmare, he looked out and saw the first light of dawn in the east. " I must look for my friends," he said. " It is time to start."

Calling his man, Pakhom ordered him to put in the horses, and set out to wake the Bashkirs. " Good morning," he said ; " we must now go out to the steppe and measure off the land."

The tribe were soon gathered together, and in a few minutes were joined by the Chief. They breakfasted on koumiss, and offered Pakhom tea ; but he was in too great a hurry to wait. " Let us start, let us start ! " he cried.

And so they all set out, some of them mounted and others in the light carts of the steppe ; and they had no sooner reached the steppe than the dawn was ruddy in the sky. The tribe halted at the foot of a low hill, and ascending it, all stood there together. The Chief waved his hand over the horizon.

" There you are," he said. " The land is ours as far as you can see. Make your own choice."

Pakhom's eyes gleamed. The entire expanse was covered with waving grass. It was a vast level of the darkest and richest hue, and the watercourses were marked out by many-coloured bushes and stunted trees. The chief laid his fur cap on the ground at the summit of the hill. " There is your goal," he exclaimed ; " put the money in my cap. Your man shall stand beside it. From here you start, and here you must return. The land that you surround to-day is yours."

Pakhom laid the money in the fur cap, took off his cloak, tightened his belt, placed a chunk of bread in his breast, tied a water-flask to his belt, fastened his boots more securely ; and ready to set out, surveyed the land.

" It does not matter which way I start," he thought, " I will go westward." Then he stood looking toward the dawn, eager for the sun to rise above the horizon. The horsemen had now grouped themselves on the summit of the hill behind him. As soon as the disc of the sun came into view Pakhom turned his back on it and set out across the steppe, followed by the mounted men.

At first he kept an easy steady pace, and after the first mile he ordered them to plant a post. As he went on, his limbs became more supple and his pace increased, and before long another post had been set up. Looking backward now, he could still see the summit of the hill, and even the tribe grouped upon it, and guessed that he had come five miles at least. And now the pace began to tell. He was bathed in perspiration. He threw off his coat and tightened his belt again. He ran five miles more, and the sun grew very hot. It was quite breakfast-time. " Now I have done one stage," he thought ; " four stages are as much as any one does in a day. I don't need to turn back yet, but I had better ease my boots." This made the running much easier, and the eager man, noticing how excellent was the land over which he passed, determined to do another five miles and then turn to the left. But as he went on, the quality of the land became better and better, and he could not turn aside from his straight course. When once he looked round, the hill was scarcely to be descried upon the horizon.

" I have done enough in this direction," he said at last. " I must turn in time." The heat was dreadful and he was very thirsty ; so he raised his flask and drank eagerly, had another post fixed in the ground, and turned sharply to the left. Still he went onward through the stiff high grass. The heat was overwhelming, and the position of the sun showed that it was dinner-time. " I must rest," he said as he stood still and bit at his loaf, " but I must not sit down, for then I should lie down, and then I should go to sleep."

Having regained his breath, he forced the pace again. At first it was fairly easy, for the food had given him strength. But the sun beat down cruelly, and he was tired almost to death. " Stick to it," he said, " stick to it for an hour, and live like a king for the rest of your days ! "

For ten miles he continued in this direction, and was just about to turn once more to the left, when he caught sight of a lovely cool well-watered dell. This at least must not be left out ; it was perfectly adapted for growing flax. So again he went straight on, and passing the dell, made them set up another post, and turned his second corner. Pakhom looked away toward the hill, which was about fifteen miles away, and concluded that as the first two sides of his estate had been very long, this last one must be as short as possible. With long painful strides, he set out upon it. The sun had already begun to descend in the heavens. Thinking that he had got enough land at last, he ran swiftly toward the hill.

And now the work began to be very heavy. Again and again he stumbled and nearly fell. His limbs were in torment and seemed on the point of giving way altogether. He would have given anything for a rest ; but that was now impossible, for the sun seemed actually to be falling down toward the horizon. And now for the first time a doubt began to form itself in his mind. " Have I made a fool of myself ? " he wondered. " Have I tried for too much ? What if I don't get there in time ? Oh, how far it is ! What if all this trouble should go for nothing ! " He pulled himself up, and fell into a lame trot. His feet were bleeding. He threw away his boots, his flask, his hat. " I have been too covetous," he moaned ; and his heart was filled with terror. His clothes, streaming with sweat, stuck to his limbs. His mouth and throat were dry and hot as a furnace. His lungs laboured like the bellows of a smithy, and his heart beat like the hammer on the anvil ; and now he had a strange sense that his feet and legs no longer belonged to him. He had no more thought of the estate, but only feared dying of exhaustion. Yet, though he was afraid to die, he could not bring himself to stop.

What strange sound was this ringing in his ears ? The tribe were shouting, encouraging him to run the race, and their friendly cries renewed his courage. One glance backward showed that the sun was touching the horizon, but a few minutes would be enough to bring him to the goal. The folk on the hill were waving their arms to him, and their shouts spurred his fainting strength. Very soon he saw the fur cap on the ground, which held the money, and beside it was the Chief, laughing. That dreadful dream came back to Pakhom. " My land is great and wonderful," he thought, " most wonderful and plenteous ; but—will God let me enjoy it ? Ah ! I have lost myself, *myself* ! "

Still giddily he stumbled on. One glance back at the sun showed that its great lurid disc was nearly gone ; and when he had struggled to the foot of the hill, it had fallen quite below the horizon. The man groaned aloud, thinking that everything was lost ; and then he suddenly realised that though he could not see the sun, it must still be visible from the summit of the hill. With a last effort he plunged upward, and staggered toward the fur cap. Yes, it was there still ! Near it he gave way altogether, and falling on the ground stretched out his hands toward the prize.

" Well done, my lad ; well done ! " shouted the Chief of the tribe. " You have indeed won a great estate ! "

Pakhom's man ran to his master to lift him up ; but he found his master dead, with blood oozing from his lips. The servant moaned in despair ; but the Chief still sat on the ground, swaying with inextinguishable laughter.

At last the Chief arose and took the money from the fur cap, saying to Pakhom's servant, " Dig, dig ! " Then, with all his tribe, he went away.

The man was left alone with the body. He dug a grave and buried his master. The grave was just six feet long, for Pakhom had been six feet tall.

THE LONG EXILE

Count Leo N. Tolstoy

" God sees the truth, but bides His time."

ONCE upon a time there lived in the city of Vladímir a young merchant named Aksénof. He had two shops and a house.

Aksénof had a ruddy complexion and curly hair ; he was a very jolly fellow and a good singer. When he was young he used to drink too much, and when he was tipsy he was turbulent ; but after his marriage he ceased drinking, and only occasionally had a spree.

Once, in summer, Aksénof was going to Nízhni [1] to the great Fair. As he was about to bid his family good-bye, his wife said to him :

" Iván Dmítrievitch, do not go to-day ; I had a dream, and dreamed that some misfortune befell you."

Aksénof laughed at her, and said : " You are always afraid that I shall go on a spree at the Fair."

His wife said : " I myself know not what I am afraid of, but I had such a strange dream : you seemed to be coming home from town, and you took off your hat, and I looked, and your head was all grey."

Aksénof laughed. " That means good luck. See, I am going now. I will bring you some lovely presents."

And he bade his family farewell and set off.

When he had gone half his journey, he fell in with a merchant of his acquaintance, and the two stopped together at the same tavern for the night. They took tea together, and went to sleep in two adjoining rooms.

Aksénof did not care to sleep long ; he awoke in the middle of the night, and in order that he might get a good start while it was cool he aroused his driver and bade him harness up, went down into the smoky hut, settled his account with the landlord, and started on his way.

After he had driven thirty miles, he again stopped to get something to eat ; he rested in the vestibule of the inn, and when it was noon he went to the doorstep and ordered the samovár to be got ready ; then he took out his guitar and began to play.

[1] Nízhni Nóvgorod : it means Lower New Town.

Suddenly a carriage with a bell dashed up to the inn, and from the equipage leaped an official with two soldiers; he came directly up to Aksénof and asked: "Who are you? Where did you come from?"

Aksénof answered without hesitation, and asked him if he would not have a glass of tea with him.

But the official kept on with his questions: "Where did you spend last night? Were you alone or with a merchant? Have you seen the merchant this morning? Why did you leave so early this morning?"

Aksénof wondered why he was questioned so closely; but he told everything just as it was, and asked: "Why do you ask me so many questions? I am not a thief or a murderer. I am on my own business; there is nothing to question me about."

Then the official called up the soldiers, and said: "I am the police inspector, and I have made these inquiries of you because the merchant with whom you spent last night has been stabbed. Show me your things; and, you men, search him."

They went into the tavern, brought in the trunk and bag, and began to open and search them. Suddenly the police inspector pulled out from the bag a knife, and demanded: "Whose knife is this?"

Aksénof looked and saw a knife covered with blood taken from his bag, and he was frightened.

"And whose blood is that on the knife?"

Aksénof tried to answer, but he could not articulate his words: "I—I—don't—know— I— That knife—it is—not mine——"

Then the police inspector said: "This morning the merchant was found stabbed to death in his bed. No one except you could have done it. The tavern was locked on the inside, and there was no one in the tavern except yourself. And here is the bloody knife in your bag, and your guilt is evident in your face. Tell me how you killed him and how much money you took from him." Aksénof swore that he had not done it, that he had not seen the merchant after he had drunk tea with him, that the only money that he had with him—eight thousand roubles—was his own, and that the knife was not his.

But his voice trembled, his face was pale, and he was all quivering with fright, like a guilty person.

The police inspector called the soldiers, commanded them to bind Aksénof and take him to the carriage.

When they took him to the carriage with his feet tied, Aksénof crossed himself and burst into tears.

They confiscated Aksénof's possessions and his money, and took him to the next city and threw him into prison.

They sent to Vladímir to make inquiries about Aksénof's character, and all the merchants and citizens of Vladímir declared that Aksénof, when he was young, used to drink and was wild, but that now he was a worthy man. Then he was brought up for judgment. He was sentenced for having killed the merchant and for having robbed him of twenty thousand roubles.

Aksénof's wife was dumbfounded by the event, and did not know what to think. Her children were still small, and there was one at the breast. She took them all with her and journeyed to the city where her husband was imprisoned.

At first they would not grant her admittance, but afterward she got permission from the chief, and was taken to her husband.

When she saw him in his prison garb, in chains together with murderers, she fell to the floor, and it was a long time before she recovered from her swoon. Then she placed her children around her, sat down amid them, and began to tell him about their domestic affairs, and to ask him about everything that had happened to him.

He told her the whole story.

She asked: "What is to be the result of it?"

He said: "We must petition the Tsar. It is impossible that an innocent man should be condemned."

The wife said that she had already sent in a petition to the Tsar, but that the petition had not been granted. Aksénof said nothing, but was evidently very much downcast.

Then his wife said: "You see the dream that I had, when I dreamed that you had become grey-headed, meant something after all. Already your hair has begun to turn grey with trouble. You ought to have stayed at home that time."

And she began to tear her hair, and she said: "Ványa, my dearest husband, tell your wife the truth: Did you commit that crime or not?"

Aksénof said: "So you, too, have no faith in me!" And he wrung his hands and wept.

Then a soldier came and said that it was time for the wife and children to go. And Aksénof for the last time bade farewell to his family.

When his wife was gone, Aksénof began to think over all that they had said. When he remembered that his wife also had distrusted him, and had asked him if he had murdered the merchant, he said to himself: " It is evident that no one but God can know the truth of the matter, and He is the only one to ask for mercy, and He is the only one from whom to expect it."

And from that time Aksénof ceased to send in petitions, ceased to hope, and only prayed to God. Aksénof was sentenced to be knouted, and then to exile with hard labour.

And so it was done.

He was flogged with the knout, and then, when the wounds from the knout were healed, he was sent with other exiles to Siberia.

Aksénof lived twenty-six years in the mines. The hair on his head had become white as snow, and his beard had grown long, thin, and grey. All his gaiety had vanished.

He was bent, his gait was slow, he spoke little, he never laughed, and he spent much of his time in prayer.

Aksénof had learned while in prison to make boots, and with the money that he earned he bought the *Book of Martyrs*, and used to read it when it was light enough in prison, and on holidays he would go to the prison church, read the Gospels, and sing in the choir, for his voice was still strong and good.

The authorities liked Aksénof for his submissiveness, and his prison associates respected him and called him " grandfather " and the " man of God." Whenever they had petitions to be presented, Aksénof was always chosen to carry them to the authorities; and when quarrels arose among the prisoners, they always came to Aksénof as umpire.

Aksénof never received any letters from home, and he knew not whether his wife and children were alive.

Once some new convicts came to the prison. In the evening all the old convicts gathered around the newcomers, and began to ply them with questions as to the cities or villages from which this one or that had come, and what their crimes were.

At this time Aksénof was sitting on his bunk, near the strangers, and, with bowed head, was listening to what was said.

One of the new convicts was a tall, healthy-looking old man of sixty years, with a close-cropped grey beard. He was telling why he had been arrested. He said:

" And so, brothers, I was sent here for nothing. I unharnessed a horse from a postboy's sledge, and they caught me in it, and insisted that I was stealing it. 'But,' says I, 'I only wanted to go a little faster, so I whipped up the horse. And besides, the driver was a friend of mine. It's all right,' says I. 'No,' say they; 'you were stealing it.' But they did not know what and where I had stolen. I have done things which long ago would have sent me here, but I was not found out; and now they have sent me here without any justice in it. But what's the use of grumbling? I have been in Siberia before. They did not keep me here very long though——"

"Where did you come from?" asked one of the convicts.

"Well, we came from the city of Vladímir; we are citizens of that place. My name is Makár, and my father's name was Semyón."

Aksénof raised his head and asked:

"Tell me, Semyónitch, have you ever heard of the Aksénofs, merchants in Vladímir city? Are they alive?"

"Indeed, I have heard of them! They are rich merchants, though their father is in Siberia. It seems he was just like any of the rest of us sinners. And now tell me, grandfather, what you were sent here for?"

Aksénof did not like to speak of his misfortune; he sighed, and said:

"Twenty-six years ago I was condemned to hard labour on account of my sins."

Makár Semyónof said:

"But what was your crime?"

Aksénof replied: "I must, therefore, have deserved this."

But he would not tell or give any further particulars; the other convicts, however, related why Aksénof had been sent to Siberia. They told how on the road some one had killed a merchant, and put the knife into Aksénof's luggage, and how he had been unjustly punished for this.

When Makár heard this, he glanced at Aksénof, clasped his hands round his knees, and said:

"Well, now, that's wonderful! You have been growing old, grandfather!"

They began to ask him what he thought was wonderful, and where he had seen Aksénof. But Makár did not answer; he only repeated:

"A miracle, boys! how wonderful that we should meet again!"

And when he said these words, it came over Aksénof that perhaps this man might know who it was that had killed the merchant. And he said:

" Did you ever hear of that crime, Semyónitch, or did you ever see me before ? "

" Of course I heard of it ! The country was full of it. But it happened a long time ago. And I have forgotten what I heard," said Makár.

" Perhaps you heard who killed the merchant ? " asked Aksénof.

Makár laughed, and said :

" Why, of course the man who had the knife in his bag killed him. If any one put the knife in your things and was not caught doing it—why, it would have been impossible ! For how could they have put the knife in your bag ? Was it not standing close by your head ? And you would have heard it, wouldn't you ? "

As soon as Aksénof heard these words he felt convinced that this was the very man who had killed the merchant.

He stood up and walked away. All that night he was unable to sleep. Deep melancholy came upon him, and he began to call back the past in his imagination.

He imagined his wife as she had been when for the last time she had come to see him in prison. She seemed to stand before him exactly as though she were alive, and he saw her face and her eyes, and he seemed to hear her words and her laugh.

Then his imagination brought up his children before him ; one a little boy in a little fur coat, and the other on his mother's breast.

And he imagined himself as he was at that time, young and happy. He remembered how he had sat on the steps of the tavern when they arrested him, and how his soul was full of joy as he played on his guitar.

And he remembered the place of execution where they had knouted him, and the knoutsman, and the people standing around, and the chains and the convicts, and all his twenty-six years of prison life, and he remembered his old age. And such melancholy came upon Aksénof that he was tempted to put an end to himself.

" And all on account of this criminal ! " said Aksénof to himself.

And then he began to feel such anger against Makár Semyónof that he almost fell upon him, and was crazy with desire to pay off the load of vengeance. He repeated prayers all night, but could not recover his calm. When day came he walked by Makár and did not look at him.

Thus passed two weeks. Aksénof was not able to sleep, and such melancholy had come over him that he did not know what to do.

Once during the night, as he happened to be passing through the prison, he saw that the soil was disturbed under one of the bunks. He stopped to examine it. Suddenly Makár crept from under the bunk and looked at Aksénof with a startled face.

Aksénof was about to pass on so as not to see him, but Makár seized his arm, and told him how he had been digging a passage under the wall, and how every day he carried the earth out in his boot-legs and emptied it in the street when they went out to work. He said:

" If you only keep quiet, old man, I will get you out too. But if you give me away, they will flog me; but afterward I will make it hot for you. I will kill you."

When Aksénof saw his enemy, he trembled all over with rage, twitched away his arm, and said: " I have no reason to make my escape, and to kill me would do no harm; you killed me long ago. But as to informing about you or not, I shall do as God sees fit that I should do."

Next day, when they took the convicts out to work, the soldiers discovered where Makár had been digging in the ground; they began to make a search, and found the hole. The chief came into the prison and asked every one, " Who was digging that hole?"

All denied it. Those who knew did not name Makár, because they were aware that he would be flogged almost to death for such an attempt.

Then the chief came to Aksénof. He knew that Aksénof was a truthful man, and he said: " Old man, you are truthful; tell me before God who did this."

Makár was standing near, in great excitement, and did not dare to look at Aksénof.

Aksénof's hands and lips trembled, and it was some time before he could speak a word. He said to himself: " If I shield him— But why should I forgive him when he has been my ruin? Let him suffer for my sufferings! But shall I tell on him? They will surely flog him? But what difference does it make what I think of him? Will it be any the easier for me?"

Once more the chief demanded:

" Well, old man, tell the truth! Who dug the hole?"

Aksénof glanced at Makár, and then said:

" I cannot tell, your Honour. God does not bid me tell. I will not tell. Do with me as you please; I am in your power."

In spite of all the chief's efforts, Aksénof would say nothing more. And so they failed to find out who dug the hole.

On the next night, as Aksénof was lying on his bunk, and almost asleep, he heard some one come along and sit down at his feet.

He peered through the darkness and saw that it was Makár.

Aksénof asked :

" What do you wish of me ? What are you doing here ? "

Makár remained silent. Aksénof arose, and said :

" What do you want ? Go away, or else I will call the guard."

Makár went up close to Aksénof, and said in a whisper :

" Iván Dmítritch, forgive me ! "

Aksénof said : " What have I to forgive you ? "

" It was I who killed the merchant and put the knife in your bag. And I was going to kill you too, but there was a noise in the yard ; I thrust the knife in your bag, and slipped out of the window."

Aksénof said nothing, and he did not know what to say. Makár got down from the bunk, knelt on the ground, and said :

" Iván Dmítritch, forgive me, forgive me for Christ's sake. I will confess that I killed the merchant—they will pardon you. You will be able to go home." Aksénof said :

" It is easy for you to say that, but how could I endure it ? Where should I go now ? My wife is dead ! my children have forgotten me. I have nowhere to go."

Makár did not rise ; he beat his head on the ground, and said :

" Iván Dmítritch, forgive me ! When they flogged me with the knout, it was easier to bear than it is now to look at you. And you had pity on me after all this—you did not tell on me. Forgive me for Christ's sake ! Forgive me though I am a cursed villain ! "

And the man began to sob.

When Aksénof heard Makár Semyónof sobbing, he himself burst into tears, and said :

" God will forgive you ; maybe I am a hundred times worse than you are ! "

And suddenly he felt a wonderful peace in his soul. And he ceased to mourn for his home, and had no desire to leave the prison, but only thought of his last hour.

Makár would not listen to Aksénof, and confessed his crime.

When they came to let Aksénof go home, he was dead.

A CANDLE

COUNT LEO N. TOLSTOY

THE incident took place at a time when the landowners were all-powerful. They were of various kinds; some of them feared God, and remembered death, and had pity on the poor; others, if I may use the word, were little better than dogs. But none of them was worse than the stewards who had risen from being serfs. They were like rulers who had risen out of the mud; and they made the life of the peasants intolerable.

A steward of that kind ruled over the estate of a great landlord. There were many peasants, much good land, plentiful water, and good meadows and woods. There was plenty for lord and peasants alike, but this landlord brought one of his serfs from another of his estates to be steward. This man was very overbearing and oppressed the peasants. He came with his wife and two daughters, who were married. He was already well off, and might well have lived a blameless life, had not covetousness led him into evil. He made the peasants do more than their proper day's work on the estate; and besides that he started a brickyard, forced both men and women to work upon it, and made a profit by the sale of the bricks. The peasants vainly complained to the landlord at Moscow; he sent them away disappointed, and did not bring the steward to book. The latter soon found out that the peasants had reported his actions, and quickly took his revenge, so that their state was worse than before. Moreover, some of the peasants were tale-bearers, so that the estate was soon in a very bad way, and the steward became more ferocious than ever. At last he became so hard and cruel that he was more feared than a wild beast. Men and women alike would hide from him as from a wolf, doing everything to escape his sight. Of course, the man soon saw this, and their fear only increased his rage. He pursued them with violence and oppression, so that their sufferings were unendurable.

It often happened that criminals of this kind were done to death, and the peasants began to mutter of assassination. They met furtively from time to time, and the bolder spirits would say: "Must our sufferings go on for ever? It is no sin to kill a man like him!" On one of these occasions, just before Easter, the peasants were gathered at dinner in the forest, whither the steward had sent them to cut wood. "How are we to live?" said one. "The man will be the death of us. Neither our wives nor we can rest by day or night. Whenever he is angry he uses the whip. So Semyón died, and Anisim was tormented by the stocks. The same will be our fate. He will be here to-night and is sure to raise trouble. Let us pull him off his horse and hit him on the head with an axe and bury him like a dog. No one can ever know anything about it. But we must all stick together; no one must tell!"

These were the words of Vasili Minaef, who was angrier than any one else, for the steward beat him every few days and had taken away his wife to be his servant.

As expected, the steward came on horseback in the evening, and no sooner had he arrived than he began to scold. He found a few lime-branches among the cut wood. Now he had forbidden this wood to be cut. "Confess who did it," he said, "or I will beat you all." Then he ascertained whose pile contained the lime-wood. It had been cut by Sidor, and the steward beat him until the blood came. Then he beat Vasili because he had done too little work; and growling, went away.

That same evening the peasants met once more, and Vasili harangued them. "You are not men," he said, "but sparrows. You promised to stand all together, but when the opportunity comes all fear to act. When he beat Sidor you should all have joined and put him to death. But after promising to stand together, you are like sparrows who fly into the bushes when the hawk swoops down on one of them."

The anger of the peasants gathered force, and at last they determined to put an end to the steward. He told them on Good Friday that they must plough for the landlord on Easter Sunday, to prepare the land for oats. This was an unheard-of proposal. On Good Friday they met behind Vasili's cottage and consulted. "He has forgotten God," they said. "If he commands such sins we must kill him. We are lost in any case."

There was among them a very peaceable peasant named Piotr Mikhyeef, who did not at all agree to this. "Brothers," he said, "you are proposing a great sin. Nothing is worse than to kill a soul.

What about your own souls? The misfortune is his, because it is he who does the evil. As for us, brothers, we must suffer in silence."

This counsel annoyed Vasili exceedingly. "You say that it is a sin to kill a man! You repeat the same thing again and again. Now it is a sin to kill an honest man, but God Himself has commanded that we should kill a dog like this one. A mad dog must be slain that men may be safe. It would be a greater wrong not to kill the steward, who is our ruin. Even though it should bring us into trouble, we ought to do it for the sake of others. They will be grateful to us. You talk mere nonsense. It would be a greater sin for us all to work on Easter Sunday. Even *you* would not do that."

But the peaceful peasant was ready with his answer. "Certainly I will plough," he said, "when they send us, though I would not plough for myself. God will know where the sin lies. It only matters that we should not be forgetful of Him. God has not told us to render evil for evil, but to do exactly the opposite. If you do wrong, it is you who will suffer in the end. If you slay a man your soul will be stained with blood. You think that you will have killed a bad man, or that you will have destroyed a plague-spot, but in point of fact you will have done a far greater wrong to yourself. If you give way to fate, fate will give way to you." This speech had much effect, and the peasants were divided in opinion, some thinking that the steward should be slain, and others agreeing with Piotr that it would be better not to sin, but rather to bear their sufferings.

The peasants were celebrating the great festival of Holy Saturday when the village elder came round and informed them that the steward had given orders that all the men were to plough the oatfields on the following day. Together with police officials, he went all through the village, shouting to one man on the river and to another on the road, saying that every man must plough. The unhappy men mourned, but could only obey; and on the morrow they brought their ploughs and set to work. The first mass was being celebrated at church and all the air was full of the Easter festival, but the peasants were ploughing.

Late in the morning the steward arose and rode over to the farm. His family were dressed in all their best garments, horses were harnessed to the little carriage; they went and heard mass. On their return the servants made the tea, and when the steward came in they began to drink it. After the steward had finished his tea he lit his pipe and sent for the village elder.

" Have you set the men to work at ploughing ? " he asked.

" I have," was the reply.

" And did all of them go ? "

" Every one of them. I set them to work myself."

" That is very good, but I wonder whether they are really working. I want you to go and see, and tell them that I shall come out after dinner to see that each of them has covered sufficient ground, and has done it well too. If I have any fault to find, there will be no festival for them."

The village elder had not gone far when the steward called after him. He hesitated, wishing to give some order, but did not know how to choose his words. At last, with some hesitation, he brought it out.

" I want you to tell me what those scoundrels say about me. Find out which of them is grumbling and let me know what he says. I know the lazy villains ; they hate working ; and unless I kept them tightly in hand they would do nothing. They like feasting and holidays, but not ploughing. Just keep your ears open to what they say and report to me. I want to know all about it." At this the village elder mounted his horse and rode off to the fields where the peasants were working.

Now the steward's wife, a peaceable, tender-hearted woman, had overheard this conversation, and came to speak with her husband and plead for the peasants. In fact, she always stood up for them whenever she could.

" My dear husband," she said, " do take care you do not commit a sin on this great festival of Our Lord. Dismiss the men from their work, I ask you for Christ's sake."

But the brutal man only laughed at her. " It seems to me that you want a good thrashing," he growled. " How dare you meddle with my affairs ? "

" My dear love," she said, " I dreamed about you last night ; it was a dreadful dream. Do listen to me and dismiss the men."

" I shall have something to say about that," he replied ; " if you give me any more cheek I will beat you. So take care ! " He was very angry ; and thrusting his pipe into her face, told her to fetch dinner. After an abundant repast, at which he drank freely, the steward called for the cook and made her sing, while he accompanied her voice with his guitar. He was still gaily chatting with the cook and playing his guitar, when the village elder returned to report upon the men at work.

" Are they ploughing ? " asked the steward. " Will they get their task done ? "

" They have done more than half of it already."

" And done it well ? "

" Very well, sir. They dared not do otherwise."

" How does the ground look ? "

" In excellent condition, and turns up easily."

After a long silence the steward resumed. " And what are they saying about me ? No good, I suppose ? "

The old man hesitated, but the steward called on him to speak freely. " Tell me everything ; it is not your own words I ask you to repeat, but those of others. I will make it worth your while to tell the truth, but take care you don't hide anything. Here," he continued, addressing the cook, " give him a glass of spirits."

The old man, thus refreshed, took courage and spoke. " They don't speak any good, sir ; they grumble a good deal."

" I dare say ; but what do they actually say ? "

" Always the same thing, sir,—' He does not believe in God.' "

" Who says that ? " asked the steward scornfully.

" All of them. They say : ' He has sold himself to the Devil.' "

" Very good," said the steward, chuckling. " Now tell me, does Vasili say that ? "

Unwilling as the elder was to tell tales of his companions, he had long been on bad terms with Vasili, and admitted that Vasili grumbled more than any of the others.

" Can't you speak out, man ? " said the steward. " What does he say ? "

" It is a dreadful thing to tell you. He says that you cannot escape a violent death."

" Aha, he's a fine fellow ! I suppose he lies in wait for me ? No, no, Vasili, you cannot touch me ! I'll see about you, my man ! Now, then, what does Tishka say ? He, too, I suppose, the dog ? "

" Yes, sir, they all say dreadful things, hateful."

" Come on, man. Don't be afraid to speak."

" Well then, if I must : they all say that you will burst asunder and your entrails will fall out."

The steward was hugely delighted and howled with laughter. "Aha, we shall see who will first meet that fate! Who is it says that?"

"No one has anything good to say; all are very threatening."

"What about Piotr? He grumbles too, I suppose?"

"No, sir; he alone among all the men has nothing to say. He is a deep fellow, is Piotr. I can't understand him."

"What do you mean?"

"All the men are wondering and talking about it. He is ploughing on the upper field. I came near him and heard him singing, and saw that he was carrying something very carefully; and there was a bright light between the handles of his plough, just as it might have been a tiny fire flickering. When I came near I saw a little candle, might be a twopenny one, standing burning on the cross-bar of the handles; and it would not go out for all the wind. Piotr, in his Sunday clothes, went up and down the furrows singing as they sing in church. With all the shaking the candle would not go out. I was close up to him when he lifted and turned the plough; and the candle burned steadily and would not go out."

"What did he say?" inquired the steward.

"Not a word, sir; he only looked at me, made the sign of the cross, and then began to sing."

"Did you not speak to him?"

"No, sir, but some of the men came up and began to chaff him, saying that his prayers would not save him from punishment for ploughing on a holy day."

"And did he speak?"

"Only these words—'On earth, peace to men of good-will.' And then he jerked the reins, and into his songs again, and the plough went away across the hill. And still that candle burned and would not go out, sir."

The steward laughed no longer, but throwing aside his guitar, let his head fall upon his breast, as he pondered this portent. Long he sat there before he sent away the cook and the old man; and then he lay down on his bed, and sighed and groaned as if he had been buried beneath a stack of wheat. His wife entered and spoke to him, yet could get no reply but this: "He has won the day; it is all up with me!"

The good woman seized on the opportunity. "Do dismiss the men, dear. Don't be afraid; no harm has been done."

" It is all up with me," the wretched man repeated ; " he has won the day ; he has conquered me."

His wife raised her voice imperatively. " Get up and dismiss the men, and all will be well. Get up while I saddle your horse."

The steward mounted at the gate, and rode forth to dismiss the men. As he came near the village a woman opened the gate for him ; and as he rode down between the houses the street was cleared as if by magic, every soul running to cover, some within doors and others in their gardens. So he passed throughout the village and came to another gate. This was shut, and he failed to open it while mounted. He shouted again and again for some one to open it, but no one came forward. Dismounting, he set the gate wide open, and was about to mount his horse. His foot was in the stirrup, and he was just throwing himself into the saddle when the restive horse shied at a running pig and leapt sideways against the fence. The corpulent steward failed to reach the saddle, and was thrown forward upon a sharp post that supported the fence. He fell with his belly right on its sharpened point ; and it tore him open, and then he fell to the ground.

The men were returning in haste from their work, their mouths full of bitter sayings. When they came with their horses to the gate they saw the dead steward lying on his back with outstretched arms ; his eyes were glazed, and his blood was about him like a pool, of which earth itself refused to drink. The terrified men urged their horses onward. But Piotr threw himself from his horse and, coming to the dead man, closed his eyes ; then putting his horse into a cart, brought the body to the manor-house.

Having heard the whole matter, the lord of the manor remitted to his men their annual tax. And the peasants, for their part, knew that the power of God works by goodness and not by sin.

THE THREE HERMITS

COUNT LEO N. TOLSTOY

A CERTAIN bishop set out to sea in a ship sailing from the city of Archangel to Solovki, a port on the River Dwina. With him were many going on pilgrimage to a holy shrine. There was a fair breeze, the sea was smooth and the skies blue. And as they fared forth over the waters the pilgrims held converse together, whether lying or sitting on the deck or taking their meals.

One morning the bishop came up on deck and paced to and fro upon the poop. Then, seeing the ship's company and passengers thronging the bow, he went forward to join them. A young lad was pointing away far over the sea, and those about him were listening to what he said. The bishop scanned the horizon to which he pointed, but could see nothing but the far glittering of the ocean. Approaching nearer to hear what the lad had to say, the bishop was saluted with great deference by all the company.

"Do not let me interrupt you, my brethren," he said. "I only wanted to hear what you are saying, my lad."

"The boy, a fisherman in these waters," said a trader, "has been telling us about certain hermits."

"What hermits? I should like to hear," said the bishop, taking his seat by the bulwarks. "What were you pointing at?"

"That little island just in sight on the port bow," replied the fisher-boy. "There are three hermits living there for the good of their souls."

"But where is this island?" the bishop inquired.

"Look, sir, right along my arm, just to the left of the little cloud. You will be able to see it."

The man of God peered forth across the glittering waters, but could make out nothing in the vast expanse. "I see nothing," he exclaimed. "What kind of hermits are they?"

"Some sort of monk," the lad replied. "I have heard of them often, and last summer I saw them." Then he told how he had been driven by contrary winds to the shore of the island, not knowing where he was. He had explored the island and had come upon a lowly mud cabin. Here he had found one of the hermits, and then the two others had come into the cabin. They had given him food and dried his clothes, and had helped him to mend his fishing-boat.

" What were they like ? " the bishop inquired.

" Well, sir, the first I saw in the hut was a very, very old man, I should think a hundred years old ; a tiny little man he was, with a round back, and he wore an old cassock. His beard was quite white, and he smiled, sir, smiled like the pictures of the saints. Then the next, he was old too, with a long yellow beard ; taller, he was, and had a ragged coat ; I can tell you he *was* strong ; he could turn my boat over by himself. Lively and happy he was. Then the other was a great tall white man, white as the moon, and his beard came down to his knees. He was severe and sad to look at, and his eyes shone as out of caves. He wore nothing except a belt round his middle."

" What did they say ? "

" They would hardly speak a word, sir, and said very little to each other ; if one of them looked, *so*, the others would understand. I asked the tall one how long they had been there, and he frowned and looked angry and growled at me ; but the little old, old man took his hand and smiled at him, and the big tall man was quiet then. And then the old man smiled again and said to me, ' You must excuse us.' "

While this story was going on the ship was gradually approaching the island. " There now, reverend Father," exclaimed the trader, " the island is quite plain now ! " and pointed away over the sea. And this time the bishop was just able to make out a tiny dark speck, which was indeed the island. For long the man of God gazed upon it ; then, taking some resolution, he walked aft and spoke to the steersman.

" What is that little island called ? " he inquired.

" Well, sir, I don't suppose it has a name. There are many like it in these waters."

" I am told that certain hermits live on it. Do you know if that is the case ? "

" You can't believe all you hear," the man replied. " They do say that there are hermits there, and that the fishermen have seen them. I am sure I don't know."

" I should like to put ashore," said the bishop, " and visit the hermits. Can it be done ? "

" Well, your reverence, we cannot take the ship alongside," the man answered. " Of course you could land in the boat, but that is a matter for the skipper. There he is."

" Captain," said the bishop, addressing him, " I should very much like to see those hermits. Can you see your way to putting me ashore ? "

The skipper was very unwilling to do anything of the kind. " It is easy enough, my lord," he said, " but it would only be a waste of time. I can assure you that they are not worth your trouble. I have been told that they are out of their wits ; cannot understand what you say nor say anything themselves ; little better than shell-fish."

" That may be," the bishop replied. " But I wish to land and am willing to pay for the time and trouble."

It was difficult to refuse a man of his dignity. The necessary orders were given ; the ship was laid on the other tack and swiftly bore down on the island. They fetched a seat for the bishop, who then sat right in the bow and looked steadily at the island, while the ship's company gathered behind him. Soon the more far-sighted seamen made out the rocks, and presently the little cabin, and at last one of them thought he saw the three hermits. Then the skipper fetched his glass, and having studied the shore gave it to the bishop, saying, " Right you are. There are three men standing on a rock on the shore." The bishop took the glass and presently made out the three men, one very tall, the second shorter, and the third very short indeed, standing together on the shore and holding one another's hands.

Then said the captain : " We cannot go farther, sir. We must anchor here. If you still wish it you can go ashore in the ship's boat." So the helm was put down and the ship ran up into the wind ; the anchor was thrown over and the sails lowered ; and the vessel rolled in the swell of the sea. The boat was put over the side and manned by its crew ; the bishop climbed down the ladder and sat in the stern ; the oarsmen beat the water and the boat sped on its way like a stone from a sling. Plainer and plainer became these three old men standing together and holding one another's hands. Soon the boat came alongside the rocks ; a seaman caught them with the hook, and the bishop climbed ashore. The hermits came forward and made obeisance. He gave them his blessing, and they bowed again. Then the bishop spoke :

" I have been told that you are living here as followers of Our

Lord Christ, to worship God and to work out your salvation. By the grace of God I too am a servant of Our Lord, though an unworthy one, and have been called to be a shepherd of His flock. So I wish, if possible, to come and give you some instruction, for you are God's servants."

The hermits found nothing to say, but only looked at one another and smiled.

" Will you tell me," inquired the bishop, " how you seek your salvation and serve God ? "

The two taller hermits sighed and looked toward that venerable ancient little one. And he in turn smiled and said, " O servant of God, we are not able to serve God. We serve ourselves by seeking our food."

" But how do you pray to God ? " said the bishop.

Then the old man made reply, " This is what we say : *You are three ; we are three ; have mercy on us*." And no sooner had he spoken than all three hermits lifted their eyes to the heavens and cried in chorus : " *You are three ; we are three ; have mercy on us*."

The bishop was touched, and smiled. " You have been rightly taught," he said, " about the Holy Trinity, but that is not the way to pray. Your devotion pleases me, my children. It is plain that you wish to serve God, but you do not know how to do so. Listen to me ; let me teach you. I am not going to teach you my own words, but will teach you from Holy Scripture how God wishes all men to pray to Him." Then he explained to the hermits the mysteries of Revelation, telling them all about God the Father, God the Son, and God the Holy Ghost, and continued, " The Son of God came to earth to save us all and taught all men to pray thus,—Listen and say the words after me,—*Our Father*."

One hermit repeated *Our Father*, and the second after him, and lastly the third also.

" *Who art in heaven*."

The hermits tried to say, *Who art in heaven*, but none of them could make anything of it. The tall naked man's lips were ungovernable so that he could not speak. The most ancient of the three failed to make the words intelligible ; and the other mixed them up hopelessly.

Undiscouraged, the bishop took his seat on a rock while the hermits stood before him, and they repeated that phrase after him until at last they had it by rote. All the long day until nightfall the bishop persevered, repeating every word a hundred times, until the hermits were able to speak each phrase. And when, as often happened, they got it all mixed up, he stopped them at once and began all over again. He did not leave them until they had learned the whole of the Lord's Prayer, and could repeat it together and separately.

Night had already fallen, and the moon had climbed up from the sea, before the bishop arose to say farewell. They made obeisance as before and he kissed them, enjoining them to pray as he had taught them. Then he entered the boat again, and as the seamen rowed him toward the ship the voices of the hermits followed him, shouting the *Our Father*. Having climbed aboard the ship, he could no longer hear the sound of prayer, but there in the moonlight were the three old men standing upon the shore.

The sails were set and the anchor raised and the swift ship sped on her course. Seated in the stern, the bishop still gazed at the rocky island. Soon he lost sight of the hermits; presently the island itself faded from vision; and there was only the sea with the wide pathway of the moon. The pilgrims were asleep, and there was not a sound on board. But there was no sleep for the bishop, seated alone in the stern, rejoicing in his good hermits and in the instruction they had received, and thanking God that he had been able to help them.

Thus he sat thinking, his eyes dazzled with the moonlight dancing on the waves, when he was suddenly aware of some gleaming white fleeting object coming down the pathway of the moon. Was it a sail, or some bird pursuing them? The bishop peered over the water. This strange object was swiftly gaining upon the vessel. It was not a boat, nor a bird, nor a fish, but rather like the figure of a man of great stature. Yet that could not be, for how could a man be fleeting over the surface of the waters?

The bishop hailed the steersman. "See, brother," he cried, pointing, "what is that?" But he knew already. The three hermits were fleeting over the sea with shining beards, and they overhauled the ship as though she had been at anchor. The frightened steersman left the tiller, and screamed, "God save us! The hermits, the hermits! They run as though upon the land!"

The alarm brought the whole ship's company on deck, and they clustered affrighted about the stern. And still the hermits, holding one another's hands, fleeted over the moonlit waters, waving to the vessel to lie to; and though they ran as on dry land their feet were not seen to move. Before ever the ship had run up into the wind the hermits had come up and scaled the side. Standing on deck before the astonished company, they said, "O servant of God, we have forgotten all, all that you taught us. We remembered it so long as we were repeating it; but when we stopped saying it for an hour, we had lost one of the words. We could not recall it, and presently the whole was gone. We remember not a word of it; please teach us again."

The bishop made the sign of the cross, and knelt before the hermits, saying, "God has accepted your prayer, O holy hermits. There is nothing I can teach you. Only, pray for us sinners." So he bowed himself before their feet.

For a moment the hermits stood, then turned and fleeted away over the sea. And next morning the deck was seen to shine where they had stood.

ELIAS

Count Leo N. Tolstoy

ONCE upon a time there lived in a remote Russian district a man of the name of Elias. His father had left him but little wealth, but had found a wife for his son, and had died a year later. Then Elias was the owner of seven mares, two cows, and twenty sheep. But as soon as Elias had become his own master he began to get on. He and his wife worked from dawn to sunset; he was more laborious than any other man, and grew richer year by year. After thirty-five years of arduous labour he had amassed great wealth. For now he had two hundred horses, a hundred and fifty cattle, and twelve hundred sheep; and employed many herdsmen and horsemen, and many dairymaids to make koumiss and butter and cheese.

Elias was the envy of all who knew him; and people used to say, "What good fortune the man has! He has abundance of everything!" Even the best people began to make his acquaintance, and visitors came to him from far away. Elias gave a welcome to every one, and plenty to eat and drink; there was always abundance of koumiss and tea and sherbet and mutton. As soon as a guest came a ram was killed, and if there was a large company they killed a mare.

Elias had two sons and a daughter; for the former he had procured wives, and his daughter had been given in marriage. So long as the father had been poor the sons had worked for him as herdsmen, but when wealth came the lads took to dissipation, and one of them to strong liquor. The elder fell in a drunken quarrel, and the younger came under the dominion of a proud wife and no longer respected his father, so that Elias had to portion him off and send him away. He gave him a house and herds of cattle, and thereby Elias lost much of his wealth.

And now troubles began to accumulate. Many of the old man's sheep perished by a fell disease. Then followed a year of drought such that no grass would grow, and for lack of hay many of his cattle died in the winter. Not long afterward a bandit tribe came and drove away most of his horses, so that Elias was impoverished yet further. He fell from one sorrow to another, and his natural strength was abated. At last, when he was seventy years old, he had to sell his furs and carpets and waggons ; and then the day came when his last cow and last sheep had been sold, so that Elias had come down to nothingness. He realised that he had now absolutely nothing, and that he and his wife must now live among the very poorest. He had nothing to call his own but the clothes he wore, a fur cloak, his hat and shoes ; and his aged wife was equally destitute. The son had gone away to a far country and the daughter was dead ; and there was no one to help the poor old couple.

But a neighbour of theirs, Muhamedshah, was sorry for the poor old folk. He was not rich, neither was he poor, but lived comfortably and had a good heart. He did not forget that he had eaten bread and salt with Elias ; and touched with pity, he said to him, " Come and live with me, Elias, together with your wife. In summer you may do what you can in the melon-fields, and in winter you may feed the cattle, while your wife does the dairywork and makes koumiss. I will give you both food and clothing, and whatever else you may desire and ask for."

The grateful old man thanked Muhamedshah, and with his wife dwelt in his house as a servant. It was hard enough at first, but they soon became accustomed to it. So the aged couple lived and did what work they were fit for. They were very profitable to their master, because they themselves had been master and mistress, and knew the right way of doing things ; moreover, they were never idle, but did all that they could. Only, their employer was sorry to see his old friends fallen to so humble a state in life.

One day it happened that some of his relatives came to visit Muhamedshah, and a priest came with them, and Elias was ordered to choose a ram and prepare it for the table. The visitors feasted on the meat and drank tea and then koumiss. They sat with their host on cushions on the floor and had pleasant talk, while Elias pursued his duties, and happened once to pass by the open door. As he did so, Muhamedshah exclaimed, " Did you see that old man who just now passed the door ? "

" Yes," said one of the guests, " what about him ? "

" There is this to tell about him. There was a day when Elias was the wealthiest of us all. You have surely heard of him ? "

"Of course I have heard of him," was the reply. "His reputation was all over the countryside."

"Well, he is nothing now. He lives here as my servant, and his wife looks after the cows."

The visitor was amazed. He sighed, and shook his head and exclaimed: "Surely fortune goes round like a wheel, raising one upward and throwing another down! But tell me, is the old man unhappy about it all?"

"Who can say? He is very quiet and gentle, and seems happy enough."

"May I have a few words with him?" continued the guest. "I should like to ask him one or two questions."

"Of course you may," the host replied, and sent for Elias.

The aged couple came to the door. Elias saluted his master and the visitors, muttered a prayer, and knelt down at the door, while the wife went to her mistress behind the curtain. Elias was given a cup of koumiss, and after drinking the health of the company, laid down the cup.

"Would you tell me, grandfather," said the visitor who had spoken; "does it not pain you, when you come among us, to remember your former happy and fortunate life, and to think of your present lowly position?"

Elias smiled. "You would not believe me, sir, if I were to speak of what is good fortune and what is misfortune. It would be better to ask my wife about this. Being a woman, she says all that is in her heart; she can tell you all that there is to know about your question."

The visitor turned toward the curtain, and said: "Tell me, old mother; what do you think about the good fortune of the old days and the troubles of the present?"

An aged voice came from behind the curtain. "This, sir, is what I think. My old man and I have lived together for fifty years. We sought for happiness, but could not find it. And this is only the second year in which we have wanted for nothing. We live as working people, and are really happy, and have need of nothing."

Not only the guests but even their host was amazed; he rose to his feet and drew aside the curtain to see the old wife. She was standing just behind it with her arms folded; she smiled as her eyes fell on her old man, and he returned the smile. "I mean what I say," she continued. "I am not jesting. For half a hundred years we sought for joy, and so long as we were rich we never found it. But now that we have nothing of our own and live among the peasants we have found greater happiness than I can say."

" What causes this happiness of yours ? "

" This is what causes it, sir. So long as we were rich my old man and I had never a quiet hour together ; we had no time to talk, nor to care for our souls, nor to pray to God ; for we were burdened with endless cares. Often guests came to us, and we were concerned how to provide for each of them, and what presents to give lest we should go down in their esteem. We were always worrying lest the wolves should catch our lambs and kids, or robbers drive away our mares ; and even when we went to bed we stayed awake fearing that the sheep might smother the lambs. Then we would rise and walk about in the night, but no sooner had we set our minds at ease than a fresh question would come to us, such as how to procure hay or find pasturage for winter. So it went on and on. But this was not so bad as the quarrels between my husband and myself. He would say : ' We must do this,' and I would reply : ' No, we must do that,' and then we would fall into ill words, and so into sin. So we lived, going on from care to care, and from one sin to another, and there was no happiness for us anywhere.

" And what about your present state ? "

" My husband and I rise in the morning together and agree in everything ; our talk is all loving ; there is nothing to trouble us nor to dispute about ; our only desire is to serve our master. We are glad to work for his prosperity. When we come up to the house we find dinner or supper or koumiss. In cold weather there is a good fire and plenty of furs. And we always have time to talk with one another, to care for our souls, and to pray to God. We sought happiness for fifty years, and have only found it now."

The visitors laughed among themselves, but Elias continued : " My brothers, do not laugh ; this is not a jest, but the very truth of human life. In the first days my wife and I were foolish enough to weep that we had lost all ; but now God has shown us the very truth ; and we tell it to you, not to amuse ourselves, but that it may help you."

Then said the priest : " These are wise and true sayings. Elias has spoken the very truth. Moreover, every word of it is set forth in Holy Scripture."

The guests laughed no more, but thought deeply in their hearts.

THE GRAIN OF WHEAT AS LARGE AS AN EGG

Count Leo N. Tolstoy

SOME children at play happened to find in a crack in the ground a curious object very like an egg, but with a groove running down it such as is found in a grain of wheat. A wayfarer, attracted by its curiosity, gave the children a penny for it, and having brought it up to the city sold it to the King. He then sent for the learned men of his Court and asked them what this object could be, and whether it was a grain of wheat or a hen's egg. The men of learning thought deeply on the matter, but were still unable to give any reply.

But the question was soon solved. This remarkable object was lying on the window-ledge when a bird alighted beside it and eagerly pecked at it, and so dug a cavity deep into its middle. The bystanders were astonished to see that it was indeed a grain of corn. So the men of learning went up to the King again and reported that it was a grain of wheat. The King was amazed, and commanded these learned men to find out in what place and at what time monster grain such as this had been grown.

The men of learning thought on the matter and consulted ; they searched the volumes in their libraries, and all without result. They returned to the King's presence and said : " Your Majesty, we have not been able to find out, for our books contain nothing concerning this thing. It will be well to ask the peasants whether they have heard from their forefathers anything about the growing of wheat like this. So the King commanded that one of the oldest of the peasant elders should be fetched into his presence.

This aged man tottered painfully into the presence, supported by crutches. His face was white, he was without teeth and could hardly see. The King placed the grain of wheat in his hand. The old man turned it about, peered at it, and felt it over with his fingers, and at last formed some dim idea of its nature.

" Do you know, old man," said the King, " where corn like this is to be found? Have you ever grown wheat like this, or do you remember buying it?"

For long the old man made no reply. His hearing was almost gone, and his mind moved very slowly. But at last he raised his voice, saying, "No, sire, I have never sown nor reaped grain like this, nor bought of it in the market. All the corn we have had to do with has been of the small-grained kind. But perhaps my father may have heard tell of wheat like this. Let Your Majesty ask him."

So the King commanded them to fetch the old man's father, and they found him and brought him into the presence. This venerable man used but a single crutch, and had still the use of his eyes. The King put the grain of wheat before him, and one glance was enough for him. "Do you know, my venerable man," said the King, "where grain like this has been grown? Have you ever grown any like it, or bought it in the market?"

The venerable man was indeed hard of hearing, but was not nearly so deaf as his son. "No, sire," he replied, "I have never cultivated wheat like this; nor have I ever purchased any, inasmuch as we knew nothing about money in our time. Every man lived on the corn grown on his own land, and had wherewithal to furnish his neighbour's need. I do not know where wheat like this was grown. Ours was of larger grain and the yield was greater than that in the present day; but I have never seen anything like this. But I remember my father's saying that wheat was better and the grain larger in his time than it was in my day. It would be well to send for him."

So the King sent them to fetch the father of the venerable man, and soon they brought this ancient patriarch into the presence. This ancient man came before the King without any crutch; his footstep was alert, his eyes gleamed, and his speech was distinct. The King placed the grain of wheat in his hand.

The ancient grandfather glanced at it, and rubbed it between his fingers. "Holla!" he exclaimed; "this is a grain of the good old kind!" He bit the grain and tasted it. "It is the very same," he said.

Then said the King, "Can you tell me, ancient grandfather, in what place and at what time they grew wheat like this? Have you ever cultivated this great wheat or bought of it in the market?"

"In my time, sire," the ancient man replied, "all the wheat was just such as this is. My family and I always lived on grain like this. And all my youth I sowed and reaped and threshed this wheat."

Then replied the King : " Did you buy this corn, old man, or grow it in your old fields ? "

" In those days," returned the ancient man, " no one ever thought of so great a sin as the buying or selling of grain. None of us knew anything about money. There was as much wheat for every one as he could wish."

" Tell me once more, old man, on what land did you sow corn like this ? Where were your fields ? "

Then answered the ancient grandfather : " My fields were as wide as God's own world. Wherever I drove my plough there was my land. The soil was free to every man. No one ever said : ' This is *my* land.' A man called nothing his own except the work of his own hands."

The King pondered and said : " I have yet two questions to ask. In the first place : Why can we not grow wheat like this in our day, though you were able to grow it in your day ? And, secondly : Why does your grandson need two crutches, and your son one crutch, while you yourself, ancient as you are, have a light and firm step, and your eyes are bright, and your teeth are strong and sound, and your speech is distinct, and your voice is pleasant to the ear. Can you tell me, old grandfather, what is the meaning of all this, and why such things as these do not come to pass in our day ? "

Then answered the ancient patriarch : " Such grain as this no longer grows, and the aged are afflicted by every ill, because men no longer live only by the work of their own hands, but covet instead the property of their neighbours. In the days of old they lived far otherwise. In the days of old they walked with God, and peacefully ruled their own households, and had no desire for the possessions of others."

CHILDREN WISER THAN THEIR FATHERS

COUNT LEO N. TOLSTOY

EASTER was early that year, and people were still going about in sledges. The roofs were covered with snow, and streamlets were running all about the countryside. A large pool lay across the roadway between two cottages and had attracted two little girls, one a very tiny child and the other a little older, from these cottages. The two girls had both been dressed by their mothers in new frocks ; the smaller child was in blue and the elder in yellow with a pretty pattern, and each had a smart handkerchief fastened about her head. They had finished dinner, and had run out to play by the pool and to show one another their little presents.

Then, of course, they wanted to paddle in the dirty water. The baby stole down to the edge of the pool in her dainty shoes, but her companion cried, " Stop, Malashka, don't go in, mother will be angry. Take off your shoes if you like, and I will take off mine too." So they took off their shoes and tucked up their frocks, and stole into the pool.

Malashka's ankles were soon covered, and she cried, " I am afraid ; it is so deep ! "

" Oh, no, it's quite safe," said Akulyushka. " It is no deeper in the middle. Come right across."

They approached one another, and the elder girl said, " Take care, Malashka, you are splashing too much. Do walk more gently."

But she had hardly spoken when Malashka's little foot made a great splash and wetted Akulyushka's pretty frock all over, and the water even wetted her face and got into her eyes. When Akulyushka saw that her frock was spoiled, she lost her temper and raged at Malashka, and flew at her with her little fists clenched. Thoroughly frightened, Malashka fled from the pool for the shelter of home.

At this moment, the mother of Akulyushka came past and saw her child's frock splashed from neck to knee. " What have you been doing, you dirty child ? " she cried.

" It was Malashka," was the reply. " She did it on purpose."

The infuriated mother pursued Malashka and hit her on the head.

The child's cries rang down the street, and her own mother, running out from her cottage, fell to scolding the other woman, saying, " What right have you to hit my child ? "

Soon the two were engaged in a hearty duet of abuse, and the cottagers all down the street came out and gathered in a crowd around them ; the men all growling and the women all shrilling, and no one giving heed to any word of his neighbour. Curses and oaths were followed by blows, and there was a mob fight until the arrival of an aged woman, the grandmother of Akulyushka.

" Come, come, my children, this is too bad. This is no way to spend Easter. We ought all to be giving thanks, and not to be sinning with our words." Her appeal was in vain, and they even hustled the poor old woman. She would never have succeeded in calming them if it had not been for the two little girls. While the acrimonious conflict was still going on, the elder child had dried her frock and returned to the pool. Using a stone to excavate the earth, she began to throw it into the pool so as to send the water into the main street ; and Malashka came out to help her dig a channel to direct its flow. Still the peasants argued and disputed, while the water ran down through the tiny ditch the girls had made and came at last to the feet of the angry peasants and the old woman who was trying to pacify them. The happy children were running one on each side of the little water-course which they had made.

" Stop it, Malashka, do stop it," Akulyushka cried, as well as she could for laughing. But the little one was unable to do anything or even to speak through happy laughter.

So they danced down beside their rivulet, delighted with a little bit of wood which was tumbling down its rapids ; and so they danced right into the middle of the crowd.

Seeing this, the old woman raised her voice once more. " Have you no fear of God, that you quarrel so miserably ? Here you are all angry and disputing about these two little girls, although they have forgotten all about it long ago, and—dear little hearts—are happily playing together again. Are they not wiser than you ? "

The peasants, now silent, looked at the two children and were ashamed of their contentions. Then, laughing at their own folly, they separated and went home to their several cottages.

" Unless you become as little children, you cannot enter the Kingdom of Heaven."

NICOLAI S. LESKOV
1831–1895

THE GHOST OF THE ENGINEERS' CASTLE

I

HOUSES, like people, have their own reputations. There are houses that by general opinion are considered impure, that is, where there have been indications of some impure or, at any rate, incomprehensible power. Spiritualists have done much to explain such phenomena, but as their theories are not generally accepted the matter of haunted houses is still as obscure as ever.

In St. Petersburg, one of the many houses that possessed such an undesirable reputation was the characteristic castle of Paul, known at the present day as the Engineers' Castle. The mysterious manifestations, put down to ghosts and spirits, were observed almost from the very foundation of the castle. Even during the lifetime of the Emperor Paul, they say that the voice of Peter the Great would be heard there and that the Emperor Paul himself saw the ghost of his great-grandfather. The latter event was recorded in the foreign reviews that found space to write about the death of Paul, and in the latest Russian book by Mr. Kobeko, and no refutation appeared. It seems that Peter rose from his grave to warn his great-grandson that his end was near, and the prophecy was fulfilled.

However, Peter's ghost was seen on the walls of the castle, not only by the Emperor Paul but also by some of his suite : in a word, the house was sinister because it was haunted by ghosts and apparitions who spoke of terrible things that came true into the bargain. The sudden and unexpected end of the Emperor Paul—on which occasion people instantly recalled the ghosts met by the late Emperor in the castle—exaggerated still more the mysterious and forbidding reputation of the gloomy house. From that time the castle lost its former importance as a royal residence and, as they say, " went to the cadets."

At the present time this former palace is used by the cadets of the engineering department, but before that it was lived in by the former engineer cadets. This was a still younger crowd of boys not yet free from childish superstitions, who were, besides, sportive, mischievous, daring, and curious. Of course they all knew something of the terrible tales told of their gloomy castle. The children were very much interested in the details of these harrowing stories and fed on their terrors, while those who were sufficiently acclimatised loved to frighten the others. This was in great fashion among the engineer cadets, and the principals could in no way break them of this bad habit until an event occurred which cured them of it once and for all.

It is with this event that our story deals.

II

It was especially the fashion to frighten the new boys, the " little ones " as they were called, who on their arrival would hear so many weird stories about the castle as to make them superstitious and timid to the extreme. They were most afraid of a certain room at the end of a corridor that had served as bedroom to the Emperor Paul, where he had gone to bed one night quite well, and had been carried out dead next morning. The " old boys " maintained that the spirit of the Emperor haunted that room and came out of it every night to inspect his beloved castle, and the " little ones " believed it. The room was always securely fastened with several locks, but to a spirit no lock or bar is of significance. Besides, it was said that it was possible to get into the room, and this turned out to be true. At any rate, a few of the older cadets managed to get in, and continued to do so until one of them committed an outrageous piece of mischief for which he had to pay cruelly. He opened some sort of secret aperture into the terrible bedroom and managed to hide a sheet there. At night he went there, covered himself from head to foot in the sheet, and stood by the dark window that looked out into Sadov Street, where he could be seen by any one who happened to be walking or driving past.

In playing the part of a ghost, the cadet certainly managed to bring terror upon many superstitious people who lived in the castle or who happened to pass by it and see the white figure, all taking it for the shade of the late Emperor.

This piece of mischief continued for several months, and caused a persistent rumour that the Emperor Paul walked about his bedroom at night and looked out on St. Petersburg from this window. Many were certain that the white ghost at the window shook his head and bowed to them more than once; the cadet, of course, was capable of doing these things. All this caused general discussion and prophetic explanations, and ended with the culprit who had caused this anxiety being caught red-handed. He received "exemplary corporal punishment" and disappeared for ever from the institution. There was a rumour that, at one of his appearances at the window, the hapless cadet had the misfortune to frighten some important person who happened to be passing by, and that was why he was so severely punished. To put it more bluntly, the cadets said that the unfortunate boy had "died under the rod," and as at that time such a thing was not looked on as impossible, this, too, was believed and the cadet himself became a new apparition. His comrades began to see him "slashed all over," with a wreath on his forehead, and on the wreath was written the inscription:

I did but taste a little honey, and lo, I must die!

The allusion is very touching if one recalls the Biblical story from which it is taken.

After this cadet's downfall, the bedroom that was the cause of all the terror in the Engineers' Castle was thrown open and put to such a use as to destroy its uncanny reputation, but nevertheless the tradition of the ghost lived on for a long time. The cadets continued to believe that their castle was haunted by a ghost that appeared at night. This was the general conviction held equally by young and old cadets, with the difference, however, that the younger ones believed blindly in the apparition while the elder ones sometimes personally arranged its appearance. This did not prevent those responsible for the apparition from being afraid of it. In the same way "false makers of miracles," who produce the miracles themselves, bow down before them and believe in their reality.

The younger cadets did not know "the whole story," about which it was strongly forbidden to speak after the event of the cruel corporal punishment, but among the older cadets there were some who had been either whipped or flogged and knew the whole secret of the apparition. This gave the elders great prestige, which they enjoyed until the years 1859 or 1860, when four of them went through a very trying ordeal which I shall relate from the story of one of the participants in the misplaced joke at the coffin.

III

In 1859 or 1860, General Lamnovsky, the head of the Engineers' Castle, died. He can hardly be said to have been beloved by the cadets, and it was said that he did not enjoy a good reputation with the governors. They had many reasons for this; they found that he treated the boys in a severe, unsympathetic manner, did not investigate their needs, did not trouble himself about their food, and, above all, was troublesome, quarrelsome, and severe in petty things. In the corps it was said that, left to himself, the general would have been still harsher had not his unreasonable severity been mitigated by his angelic wife, whom no one had ever seen because she was always ill, but who was considered the good genius, protecting every one from the general's extreme ferocity.

Together with his severe disposition, General Lamnovsky had exceedingly unpleasant manners. Some of them were comic, and these the children seized on, and when they wanted to imitate the unpopular head they would take off one of his absurd habits, exaggerated to caricature.

One of the general's most comic habits was that, when making a speech or doing something imposing, he always stroked his nose with all the fingers of his right hand. This, according to the cadets, made it appear as though he were "milking the words out of his nose." The deceased was not distinguished by his eloquence, and it would sometimes happen that he would be at a loss for a word to point a homily, and at every such pause the "milking" would increase, at which the cadets would be unable to maintain their seriousness, and would begin to exchange smiles. Noticing this insubordination, the general would grow still angrier and punish them. Thus the relations between the general and the cadets grew worse and worse, and through it all, according to the cadets, "the nose was most to blame."

Having no love for Lamnovsky, the cadets lost no opportunity of annoying him or of revenging themselves on him and of impairing his reputation with his new colleagues. For this purpose they spread a rumour in the corps that the general had dealings with the black art, and made demons carry the marble for a memorial he had erected in some building, the Isaac Cathedral, I believe. But as the demons were tired of the work, the story goes on, they were anxiously waiting for the general's death, which would bring them their freedom. And to make this more credible, on the evening of the general's nameday the cadets caused him a great deal of unpleasantness by arranging a mock funeral. It was arranged so that when the guests began to arrive in Lamnovsky's private quarters a mournful procession marched down the corridor of the cadets' quarters. The cadets, covered in sheets, with candles in their hands, singing dirges, were carrying a bier on which lay the dummy of a man with a long-nosed mask. The ringleaders who had arranged this ceremony were discovered and punished, but on Lamnovsky's next nameday the unpardonable jest of the mock funeral was repeated. Thus things went on until the year 1859 or 1860, when General Lamnovsky really died and it was necessary to arrange a real funeral. According to the custom of the time, the cadets had, in turn, to be on guard at the coffin, and it was then that there happened the terrible event that frightened the very heroes who, for so long, had been frightening others.

IV

General Lamnovsky died late in autumn—in November—when St. Petersburg has a most man-hating appearance; cold, penetrating damp, and mud; the peculiar misty, foggy light has a depressing effect on the nerves and through them on the brain and imagination. All this produces an abnormal inner disturbance and excitement. Molechott, in his learned deductions on the influence of light on life, could have got some very curious data from us at this time.

About the time that Lamnovsky died the days were particularly depressing. The deceased was not carried into the castle church, as he was a Lutheran; the body was placed in the large, mournful drawing-room in the general's quarters, and it was here that the cadets had, in turn, to be on guard. In the church, according to the Orthodox custom, there was one mass for the dead during the day and another in the evening. All the inmates of the castle, cadets and servants alike, had to appear at both services, and this rule was observed strictly. In consequence, when a service was going on in the church, all the inmates of the castle were gathered there, and the rest of the enormous house, with its long corridors, was quite deserted. In the drawing-room there was no one except the relief guard, who, in parade dress and with rifles, were watching the coffin.

An uncanny weirdness was over the place; all felt uncomfortable and began to be afraid of something; and then they began talking of people "rising" and "walking" again. It became so unpleasant that they began to stop each other, saying: "Shut up, do! Damn your stories! You only ruin your own and other people's nerves." Then they would start again in the same strain, and be again repressed. Towards evening they were all afraid. Their fear became particularly acute when one of them called out plaintively for "Batya," one of the priests.

The priest made them feel ashamed of their joy in the general's death. He had a gentle way, but he understood how to touch their feelings.

"He walks," he said, repeating their words. "You do not and cannot see him, but he has a power which you cannot escape. He is the grey man. He does not arise at midnight, but in the twilight when everything turns grey and every one wants to express the evil in their thoughts. This grey man is conscience. I advise you not to disturb him with your petty joy over another's death. Every man loves some one, pities some one,—take care that the grey man does not take some of those you love and give you a severe lesson."

The cadets took this to heart, and as it began to get dark that day they began peering round for the grey man. We know that in the twilight all sorts of sensitive feelings arise in the heart—a new world arises to take the place of the one we knew by day; well-known objects of familiar form become fanciful, incomprehensible, and even terrible. At such a time every sensation seems somehow to try to find for itself a vague enhanced expression; the moods of thought and feeling are constantly wavering, and in this strange, crowded discord, all the inner world of man begins its work of fantasy; the world turns into dreams, and dreams into the world. This is alluring and terrifying; the more terrifying it is, the more alluring and enticing it becomes.

The majority of the cadets were in such a condition, particularly when on night duty at the coffin. On the last evening before the funeral, many high personages were expected to mass in the church, so that besides the ordinary inmates of the castle there was a large number of people from the town. Even every one from Lamnovsky's household went to the Russian church to see the gathering of the famous people. The dead man remained alone with four young guards. The guard consisted of the cadets G——, B——, Z——, and K——, all still living happily and now occupying important military as well as social positions.

V

Of the four youngsters composing the guard, one particularly, K——, was a most mischievous scamp who had annoyed the late Lamnovsky more than all the rest, and the general, in his turn, had punished K—— more than any one else. The deceased particularly disliked K—— because he could mimic him beautifully about the "milking of the nose," and because he had taken an active part in the arrangement of the funeral processions that took place on the general's namedays.

On the occasion of the last of these processions K—— had himself played the part of the general, and had even made a speech from the coffin with so many grimaces and in such tones as to amuse every one, even the officers sent to scatter the mock procession.

It was known that this event had brought the late Lamnovsky into an extreme fit of wrath, and among the cadets there was a rumour that the enraged general had sworn "to punish K—— so that he would remember it for the rest of his life." The cadets believed this, and taking into consideration the well-known character of their head, did not in the least doubt that he would carry out his oath. For a whole year K—— had been looked upon as "hanging by a hair," and as by the liveliness of his nature it was difficult for this cadet to keep away from dangerous and risky escapades, his position was considered very precarious, and it was expected by everybody that some day K—— would be found out in something, and then Lamnovsky would make short work of him and bring all his might to bear on the famous "I will make him remember for the rest of his life."

K—— was so greatly afraid of the head's threats that he made desperate efforts over himself, like a drunkard does over wine; he avoided all pranks, a thing that made the others quote the old proverb to him, "A peasant may not drink for a year, but when the devil seizes him he drinks without stopping."

The devil seized K—— at the general's very coffin. The latter was reposing without having fulfilled a single one of his threats. The general was no longer terrifying to the cadet, and the boy's long pent-up playfulness at last came out, breaking out like an overstrained spring. He simply went mad.

VI

The last mass for the dead man, at which all the inmates of the castle were to be present, was fixed for seven o'clock in the evening, but as certain famous people were expected, after whom it would not have been decorous to enter the church, they all went much earlier. In the dead man's drawing-room there only remained the youthful guard, G——, B——, Z——, and K——. There was not a soul in any of the large neighbouring rooms.

At half-past seven the door opened, and the adjutant appeared for a moment, to whom there happened an absurd incident that increased the general weirdness. The officer, going up to the door, was either alarmed at his own footsteps, or imagined that some one was running after him ; at first he stopped to let the person pass, and then cried out suddenly :

" Who is that ? Who is that ? " and quickly thrust his head through the door.

The second half of the door shut of itself and made him cry out again as though some one had seized him from behind. Needless to say that he went away after that, casting a quick anxious glance over the mournful room, and guessing by its deserted state that every one was in church, he again shut the door, and loudly clanking his sword, he ran down the corridor to the church as fast as he could.

The cadets standing by the coffin noticed that even the grown-ups felt there was something to be afraid of, and fear is infectious to all.

VII

The cadet guard listened to the sound of the retreating footsteps and with every step they felt themselves more deserted—as though they had been immuned with the dead man for some unforgotten, unforgiven insult, and for which he would arise and revenge himself. And this indeed he did, in the manner of the dead. . . . It was only necessary to have the proper hour—the mystic hour of midnight,

When the cocks crow
And the dead roam about in the darkness. . . .

But they were not going to remain there until midnight, they would be relieved, and besides, they were not only afraid of the dead but also of the grey man who walks in the twilight.

Now it was dense twilight; the dead man was in his coffin and all around was the weirdest stillness. Outside the wind blew with a raging fury, beating the heavy autumn rain against the huge windows, in terrific gusts, smiting the leaves against the tiles in the angles of the roof; the chimneys moaned and howled. All this did not conduce to sobriety of feelings or calmness of reason. The oppression of these sensations was made still worse for the youngsters by the fact that they had to stand and maintain a strict silence: everything was in a state of alarm; the blood rushing to the head beat against the temples so that the sound it produced was like the monotonous grinding of a mill. Those who have experienced this sensation will know it well; it is as though a mill were grinding, not grain, but its very self. This soon brings a man into an oppressive nervous state, and it is rather like the feeling inexperienced people have when going down the shaft of a mine as the customary daylight suddenly changes to the murky light of lamps. . . . To maintain silence becomes impossible—you are seized with a desire to hear your own voice, or to crawl under something and hide, or do most unreasonable things.

VIII

One of the four standing at the general's coffin, K—— himself, feeling this sensation, forgot discipline, and whispered as he stood with his rifle:

" Ghosts are coming to us for Papka's nose."

Lamnovsky was sometimes called " Papka " in fun, but the joke failed to amuse the others, in fact it increased the general weirdness. Noticing this, one of them said to K——:

" Shut up! We are frightened enough as it is," and all looked anxiously towards the shroud that covered the dead man's face.

" That was why I said it," K—— replied. " As for me, I am not a bit afraid; he can't do anything to me now. You must be above such prejudices and not be afraid of such nonsense—a corpse cannot harm you; I'll show you."

" Don't, please! "

" Yes, I will! I'll show you that Papka can't do anything to me now, not even if I take hold of him this minute by the nose."

And with this unexpected remark, K—— put his rifle under his arm, walked quickly up the steps of the catafalque, and taking the dead man by the nose, called out loudly and merrily:

"Oh, Papka, you are dead and I am alive! I am pulling your nose and you can't do anything to me!"

His comrades were stunned by this prank; they had scarcely time to utter a word when suddenly they all heard, plainly and distinctly, a deep, painful sigh. It was like the sound of air escaping from an inflated rubber air-cushion when the valve is loose, and this sigh, it seemed to all, came from the very coffin.

K—— seized his gun quickly and flew down the steps of the catafalque with a loud clatter; the other three, scarcely knowing what they were doing, put down their guns to defend themselves against the rising dead.

But this was not all; the dead man not only sighed, but actually either ran after the mischievous boy who had insulted him or caught him by the hand, for a whole wave of the muslin on the coffin came down after K—— and he could not extricate himself from it. With a loud cry he fell to the ground. . . . The wave of muslin was really an inexplicable and terrifying phenomenon, the more so as now the dead man lay completely uncovered, his hands folded over his breast.

The boy lay on the floor; he dropped his gun and, covering his face with his hands, made the most awful groans. He was evidently in full possession of his senses and just waiting for the dead man to dispose of him in his own fashion.

Meanwhile the sigh was repeated, and a faint rustling was heard. It was a sound that might have been produced by the rubbing of one linen sleeve on another. Evidently the dead man was moving his hands—and suddenly there was a gentle noise followed by a draught of air that blew over the candles, and at the same moment, in the moving curtains that covered the door, an apparition appeared. It was the grey man! Yes, to the eyes of the terrified boys there was presented an apparition in the form of a man. Was it the soul of the dead man in a new shape that he had acquired in the other world—from which he had returned for a moment to avenge the insult? or was it the still more terrible guest, the spirit of the castle, who had come out of the floor of the next room from out the earth?

IX

The apparition was no trick of the imagination ; it did not disappear nor remind one by its form of Heine's description of the " Mysterious Woman " he had seen. At the same time, this apparition, like Heine's woman, seemed like a corpse with a human soul imprisoned in it. Before the frightened boys there was an extraordinary emaciated figure, all in white, but in the shadow it appeared grey. It had a terribly thin pale face and a long, thick, tangled mass of hair which also was grey and which, flowing down in disorder, covered the bosom and shoulders of the apparition. . . . The swollen eyes were bright and sparkled with a feverish fire. They looked out from deep hollows like two living coals of fire. The apparition had thin emaciated hands, like those of a skeleton, and with these hands it was holding on to the heavy drapery over the door. Convulsively clutching the material in feeble fingers, these hands produced the dry rustling heard by the cadets.

The apparition's lips were black and parted, and through them at intervals there issued with a whistling and wheezing that half groan, half sigh that the cadets had first heard when K—— had held the dead man's nose.

X

Seeing this terrible apparition, the three guards who remained standing were petrified in their defensive attitudes. They were more afraid than K——, who lay on the floor entangled in the shroud.

The apparition paid no heed to this group. Its eyes were fixed on the coffin where the dead man lay completely uncovered. It swayed gently from side to side, evidently trying to move. At last it succeeded. Supporting itself against the wall, the apparition moved slowly, with halting steps, towards the coffin. Its movements were terrible. Shuddering convulsively at each step, and trying, with pain, to draw air through those parted lips, it emitted from its chest those awful sighs that the cadets had thought issued from the coffin. Another step, and another ; it was nearer ; at last it had approached the coffin, but before walking up the steps of the catafalque, it stopped, and taking the trembling K—— by the hand with its gentle dry fingers it disentangled the shroud that had got caught in one of the unfortunate boy's buttons, then, looking at him with an expression of unutterable sadness, waved an admonishing finger and made the sign of the cross over him. . . . Then, scarcely able to stand on its trembling legs, it walked up the steps of the catafalque, and catching hold of the edge of the coffin it put its skeleton arms round the dead man and burst out into sobs. . . . It seemed as though the two dead were embracing in the coffin, but soon this ceased. Sounds of life were borne from the other end of the castle; the mass was over and the vanguard was hurrying from the church to the general's quarters, to be there before the arrival of the dignitaries.

XI

The cadets heard firm footsteps approaching down the corridor, and from the open door of the church sounded the last notes of the funeral hymn. The sudden change of impressions caused the cadets to gain courage, and the force of habitual discipline put them in their proper places and positions.

The adjutant, the last person who had looked in before mass, was the first to run in hastily.

" My God ! How did she get here ? " he cried.

The inert body in white, with the tangled grey hair, was lying with its arms round the dead man and seemed herself to be no longer breathing. The matter was explained. The apparition that had frightened the cadets was the late general's widow, herself at death's door. From extreme weakness, she had for long not been able to rise from her bed, but when all had gone to the State mass, she crawled from her own death-bed and, supporting herself with both hands against the wall, had appeared at the dead man's coffin. The dry rustling that the cadets had taken for the movement of the dead man's sleeves was her touch against the wall. Now she was in a deep faint, in which condition the cadets, by the order of the adjutant, carried her out in an arm-chair into the next room.

This was the last fright in the castle, and according to the man who told the story it left a lasting impression. " Since that event," he said, " we could never bear to see any one pleased at another's death. We always remembered our unpardonable prank and the blessing hand of the last ghost of the Engineers' Castle, that alone had the power to forgive by the holy right of love. From that time fear of apparitions disappeared from the corps. The one we had seen was the last."

NICOLAI V. USPENSKY

1837–1889

THE VILLAGE SCHOOLMASTER

AN elderly gentleman, sitting on the verandah of his house, called to a workman who was passing with a water-cart:

" Hi! Prokòfyi! Prokòfyi!"

The cart stopped.

" Are you deaf?"

" The wheels makes such a noise, Grigòryi Naòmich; one can't hear anything. They wants greasing."

" Oh, they're all right. What have you got there? water?"

" Yes, sir."

" From the pond?"

" Yes, sir."

" All right," said the master after a moment's pause, " you can go."

A soldier came up to the verandah.

" Wish your honour good-day!"

" Who are you?"

" From Verkhogliàdov in the Merkoùlovsky district; perhaps you know it?—by the river Kostra . . ."

" What d'you want?"

" I'm looking for a place, sir, as doorkeeper, or bailiff."

" What have you been up till now?"

" Well, when I served in the army I used to be postillion for the commander; then, in Mouràvki, I was cook for the examining magistrate. I'm a Jack-of-all-trades, your honour—gardener, whipper-in, cook—anything you like!"

" Can you break stones?"

" Why, no, your honour, I can't do that kind of work!"

" Why?"

" Well, you see, the army life breaks a chap down so; I was in a line regiment, not in the guards, and a man never gets over that."

" Oh, you're healthy enough, I can see that, and yet you want to do such little fiddling work! What sort of career is it to be a bailiff or a whipper-in?" . . .

"Surely, your honour, it's better than stone-breaking!"

"I think stone-breaking a very fine occupation. . . . H'm. . . . Have you recommendations from your former employers?"

"No, your honour."

"I can't take you without a character, my good man."

"Yes, sir, you're quite right, sir."

"Perhaps you're some good-for-nothing fellow—a thief or drunkard for all I know. . . ."

"Just so, your honour."

"You must bring me a character."

"Yes, sir; good-morning, sir."

The soldier went away. Presently the steward came up to his master and announced—

"If you please, sir, a strange gentleman came while your honour was asleep; he calls himself a village schoolmaster."

"Where is he now?"

"Sitting in the office."

"Let him in."

There came on to the verandah a sunburnt man of about forty, in a nankeen coat and high boots. The master of the house offered him a chair.

"Who are you?"

"Schoolmaster from the Pobiràkhinsky district, from the village of Bezzùbov. I humbly venture to trouble you with a request; can I not obtain some kind of situation?"

"I don't want a schoolmaster," said the owner of the house.

"I can take other situations. I have heard that you are looking for a clerk?"

"Why did you leave your situation in Bezzùbov?"

"The school was destroyed by fire."

"Long ago?"

"On All Souls' Day. The cause is not known—the whole village was burnt down."

"Yes, one is constantly hearing of fires nowadays. A village close to us has been burnt down too. . . . Allow me to ask, though, how did you become a teacher?"

"After completing my education I lived in my brother's house in the village of Khmyèlnoye. I did not work, but he supported me. Then I took a situation as tutor in a country gentleman's house at

Ogoùrtzov, at a salary of two roubles a month. But I did not stop with him long, and while there I served chiefly as coachman. . . ."

"But why?"

"Because my pupil did not like studying, and his parents let him have his own way, and employed me temporarily as coachman. . . ."

"That's strange!"

"I did the work properly! I had no choice. . . ."

"How much did you get for it?"

"Nothing! only board and lodging, and a cast-off dressing-gown that the gentleman gave me. In that dressing-gown I went back to my brother, and he said: 'What are you hanging about here for, doing nothing? Can't you set to and learn something, if it's only singing?—you might get to be choir-master in time.' So I began to study singing, and then my brother got tired of hearing me. 'Confound it all!' he said, 'I'm sick of this; go home to father.' Well, then, I went home. Of course my people abused me:—'Always hanging about in the way! We've had enough of this!' What would you have me do, sir, when I couldn't get a situation anywhere? I thought one time of going into a monastery; but just then I got a letter from my brother telling me to come to him. I went, and he said, 'The prince's steward wants to start a choir. You must engage yourself as choir-master.' I asked him how did he suppose I was to do that when I didn't know how to sing myself? But all he would say was: 'Don't be afraid! you'll learn in teaching your class.' So I took the post. They gave me a tuning-fork——"

"May I ask," interrupted the gentleman, "whether you were attired in the dressing-gown?" . . .

"No, in my mother's cloak; the dressing-gown was worn out. . . . It was a short cloak, . . . home-made. . . ."

"Well, and how did you get on?"

"Very well. There was quite a fair choir. My brother sang tenor; Ivàn Alexèyich (at the present moment a teacher of patrology and hermeneutics) bass; then there were a few more volunteers. We got perfect in 'Kol Slàven,' [1] and two sort of . . . a . . . choral part-songs, 'Vzyde' and 'Polozhil yesi.' The steward was quite surprised at us; he was a critic in musical matters; and he wrote a letter to Moscow, to the prince, about a salary for the choir-master. Meanwhile we began to practise 'Kto Bog?' and 'Kheruvìmskaya Razòrennaya' [2] . . .

[1] Russian hymn. [2] Russian sacred songs.

All of a sudden the prince wrote back, 'I don't want a choir; I am going away for my health.' . . .

"So after that I got appointed at the village school at Bezzùbov. The people there are very poor; many of the peasants used to sleep in their ovens in winter-time. One day the priest came into a cottage to bless the household; he looked round, and there was no one there, so he began to sing the *tropar*.[1] Suddenly the people crawled out from the oven and came up to kiss the crucifix. . . . A good many of my pupils went about begging. For all that, though, a great gentleman from St. Petersburg passed through our village, and he said the people were not averse to education—really."

"Do you mean that ironically?" asked the master of the house.

"Oh dear no!"

"Of course, even a poor man may desire education; just take the case of Lomonòsov: he was a peasant and became an academician."

"Exactly so."

"Well, what else did the great gentleman from St. Petersburg remark?"

"He said that it would be a good thing for our administration to introduce a uniform for the scholars."

"A capital idea!" exclaimed the master of the house; "there ought to be discipline in a school. Without discipline no institution can exist. H'm. . . . What subjects were taught in your school?"

"We used the New Testament in the Russian and Slavonic tongues, a hundred and four selections from the Old and New Testaments, the 'Elements of Christian Doctrine,' 'Examples of Piety,' and the Breviary for the children to learn by heart; the first hour's division[2] of the Thirty-third Psalm, and the Book of Six Psalms, with 'All that has breath.'" . . .

"Is that all?"

"No, we had a library, containing the following books:

"'Selected Passages from Schreck's "Universal History."'

"'The Programme for Acceptance into the Military Service.'

"'Food for the Mind and Heart.'

"The Psalter, without red lettering.

"The Breviary, with red lettering.

"A work of Glinka, entitled, 'Hurrah.'

[1] Special canticle on a Saint's day.

[2] In the Greek Church the psalms are divided up into a kind of rosary.

" 'The Life of St. Prokopius the Natural.'

" 'Reader for the People.'

" 'Domestic Conversations.'

" 'The Clever Reader.'

" And a few others."

" The books are good," remarked the gentleman; " I'll order 'Domestic Conversation' and the 'Clever Reader' myself. How long did you retain your post ? "

" Eight years. I received no rise in my salary for the whole time. One day the inspector came, and he asked me, 'How long have you been teaching here ? ' 'Eight years,' said I. 'Has your salary been raised ? ' 'No,' said I; 'I receive the minimum salary.' 'Why is that ? ' 'I don't know.' Then he turned to the chief of the district and said, 'The teacher is to receive a rise in his salary.' The inspector observed, too, that the schoolhouse garden was neglected, and ordered it to be put to rights, saying 'that it would then have a favourable moral influence on the minds of the scholars, who would, in time, become agriculturists.' "

" I agree with him. The bad tendencies must be restrained in these people from the very tenderest years."

" The inspector ordered flowers to be planted in the garden——"

" H'm, in my opinion that is superfluous. He should have had birch trees planted; that would have influenced the pupils more favourably."

" There were birch trees already——"

" Ah! Birch trees are as valuable as the 'Clever Reader' and 'Domestic Conversations.' Are you married ? "

" I should have liked to marry, but I was afraid to. The parish clerk of Ogoùrtzov offered me his sister-in-law in marriage. I knew her—she was a first-rate girl. I went to see her."

" Was she clever ? "

" A-a! Really, sir, I don't know whether she was clever or not."

" But you talked with her ? "

" Oh, yes, of course! I said, 'We are acquaintances, Olga Mitrevna.'

" 'Oh, yes,' she said, 'I am quite aware of that.'

" 'I have been brought here,' said I, 'to ask you in marriage.'

" 'Indeed!' said she.

" 'Do you know where I have seen you ? At a christening at Ogourtzov,' said I, and she answered:

" 'Yes, I remember. And you are from Khmièlnoye?'

" 'Yes,' said I.

" 'Ah! the scenery is pretty round there.'

"And that was about all her cleverness! . . . Her father kept on begging me to marry quickly, because a man can't live properly without some one to keep his house. 'We shall get on much better together,' she used to say. . . . So we stayed up till dawn, singing and dancing."

"Sacred songs?"

"No, sir, various—sacred and secular."

"Well, and did your betrothed sing?"

"No; afterwards, when I left her—she sang that romance—you know—

> "'Twas my fault for thus betraying
> All too soon my love to thee;
> Now thou hast beheld my weakness,
> Ah! thou hast forsaken me."

"That's to say you jilted her?"

"I don't know—anyway, I hadn't anything to keep her on."

"H'm—so you say the school was burnt down?"

"To the ground."

"And are all the books and things burnt too?"

"No; they were saved. The fire was in the day-time, and our people had time to get the books out."

"That's good. So I suppose it will soon be built again, and you can go on being teacher?"

"I don't wish to take that work."

"Why not?"

"I'm sick of it! You wouldn't believe me, I've often thought of putting an end to myself."

"So you prefer to be a clerk?"

"Yes, sir."

"H'm'm—I am sorry that I can't help you; it's true that I've just dismissed my clerk, but I don't want another. You see, in these times one must look after everything oneself. I do all my accounts myself. Now, I have a vacancy for a bailiff, but you wouldn't care for that . . . the salary is so small . . . three roubles a month."

"That is very little," said the teacher.

"There you see! and I don't want a clerk. Besides, I can't understand why you don't wish to be a teacher."

"I can't stand it, indeed I can't!"

" It's true that the root of learning is bitter, but, you see, the fruits are sweet. . . . No, I would advise you to disseminate instruction among the people. . . . At the present time, when education has become a positive necessity, we ought all of us to assist in the work, to the limit of our powers. For my part, I am quite willing to do what I can. I will make a donation of books to your school. Here! Aliòshka! Fetch the hamper that stands under the ante-room sofa."

The footman brought in a hamper of books, gnawed all over by rats. " Now," said the gentleman, " here's a book for you, 'Nature's Vengeance,' a capital book; I've forgotten what it's about. Ah! and here . . . 'The Oath, taken at the Holy Sepulchre.' . . . In fact, you can have the whole lot. When your new school is built, kindly range all these works in your library with an inscription: 'Presented by Mr. Yàkov Antònovich Svinooùkhov,[1] the squire of Prokhòrovka.' Posterity will remember me. . . . I am very glad that fortune brought you here, otherwise my books would have lain by uselessly, but now they will do good; and not to one generation only, but to future ages. . . . Hi! Aliòshka. Tell the man to harness a horse and conduct these books and the schoolmaster with them to the village of Bezzùbov."

. . . .

Two months later the new school was built. The educational library had been enriched by the following works, the gift of Mr. Svinooùkhov:—

" The Correspondence of the Nobility of Hell."
" Hunting with the Hounds."
" The Russian Theatre."
" Nature's Vengeance."
" The Works of Bulgarin."
" Political and Moral Fables."
" *The Moscow Gazette.*"
" A New Latin Alphabet."
" Words to Scholars, Concerning the Attributes of True Wisdom."
" A Guide to Didactics."
" A Short Dissertation upon the Rules of True Wisdom."

Etc., etc.

Nothing was wanting, except a teacher. The former teacher, it is said, had hanged himself.

[1] Literally " Pig's ear."

DMITRI MAMIN-SIBIRIAK
B. 1852

IN THE HEART OF THE URALS

I

THE village of Shalaika was situated in the very heart of the forest on the high bank of the river Chusovoi. The road for vehicles ended at Shalaika, and beyond it there was no road. No one ever came to Shalaika except the priest who lived on the Borovsky Works some twenty miles away, and whenever he came he invariably expressed his surprise that all the inhabitants of the village were surnamed Shalaev. Rightly speaking, there were no surnames, merely a nickname after the village.

" How shall I enter you in the book ? " the priest would ask. " For instance, in the present year, three Ivan Shalaevs have died and three Ivan Shalaevs were born, and last year we had the same thing happen with Matrenas—two Matrenas died and two were born ! You seem to mix them all up."

" It has been so from time immemorial," the elder explained, " all are Shalaevs and there is an end to the matter. Our great grandfather was called Shalaev and we are all called Shalaev after him. The authorities also are vexed about it. Some five years back, I took our young fellows who were called up for soldiers, and, as though on purpose, they turned out to be three Sidors, and all were Ivanitch. The military commander got quite angry."

" We must invent some surname though," the priest said. " It will be more convenient for you."

" What do we want surnames for, father ? We have lived in the forest from time immemorial and know each other well. . . . And as for the dead, the Lord our Father will be able to distinguish them for what they are worth without our help."

From the distance, Shalaika was very beautiful, especially when seen from the river—the huts shone in the sun like firm white teeth, each more beautiful than the other, thanks to the forest that was near at hand and surrounded the village like a massive green wall. There was little ploughing, for the Shalaevs mostly worked in the forest, and in the mountains the summers are cold and the soil not very fertile. If hay were needed, it could be cut in the glades of the forest or on the banks of the river Chusovoi. There were twenty-seven dwellings in Shalaika, and the Shalaevs were like a huge family, all related to one another.

Pimka's hut stood right by the river-bank, that is to say, almost on a cliff. In the summer the river could be seen from the little window for about five miles, for there was a reach here. By the river stretched the limitless forest, and no one in Shalaika knew where it ended, as though the village were at the very end of the earth. Pimka was in his tenth year and he had not been anywhere or seen anything except his own village. It must be said that the Shalaevs were very fond of their village and even proud of it too. When the young fellows were called up as soldiers they took leave of their native village with such tears as were not shed by St. Petersburg or Moscow recruits. One would have thought that the only possible place to live in was Shalaika. Pimka remembered how his elder brother Yefim had gone off as a soldier with the other young fellows and had also cried like the others.

"Leave off, you fools!" Uncle Akintich said to them, "why are you crying? You are not going to live with wolves, but with kind people; you will, at any rate, see how other people live and learn from them. Passing the whole of your lives in the forest at Shalaika is not such a great joy!" No one believed the soldier Akintich. It was all very well to talk after you had finished your service. If it was so very pleasant in those strange lands, then why did he come back again to Shalaika? Akintich lived with Pimka's father, because his own family had somehow got separated; the old people had died, his sisters had got married and he could not get on with his married brothers. Pimka was passionately fond of the soldier Akintich, who knew everything and could tell such good stories, even better than grandmother, who only knew fairy stories about "long ago." When brother Yefim went away as a soldier, Akintich took his place. Though the family was large, there were only two real workers, father Yegor and the second brother Andrei. There was also grandfather Tit, but he could no longer go out to work, and lived for the most part in the forest, which he very rarely left. The women were not counted. The mother Avdotia looked after the house, and the elder sister Domna was "not quite right" in her mind. This is what had happened to Domna. One summer the women had gone out to gather raspberries in old Matugin's charcoal works, and Domna was with them. She was still quite a child, and somehow strayed from the company. The women hunted high and low but could not find her. For three whole days they searched the forest round the village and then came to the conclusion that she had been torn to pieces by a bear. On the fifth day, grandfather Tit found her, hidden on a silver birch to which she was clinging and making no sound. The old man could scarcely get her down, and brought her home half dead. From that time Domna had not been quite right in her mind. She never spoke, no matter what was said to her. She worked when her mother made her, and generally was like a small child. The village children loved to tease her. They would come in a crowd shouting:

"Domna, show us how the werewolf laughed."

They had only to say this, and Domna would begin to laugh wildly, rolling her eyes and looking terrible. It was thought that she had seen a werewolf and he had frightened her with his laughter. Besides Domna there were some other children, but these were quite tiny and did not count at all.

The whole of Shalaika worked in the forest, including Pimka's family. Even grandfather Tit worked at the charcoal works under father Yegor. Some cut the wood and carted it to the river, where it was placed on rafts, some rowed it to the lower wharves. The work was not light, but all were used to it and desired nothing better. And what more can a man want after he is fed, clothed, and warm? Pimka knew that he too would work in the charcoal works, and often said to his father:

"Father, when will you take me to the forest?"

"Wait, your time is before you, Pimka. . . . You will work in the charcoal works when the time comes."

And Pimka waited. It seemed to him that when he departed for the charcoal works he would be grown up. The works were about twenty miles away, and you could only go there over the winter roads. Grandfather Tit sometimes stayed there all summer. Pimka was disturbed by one thought only. In the forest they "bewitch" you as Domna was bewitched. You have to look out and see that the werewolf does not make you lose your way in the forest. However, the werewolf played his pranks even in Shalaika, particularly near the Chusovoi. Many times had grandmother Akulina heard him sighing in the night, and once he had killed a woman at the hay-making. Still more terrible was the werewolf's wife who had lived in the waters of the Chusovoi. Even the grown-ups were afraid of her; when she splashed about in the water, the sound could be heard from afar. She loved to look for children who happened to be bathing in the river on hot summer days; she would seize them and carry them away to her pool. Every one knew that she lived in a pool about a mile from Shalaika, where the bottomless river flowed under a high cliff. Grandfather Tit had seen her with his own eyes, only he did not like to talk about it; she was quite black, covered with hair, and had eyes like those of a wolf. Only the soldier Akintich was not afraid of either the werewolf or his wife and even went at night to fish in the pool. "The old woman tells you foolish things, Pimka," he said gently. "Don't you be afraid of anything—of nothing at all; and you will never be frightened. Do you understand?"

"And suppose the werewolf's wife catches hold of my leg?" Pimka asked.

"She won't; but if she does, hit her in the jaw. The werewolf, too, is all nonsense. Should he sigh, you sigh too; if he cries like a baby, you cry. Let him frighten women, but don't you fear anything, Pimka, and you will never be frightened."

We have already said that no one ever came to Shalaika and there was nowhere further to go. Of "strange folk" occasionally some charcoal contractor would come or sometimes a hunter who lived by catching wood-hens and squirrels in late autumn. The soldier Akintich also did a little hunting in his spare time, and made friends with all the hunters. They always stayed at Yegor's hut. Pimka, lying in the loft, loved to listen to the hunters' tales, especially when they talked of the pranks of bandy-legged bruin. Grandfather Tit had killed more than a dozen bears, but he did not like to speak of it. He had given up hunting when the last bear had so mauled his leg that he remained lame for the rest of his life. Akintich, after a couple of drinks, would boast of his feats and would tell the hunters imaginary tales of his prowess, until brother Yegor would stop him:

"That will do, brother Akintich. . . . You have exaggerated enough."

The gayest time in Shalaika was spring, when a caravan would come down the Chusovoi. The river rose about two feet, and over it hundreds of boats sped along quickly. All the village came out on the banks to watch. Pimka, too, looked on, thinking of the places to which the boats were going, and of the people there. Akintich was the only man in the village who had ever been in a boat, and he told wonderful tales of how the river beat against the banks, how boats struck on rocks and people were drowned. Akintich knew everything there was to know in the world, and would mention some wonderful places where the boats were going.

"The people who live there are rich, brother," he would explain. "They will buy everything that you care to bring: timber and iron and copper, squirrels and wood-hens—you have only to take them there. The houses there are built of stones and there are steamers on the river."

II

Pimka was in his thirteenth year when his father said to him: "Well, Pimka, you must get ready to come to the charcoal works. It is time, my son, that you turned into a peasant."

It was at the beginning of the winter, when the winter roads were forming. Pimka was glad, yet afraid. In the charcoal works there were of course no werewolves, but there were bears. He told no one of his fears, because a real peasant was not afraid of anything. In the summer the mother had prepared the future peasant's garments; a short sheepskin coat, gauntlets, and long felt boots, and the kind of cap that a real peasant should wear. Sometimes the frosts were so terrible in the winter that the birds froze in the air, and the only protection for one was dogskin. The charcoal workers who took the charcoal to the Borovsky suffered terribly, and sometimes a man would have his nose or ears frozen. His mother was sorry for Pimka and cried when she took leave of him.

"Mind you don't catch cold, Pimka. . . . You are going to live in camp and the draughts there are terrible."

"Don't be afraid, mamma," Pimka replied gaily. "I shall live with Akintich, and he knows everything.... He and I are going to kill bears."

"That's right, mind you don't get your ears frozen."

"I will let him do the cooking," explained his father. "Why should he waste his time at home when there is work to do there? You can't make a cook out of a cat, can you, Pimka? Grandfather Tit will be pleased to see you. Old and young—and you will live in camp."

"I am not afraid of anything, father."

"Why should you be afraid? You are going to live with other people."

The road to the charcoal works ran through the forest and pleased Pimka very much. The snow had only just fallen and the bogs were not yet properly frozen. They travelled in the cart plaited out of bushwood by grandfather Tit. The old man had remained in the forest the whole summer, making sleighs out of birch and plaiting carts. He could make everything for the charcoal works or for the house: hatchets for the men, troughs and rolling pins for the women—all were useful. The forest was only just covered by its first snow. The slumbering birches stood in rows, one behind the other, like soldiers. On old clearings there stood young aspens and birches, which, in the winter, had a very bare appearance. The father drove the horse, saying every now and then to Pimka:

" Look, there is a hare's trail! See the little dents he has made in the snow. They make such patterns that you can't mistake them. And there a fox went by; the fox, like the sheep, covers its traces with its tail."

At one place Yegor stopped the horse, stared for a long time at the trail, and then said:

" A pack of wolves went by here. . . . They are like soldiers, my son, each walks in the same footsteps. A whole pack went by, yet there is only a single trail. Our wolves are not dangerous because they get plenty of food in the forest. They catch hares, wood-hens, and moor-hens. They are cunning beasts!"

At another place Yegor pointed out a big trail to Pimka, and explained what it was:

" That was a moose-deer. See how he hurried away. Our soldier must try to get him—he would feed the lot of us, and we could sell his skin at the works. I must tell him and he will go after its trail."

It was night when they got to the charcoal works. Pimka was huddled up at the bottom of the cart and was dozing. The clearing could be seen from a distance by the light cast by the burning piles of wood. To one side stood four huts. Yegor went to the one occupied by grandfather Tit. When still some distance away, the guests were greeted by the barking of the dog Liska, who looked very sheepish when she recognised the horse. With the sound of the barking, persons appeared from all the huts.

" Is that you, Yegor?"

" Yes, it is I. . . . Look at the animal I have brought you. Pimka, come out."

Akintich came forward and pulled Pimka from the cart, but the boy could not wake up. When Akintich shook him, the boy felt very cold. In the hut, grandfather Tit was watching the pot of porridge on the fire, cooking for that night's supper. When he caught sight of his grandson the old man was very pleased.

" Come, come, sit down like a visitor," he said. " Are you cold ? Wait, when you have eaten some porridge you will be quite warm."

It was a large, low hut without windows or chimney. The rear half was taken up with large bunks made of yew. To the right of the low door a fireplace had been built out of big stones. In the place for a chimney there was a hole in the roof, and the hut was filled with smoke so that it was impossible to stand, and Pimka began coughing violently as he swallowed the smoke. The walls and ceiling were covered with soot.

" Don't you like our place ? " Akintich said teasingly. " Sit down on the floor, Pimka, near grandfather."

Old Tit was immensely pleased with his grandson, and made him sit down near him on a log of wood. The old man was about eighty, and his grey beard had turned yellow, but he was still strong and did not take second place in work with the youngest peasant. Unfortunately, however, his back had begun to ache and he had constant pains in his legs.

" Another hand for you, grandfather," the peasants who had gathered in the hut said in fun. " When it comes to eating, he will make an excellent assistant."

All the wood-cutters and wood-burners looked like chimney-sweeps owing to the life in the charcoal camp. It was all the same whether you washed or not, you could not get away from the soot. They were all pleased to see a new face, and teased the youngster in every way they could think of. But Pimka was perfectly happy. The peasants were all his own people and he knew them all by sight. Pimka's father had brought all sorts of things with him, and these he handed out—bread for one, a coat for another, a shirt for a third.

Pimka ate his porridge with more relish than he had ever experienced before in eating, and instantly fell asleep sitting on the log beside his grandfather.

" Well, we must put the youngster on the feather-bed," said Akintich jestingly, making a bed for him out of hay on a bunk. " We will put some green down here so that he can sleep well."

He carried the sleeping Pimka over in his arms, laid him on the hay, and covered him over with his coat.

" How sleepy the young beggar is ! " said the peasants. " He must have got cold on the way, and coming straight into the warm room sent him off ; besides, he is tired."

One after another the peasants left grandfather Tit's hut. All had to rise early in the morning.

On the following morning Pimka was awakened early by the terrible cold. It was warm in the hut so long as there was a fire, but as soon as the fire went out, the heat escaped through the hole in the roof and through the badly fitting door. It was terrible waiting until the fire gave out some heat and the smoke began to come. Then grandfather Tit climbed on to the roof and covered the hole with a piece of yew bark and some maple leaves over the top. It was either very cold or very hot in the hut.

The work in the camp was already in full swing when Pimka emerged from the hut. Grandfather Tit was harnessing the new sledge just outside the door. Somewhere in the forest the axes cutting the frozen wood could be heard, and in the new clearing there were about ten smoking piles. These piles were about seven feet high and four feet broad. The wood was placed upright in the centre and allowed to burn or rather smoulder slowly. The whole secret consisted in not letting the wood rot, so as to get firm charcoal. The piles burned for about two weeks until all the wood was turned into charcoal. Every group of piles had its stoker, who had to look after the whole set. All the work would be wasted if the fire were allowed to burn through the sods, as then the wood burned quite away. The stokers never left their piles, day or night. This was the most difficult and responsible work. The wood-cutter ran no risks, nor did the carrier, but the stoker was responsible for all. Only the most experienced workmen became stokers. From a distance the piles looked like huge ant-hills, with the difference that no smoke issued from the latter, while from the former a thick smoke rose night and day. A burnt-out pile had to be left for quite a long time until the charcoal was quite cold. Grandfather Tit had been a stoker for forty years and now his son Yegor had taken his place.

From the very first day Pimka adapted himself to the conditions of the camp life. They rose at daybreak, ate whatever there was, and then worked till dinner. After dinner there was a little rest, and then work again as long as there was light. Everybody's task was hard, and only those accustomed to it could stand it. The wood-cutters reeled home like drunken men, so tired were their backs and hands. The wood-carriers dropped on the road, especially in the hard frosts when the cold beat against their faces. And it was worse still to live in the dark huts, with poor food, black bread, and something hot—generally porridge. How could a peasant arrange for cooking ?

" What a life ! " the soldier Akintich would grumble, his years of service having disused him from the heavy work. " I'll throw it all up and go away somewhere. The worst of it is that there are no baths. . . . You look as if you've just got out of a chimney."

The whole camp dreamt of baths and envied every one who went to the village. Going to the village meant having a bath. They went in turns, and the whole winter through each man would have been twice only. Pimka had only been in camp a few days when he grew terribly home-sick. It was hard living in the forest, and the boy agreed with uncle Akintich that it was better to go away anywhere. Pimka even cried when there was no one to see him.

III

The most trying time was holidays. Of course they could have gone to Shalaika for the day, but they did not like to tire the horses unnecessarily. It was about forty miles there and back, over a bad forest-road. It was wicked to work on a holiday, so they killed time somehow or other. It was wearisome sitting in the dark huts all day, so they gathered in the " street." They lit a big fire, sat round it and talked. The principal talker was of course Akintich, who had been to Moscow in his soldiering days. The others had never been farther than the Borovsky works. Akintich, too, loved to tell impossible tales.

" Mind you don't tell us lies, soldier ! " the peasants would say.

" Why should I tell lies ? You have never seen anything, that is why everything seems so wonderful to you. Take a steamer, for instance. It is enormous ! A thousand people could go in it, and it does not even trawl a single boat after it. The whole of Shalaika could go in it at the same time. And then there is the railway train, that is even more wonderful—one whistle, and away you fly. That, too, can take ever so many people and all sorts of things. You have hardly time to look round when there goes another whistle and this means that you have arrived. If only there were a railway to Borovsky you could get there in an hour, whereas now you crawl along for eight and get tired on the way."

"You are telling lies, soldier!"

"How can I talk to you if you won't understand anything?"

To Pimka, too, it seemed that the soldier lied, especially when he described the mode of life in various towns. To Pimka it seemed that all people must chop wood and make charcoal, and here were suddenly stone houses, stone churches, steamers, trains, and suchlike wonders. The peasants sometimes made fun of the soldier.

"Have you flown in the air, soldier? It won't cost you any more to say so."

Then Akintich would grow angry and begin to quarrel. He was quite absurd when he got angry, and all laughed.

"I shall go away from you, and that will be the end of things! I am tired of living with you in darkness. I'll go to the town, and become a handyman to a merchant. The work is very easy; you have to sweep the yard, carry the wood, groom the horse, and that is all. You can go to the baths every day if you like. Your clothes are clean, and you get as much food as you want. You get soup with plenty of fat, and porridge in which the spoon will stand up. But the nicest thing of all is tea. . . . I can't tell you how much I love tea, brothers!"

"How do they prepare it, this tea?"

"It is a kind of herb—Chinese."

"Do they put groats or beef with it?"

"Heavens! What can one do with you? You don't seem to understand anything. They drink tea with sugar! Do you understand now? But how can you? Take a lamp now. You have never seen one, but it is a most necessary thing. In Shalaika we use splints, but enlightened people have lamps. It is like a small glass bowl filled with an oil called kerosene, a wick is put in, you take a match and you get a light! The best thing about it is that you can make the light weaker or stronger as you will, not like a tallow candle. . . . Do you understand now?"

"It is sinful, all this," grandfather Tit said. "Suppose I drink this tea of yours, eat soup and porridge, go away in trains and steamers, who will do the work, eh? Suppose I run away from hard work, then you, then Pimka, and after us the whole of Shalaika, who will make the charcoal?"

" Your charcoal is of no use to any one, grandfather," the soldier said. " There is the mineral coal which they get straight out of the earth."

" Who put it there for you, eh ? Oh, soldier, soldier . . . another story of yours."

Grandfather Tit did not like Akintich, because of his frivolity and because he had become spoiled in service and loved to talk about the easy life there. The man had got quite unaccustomed to real peasant labour. The old man often quarrelled with Akintich on account of his soldier's pipe and frequently chased him out of the hut. No one smoked in Shalaika, and the peasants took advantage of this to complain to the old man.

" Grandfather, the soldier says that in the town every one smokes and they even put tobacco in their noses."

" Nonsense, it is not true," grandfather said. " It is a sin to listen to such things. He doesn't like work, that is the chief reason. That is why he does not know that God loves him who labours. What sort of a man would I be if I did not work ? Every creature must do its work, according to its needs, because nests must be built and the young must be fed."

" In towns they work according to their need, grandfather," exclaimed the soldier, " only there the work is cleaner than ours. . . . They do not work less than we do . . . perhaps more. Not every one need make charcoal—there are many other trades. Some make cotton and cloth, others boots, and others are locksmiths."

" That is all nonsense ! " grandfather said. " In the olden days they lived without cotton, and cloth was woven by the women at home. It is all nonsense ! The principal workman is after all the peasant who sows the corn. You can't live without bread, and the rest is all nonsense. Indulgence . . . " Pimka began to think of how other people in this wide world lived. If he could only look at them—with one eye only ! Perhaps the soldier did not lie. He had told them of places where there was no winter, and that he had seen, with his own eyes, the biggest animal in the world, an elephant, that was as big as a huge bath. Pimka's childish curiosity was satisfied by an unexpected event.

One day the whole camp was in a deep sleep. There was a hard frost and even the dogs went into the huts. Suddenly, in the middle of the night, Liska growled angrily. He had particular growls for beast and for man, and now his growl was for man. Soon loud voices were heard. It was a party of railway engineers who were surveying a road for a new railway. There were about ten of them; two engineers, their assistants, simple peasants—and a guide. The latter had lost his way, and had brought the party to the camp instead of to Shalaika. The soldier Akintich shot out and invited the chief into his hut.

"Welcome, Your Honour. We will do the best we can for you. We will light a fire in a moment and boil some water. You must excuse us, Your Honour."

This was the first time that Pimka had ever seen strangers, and he stared at them as though they were from another world, with all the wonder of a young barbarian. Then he was struck by the alacrity with which Akintich looked after the guests, excusing himself at every step. The chief was angry, however—angry with everything: with the sooty hut, the smoky fire, with the guide who was responsible for their having lost their way, and even with the hard frost of the forest.

"It certainly does smoke, Your Honour," Akintich said, "and the frost is very bad indeed. . . . You must excuse us because we live in the forest and know no better, Your Honour."

"Have you been a soldier?" the chief asked.

"Yes, Your Honour . . . I have been to Moscow. Yes. . . . And here—you must excuse us—there is only the forest and ignorance."

Pimka saw the gentlemen drink tea, eat their own food, and smoke cigarettes. He even tasted the tea himself, that is, he ate several leaves and decided that the soldier had lied. There was no sweet taste, it was only a weed, and black.

Early in the morning the party went on farther. Akintich himself accompanied them, not knowing what to do to please the gentlemen.

"It is as though a snake were uncurling itself," grumbled grandfather Tit, shaking his head. "Ah, soldier, soldier, you will betray the lot of us!"

The chief grumbled the whole morning: it was cold in the hut, and the water in the pot smelt badly; the dogs had barked all night,—he was discontented with everything. Pimka stood with his mouth open, fearing that the chief might strike him. However, things went off smoothly.

When the guests departed, the camp seemed empty, it was so quiet. The whole camp gathered in a crowd to discuss the departed guests.

" And the soldier foretold all this," Pimka's father said. "The railway—and here it has come to us."

The peasants wondered whether it would be good or bad for them when the railway ran through their forest.

" Of what use will a railway be to us ? " grandfather Tit grumbled. " It is only indulgence, and probably sinful. . . . Ah, it is time I were dead. . . ."

Exactly three years later, an iron railway bridge stretched across the Chusovoi a little below Shalaika, and the soldier Akintich was appointed watchman. He had his own sentry-box, a samovár, and a new pipe. He was perfectly happy.

The whole of Shalaika turned out to see the first train go by—even grandfather Tit. The old man no longer went to the charcoal camp, because he was too ailing. He gazed for a long time at Akintich, who was pacing up and down outside his sentry-box, with a green flag in his hand, and at last the old man said :

" That is the very place for you, Akintich. No work at all and you get wages for nothing."

Pimka trembled all over when the sound of the first train was heard in the distance. Soon it crawled out from behind the mountain like an iron serpent, and emitted its first shriek, destroying for ever the stillness of the forest. Akintich drew himself up erect in military fashion and, raising his flag, cried to the first train : " Zdravia jelaem ! " [1]

[1] The Russian military greeting from soldiers to their officers.

"THERE IS NO REPLY"

DMITRI MAMIN-SIBIRIAK

I

"AND you say that we shall have an apple orchard also?" she asked, dexterously applying the pencil beneath the left eyelid.

"Yes—and the apple trees are lovely in full bloom," he replied, watching her as she quickly went on with her make-up.

"And the Volga flows below?"

"My estate lies on the very slope of the hill. There is a fine view from the verandah, and in spring the Volga spreads out for more than seven versts."

"Very nice, indeed—that is, the slope of the hill, the spreading of the Volga, and the blossoms of your apple trees—it is all very beautiful. But, do you know, there is something your orchard lacks?"

She turned her painted face and looked at him with smiling eyes. It was a remarkable face, which drew him to her like an electro-magnet. What beautiful eyes she had, grey and lustrous, a rosebud mouth showing with every smile two lines of pearly teeth; pink, shell-like little ears; a charming dimple in the chin; a small but beautifully sculptured brow; everything, even to the tiny birth-mark on the left cheek, was lovely and like a picture in its living frame of soft, slightly curling fair hair with a golden glint in it.

"Yes, the only thing your garden lacks is orange-blossoms," she said slowly, drawling the words.

He did not catch her meaning, and replied quite seriously:

"Orange-blossoms? Oranges do not grow in our climate."

"Really? Ah, why did you tell me that? I think orange-blossoms are so beautiful, something like a lily, emblematic of youth and purity."

He still did not catch her meaning, and his face wore the same confused smile. She playfully struck him on the shoulder with her fan and said in a more serious tone:

"Well, and what should we do in your garden?"

"We should roam in it every day."

"And upon the estate?"

"Oh, we should settle down and live upon it pleasantly and peacefully."

She threw back her head and laughed. He could see her beautifully sculptured neck, her rounded breast, her sloping shoulders which were shaking with laughter.

"Roam in a garden—live on an estate!" she repeated, wiping the tears of laughter from her face. "See, you have spoiled my whole make-up. Oh, you dear child! How old are you?"

"I shall soon be twenty-three."

"A beautiful age. I can only be envious of you. And how old do you think I am? But, after all, better not try to guess. In fact, I myself am beginning to forget my chronology."

They were in the dressing-room of one of the merry summer theatres of St. Petersburg. Upon the small strip of paper pasted on the outside of the door was written: "Maria Ivanovna Guliaeva." The interior of the room struck a newcomer with its look of poverty. The walls were built of the badly joined boards of an old boat, full of holes from the pulled out wooden spikes, through which a continual draught entered in spite of the plugs of rags, wadding, and paper. The furniture consisted of a dilapidated sofa, a couple of chairs, a toilet-table, and a washstand. In a corner several theatrical costumes hung in artistic disorder. The stale air was impregnated with the smell of eau de cologne, face powder, and cheap, strong perfumes. The only window, facing the garden, was curtained with a piece of muslin yellow with age. During the performance, when Maria Ivanovna was dressing, the window had, as a matter of course, to remain closed; during the rest of the day and night there was no necessity for keeping it open. But even such a dressing-room was a certain luxury which only the "stars" of summer-garden companies could obtain. Maria Ivanovna had already reached that period when an actress struggles desperately against the mercilessly approaching "artistic" age. She well knew that her reign would not last long, but she was as yet queening it on the stage of the summer-garden theatres, thanks to her great name. In every walk of life and in every profession there are great names.

The young man who stood before her was neither handsome nor plain. He was only young, young with an uncorrupted youth. A thick, blond little beard gave him a more steadfast and mature appearance than his years warranted, and his earnest brown eyes looked unusually simple and trustful. Judged by his elegant summer clothes and general well-groomed appearance he could be easily classified as belonging to people of "society." Maria Ivanovna, who had studied well her summer-theatre zoology, noticed that from the first. She liked his air of breeding, and allowed him to visit her in her dressing-room. But to-day he surprised her so much that even she lost control over herself while trying to impart a jesting tone to his proposition.

"Please do not forget that I have spoken in all seriousness," he remarked in a slightly dulled voice; his throat had become parched from excitement.

"Yes? Oh, yes—please do not bother me with your jests. It soon will be my turn. What shall I sing for you?"

"Whatever you please."

"Very well, I know just what you care most to hear."

She wanted to say something more, when some one tapped at the door; it was the call of the stage manager. She rose quickly from her seat, gathered her long train, and, rustling her silk skirts like a snake in its dry skin, hurriedly left the room. Going through the dirty, sparsely lighted corridor, she smilingly repeated to herself:

"Oh, what a funny creature! How foolish he is—the dear!"

The door of the dressing-room remained open, and he could hear the deafening applause and that remarkable noise of a human crowd which recalls the roar of sea-breakers. She had appeared before the footlights, and the public were greeting her with a voice like that of a bloodthirsty, hungry beast to whom a piece of fresh meat is flung. They quieted down soon, and the first words of the romance which he loved so well reached his ears.

He listened numb with excitement, absorbing with intoxicated delight every note. Yes, she was singing for him, confessing her love in another's words.

The sounds ceased. A brief pause and again a storm of applause like the thousand-voiced echo of a summons and a caress. He rose and began to walk quickly up and down the dressing-room. In his heart also raged a tempest, but a silent one, like a gathering storm. Oh, how he hated it all now—this madly roaring mob and the whole setting of this low cabaret, even the air impregnated with the peculiar miasmas of unrestrained debauch. The place was a putrid swamp emanating vile, poisonous stenches and corrupting everything that dared to come close enough—and she, this pure water lily, whose chaste whiteness could not be ruined by all the miry poisons together! A low cabaret and the first lisp of love!

The public continued their violent clamour, forcing her to sing song after song. Maria Ivanovna sang pieces from *The Geisha* and the new gipsy songs which were then the rage.

She returned to the dressing-room tired out, with red spots on her face and eyes troubled. In her hand she held several visiting cards, which she carelessly threw upon the toilet-table. To the dumb question in his eyes she wearily replied:

"Oh, these are all invitations to suppers in private rooms. My dear admirers seem to think that I have seven stomachs, like a dromedary. And all of them are our esteemed provincials, fathers of families and elderly men. At home they would be ashamed to take supper with a singer in a private room, but here, where no one knows them, they are glad to take advantage of the opportunity to enjoy themselves." Catching an expression of jealousy in his eyes, she quickly added, with a smile: "Don't be afraid; you have no rivals. I want to be only my own self to-day; it is an almost unobtainable luxury for me. Only one evening to be my own self——"

Then she put her round, white arms upon his shoulders and, gazing searchingly into his eyes, whispered, "And I do not receive a declaration of love and an offer of the hand and heart every evening."

He dropped his eyes, and she felt she had been wanting in tact.

II

After the performance they walked over to the farthest end of the summer garden, where, in a low, stone building, were the private rooms of the garden restaurant. She took his arm and looked around continually, as if fearing to meet an acquaintance. He also felt her fear, and attentively scanned the faces of the people. They met two actors —one stout and red-faced, the other a handsome, dark man with bold, black eyes. The two exchanged glances, and the stout man whispered something which evidently concerned Maria Ivanovna. The handsome actor only smiled with his eyes and shrugged his shoulders.

"The scoundrels!" thought Maria Ivanovna, hurrying her steps.

The private room looked like all such places—a pothouse den. A motley collection of dirty, dilapidated furniture, a dim, scratched mirror, a carpet worn and soiled, and so on. At the door of the room they were overtaken by the box-opener, who stealthily tried to hand two more visiting cards to Maria Ivanovna, but she pettishly pushed him away.

"Enough, enough! Tell them I am dead—yes, dead."

When the door closed after them she sank into a chair.

"How tired I am!" she said in a weary voice. "If you could only know! By the bye, I have forgotten your name—forgive me."

"Pavel Konstantinich Ruzhishchev."

"Yes, yes; please forgive me. I have such a bad memory, and besides——" She was going to add, "And I have so many acquaintances and new ones every day," but she caught herself in time. He looked over the menu, not knowing what to offer her.

"Pavel Konstantinich, to-night I would like to choose for myself something cheap and plain: a plate of beet soup, sausages and cabbage, or creamed liver——"

"And I wanted to order a steamed sterlet."

"Ah, no, I am sick to death of all these delicacies. I want something simple."

"And the wine?"

"No wine at all—order a bottle of cheap beer. Let us eat like a pair of student comrades. I shall order some nice hot sausages—you know the kind, those you can slice in fine round slices with the skin on—and a piece of cheap domestic cheese that crumbles under the knife. That will be splendid!"

He laughed contentedly at her whims and fantasies. And the waiter who received the order looked at him contemptuously—was this the way to treat Maria Ivanovna? Their first star, and—a bottle of beer!

"Splendid, first-rate!" she continually kept repeating, gazing at Pavel with narrowed eyes.

She took off her lace cape and approached the window, through which the noise of the public, now scattered over the whole garden, reached them like a far-away rumble.

"We should have gone away from here and supped somewhere at a cheap little restaurant," she murmured meditatively, "where the air is always saturated with the smell of burned butter, fried onions, and herring. But I think all the restaurants except the most expensive ones are closed at this time of night."

The supper turned out a very homely affair. Maria Ivanovna, who usually took a tiny glass of vodka at night "for the nerves," as she explained, looked very charming with her slightly heightened colour. The impression was marred only by the traces of make-up near the eyes. Pavel looked at her admiringly, and listened attentively to the endless flow of her feminine prattle.

"Am I wearying you?" she asked him several times, with a kind of guilty smile. "And I would like to tell you everything—that is, not quite everything, but what would interest you. I was born and brought up far from here, in the South. My family was neither poor nor well-to-do, but middling—managing to pull through somehow or other. My childhood was spent tediously and uninterestingly till I passed the fourth form at school—I was then just fourteen years of age, but I looked much older, and my short, brown dress-uniform gave a sort of piquancy to my whole appearance. Oh, I very early found out my personal value—probably this was the real reason for all the misfortunes of my subsequent life. You men cannot imagine how joyfully the woman awakes in the girl-stripling. Why are you sitting in that chair, Konstantin Pavlowich?"

"Pavel Konstantinich."

"Pardon me—come, sit here, close by me on the sofa; let us touch glasses! Yes, it was very nice. I can see myself now, just a bit of a girl. I was splendidly built and had a long, thick, luxurious braid of hair, a wonderful complexion, and beautiful, gentle eyes. I can speak of myself like that now because it was so long ago that I can talk of myself as if I were an entire stranger, as I would speak of those young girls whom I often meet in the street and in whose beauty I take such delight. Come, sit close by me, closer! What a strange man you are! But wait, I will move nearer myself—so!"

Her shoulder almost touched his, and he could feel the warmth of her body and the odour of powder. He was slightly dazed, and his eyes became overcast with a mist. It was at the same time painful and pleasant, and he felt like telling her so, and in such wonderful language—in words which are as difficult to grasp as one's shadow. And she prattled on, sipping the beer from her glass and bestrewing her dress with cheese crumbs.

"You have noticed, Konst—that is, Pavel Konstantinich, the expression of human eyes? How beautiful they are in children—I mean, very little children! In boys this purity of expression is lost at a very early age, but girls preserve it till nearly sixteen. Yes, exactly, purity. It is as pleasant to gaze into such eyes as it is to gaze into calm waters unruffled by the wind. In such eyes one sees the whole soul, while it is as yet pure and untroubled. Yes, and thus I was passed into the fifth form ; and afterward, when I passed into the sixth, I began to feel uncomfortable in my short frocks."

She sighed and leaned her head on the back of the sofa with half-closed eyes. He took her hand and softly patted it. She did not draw it away nor open her eyes. In a sweet drowsiness Maria Ivanovna continued to see herself a half-grown girl.

"Yes, it was a beautiful time," she whispered, as if awaking from sleep. "And afterward——"

"I know what happened afterward," he interrupted. "That is, I can guess——"

She was suddenly possessed by a passionate longing to tell him everything, to tell the story of her whole life, to him, who was so gentle and good and pure, and who ought to know what kind of a woman he wanted to bring to his ancestral home, into his beloved apple orchard. It was true he would turn away from her in disgust, but that was preferable to base deceit. Oh, she had lied so much, lied her whole life long, every word she had uttered was a lie. When he first proposed marriage to her she had taken it for one of those jests that are often essayed for closer intimacy with such women as she. In her life history she had had several such experiences. But this time she felt with her whole being that he meant it earnestly, as she felt his wonderful gaze—he looked at her also with his whole body, with every drop of his pure, uncorrupted blood.

For a few moments they were silent, but the silence was more eloquent than words ; he understood what she was thinking of and forestalled her.

"Yes, I know," he said, choosing his words with difficulty. "I know that you have a past. But it does not concern me. I do not want to know it. There are feelings which cleanse everything, just as fire clears metal from rust. I am fully conscious of the step I am taking and what I intend to do. But one condition I beg of you, for the love of God—never, not with a single word, mention that past ! It would pain me very much, horrify me to hear it—especially from you."

She was silent, feeling suddenly a queer dizziness, and it seemed as if she saw many-coloured disks whirling before her eyes.

" No, never, never ! " he repeated, firmly pressing her hand. " A human being should not be judged by his mistakes, but by his heart."

He spoke further in the same strain, seriously and simply, like a brother to a sister, while from the garden the clamour and noise of the revellers and the sound of music came up to them. To Maria Ivanovna it seemed as if the great crowd were calling to her, and she wanted to hide herself far, far away, leaving behind for ever the Maria Ivanovna whom this public knew and whom it considered its property. Thus think the sick, who dream of going away in the vain hope of leaving their sickness behind them.

" You are good and noble," she said in a motherly tone. " There are so very few really good people in the world. No one can become good—it is in one's blood. Your father and mother must also be good people."

" Yes, they are."

They sat very late into the night, speaking quietly of trifles which had suddenly gained an unwonted importance in their eyes. On parting she kissed him. It was their first kiss, and she was surprised to find her heart beating faster than usual.

It was a white, moonless night. Only a few late guests were left in the garden. From one of the private rooms came the sounds of a drunken quarrel. Tired waiters hurried past with trays upon which were piled empty dishes and bottles. The air was filled with the fumes of drunken revelry.

Pavel escorted Maria Ivanovna to a carriage and helped her in.

" I do not like to be accompanied home," she informed him gently, with an enigmatic smile.

III

The following nights were also white and moonless, those white nights of St. Petersburg.

Maria Ivanovna was very miserable. She felt as if something were pressing on her. She wept and was angry with herself.

" You old fool, you old fool ! "

She went to the mirror and, looking intently at her slightly faded face, smiled bitterly.

" Old, quite old."

There had been a time when Maria Ivanovna laughed at the women age had caught in its merciless grasp, who yet tried desperately to appear young. And now her turn had come! Time knows no pity. She caught her head in both her hands, cursed herself and again wept. She was of a different mind about the matter ten times a day. She would certainly never marry Ruzhishchev; that would be simply ridiculous—a husband of twenty-four and a wife of thirty-seven—a whole abyss of thirteen years. No, she would just go on loving him, simply and without any obligations on his side, for so long as his love might last—a year, maybe two. To be superfluous, to be unloved—that would not matter; but to be ludicrous was more than she could bear. On the other hand, do not old men marry very young girls? There are marriages based upon mutual respect, and there are some men who love only once in their lives and find in their wives the better part of themselves. Was it not possible that she might die in the height of their happiness and he also? And, after all, she could always leave him as soon as she noticed a change in his feelings and give him back his full liberty.

Her infatuation was no longer a secret among her comrades of the profession. She was met with meaning smiles, and the stout comedian Butusov paraphrased a well-known French jest: "Our Maria Ivanovna wants to exchange her forty-franc piece for two twenty-franc pieces; one cash down and the other on credit. That is called the conversion of a domestic loan."

Her good friends certainly did their best to acquaint Maria Ivanovna with all this tittle-tattle and the cheap witticisms circulated about her. She was exasperated, but had always the same reply: "They do not understand, therefore they are angry."

Among the members of the International chorus there was a fair young girl by the name of Tania. She was a newcomer on the stage and had not as yet lost her maidenly modesty. Maria Ivanovna took an interest in her, and often invited her into her dressing-room to pin a bunch of fresh flowers on her corsage or to give her a box of bon-bons.

Tania looked up to Maria Ivanovna as to an unattainable ideal. She waited for her in the corridor before going on the stage, caught her every glance, and followed her with loving eyes. This mute adoration highly amused Maria Ivanovna, and she instinctively pitied the lovable young girl. After listening for some time to the gossip in the wings, Tania watched for Maria Ivanovna in the corridor and, assuring herself that she was alone, went uninvited into the dressing-room.

" Do you need anything, Tania ? " asked Maria Ivanovna.

" No—that is, yes," the girl said, confused ; then she faltered : " They all say that you are in love."

" Oh, what foolishness, Tania ! And why must you repeat what others are saying ? "

" But I know, Maria Ivanovna, that you are in love."

" Well, let us suppose that it is so—what of it ? "

" I wanted to ask you how it feels."

Maria Ivanovna broke into a merry peal of laughter.

" Oh, you little silly ! I suspect you are in love, too ? "

" I do not know. I am being courted by two men : the head boxkeeper and the hairdresser."

" And whom do you love ? "

" I like them both the same."

" Ah, you foolish, foolish little girl ! If you like them both, then you do not love either one. You can love but one. Your time has not yet come, Tania. When one loves one asks no one about it."

Maria Ivanovna took the ingenuous girl in her arms and kissed her many times.

" Everybody loves you, Maria Ivanovna. Everybody courts you," whispered Tania, pressing her fair little head on Maria Ivanovna's shoulder ; " you do not want to tell me, but you know everything. The boxkeeper went on a spree from sheer despair, and Alfred, the hairdresser, is threatening to blow his brains out, and I do not know what to do."

Maria Ivanovna laughed heartily as she told Ruzhishchev about this, but Ruzhishchev found little in it to laugh at.

They met every day. Ruzhishchev, as if in duty bound, spent every evening in the garden. He knew by sight not only all the artists, boxkeepers, and waiters, but even the hangers-on and habitués of the garden, and the closer his contact and acquaintance with the place the more he hated it. It was all horrible, ugly, and hopeless. He suffered terribly at the sight of the actors and actresses who were employing all the tricks of their trade for the edification of the drunken crowds. The boldness of the actresses as they vied with each other especially distressed him.

Maria Ivanovna was no better than the rest when she sang her spicy chansonettes, accompanied with gestures and intonations. Her painted face, her neck and arms covered with false diamonds, her bold smiles and gestures horrified Ruzhishchev. At supper every evening he would repeat the same words to her :

" Maria, let us go away from here. It is terrible ! You cannot imagine how it hurts me to see you grimacing upon this accursed stage. I no longer recognise you. Your face becomes strange, and your smile, your motions, your voice——"

" My dear, it is simply because you are not used to it. Our cynicism does not exist for ourselves personally ; we do not feel it any more than the hucksters and fishmongers in the market do the continual abuse and cursing in which they indulge with so much gusto on the least provocation : they are used to it, and therefore do not care. As to my leaving at present, I cannot do it ; my contract will not permit it ; I should have to pay a large forfeit."

" I will pay the forfeit."

" But my reputation ? What manager would engage me again if I once broke my contract ? Our artistic reputation is our whole capital. To-day you love me, and everything is well ; but who knows what may happen to-morrow ? "

" For the love of God, Maria, do not speak like that ! "

Ruzhishchev was too modest to talk much about himself and his private affairs ; but in the theatrical world in which Maria Ivanovna lived there are no secrets, and Maria Ivanovna knew through others that he was the only son of a very wealthy landowner on the banks of the Volga, had graduated from a university, and served in one of the minister's offices without remuneration.

There was one man, a very questionable character, whose business lay with the actors at summer gardens and cafés chantants. He wore a high hat and gold spectacles, and spoke several languages. He seemed to know everything and everybody, and served the actors—especially the women—in the capacity of theatrical agent. His name was Astmus. Rumour gave him a very shady reputation and held him as ready for any kind of rascality. His specialty lay in procuring profitable acquaintances for his clients, writing laudatory criticisms, and circulating scandals or slanders. Maria Ivanovna had known him for several years and had often made use of his services. She now feared him with a deadly fear. She knew that Astmus was intimately acquainted with the whole of her turbulent life, and could spoil her growing happiness in a moment by a few anonymously written lines.

Astmus himself thoroughly understood the situation, and behaved toward her with provoking familiarity.

"So, so; we have a nice little love affair, Maria Ivanovna?" he jested, looking straight at her with his cruel eyes. "Well, you must not lose valuable time, my dear. You can depend on my discretion, because I am the living grave of all women's secrets. That is my principle, Maria Ivanovna. But why do I tell you this? You have had enough opportunities to find out how honest I am in my dealings. By the bye, Maria Ivanovna, you could easily win my friendship by doing me a small favour. You know the little chorus girl Tania. I like her extremely, but she chooses to play the prude, taking offence at the least hint. If I could meet her at your rooms—accidentally, of course—well, what do you say? Besides, I am well aware that she adores you, and you, like a clever and practical woman, could easily influence her."

"Pardon me, Monsieur Astmus," Maria Ivanovna sharply interrupted him, red with anger. "I have nothing to do with affairs of that sort."

"You are afraid of a new rival, my dear, eh? Oh-h-h! I really didn't expect it."

After this conversation there was nothing for her to do but run away from the place as quickly as possible. Yes, run—not leave it but run.

IV

Ruzhishchev was beside himself with joy when she told him that she had decided to leave the stage.

"I sing to-day for the last time," she declared, watching him with eyes beaming with joy. "To-morrow I shall announce it to the manager. I am a little conscience-stricken, because I am leaving at the height of the season. After all, I have been a good attraction, and the public liked me. My leaving may have a detrimental effect upon the business of the whole company."

"My beloved, somebody will surely be found to replace you."

"You forget that I shall have to pay a large forfeit—something like six thousand roubles. I have only two thousand, which I had saved up for a rainy day."

"Do not worry about money."

"It looks very much as if you were ransoming your future wife out of captivity!"

"Precisely. You are perfectly right! And so this is your last appearance?"

"Yes, my beloved. And to-night we shall sup for the last time in the cabaret."

They embraced lovingly. She turned to her make-up while he went out into the theatre to look on for the last time at his shame. The low cabaret, with its hangers-on, confidence tricksters, and revelling elderly provincials, who came to the capital on business—everything vanished from before his eyes like a bad dream. Ruzhishchev could not even distinguish the various faces—everything was mixed into one absurd living and moving spot, like a drop of infected blood under a microscope. "Oh to escape from here into the fresh air!" he thought. "Oh to be able to carry away my happiness to the banks of my native Volga!"

It seemed to him as if time had stopped—like flowing waters meeting an irresistible barrier in their way. Maria Ivanovna was the last on the programme, and the public, as if anticipating the speedy retirement of its idol, was tireless in calling her before the curtain.

Ruzhishchev kept continually repeating to himself: "Enough! Enough! Leave her alone!"

He was surprised at Maria Ivanovna's whim to sup for the last time in a private room of the garden restaurant. In his opinion they should have run away from there without one backward glance. But who can account for a woman's caprices? Besides, she probably intended it as a last good-bye to the past, a last tribute to a bad habit.

He awaited her in his private room, which somehow did not appear to him to-night so dirty and disgusting as usual.

She came rather late, looking happy, agitated, and joyful.

"Is everything done with?" he asked.

"Yes."

"Did you see your manager?"

"For a moment. I told him what I intended to do. Let us not speak of it," and she laughingly tossed half-a-dozen visiting cards on the table.

"Those dear old men from the provinces won't leave me in peace," she explained, making a wry face. "Oh, how I despise them—I hate them from my very soul. It is not the young who are depraved and debauched, but these esteemed fathers of grown-up families, these virtuous husbands, these living examples of family happiness."

She could have told him also that some of these cards were delivered through the friendly offices of Monsieur Astmus, who was the go-between.

Again they ordered a plain student's supper, and sat on the sofa, holding each other in a close embrace and recalling the details of their first meeting. Maria Ivanovna gazed at Ruzhishchev with loving eyes.

"Heavens, how quickly it has all happened!" she exclaimed. "Just like a dream! Let us see, how was it we became acquainted? I really cannot recollect."

"Oh, well, how we became acquainted is not very interesting. It was in just such a private room as this. Have you forgotten?"

"Let me see; you had two old men with you. Yes, one of them was such a funny creature, a little bit of a man, and he said his name was Dr. Kinderbalsam. He told me that he had formed your acquaintance only that very evening here in the garden."

"No, he was only humbugging you, Maria." Ruzhishchev laughed and added: "This must be our little secret, Maria—you see, my father is a very good and kind man, but sometimes he likes to go on a spree!"

She tore herself away from his arms, sprang up from the sofa, and trembling all over, her face white, said in a choked voice:

"That—that was your—father?"

He rose, took her hands in his and tried to draw her back upon the sofa.

"Yes, my father. He is a very good man, though he has his little shortcomings."

"Father!" she repeated, listening to the sound of her own voice. "Father!"

Again she tore herself away from him and sank, weak and helpless, into a chair.

"Maria, Maria, what ails you? Such nonsense——"

But she made no reply and only covered her face with her hands.

"Maria, you will forgive him! It is such a trifle!"

But she could only groan and press her head in her two hands.

"It is nothing. I often have them," she explained, without removing her hands—"violent pains in the head. Do not be angry. I must go home immediately. You will receive here my final decision to-morrow evening. I must first speak with the manager."

"I will accompany you, Maria."

"Oh, for the love of God, don't; it is unnecessary!" Maria Ivanovna exclaimed in a frightened voice. "Tania will see me home."

He escorted her back to her dressing-room. Tania, who was ready to start for home, was delighted at the thought of accompanying Maria Ivanovna and sitting with her alone in a carriage. Ruzhishchev helped them into the carriage and remained standing on the pavement long after. He could not make it out. Maria Ivanovna had gazed so long into his eyes at parting and had embraced him so lovingly.

As soon as the carriage rolled off, leaving Pavel behind, Maria Ivanovna broke out into bitter weeping, unheeding the crowds of people thronging the pavements on their way from the gardens.

"Maria Ivanovna! Darling, what ails you?" murmured the frightened Tania, embracing her adored one. "Maria Ivanovna, tell me!"

Maria Ivanovna looked at her with wild eyes, and wiping away the tears that were rolling down her face, she said in a choked voice:

"There is no longer any Maria Ivanovna. She is dead. Oh, my God! So this is how retribution has overtaken me!"

"Darling Maria Ivanovna, men are all like that—they are all deceivers."

"Ah, it is not that, Tania. He is noble and pure. You will stay with me to-night, will you not? I am afraid. I cannot explain to you what has happened."

The distance from the garden to Maria Ivanovna's rooms was very short—a few streets only, but it gave her time to think it all over and arrive at a decision. Thoughts chased each other quickly through her head as if storm-driven. And the fatal word "father" was beating in her brain like a hammer. Yes, father! she could see him before her at that very moment, and it sent a shiver through her whole body. After she had formed his acquaintance, brought about by Astmus, in a private room of the garden restaurant, he had visited her several times at her rooms, bringing her flowers, bonbons and costly trinkets. He was a well-preserved, provincial old man, brimming over with the joy of life. And each time after the visit of Dr. Kinderbalsam Maria Ivanovna found on her little night-table under her powder-box a hundred-rouble note. These facts burned in her now like a red-hot iron. She could hear the voice of Dr. Kinderbalsam:

"The young men of to-day are no good. What do they understand, the striplings! But Dr. Kinderbalsam is a specialist in women, for whom the best prescription is a nice cheque or bank-note, easily filled by a first-class jeweller."

Maria Ivanovna felt that she was drowning in this mire in which she had wallowed all her life. Could she marry the son after this? Enough! And she, such a low, vile, disgusting being, dared to love! No, there was no punishment too heavy for her!

On the evening of the next day Ruzhishchev sat impatiently awaiting the promised reply from Maria Ivanovna. Tania found him in the garden and silently handed him an envelope. He opened it, and found written on a single sheet the laconic phrase of Marguerite Gautier: "There is no reply."

VLADIMIR KOROLÉNKO
B. 1853

EASTER EVE

IT was Holy Saturday, one year in the 'eighties.

Evening had long since enfolded the silent earth. The ground, warmed during the day by the rays of the sun, was now cooling beneath the invigorating influence of the night-frost. It seemed as if sighing, while its breath, forming a silvery mist, rose glistening in the rays of the starlit sky, like clouds of incense, to greet the approaching feast.

All was still. In the cool night-breeze the small provincial town stood silent, waiting to hear the first stroke of the bell from the high cathedral tower. But the town was not sleeping ; a spirit of expectancy brooded beneath the veil of darkness, breathing through the shadows of the silent and deserted streets. Now and then a belated workman, who had just escaped from his servile task ere the festival began, passed, hurrying on his way ; once in a while a cab rattled by, leaving silence behind it. Life had fled indoors and hidden itself, in mansion and hovel, from whose windows the lights shone far out upon the street, while over the city and the fields hovered the spirit of Resurrection.

Although the moon stood high above the horizon, the town still rested in the broad, deep shadow of a hill, crowned by a gloomy and massive edifice, whose peculiarly straight and severe outlines were sharply defined in the golden atmosphere. The sombre gates were hardly to be distinguished amid the gloom of its deeply shadowed walls, while the towers on the four corners stood out boldly against the azure sky, and gradually over all the moon poured its flood of liquid gold.

Suddenly on the sensitive air of the expectant night came the first stroke from the high cathedral belfry ; then another, and still another. A minute later and the whole air throbbed and swelled, as the countless bells rang out, uniting in one harmonious peal. From the gloomy building overshadowing the town there came a faint, broken harmony, that seemed to flutter helplessly in the air, and thence to rise into the ethereal light, and join the mighty chorus. The singing ceased, the sounds dissolved in air, and the silence of the night gradually resumed its sway; a faint echo seemed to hover for a while, like the vibration of an invisible harp-string. Now the lights were gradually extinguished, the church windows shone forth brightly, and Earth seemed ready to proclaim once more the old tidings of peace, love, and good-will.

The bolts of the dark gates in the gloomy building creaked, and a band of soldiers, with clanking arms, sallied forth to relieve the night sentinels; on approaching the corners, they would halt, and a dark form, with measured steps, would detach itself from the rest, while the former sentinel took his place in the ranks, and the soldiers went on their way, skirting the high prison wall, that glistened in the moonbeams.

As they reached its western side, a young recruit stepped forward from the ranks to relieve the sentry who was posted there; a rustic awkwardness still showed itself in his movements, and his young face betrayed the absorbed attention of a novice who was to occupy for the first time a responsible post. He faced the wall, presented arms, made two steps forward, and shouldering his rifle, stood beside the sentry he was to replace. The latter, turning slightly toward him, repeated the usual formula, in the sing-song tone of discipline:

"From corner to corner. Keep watch! Do not sleep or doze!" He spoke rapidly, while the recruit listened with close attention, and a peculiar expression of anxiety and sadness in his grey eyes.

"You understand?" asked the sergeant.

"Yes, sir!"

"Then, look out!" he added sharply; but, suddenly changing his tone, he said, good-naturedly:

"Don't be afraid, Faddeyef; you are not a woman! I hope you are not afraid of the Lyeshy!"

"Why should I be afraid of him?" replied Faddeyef. Then he added: "But I tell you, boys, I have some misgiving."

This simple and almost childish confession made the soldiers laugh.

"There's simplicity for you!" exclaimed the sergeant, in tones of contempt. Then giving the order, "Shoulder arms! March!" the sentries, with measured tread, disappeared around the corner, and the sound of their footsteps was soon lost in the distance. The sentinel shouldered his rifle, and began to pace along the wall.

Inside the prison, at the first stroke of the bell, all was in motion.

It was long since the sad and gloomy prison night had witnessed so much life. It seemed as if the church bells had really brought tidings of liberty; for the grimy doors of the cells opened in turn, and their occupants, clad in long grey garments, the fatal patches on their backs, filed in rows along the corridors, on their way to the brilliantly lighted prison church. They came from all directions—from right and left, descending and ascending the stairway; and amid the echoing footsteps rang the sound of arms and the clanking of chains. On entering the church, this grey mass of humanity poured into the space allotted to it, behind the railing, and stood there in silence. The windows of the church were protected by strong iron bars.

The prison was empty, except in the four towers, where, in small, strongly bolted cells, four men, in solitary confinement, were restlessly pacing to and fro, stopping once in a while to listen at the keyhole to the snatches of church-singing that reached their ears.

And, beside these, in one of the ordinary cells, in a bunk, lay a sick man. The governor, to whom this sudden illness had been reported, went into his cell as they were escorting the prisoners to church, and, leaning over him, looked into his eyes, that were gazing fixedly before him, and in which shone a peculiar light.

"Ivanof! Ivanof!" he called out to the invalid.

The convict never turned his head, but continued muttering something unintelligible, moving his parched lips with difficulty.

"Carry him to the hospital to-morrow!" said the governor, as he left the cell, appointing a sentry to guard the door. The latter, after a close examination of the delirious patient, shook his head, saying as he did so: "A vagrant! Poor fellow! you are not likely to tramp any more!" The governor continued his way along the corridor, and entered the church, taking up his post by the door, where, with frequent genuflexions, he listened devoutly to the service. Meanwhile the mutterings of the unconscious man filled the empty cell.

He did not seem old; on the contrary, he looked strong and muscular. He was delirious, apparently living the past over again, while a look of distress disfigured his face. Fate had played him a sorry trick. He had tramped thousands of miles through the Siberian forests and mountains, had suffered countless dangers and privations, always urged onward by a consuming home-sickness, and sustained by one hope—that he might live to see his native place, and be once more with his own people, if it were but for a month, or even a week. Then he would be resigned, even if he had to go back again. But it chanced that, when only a few hundred miles from his native village, he had been recaptured and confined in this prison. Suddenly his mutterings ceased. His eyes dilated, and his breathing became more even. Brighter dreams flitted across his fevered brain. The forest moans. He knows it well, that moaning ; monotonous, musical, and powerful. He can distinguish its various tones ; the language of each tree : the majestic pine, dusky green, rustling high overhead ; the whispering cedars, the bright, merry birch, tossing its flexible branches ; the trembling aspen, fluttering its timid, sensitive leaves. The free birds sing ; the stream rushes across the stony chasm ; and a swarm of gibbering magpies, the detectives of the forest, are soaring in the air over the path followed by the vagrant through this almost impenetrable thicket.

It seemed as if a breeze from the free forest were wafted through the prison cell. The invalid sat up and drew a long breath, gazing intently before him, while a sudden gleam of consciousness flashed into his eyes. The vagrant, the habitual fugitive, beheld before him an unaccustomed sight—an open door !

In his frame, enfeebled by disease, a powerful instinct sprang to life. His delirium either disappeared or centred itself on one idea, which, like a ray of sunlight, illumined the chaos of his thoughts. Alone, and with an open door ! In a moment he was on his feet. It seemed as if the fever had left his brain, and was only perceptible in his eyes, which had a fixed and menacing expression.

Some one had just come out from the church, leaving the door ajar.

The strains of the harmonious singing, subdued by the distance, reached the ear of the vagrant, and then died away. His face softened, his eyes grew dim, and his imagination reproduced a long-cherished scene : A mild night, the whisper of the pines, their branches swaying above the old church of his native village, a throng of countrymen ; the lights reflected in the river, and this same chant ! He must make haste with his journey, that he may hear this at home, with his family !

All this time, in the corridor, near the church door, the governor prayed devoutly, kneeling, and touching his forehead to the ground.

Meanwhile, the young recruit paced to and fro on his beat along the prison wall, which glowed with a phosphorescent light. A broad, level field, recently freed from snow, lay before him.

A light wind rustled through the tall grass, inclining him to a sad and pensive mood.

The moon hung high above the horizon; the expression of anxiety had vanished from Faddeyef's face. He stopped by the wall, and, setting his rifle on the ground, rested his hand on the muzzle, on which he leaned his head, falling into a deep reverie. He could not yet wholly grasp the idea of his presence in this place, on this solemn Easter Eve, beside the wall, with a rifle in his hand, and opposite the vacant field. He had by no means ceased to be a peasant; many things clear to a soldier were to him incomprehensible; and he was often teased by being called " a rustic." But a short time ago he was a free man, had the care of a household, owned a field, and was at liberty to work when and where he pleased, Now, an indefinite, inexplicable fear beset his every step and movement, forcing the awkward young peasant into the groove of strict discipline. At this moment he was alone. The bleak landscape before him, and the wind, whistling through the dry grass, made him dreamy; and memories of familiar scenes passed through his mind. He seemed to see his native village! The same moon shone above it, the same breeze blew over it; he saw the lighted church, and the dark pines tossing their green heads—

Suddenly he became conscious of his present surroundings, and surprise kindled his blue eyes, as though he were questioning, " What are these—this field, this wall, and rifle? " For an instant he realised where he was, but in another moment the whistling breeze wafted him back to familiar scenes; and again the soldier dreamt, leaning on his rifle.

All at once, close beside him, appeared a head over the top of the wall, the eyes glimmering like two coals. The vagrant peered into the open field, and beyond it to the shadowy line of the distant forest; his chest expanded as he greedily inhaled the refreshing breath of " mother night." He let himself down by his hands, gently gliding along the wall.

The joyful ringing had awakened the slumbering night. The door of the prison church was opened, and the procession moved into the yard. In waves of melody the singing poured forth from the church. The soldier started, lifted his cap, and was about to make the sign of the cross, when he suddenly stopped, with his hand raised in the act of prayer, while the vagrant, having reached the ground, swiftly began to run toward the tall grass.

" Stop, pray, stop, my dear fellow! " exclaimed the soldier, in a terrified voice, as he raised his rifle. At the sight of this grey figure fleeing from pursuit, all his shapeless and terrible fears took a definite form. " Duty—responsibility ! " flashed across his mind, and, raising his weapon, he aimed at the fugitive. But before pulling the trigger he pitifully shut his eyes.

Meanwhile, above the town there rose, hovering in the upper air, a harmonious and prolonged chime, marred only by the prison bell, that trembled and fluttered like a wounded bird ; and from beyond the wall the sounds of the joyous chant, " Christ is risen," reached far into the field. Suddenly, above all other sounds, came the report of a rifle, followed by a faint, helpless groan, like a plaintive and dying protest. Then for a moment all was still ; and only the distant echoes of the vacant field repeated with a sad murmur the last reverberation of the shot amid the silence of the terror-stricken night.

THE OLD VERGER

VLADIMIR KOROLÉNKO

IT is growing dark.

The little village, sheltering under the pine forest above the distant river, is bathed in that peculiar twilight of starry spring nights when thin mists, rising from the ground, deepen the shadows in the woods and cover the open space with silvered azure smoke. . . . All is still and sad. The village is quietly dozing.

The dark outlines of the wretched huts are scarcely distinguishable; here and there a light twinkles; occasionally a gate creaks; an alert dog barks; now and again, from out the dark mass of gently rustling woods, the figures of pedestrians stand out; a horseman rides by; a cart scrapes along. The inhabitants of the forest villages are about to go to church to celebrate the Easter Festival.

The church stands on a little hill in the middle of the village; its windows are illuminated by candles; the belfry, old, high, and dark, stretches into the azure.

The staircase creaks . . . the old verger Mihaitch is mounting to the belfry tower, and soon his lantern is hanging in space, like a fallen star.

The old man finds it hard to climb the winding stairs. His old legs refuse to carry him; he, too, is worn out—dimly see the eyes. . . . It is quite time for him to rest, but God does not send death. The old man has buried sons and grandsons, accompanied the young and the old to the grave, but himself lives on. How hard it is! Many times has he heralded the Easter Festival, so many that he has lost count of the number of times he has waited at the appointed hour in this same belfry. And God has brought him again. . . . The old man leans his elbows on the rail and looks down from the belfry. Below, the graves in the churchyard are just discernible in the darkness; the old crosses seem to guard them with their outstretched arms. Here and there, birches not yet covered with leaves, bend over them. To Mihaitch is borne aloft the fragrance of young buds; all seems enveloped in the calm stillness of eternal sleep. . . .

What will happen to him next year? Will he again mount up here under the copper bell and wake the night with resounding blows or will he lie down . . . there, in a dark corner of the churchyard under a cross? God knows. . . . He is ready; in the meantime God has granted him to meet another festival. "The Lord be praised!" The old lips whisper the habitual formula, and Mihaitch looks up at the millions of bright fires in the starry heavens, and crosses himself. . . .

"Mihaitch! Mihaitch!" another old, quavering voice calls from below. The aged deacon looks up at the belfry, shading his blinking tearful eyes with his hand, but does not see Mihaitch.

"What do you want? Here I am," the verger replies, leaning out of his belfry. "Can't you see me?"

"No, I can't. Don't you think it's time to strike up? What do you think?"

Both look up at the stars. Thousands of God's candles twinkle down on them. Fiery Venus is already high in the sky. Mihaitch ponders a moment.

"Not yet; I'll wait a little. . . . I know when to begin."

He knows. He needs no clock; God's stars tell him the hour. . . . The earth and the sky, the white cloud softly floating in the azure, the dark forest inarticulately murmuring, the lapping of the unseen river down below—all this is familiar to him—all this is akin to him . . . it is not in vain that he has passed his whole life here. . . . Before him the distant past comes to life. . . . He recollects how he mounted to the belfry for the first time. . . . Good God! How long ago that was . . . how long ago. . . . He sees himself, a fair little boy with sparkling eyes; the wind—not the kind that raises the street dust, but a peculiar wind blowing high over the earth, flapping its unseen wings—ruffling his hair. . . . Below, far far away, little people were walking to and fro . . . the village houses looked so small, too, and the woods had receded into the distance. The round glade on which stood the village had seemed so big as to be almost limitless. "Ah, there it is! All there!" smiles the grey old man looking out at the small glade.

"Such is life! . . . In youth you see no end to it. . . . Ah, there it is!" He sees it vividly, from the beginning to the very grave he has chosen for himself in the churchyard. . . . Well . . . God be praised. . . . It is not time for rest yet. . . . The weary road has been trodden honestly and the moist earth is his mother. . . . Soon, oh soon!

However, it is now time. Looking up at the stars, Mihaitch straightens himself, takes up his hat, crosses himself, and collects the bell ropes. . . . In a moment the night air vibrates with the resounding stroke . . . another . . . a third . . . a fourth . . . one after another flow the slow, powerful melodious notes, filling the expectant night.

The ringing ceases, and in the church the service begins. In former years Mihaitch always went down and stood in a corner by the door to pray and listen to the singing, but now he stays up above. It is hard for him—and besides, he feels a kind of weariness. He sits down on the bench and, listening to the dying vibrations of the copper bell, becomes lost in thought. Of what is he thinking? He himself could not say. The belfry tower is lit up faintly by his lantern; the deep resounding bell is merged into the darkness. Below, from the church, a faint sound of singing can occasionally be heard; the night wind stirs the bell-ropes. . . .

The old man lowers his grey head on to his breast. Disconnected pictures float before him. They are singing the "Tropar," he thinks, and sees himself also in the church. There are many young voices in the choir; the old priest, gentle Father Naum, intones the prayers in a trembling voice. Hundreds of peasants' heads bow repeatedly like ears of corn before the wind . . . the peasants cross themselves . . . all familiar faces and yet there are dead. . . . Where is it, this happiness? . . . The aged brain quickens, like the final flicker of a dying fire; his thought glides in bright, swift rays lighting up all the by-paths of his past life . . . unbearable labour, sorrow, care . . . Where is it, this happiness? The heavy burden bends the powerful back, wrinkles the young face, and teaches how to sigh. . . .

He seems to see his sweetheart, standing, with humbly bent head, to the left among the village women. She was a good woman. . . . Peace be to her soul! and she had suffered much sorrow and pain. . . . Want and work, continual womanly sorrow, withers a woman's beauty and dims her eyes; a constant expression of dull fear of the unexpected blows of life is visible midst her immense beauty. . . .

Where is her happiness ? . . . Only one son remained to them—their hope and joy, and he had suffered human injustice. . . .

Here he was, his cup overflowing with sorrow, pressing down the earth on her grave, watering it with his bitter orphan's tears ; quickly he crosses himself and bows his head in the dust. . . . Mihaitch's heart overflows in the clearness of his memories, and the dark images of the ikons look down austerely from the walls on human sorrow and human injustice. . . . It has all gone. . . . It is all in the past. . . . And now the whole world for him is centred in this dark tower where the wind blows in the darkness stirring the bell-ropes. . . . "God will judge you. . . . God will judge," whispers the old man, lowering his grey head ; and the tears course softly down his cheeks. . . .

" Mihaitch ! Mihaitch ! Have you gone to sleep ? " they call from below.

" What ? " he asks, quickly jumping to his feet. " Lord, I have been asleep. What a disgrace ! " . . . With unusually quick movements he gathers together the ropes. Below, the peasants are moving about, like a colony of ants. The choir, sparkling in their golden gowns, are filling the air with song. They have passed the cross near the church, and to Mihaitch is borne the joyful cry " Christ is risen from the dead ! " The call penetrates the old man's heart like a wave . . . and it seems to him that the tall candles burn brighter in the darkness ; the crowd is more excited ; the choir sings louder. The wind seizes the waves of sound and lifts it on high, mingling it with the loud, triumphant bells. . . .

Never before has old Mihaitch rung as he does now. The old overflowing heart seems to have entered the inanimate copper, and the bells seem to sing, laugh, and cry ; they form a wonderful crown of sound carried on high to the starry heavens. The stars shine brighter, and the trembling sounds mingle together and fall to earth again in loving embrace. . . . The big bass calls loudly, drowning the earth with its powerful tones : " Christ is risen ! "

The two tenors, trembling with the alternate strokes of the iron clappers, ring out joyfully : " Christ is risen ! " The small bells, as though in a hurry not to be left behind, chime in between the larger ones and sing after them like little children : " Christ is risen ! " The old belfry seems itself to vibrate, and the wind, fanning the old verger's face, flutters its wings and repeats : " Christ is risen ! "

The weary heart forgets about life so full of sorrow and care . . . the old verger forgets that life for him means only the cramped belfry tower, that he is alone in the world like an old tree beaten down by rough weather. . . . He listens to the sounds as they cry and sing, rising to the sky and falling to the pale earth, and it seems to him that he is surrounded by sons and grandsons, that their voices, young and old, mingle in one chorus and sing to him of the joy and happiness that he has never seen. . . . He pulls at the ropes and the tears flow down his cheeks and his heart beats with the illusion of happiness. . . .

And below people listen and say to one another that never before has Mihaitch rung so beautifully. . . . Suddenly the big bell vibrates uncertainly, then ceases. The accompanying bells, confused, trill out in an unusual peal and break off as though listening to the long sad note that, trembling and crying, gradually dies away in the air. . . .

The old verger drops helplessly on to the bench, and two last tears roll gently down his cheeks.

" Hi, send for a relief, the old verger has finished his task ! "

VSEVOLOD M. GARSHIN
1855–1888

THE RED FLOWER

(*In memory of Ivan Sergaevitch Turgeniev*)

I

"IN the name of His Imperial Majesty, His Highness the Emperor Peter the First, I proclaim a revision of the whole madhouse!"

These words were uttered in a loud, harsh voice. The hospital clerk entering the invalid's name in a large shabby book at a table covered with ink, could not repress a smile. But the two young men who accompanied the invalid did not smile; they could scarcely stand after two sleepless days and nights alone with the madman whom they had just brought by rail. At the station before the last, the fit of madness had increased; a strait-waistcoat had been procured and put on the patient with the aid of the conductor and some gendarmes. Thus he reached the town and thus he had been brought to the hospital.

He had a terrible appearance! Over the grey garments that he had torn to shreds during his fit, a broad cut jacket of coarse sail-cloth was stretched across his waist; the long sleeves kept his arms crossed over his chest and were tied behind. The swollen, wide-open eyes (he had not slept for ten days) burnt with a bright unwavering blaze; a nervous shuddering caused the corner of his lower lip to tremble; the tangled curly hair fell crookedly over his forehead; with quick heavy tread he paced the office from corner to corner, glancing inquisitively at the old shelves filled with books and papers and the chairs covered with American cloth, and from time to time looked at his companions.

"Take him to the section on the right."

"I know, I know. I was here with you last year. We looked over the hospital. I know everything; it will be difficult to deceive me," the invalid said.

He turned to the door. The warder opened it for him; with the same quick resolute tread he walked out of the office, his insane head raised, and almost at a run, went to the right, to the division for the mentally deranged. His companions could scarcely keep up with him.

" Ring the bell, I cannot ; you have bound my hands."

The porter opened the door and the travellers entered the hospital. It was a large stone building of an old Government type. Two large rooms, one a dining-room, the other a general sitting-room for the quieter invalids, a broad corridor with glass doors leading out into the garden, with a flower-bed and about twenty separate rooms where the invalids lived—this composed the first floor ; here also there were two dark rooms, one padded, the other lined with boards, where they put the restive inmates, and a large gloomy vaulted room that was the bathroom. The upper floor was occupied by the women, whence came discordant sounds, broken by yawns and groans. The hospital was built for eighty inmates, but as it served several surrounding counties, it actually contained about three hundred. In the small rooms there were as many as four or five beds. In winter, when the patients were not allowed out and all the iron-barred windows were tightly shut, it was unbearably stuffy in the hospital.

The new patient was taken to the bathroom. Even on a healthy man this room would have produced a great impression, but on an unhinged, excited imagination the impression was greater still. It was a large vaulted room with a stone floor, lighted by one corner window. The walls and vaults were painted dark green, and in the dirty black floor were sunk two stone baths filled with water. A huge copper stove, with a cylindrical boiler for heating the water, and a whole system of copper pipes and taps occupied the corner facing the window. To an unhinged mind all this must have created an unusually gloomy, fantastic atmosphere, and the warder in charge of the bathroom, a stout, silent southern, with a gloomy countenance, increased the impression.

And when the invalid was led into this terrible room to be bathed, and, in accordance with the principal doctor's system of cure, to have a fly-blister put on the back of his neck, terror and anger took possession of him. Absurd thoughts, each more wonderful than the preceding, flew through his brain. " What is this ? The Inquisition ? The place of secret punishment where his enemies had decided to make an end of him ? Perhaps it was hell itself ? " At last it entered his head that he was being tried in some way. He was undressed despite his desperate resistance. With the increased strength of his madness, he easily tore himself from the hands of the few warders, so that they fell on the floor; at last, four of them knocked him down and, seizing him by the hands and legs, put him into the warm water. It seemed boiling hot to him, and there flashed through his disordered brain a disconnected, fragmentary thought of trial by boiling water and molten iron. Held firmly by the warders, he kicked feverishly with legs and hands, panted, gulped down the water, and shouted out disconnected words impossible to imagine unless one had heard them. There were prayers and curses. He screamed as long as his strength lasted, and at last, with hot tears flowing down his cheeks, he softly uttered a sentence that had no connection with his former words:

"Holy martyr Giorgi! Into thy hands I deliver my body, but my soul—never, oh, never!"

The warders still held him, though he had calmed down. The warm bath and bladder of ice on his head had performed their task. But when they took him out of the bath, almost unconscious, and placed him on the tabouret to put the blister on him, mad thoughts came back, and his remaining strength broke out.

"Why? What for?" he shouted. "I have never wished harm to any one. Why do you want to kill me? O-o-oh! oh, God! Oh, ye martyrs who died before me, save me, I pray!" . . .

The hot contact at the back of his neck caused him to struggle desperately. The warders could not manage him, and did not know what to do. "We can't do anything," said the soldier performing the operation. "We must rub."

These simple words made the patient shudder. "Rub . . . Rub what? Rub whom? Me?" he thought, and in deadly terror shut his eyes. The soldier took up a rough towel by both ends, and rubbing firmly, passed it quickly over the back of his neck, tearing off the blister and the upper skin, and leaving a bare, raw place. The pain of this operation, unbearable even to a calm, healthy man, seemed the end of everything to the patient. With a desperate movement of his whole body he tore himself out of his warder's hands, and his naked body rolled down the stone slab. He thought they had cut off his head. He wanted to cry out, but could not. He was carried out on a stretcher in an unconscious state that gave place to a deep, dead long sleep.

II

He awoke in the night. All was quiet; from the adjoining large room could be heard the breathing of the sleeping patients. Somewhere in the distance, a patient who had been into the dark room for the night was talking to himself in a monotone; upstairs, in the women's quarters, a hoarse contralto was singing some wild song. The patient listened to all these sounds. He felt a terrible exhaustion and weakness in all his limbs; his neck hurt frightfully.

"Where am I? What is the matter with me?" flashed through his brain. And suddenly, with unusual clearness, he saw the last month of his life, and he understood that he was ill and what his illness was. He recollected the crowds of absurd thoughts and acts, and it made him shudder. "But it is all over now, thank God, all over!" he whispered, and dropped off to sleep again.

The open window behind the iron bars looked out into a narrow lane between the tall buildings and a stone wall; no one ever used this lane, and it was thickly overgrown with wild bushes and lilac which, just then, were in full bloom. . . . Behind the bushes, right in front of the window, was a dark, high wall; the tops of the trees in the large garden, bathed in moonlight, peeped over it. On the right there towered the white hospital edifice with its iron-barred windows lit up from within; to the left, the white moonlit dead wall of the mortuary. The rays of the moon streamed through the iron bars of the window on to the floor in the middle of the room, and lit up part of the bed and the pale, worn face of the patient, who lay with eyes closed; now there was nothing mad about him. He slept the deep, dreamless sleep of an exhausted man, without movement, almost without breathing. At intervals he would wake in full possession of his senses, as though perfectly well, but in the morning he was the same madman.

III

"How do you feel?" the doctor asked him on the following day.

The patient, who had only just awakened, was lying under the bedclothes.

"Splendid!" he replied, jumping up and putting on his slippers and dressing-gown. "Splendid! except for this!"

He pointed to the back of his neck.

" I cannot turn my head without pain, but that is nothing. Everything is well if you only understand it, and I do understand."

" Do you know where you are ? "

" Of course, doctor ! I'm in the madhouse. But if you understand, it makes no difference, none whatever."

The doctor looked fixedly into his eyes. His handsome nurtured face, with the well-kempt golden beard and calm blue eyes gazing out of gold spectacles, was motionless and impenetrable. The patient went on :

" Why do you look at me so intently ? You cannot read what is in my soul, but I can read clearly what is in yours ! Why will you do harm ? Why have you gathered together this crowd of unfortunate beings and keep them here ? To me it doesn't matter, I understand and am calm, but they ? Why these tortures ? To a man who has reached the state when he has a great idea in his brain, a universal idea, it makes no difference where he lives or what he feels. Even life and death are of no consequence . . . isn't that so ? "

" Perhaps," the doctor replied, sitting down in a chair in the corner of the room so as to get a good view of the patient, who was pacing the room quickly from corner to corner, shuffling his large horse-skin slippers and waving the skirts of his dressing-gown made of some cotton material with broad red stripes and large flowers. The assistant surgeon and the inspector who accompanied the doctor continued standing by the door.

" And I have it ! " the patient exclaimed. " When I discovered it, I felt myself reborn. Feelings grew more intense, the brain worked as never before. What I had reached before after much theory and speculation I now know intuitively. I have, in fact, reached what has been arrived at philosophically. I experience in myself the great idea that space and time are illusions. I live in every age. I live without space, everywhere or nowhere as you please. For that reason it is all the same to me whether you keep me here or let me go, whether I am free or bound. I noticed a few others like me here, but for the rest their position is terrible. Why don't you let them go free ? To whom is it necessary ? . . ."

" You say," the doctor interrupted, " that you live outside space and time. However, you cannot but admit that you and I are in this room, and that at present "—the doctor pulled out his watch—" it is half-past ten, May the 6th, 18—. What do you say to that ? "

" Nothing. It is all one to me where I am and when I live. And if it is all the same to *me*, doesn't that mean that *I* am everywhere and at all times ? "

The doctor smiled.

" An unusual logic," he said, rising. " However, you are right. Good-bye. Wouldn't you like a cigar ? "

" Thank you." The patient stopped, took a cigar, and nervously bit the end off. " This helps thought," he said. " This is the world in miniature. At one end is alkali ; at the other, acid. So, in the universe, opposing causes are balanced and neutralised. Good-bye, doctor."

The doctor went on farther. The majority of the patients were waiting for him, stretched out in their hammocks. No chiefs are ever accorded such respect from their subordinates as a mental specialist gets from his patients.

The lunatic, left alone, continued jerkily pacing his room from corner to corner. They brought him tea, and, without sitting down, he drank off, at one gulp, a large mugful and almost in an instant ate a large piece of white bread. Then he went out of the room, and for several hours on end paced, with his quick, heavy tread, from one end of the building to the other. It was a rainy day, and the patients were not allowed out into the garden. When the assistant surgeon came to look for the new patient, they pointed him out at the end of the corridor. He was standing and gazing fixedly at a flower-bed through the glass door that led out into the garden. His attention was taken by a flower of an unusually bright, ruby shade, a kind of poppy.

" Will you please come and be weighed ? " the assistant surgeon said, touching him on the arm, and when the patient turned towards him the surgeon nearly dropped with fright, so much wild anger and hatred burned in those mad eyes. But, catching sight of the surgeon, the patient immediately changed the expression on his face and followed obediently, without a word, as though deep in thought. They went into the doctor's study, and the patient got on to the small weighing machine of his own accord ; the assistant surgeon, after weighing him, entered his weight—109 pounds—against his name in a book. On the following day it was 107, and on the third day 106.

" If he goes on like that, he will not last long," the doctor said, and ordered him to be fed as well as possible. Yet, notwithstanding the patient's tremendous appetite, he grew thinner every day, and every day the number of pounds entered by the assistant surgeon diminished. The patient scarcely slept, and passed whole days in constant movement.

IV

He knew that he was in a madhouse; he knew even that he was ill. Sometimes, as on the first night, he would awake amid the stillness, after a day of impetuous movement, aching in every limb, and with a terrible heaviness in his head, but fully conscious. It may be that the absence of impressions in the stillness of the night, the slow working of the brain on first waking up, caused him in such moments to understand his position and regain his normal state. But the day arrived; together with the light and the awakening life of the hospital, waves of impressions that his disordered mind could not cope with swept over him, and he was again mad. His condition was a strange mixture of perfect judgment and absurdities. He knew that he was surrounded by invalids, yet at the same time, in every one of them he saw some mysterious person who was hiding or being hidden, whom he had known or of whom he had read. The hospital was inhabited by people of all ages and all countries. These were the living and the dead, the famous and mighty ones of the world, the soldiers killed in the last war but resurrected. He imagined himself in some enchanted magic circle, where all the powers of the world were gathered together, and with a divine ecstasy imagined himself the centre of the circle. All his comrades were gathered together in order to accomplish the task that appeared to him vaguely as a gigantic undertaking to destroy evil on earth. He did not know in what it consisted, but felt himself strong enough to accomplish it. He could read the thoughts of others, and see in things their whole history; the large elms in the hospital garden told him whole legends of the past, the building, that really was fairly old, he imagined had been built by Peter the Great, and was convinced that the Tsar had lived in it at the time of the battle of Poltava. He read this in the walls, in the crumbling plaster, in the bits of brick and tile he found in the garden. He peopled the little mortuary with multitudes of people long dead, and peered intently through the window of its cellar that looked out on the garden, seeing in the light, unevenly reflected through the dirty coloured glass, familiar features that he had seen somewhere, in real life or in portraits.

Meanwhile, fine clear weather set in and the patients spent whole days out in the fresh air in the garden. Their portion of the garden, though not large, was thickly overgrown with trees, and planted with flowers wherever possible. The inspector made all those who were capable of it do some work in the garden. For whole days they shoaled and scattered the paths with gravel, trimmed and watered the beds and flowers, tended the cucumbers, pumpkins, and melons, planted with their own hands. The corner of the garden had several thick cherry trees, farther on there stretched an avenue of elms, and in the middle, on an artificial mound, was the most beautiful flower-bed in the whole garden. Bright flowers grew round the border of this bed, and in the centre was a patch of large rare dahlias, yellow ones with red spots. The whole garden spread out round this bed, and one could see that many patients attached some mysterious significance to it. In the garden were all the flowers met with in Little Russia—tall roses, bright petunias, tall tobacco plants with their small pink blossoms, mint, amaranth, geraniums, and poppies. Here, too, not far from the porch, grew some poppies of a particular kind. They were smaller than the usual and were distinguished by their extraordinarily bright ruby colour. This was the flower that had attracted the patient's attention when he had looked out on the garden through the glass doors on the day after his entrance into the hospital.

On going out into the garden for the first time, the first thing he did, before even leaving the porch, was to stare fixedly at the bright flowers. There were only two of them, and as it happened they grew away from the others in an uncultivated patch, and were surrounded by thick tall grass and goose-foot.

The patients came out of the door one after another, while a warder handed each a thick white knitted cotton cap with a red cross on the front. These had come from the wars and had been bought at an auction, but the invalids, of course, attached a mysterious significance to the red cross. The patient took off his cap, looked at the cross and then at the flowers. The latter were brighter. " It is triumphant," he said, " but we will see."

And he came out of the porch. Looking round and not seeing the warder who stood behind him, he stepped over the border and stretched out his hand to the flower but could not decide to pluck it. In his extended hand he felt a stinging fire that spread over his whole body, as though waves of some unknown power emanated from the red petals and penetrated through him. He moved nearer, and putting out his hand, almost touched the flower, but the flower, so it seemed to him, defended itself by exhaling a most deadly poisonous vapour. His head was in a whirl and he made a last desperate effort to seize the stalk when suddenly a heavy hand was laid on his shoulder. It was the warder who had seized him.

"You mustn't pluck the flowers," the old southerner said, "and you mustn't walk on the border. There are many of you madmen here, and if each of you took a flower there would be nothing left of the garden." And he held him firmly by the shoulder.

The patient looked into his face, silently freed himself from the hand, and walked down the path in a state of excitement.

"Oh, unfortunate ones!" he thought. "You do not see, you are so blind that you even defend it. We will measure our strength, if not to-day, then to-morrow. And if I perish, what difference does it make?"

He walked about the garden until the evening, making acquaintances and carrying on strange conversations, in which each person he happened to be talking to heard only the answer to his own mad thoughts, expressed absurdly in mysterious words. The patient walked about, first with one comrade, then with another, and at the end of the day was more than ever convinced that "everything was ready," as he said to himself. Soon, soon, the iron bars would fall and all these exiles would go from this place and hurry away to the ends of the earth, and then the whole world would tremble, throw off its worn crust, and appear in a new wonderful beauty. He had almost forgotten about the flower, but just as he was leaving the garden and going up the steps to the door, he again caught sight of those two red sparks among the darkening grass that was already covered with dew. Then he receded from the crowd, stood behind the warder, and waited for a propitious moment. No one saw him jump over the border, pluck the flower and hide it in his bosom under his shirt. When the fresh, dewy leaves came into contact with his body, he turned as pale as death, and opened his eyes wide in horror; a cold perspiration bathed his forehead.

In the hospital the lamps were lit and most of the patients lay on their beds waiting for supper, while a few restless ones hastily paced the rooms and corridors. Among these was the patient with the flower. He walked about feverishly, pressing his hands over his breast. It seemed as though he wished to crush the hidden flower. When meeting any of the others, he walked far away from them, fearing even to touch them with the hem of his garments. " Don't come near me! Don't come near me!" he cried, but in the hospital no one took any notice of such exclamations. He walked quicker and quicker, his strides grew longer and longer; for a whole hour he walked in a kind of fury.

" I will harass you! I will strangle you!" he said deeply and viciously, and occasionally he ground his teeth.

Supper was served in the dining-room. On the large bare tables they placed big painted and gilt wooden bowls containing wheaten porridge. The patients sat down on the benches, and were given a hunk of black bread. Eight of them ate out of each bowl with wooden spoons. The few who were privileged to a better diet were fed separately. Our invalid, quickly swallowing his portion given him by the warder who had called him to his room for that purpose, was not contented with it, and went into the general dining-room.

" Can I sit down here?" he asked the inspector.

" Haven't you had any supper?" the inspector asked, pouring some more porridge into a bowl.

" I am very hungry, and I must gain strength. I depend entirely on food. I do not sleep at all, as you know."

" Have some more then, my friend. Taras, give him a spoon and some bread."

He sat down by one of the bowls and ate a large portion of porridge.

" Enough, enough," the inspector remonstrated at last, when every one had finished supper and our patient was still ladling porridge out of the bowl with one hand, holding the other firmly over his breast. " You will over-eat yourself."

" Ah, if you only knew how much strength I need, how much strength! Good-bye, Nikolai Nikolaevitch," the invalid said, rising from the table and pressing the inspector's hand. " Good-bye."

" Where are you going?" the inspector asked with a smile.

" I? Nowhere. I am staying here, but to-morrow, perhaps, we shall not see each other. Thank you for your kindness," and once again he pressed the inspector's hand. His voice trembled, and tears started to his eyes.

"Calm yourself, my friend, calm yourself," the inspector said. "Why these gloomy thoughts? Go to bed and have a good sleep. You should sleep more. If you slept well, you would soon get better."

The patient sobbed. The inspector turned to order the warders to clear the tables. Half an hour later, every one in the hospital was asleep except one man, who lay fully dressed on his bed in the corner room. He was trembling as in a fever, and beating his breast convulsively, smothered, as he thought, in an odourless, deadly poison.

V

He did not sleep the whole night. He had plucked the flower because it seemed to him he was bound to do it. At his first glance through the doors the red petals had attracted his attention, and he imagined that he had, at that moment, realised his mission on this earth. In this bright red flower was gathered together all the evil in the world. He knew that opium was made from poppies, and it may be that this thought, spreading and taking on a monstrous form, made him create this terribly fantastic illusion. The flower embodied all evil to him; it had drunk all the innocent blood that had ever been spilt in the earth—that was why it was so red—all the tears and all the sorrows of mankind. It was a mysterious, terrible being, Antichrist, that had assumed this humble, innocent form. It had to be torn up and crushed. But that was not sufficient. The evil must not be allowed to escape again into the earth. That was why he had hidden it in his bosom. He hoped that the flower would have lost its strength by the morning. The evil in it would penetrate into his breast, into his soul, and there be either conquered or conqueror, in which latter case he would die; but he would die like a gallant soldier, the supreme warrior of mankind, because, until now, no one had dared to engage all the evil of mankind in single combat.

"They did not see it, but I did. Can I let it live? Better that I should die." And he lay there, growing feebler in his illusory battle, ever growing feebler. In the morning the assistant surgeon found him scarcely alive. But in spite of this, in a little while his animation came back, he jumped out of bed and, as before, ran about the hospital talking to the other patients and to himself louder and more disconnectedly than ever. He was not allowed out into the garden, and the doctor, seeing that he kept on losing weight, did not sleep, and walked about incessantly, ordered a hypodermic injection of morphia. The patient did not resist—fortunately his mad thoughts of the moment favoured the injection. He soon went to sleep and the furious movement ceased, the sound of his own loud jerky footsteps vanished from his ears. He forgot himself and ceased to think of anything, even of the second flower that had to be plucked.

However, about three days later he plucked it before the very eyes of the warder, who was too late to stop him. The warder tried to catch him, but with a loud, triumphant yell the patient tore into the hospital, up to his room, and hid the flower in his bosom.

"Why do you pluck the flowers?" the warder asked, running into the room. But the patient, who was already lying on his bed in his usual pose—hands crossed over his breast—began to talk such nonsense that the warder merely took off the white cap with the red cross that the other had forgotten in his haste, and silently left the room. The illusory battle began again. The patient felt the evil oozing out of the flower in snaky crawling streams. They enveloped and oppressed him, crushed his limbs and filled his body with their terrible contents. He wept and prayed to God in the intervals between cursing his enemy. Towards evening the flower was quite withered. He crushed the withered flower under foot and, picking up the pieces, took them into the bathroom. Throwing them into the red-hot stove, he stood watching his enemy frizzle and shrivel up until nothing was left but tender white ash. He blew at this and it vanished.

On the following day the patient was worse. Terribly pale, with sunken cheeks and sunken blazing eyes, he continued his mad walk from end to end of the hospital. His gait was uncertain, he often stumbled, but he kept on talking, talking without end.

"I would rather not use force," the older doctor said to his assistant.

"But it is absolutely necessary to stop this activity. He only weighed ninety-three pounds to-day. If it goes on like that any longer, he will be dead in a couple of days." The older doctor grew thoughtful. "Morphia? Chloral?" he said half-interrogatively.

"Yesterday the morphia had no effect on him."

"Very well, tell them to bind him. However, I doubt whether he will recover."

VI

And the patient was bound. He lay on his bed in a strait-waistcoat, firmly bound with broad linen bands to the folding iron bedstead.

But the mad desire for movement had not ceased; it had, if anything, increased. For several hours he tried obstinately to free himself from his fetters. At last, with a tremendous effort, he managed to tear one of the bands, freed his legs, and, wriggling off the bed, began pacing the room with bound hands, shouting out wild, incomprehensible words.

"Damn you!" the warder exclaimed as he entered the room. "Gretsko! Ivan! Help! Quickly! He's unbound himself!"

The three attacked the patient, and a long struggle ensued, a struggle tiring for the attackers and painful for the man defending himself and losing the remainder of his strength. At last he was thrown on the bed and bound tighter than before.

"You do not understand what you are doing!" he cried, gasping. "You will perish! I have seen a third just coming up. Now it is out. Let me finish my task! I must kill it, kill it, kill it! Then all will be finished, all saved. I would send one of you, but only I can do it. You would die from the very contact!"

"Be quiet, sir, be quiet!" said the old warder who had remained to keep guard by the bed.

The patient suddenly quietened. He had decided to deceive the warders. They kept him bound all day, and left him in that position for the night. After giving him his supper, the warder made a bed for himself near the patient, and lay down. In a minute or two he was sound asleep and the patient began his work. He doubled up his whole body in order to reach the iron bar at the foot of his bed, and touching it with his wrists, beneath the strait-waistcoat, began to rub the sleeves against the irons, quickly and firmly. In a little while the sailcloth gave way and he put out his forefinger. Then the work went much faster. With an adroitness and litheness impossible in a normal man he untied the knot behind him that held the sleeves, unlaced the strait-waistcoat, and after this for a long time listened to the warder's snoring. But the old man slept soundly. The patient took off the waistcoat and unbound himself from the bed. Now he was free. He tried the door; it was locked from within, and the key was probably in the warder's pocket. Fearing to wake the warder, he decided not to hunt in his pockets, but to get out of the room through the window.

The window was open; it was a still, warm, dark night, and the stars shone in the black sky. He gazed up at them, distinguishing the familiar constellations, and rejoicing that they sympathised with him, as it seemed to him. Blinking, he saw the multitude of rays they sent him, and his mad resolution grew firmer. He had to bend the thick iron bars, climb out through the window into the lane overgrown with bushes, and climb over a high wall. Then there would be the last struggle, and afterwards—perhaps death.

He tried to bend a bar with his bare hands, but the iron did not yield. Then, twisting the strong sleeves of his strait-waistcoat into a cord, he put it round the bar and hung on with all his weight. After desperate efforts that used up nearly all his remaining strength, the bar gave way and a narrow opening was made. He squeezed through it, grazing his elbows, shoulders, and bare knees, wound his way among the bushes, and stopped before the stone wall. All was still; the night lights shone faintly out of the windows of the large building, but no one could be seen within. No one had noticed him; the old man guarding his bed was probably in a deep sleep. The stars twinkled, sending their rays into his very heart.

"I am coming to you," he whispered, looking up at the sky.

Tearing himself at the first attempt, with broken nails, bleeding hands and knees, he began to look for a more suitable spot. There, where the wall joined the wall of the mortuary, a few bricks had fallen out. The patient felt these hollows and made use of them. He climbed on to the wall, caught hold of the branch of an elm that grew on the other side, and quietly got down to the ground from the tree.

He set off quickly for the familiar spot near the porch. The dark head of the flower, its petals folded, could be seen clearly on the dewy grass. "The last!" he whispered. "The last! To-day it is victory or death. But it is all the same to me. Wait," he said, glancing up at the sky. "I shall soon be with you."

He plucked the flower, squeezed and crushed it, and holding it in his hand, returned to his room by the way he had come. The old man was still asleep. The patient hardly reached his bed before he dropped down on it, unconscious.

In the morning he was found dead. His face was calm and serene; the worn features, the thin lips and sunken closed eyes, expressed a kind of proud happiness. When he was laid on a stretcher, they tried to open his hand and take out the red flower, but the hand was rigid, and he carried his trophy to the grave.

FOUR DAYS

VSEVOLOD M. GARSHIN

I REMEMBER how we ran about the wood amid the whistling of the bullets, how the branches crashed and fell as they were struck, how we fought through the hawthorn bushes.

The bullets came faster. Through the edge of the wood in many places there was a glimpse of something red. Siderov, a little soldier of the first company (" How did you get in with our gang ? " flashed through my mind), suddenly sat down on the ground and looked at me with large frightened eyes. A stream of blood flowed from his mouth.

Yes, I remember that well. I remember too how, almost at the edge of the wood among some thick bushes, I came across *him*. He was a big fat Turk, but I went straight at him though I was small and weak. There was a bang ; some large thing, as it seemed to me, flashed past ; there was a ringing in my ears.

" He has fired at me," I thought. At the same moment, with a cry of horror he backed against a thick clump of hawthorns. He could have got round the clump, but in his terror he forgot everything and scrambled among the prickly branches. With one blow I knocked the gun out of his hand, with another I drove home my bayonet.

There was a cry, a groan, and I ran on farther.

Our men were shouting " Hurrah ! " Some were falling, others were firing. I remember how I too fired several shots when we got out of the wood into the open fields. Suddenly the hurrahs grew louder and we all moved forward. That is to say, our men moved forward, for I remained behind. It seemed so strange to me. And stranger still when suddenly everything vanished, the shouting and the firing ceased. I did not hear anything ; I could only see something blue. It must have been the sky. A moment later even that vanished.

I had never found myself in such a strange position before. I must have been lying face downwards, for as I gazed about I could see little pieces of earth. A few blades of grass with ants crawling from one to another just below my head, a few wisps of hay left over from last year, that was the extent of my world. And I could only see out of one eye, for the other was shut down tightly by something hard, the dead twig, no doubt, on which my head was resting.

I was very uncomfortable and could not understand why it was that I was unable to move. And so the hours went by. The only sounds I could hear were the chirp of the grasshopper and the humming of the bee.

At last I made a terrific effort, pulled out my right arm, on which I had been lying, and, resting on both hands, I tried to raise myself on to my knees.

A pain as sharp and quick as lightning flashed through my body from my knees upwards, and I fell down again.

Once more there was darkness—nothingness.

I awoke. Why do I see the stars which shine so brightly in the dark blue Bulgarian sky ? Am I not in camp ? Why did I come out of the tent ? I try to move and feel a horrible pain in my legs.

I must have been wounded on the battlefield. Badly, I wonder ? I felt my legs at the place where they hurt ; both were covered with congealed blood. When I touched them the pain grew worse. It was a pain like incessant toothache, gnawing at one's very soul.

There was a ringing in my ears ; my head felt heavy. In a vague kind of way I seemed to know that I was wounded in both legs. How is it ? Why did they not pick me up ? I wonder if the Turks beat us ? Gradually at first, and then more clearly, until I came to the conclusion that it must have been the Turks who were beaten. We could not have been beaten, for I fell (of course I had no distinct recollection of falling ; I only remembered how the others ran ahead and I could not run, but stayed behind with something blue before my eyes) in the open field on the top of the little hill, the very place our little commander had pointed out to us.

"We must get there, boys," he had shouted in his ringing voice, and we had got there, which proves that we were not beaten.

Why didn't they pick me up ? In an open field like this they could easily have seen me. I wonder if there are any others here ? The bullets were so thick. I must turn my head and look around. I could move my head more easily now ; I must have fallen over on my back after my first attempt to raise myself on to my knees. That was why I could see the stars.

I tried to sit up, a difficult thing to do with two wounded legs. I had almost given up the attempt in despair when at last, after an excruciating twinge that brought the tears to my eyes, I succeeded and sat up.

Overhead was the dark blue sky. A large star and several smaller ones were twinkling round some tall dark object. It was a clump of bushes. I was among bushes and had been overlooked! My hair stood on end. But how did I manage to get among the bushes when I had fallen in the open field? I must have crawled in here myself. How strange I should have been able to get so far when now I can scarcely move. Perhaps I was only wounded in one leg then, and a stray bullet found me here.

A pale rosy light came over the sky. The large star grew fainter, several smaller ones disappeared. The moon rose. How nice it would be to be at home!

A strange weird sound reached me as of some one moaning. Yes, it was moaning. I wonder if there is some one else lying near by with wounded legs, or perhaps with a bullet in his stomach? The sound seemed quite close and yet there was no one near me.

My God! it was I that was moaning! Softly, plaintively! Is the pain really so bad? It must be, but I do not feel it because my head is dazed and as heavy as lead. I had better lie down and sleep—sleep . . . only shall I ever wake up again? What does it matter, though?

Just as I was about t lie down again, a broad streak of moonlight lit up the place where I was lying, and I caught sight of some large dark object lying a few paces away. Another wounded man. Various objects on him flashed in the moonlight; it might have been the buttons on his uniform or his arms. Was it a corpse, I wonder!

All the same, I will lie down. . . .

It is impossible! our men could not have gone. They are here. They have beaten the Turks and are occupying this position. But why is there no sound of talking, no crackling of twigs? I suppose I am too weak to hear them, but they must be here? "Help! Help!"

Wild senseless cries escape me, but there is no answer. They resound strangely in the night air. All else is still. Only the crickets keep up their incessant chirping. The moon looks down on me sadly with her big round face.

If the man over there had been alive, my cries would have

awakened him. He must be dead. I wonder if he is one of our men or a Turk? My God, what difference does it make? And sleep once more descended upon my swollen eyelids.

I lay still with my eyes closed though I had been awake for a long time. I did not want to open them because I felt the strong sunlight through my closed eyelids and was afraid my eyes would not stand the glare. Besides, it was better not to make a movement of any kind.

Yesterday (was it yesterday?) I was wounded. A day has gone by; others will go by and I shall die. It does not matter! It is better not to move! I will lie here quietly. If only I could stop my brain from working, but thoughts and recollections will come crowding in one after another. However, this will not continue for long; the end will soon come. There will be a few lines in the papers to say that our losses were insignificant; so many wounded, and killed a private volunteer of the name of Ivanov. No, they will not remember my name, but simply say "One killed, one private," like that little dog! . . . The incident suddenly flashed through my mind. It happened a long time ago. However, the whole of my life, everything that had taken place before I found myself lying here, seemed long ago. I was walking along the street when I came across a crowd of people who stood surrounding a little white object covered with blood that was whining piteously. It was a pretty little dog that had been run over by a tramcar. The dog had died, just as I shall die. A porter who was holding forth to the crowd took the little dog by the scruff of the neck and carried it away. The crowd dispersed.

Will some one come and carry me away? No, I shall lie here and die. How nice it is to be alive. . . . How happy I was that day when the little dog was run over. I remember how I walked along in a state of rapture. What torture it is to think of these things now! Former joy is present pain. . . .

The pain and torture are bad enough without these recollections that cause despair. Despair is worse than any wound.

It was getting hot. The sun was scorching. I opened my eyes and saw the same bushes, the same sky, only this time I saw them by the daylight.

And there is my neighbour. Yes, it is a Turk—a dead Turk. How huge he is! I seem to recognise him. It is the same . . .

Near me lay a man whom I had killed. Why had I killed him? He is lying there dead, covered with blood. Why did fate bring him here? Who was he? Perhaps, like me, he too had an old mother. For how long will she sit by the door of her wretched hut and look towards the north, watching for the return of her beloved son, her supporter and bread-winner?

And I? I too . . . I would have changed places with him. How happy he must be! He does not feel the pain of his wound, nor despair, nor thirst. The bayonet had pierced straight through his heart.

In his uniform was a large blank hole surrounded with blood.

I had done that!

I did not want to do it. I had no ill-feeling against any one when I came out to fight. The thought that I should have to kill did not occur to me. I imagined only that I should expose my own breast to the bullet and nothing more.

And what had happened? Fool! fool!

That poor unfortunate Arab (he had on an Egyptian uniform) was even less guilty than I. He had probably never heard of Russia or Bulgaria before he was put into a ship and sent off to Constantinople. He was ordered to go and he went. Had he refused, he would have been flogged, or some Pasha or other might have put a bullet through him. He had made a long weary march from Constantinople into Rumania. We attacked him and he tried to defend himself, but seeing that we were not afraid and kept on advancing in spite of his English Martini rifle, his courage had failed him. When he had wanted to run away, a little man—so little that he could have killed him with one blow of his swarthy fist—jumped at him and plunged a bayonet through his heart. How was he to blame?

And how was I to blame though I had killed him? How was I?

And why am I tortured by thirst? Thirst! who knows what thirst really means? Even when we had marched through Rumania, doing forty miles a day, with the thermometer over 100°, I did not experience what I feel now. Ah, if only some one would come! Stay! There must be water in that gourd the Turk has! But how can I get to him? What efforts I shall have to make! All the same I will try!

I attempt to crawl, dragging my legs behind me. My weak hands will hardly pull my heavy body. The Turk lies about four yards away, but the distance seems greater to me than if it had been four miles.

Still, I must get there. My throat is parched and burning as though on fire. I would assuredly die sooner without water. Yet—something might turn up. . . .

So I attempt to crawl. My legs seem fixed to the ground and every movement causes excruciating pains. I moan and cry aloud but still persist. I get there at last. Here is the gourd. What a lot of water! More than half full. It will last me a long time . . . until death! My victim has saved me. I try to unstrap the gourd, leaning on one elbow, when suddenly I lose my balance and fall face downwards on my saviour's breast. He gives off a strong, unpleasant odour.

I drank my fill. The water was warm, but still wholesome, and besides there was so much of it! It will enable me to last out several days longer! I recollected how some one had said that a man could live for more than a week without food if he had water; also how a man who had tried to commit suicide by starvation had lived a long time because he had drunk water.

Well, and if I continue to live for another five days, what difference will it make? Our men are gone, the Bulgarians have retreated and there is no road near by. Clearly I am bound to die; only instead of suffering for three days I shall prolong it for a week. Would it not be better to make an end? I glanced at my neighbour's rifle, a splendid specimen of English make. I had only to put out my hand and in the twinkling of an eye all would be over. A little heap of cartridges lay near him—he had had no time to use them all.

Shall I make an end or wait? For what? deliverance? death? To wait until the Turks come and pull the skin from my wounded legs? It would be better to kill myself. I must keep up my spirits and fight to the end—as long as my strength holds out. If some one finds me I shall be saved. Perhaps my bones are not broken and I can be cured. I may once more see my native land, my mother, Masha . . . Ah God! I hope they never know the truth. Let them think I was killed outright. What would they feel if they knew that I suffered like this for two, three, four days!

My head feels dizzy. The journey across to my neighbour has sapped all my strength. And then this horrible smell. How black he has turned! What will he be like to-morrow or the day after? I haven't strength enough to move away from him. I will rest a little and then crawl back to my old place away from the bad smell.

I lay there, unable to move. The sun scorched my face and hands.

If only I could cover myself with something, or night would come. It will be the second night, I think. My thoughts are confused. I lose consciousness. . . .

I must have slept a long time, for when I awoke it was night. Nothing had changed. The pain was just as bad, and my neighbour was still lying there large and immovable.

I could not keep from thinking of him. Did I really give up all that was dear to me, tramp a thousand miles, suffer cold, hunger, heat, merely to deprive this unfortunate man of his life? And have I done anything to help the course of the war by committing this murder? Murder! Yes, I am a murderer.

When I made up my mind to go to the war, my mother and Masha did not attempt to dissuade me from it, though they wept. Wrapped up in my idea, I gave no heed to their tears. I did not understand them (though I do now). What harm I had done to these nearest me! (And what is the use of knowing when I cannot bring the past back again?)

(I remember now what some of my friends had thought of me! "Fanatic!" they had said. "He does not know himself why he is going!" How could they have said that? How could they reconcile their words with their conceptions of heroism, patriotism, and such ideals? According to their standards I possessed these qualities, yet they called me "Fanatic.")

I remember how I went to Kinenev, and they gave me my kit, and I set out with thousands of others, a few of whom were, like myself, volunteers. The rest would have stayed at home had they been free to do so. Yet, like us, they went on unthinkingly, did their thousand miles, and fought even better than we did. They fulfilled all their duties although they would have abandoned everything and gone off had they been allowed. Towards morning, a keen wind sprang up. The bushes began to rustle. The sleepy birds awoke. The stars grew dim. The dark-blue sky turned paler and fleecy clouds began to cover it. The grey semi-darkness lifted from the earth. It was the third day of my . . . what shall I call it? . . . life or purgatory here.

Three days . . . how many more remained? Not many, I should think. I was very weak and could not even move away from the corpse. Soon he and I will be alike, and then he will no longer be unpleasant. I must drink some water. I shall drink three times a day: in the morning, at noon, and in the evening.

The sun rose. Its huge disk, partly hidden by the dark branches of the bushes, was blood-red. It promised a hot day.

" My neighbour . . . what will happen to you to-day ? You are horrible enough already."

Yes, he was horrible to look at. His hair had begun to fall out. His skin, dark by nature, had turned a pale yellow and, drawn tightly over his swollen face, had burst by his ears. In the raw places worms were crawling. His feet were so swollen as to be too large for his boots, and flesh protruded between the laces. He was bloated all over. What effect would the sun have on him to-day ? To lie near him was unbearable. I must crawl away at any cost. But I—how could I ?

I could still lift my hand, open the gourd, and drink some water, but to move my heavy cumbersome body was another matter. But I must move if ever so little, even if it takes me an hour.

I spent the whole morning in the attempt to crawl away. The pain was terrible, but I paid no attention—I was used to it. I had forgotten what it was like to feel normal and healthy. At last I reached my former place. I had hoped to get some fresh air (if one can talk of there being air within a few yards of a decaying corpse), but the wind had changed and carried the disgusting smell towards me. My empty stomach began to contract, causing a sickening pain ; all my organs seemed to turn over. And still that fetid, infected air came towards me.

I was in despair and cried aloud.

Utterly crushed and broken, I lay there half unconscious, when suddenly . . . was I mistaken ? was it my disordered imagination ? I don't think so. Yes, there was a sound of voices, the clatter of horses' hoofs, and the voices of men. I was about to cry out but checked myself. Supposing they were the Turks ? To my present sufferings would be added still worse ones, so horrible that it makes one's hair stand on end even to read of them in the papers. They will skin me alive, roast my wounded leg . . . that would be bad enough, but they might even invent something worse. Was it better dying at their hands than here alone ? But what if it be our men ? Oh, those cursed bushes ! why do they surround me like a thick hedge, so that I can see nothing through them ? There was only a little opening like a small window through which I got a glimpse of the glade in the distance. A stream flowed through it, the same stream at which we had quenched our thirst before the battle. A sandstone slab placed across it served as a little bridge. They will probably cross it. The voices ceased. I did not recognise the language they had used: my hearing had become weak. Heavens! if only they are our men! I will call out to them; they will hear me even from the stream. I will do it even though I risk falling into the hands of the barbarians. Why are they so long in coming? My impatience was exhausting me. I did not even notice the smell of the corpse although it was no better than before.

Suddenly, by the little bridge, I caught sight of some Cossacks! Blue uniforms, red stripes, and bayonets. There were about fifty of them. At the head, on a fine horse, rode the dark-bearded captain. As soon as the last man had crossed the stream the captain turned in his saddle and shouted "Quick march!"

"Stop! Stop! For God's sake! Help! Help, comrades!" I cried, but the stamping of dozens of horses, the clanking of the sabres, the noisy chatter of the men, drowned my voice and they did not hear me!

Oh God! In my weakness I fell on my face and sobbed aloud. The gourd toppled over and the water began to trickle out—the water that meant life and salvation; but I did not notice it until there was only about half a glassful left, and the rest had been absorbed by the dry parched soil.

This last stroke quite numbed me. I lay quite still with half-open eyes. The wind was constantly changing, sometimes giving me a breath of fresh air and then carrying the horrible smell towards me. By this time my neighbour had become too horrible for description. Once when I opened my eyes to look at him I was terrified. The flesh on his face was already eaten away, only the bones remained. That constant bony grin was too horrible to contemplate, yet I had many times handled a skull. This skeleton in uniform, with its shining buttons, made me shudder. "Such is war," I thought; "war as it actually is."

The sun was hot and scorching as before. My face and hands were long burnt. The water was all gone. I had intended to drink the remainder in little sips, but my thirst was so overpowering that I emptied the gourd at one gulp. Ah! Why did I not call out to the Cossacks when they were nearer? Even had they been Turks, it would have been better than this. At most they would have tortured me for an hour or two, whereas now I do not know how long I shall have to lie and suffer here.

Mother! Dear mother! If you knew you would tear your grey hair, you would beat your head against the wall and curse the day on which I was born. You would curse the whole world for inventing such a torture as war!

But you are no doubt with Masha and do not know my plight. Good-bye, mother; good-bye, Masha, my sweetheart, my love! Ah how hard, how bitter it is! Something is gripping my heart! Again I see that little white dog! The porter had no pity on it, knocked its head against a wall and threw it on a rubbish heap. It was not quite dead, and must have lain there in agony for a whole day. And I am still more unfortunate, for my agony has lasted three days. To-morrow will be the fourth, and after that will follow the fifth, the sixth. . . . Where art thou, Death? Come, come and take me! But Death does not hear.

And I lie there under the blazing sun without so much as a drop of water to cool my burning throat, while the corpse is infecting me. Millions of worms are crawling over him. When they are finished with him nothing but his bones and his uniform will remain. Then my turn will come and I shall fare no better than he.

The day went by, and the night, but no change. Morning came and still no change. Another day will come. . . .

The bushes swayed and rustled gently. "You will die, die, die," they seemed to be murmuring. "You will never see your home, never, never, never," the bushes on the other side replied.

"You will never find any there—" I heard a loud voice suddenly near me.

I started and came to myself in an instant. The gentle blue eyes of Hakoolev, our corporal, were looking down at me from among the bushes.

"Bring the spades!" he shouted. "Here are two more. One of our men and one of theirs."

"You will not need spades—don't bury me. I am alive!" I wanted to cry out, but only a faint moaning escaped my parched lips. "My God! Can he be alive? Mr. Ivanov! Here, boys! Quickly! Our gentleman is alive—call the doctor!"

In an instant they were pouring water down my throat—vodka and something else. Then all vanished.

The stretcher moved along with a gentle swing, with a motion soothing as a lullaby. One moment I am awake, the next, again unconscious. My bandaged wounds no longer hurt me.

An inexpressible feeling of joy pervaded my whole body.

"Stop! Lower! Men of the four relief, March! To the stretcher! Take hold! Lift!"

Thus commanded Peter Ivanitch, our field hospital captain, a tall, gaunt, good-natured man. He was so tall that as I raised my eyes to look at him I could only see his enormously long beard and his shoulders, though the stretcher was being carried by four tall soldiers.

"Peter Ivanitch!" I whispered.

"What is it, old man?" He leaned over me.

"Peter Ivanitch, what did the doctor say? Shall I die soon?"

"Nonsense, Ivanov! You are not going to die. Not a bone in your body is broken. Lucky beggar! All your bones and arteries are whole. How did you manage to exist these three and a half days? What did you eat?"

"Nothing."

"And drink?"

"I took the Turk's gourd. I can't talk much now; I will tell you later."

"Well, God be with you, comrade. Try to sleep."

Again sleep, oblivion. . . .

I awoke in the field hospital. The doctor and a nurse were standing over me, and beside them was a famous professor from St. Petersburg who was bending over my legs. His hands were stained with blood. For a while longer he occupied himself with my legs and then he turned to me.

"God has been good to you, young man! You will live. We have only cut off one of your legs, but that is nothing serious. You may speak if you want to."

I spoke, and told them all that I have written here.

THE SIGNAL

Vsevolod M. Garshin

SEMEN IVANOV served as a surfaceman on the railway. His cabin was twelve versts distant from one station and ten from the other. The year before, a large weaving mill had been established about four versts away, and its tall chimneys looked black from behind the trees of the wood; and nearer than this, apart from the other cabins, there was no human habitation.

Semen Ivanov was a sickly, broken-down man. Nine years before he had gone to the war: he served as orderly to an officer and had remained with him during the whole campaign. He starved and froze, and baked in the hot sun, and marched from forty to fifty versts in the frost or in the burning heat. It also happened that he was often under fire, but, thank God, no bullet ever touched him.

Once his regiment was in the first line; for a whole week the firing was kept up constantly on both sides: the Russian line on this side of the hollow and the Turkish lines just across, and from morning till night the firing was going on. Semen's officer was also in the front lines, and three times a day, from the regimental kitchens in the hollow, Semen carried the hot samovar and the food. Semen walked through the open space while the bullets whistled over his head and cracked the stones. Semen was afraid, but he went on; wept, and went on. The officers were very much satisfied with Semen's services: the officers always had their hot tea.

Semen returned from the war without a wound, but with a rheumatic pain in his legs and arms. And he had suffered a good deal of sorrow since that time. His old father died soon after his return, then his little son, a boy of four, also died from some throat trouble; and Semen was left alone in the world with his wife.

Their work on the little piece of land allotted to them also proved unsuccessful, it being too hard for a man to till the soil with swollen arms and legs. And so they could not get along in their native village, and decided to go into new places in search of better luck. Semen lived with his wife on the Done for some time, and in the Government of Cherson; but somehow they could not get along very well anywhere. At last his wife went into service, and Semen continued his roving life as heretofore.

Once he happened to go by rail, and at one station he noticed the station-master, who seemed rather familiar to him. Semen looked at him intently, and the station-master also peered into Semen's face. They recognised each other: it was an officer of his regiment. "Is it you, Ivanov?" said the man.

"Yes, Your Honour, my very self."

"How did you get here?" And so Semen told him the story of his misadventures.

"Well, where are you going now?"

"I cannot say, Your Honour."

"How is that, you absurd fellow; you cannot say?"

"Just so, Your Honour, because I have nowhere to go to. I must look for some kind of employment, Your Honour."

And the station-master looked at him for a moment and fell to thinking, then said to him: "Well, brother, stay here at the station in the meantime. But it seems to me that you are a married man? Where is your wife?"

"Yes, sir, I am married; my wife is serving at the house of a merchant at Kursk."

"Well, then, write to your wife to come here. I shall get a free ticket for her. We shall soon have a vacant cabin on the line, and I will ask the division-superintendent to give you the place."

"Many thanks, Your Honour," replied Semen.

And so he remained at the station, helping in the station-master's kitchen, cutting wood, sweeping the courtyard and the platform. In two weeks his wife arrived, and Semen went on a hand-car to his new home.

The cabin was new and warm, wood he had in plenty, the former watchman left a small garden, and there was a little less than one and a half acres of arable land on the two sides of the line. Semen was overjoyed: he began to dream of a little homestead of his own, and of buying a horse and a cow.

He was given all the necessary supplies: a green flag, a red flag, lanterns, a signal-pipe, a hammer, a spanner for tightening the screw-nuts, a crowbar, shovel, brooms, nails, bolts, and two books with the rules and regulations of the railroad. At first Semen did not sleep at night, for he was continually rehearsing the regulations. If the train was due in two hours, he had already gone his rounds, and would sit on the little bench at the watch-house and look and listen: were not the rails trembling, was there no noise of an approaching train?

At last he learned by heart all the rules; though he read with difficulty and had to spell out each word, nevertheless he did learn them by heart.

This happened in summer: the work was not hard, there was no snow to shovel, and, besides, the trains passed but rarely on that road. Semen would walk over his beat twice in twenty-four hours, would tighten a screw here and there, pick up a splinter, examine the water-pipes, and go home to take care of his little homestead. The only thing that bothered him and his wife was: no matter what they made up their minds to do, they had to ask the permission of one official, who again had to lay the matter before another, and when permission was at last given the time had already passed, and it was then too late to be of any use to them. On account of this, Semen and his wife began, at times, to feel very lonely.

About two months passed in this way; Semen began to form acquaintance with his nearest neighbours, surfacemen like himself. One was already a very old man, whom the railway authorities had long intended to replace; he could hardly move from his cabin, and his wife attended to his duties. The other surfaceman, who lived nearer to the station, was still a young man, thin and sinewy. Semen met him for the first time on the permanent way half-way between their cabins, while they were making their rounds; Semen took off his cap and bowed. "Good health to you, neighbour," he said.

The neighbour looked at him askance. "How are you?" he replied, turned, and went his way.

The women also met afterwards. Arina, Semen's wife, greeted her neighbour affably, but this neighbour, also not of the talkative kind, spoke a few words and walked away. On meeting her once, Semen asked:

"Why is your husband so uncommunicative, young woman?" After standing for some time in silence, she said: "But what should he talk to you about? Everybody has his troubles—God speed you."

But after another month had passed, their intimacy grew. Now, when Semen and Vasili met along the line, they sat down on the edge, smoked their pipes, and told each other of their past life and experiences. Vasili spoke but little, but Semen told of his campaign life and of his native village.

" I have seen plenty of sorrow in my time, and God knows I am not so very old either. God has not given us much luck. It just depends : the kind of a lot the dear Lord portions out to one—such he must have. That is the way I make it out, Vasili Stepanich, little brother."

And Vasili struck the bowl of his pipe on the rail to empty it, and said : " It isn't luck nor fate which is eating your life and mine away, but people. There is not a beast more cruel and rapacious than man. A wolf does not devour a wolf—but man eats man alive."

" Well, brother, wolf does eat wolf—that is where you are wrong."

" It came to my tongue, so I said it ; anyhow there is not a more cruel beast. If it were not for man's viciousness and greed, 'twould be possible to live. Every one is on the look-out to grasp at your vitals, tear off a piece, and gobble it up."

" I don't know, brother," said Semen after thinking a bit. " Maybe it is so ; but if it is so, then the great God ordained it in this way."

" And if it is so," spoke Vasili, " then there is no use of my speaking to you. A man who attributes to God every kind of iniquity, and himself sits and patiently bears it, cannot be a man, brother mine, but an animal. There you have my whole say ! " And he turned and went off without even saying good-bye. Semen rose also and called after him : " Neighbour, what are you abusing me for ? "

But the neighbour did not even turn round, and went his way.

Semen looked after him till he was lost from sight at the turn of the road, then he returned home and said to his wife : " Well, Arina, what a venomous man that neighbour of ours is ! " Nevertheless they were not angry with each other ; and when they met again they spoke as if nothing had happened and on the very same topic.

" Ah, brother, if it were not for the people, we should not sit here in these cabins," said Vasili.

" Well, what if we do live in a cabin ? It is not so bad to live in one, after all."

" Not so bad to live, not so bad—— You have lived long, but gained little ; looked at much, but seen little. A poor man, no matter where he lives, in a railway cabin or in any other place, what sort of a life is his ? Those leeches eat your life away, squeeze all your juice out, and when you have grown old they throw you out like some swill, for the pigs to feed on. How much wages do you get ? "

"Well, not much, Vasili Stepanich, twelve roubles."

"And I thirteen and a half. Allow me to ask you why? According to the by-laws of the administration, every one of us is supposed to get the same amount—fifteen roubles a month, and light and heat. Who was it that allotted you and me twelve, or say, thirteen and a half roubles? Allow me to ask you? And you say it is not so bad a life? Understand me well, it is not about the three, or one and a half roubles I am wrangling about, but even if they paid me the whole amount—— Last month I was at the station when the director happened to pass. I saw him there. Had the honour. He occupied a whole private car by himself; at the station he alighted and stood on the platform, looking—— No, I will not stay *here* long; I shall go where my eyes lead me!"

"But where will you go, Stepanich? Let well alone. You will not find it much better anywhere. You have a home here, warmth, and a bit of land. Your wife is an able workwoman——"

"Land! You ought to see the land I have—why, there isn't a stick on it. This spring I planted some cabbages. Well, one day the section-inspector passed: 'What is this?' he says. 'Why did you not report it? Why not have waited for permission? Dig it up at once; not a trace must be left of it.' He was half boozed. At another time he would not have said a word. Three roubles fine!"

For some moments Vasili pulled at his pipe in silence, then said in a low voice: "It needed but little more and I should have made short work of him."

"Well, neighbour, you *are* a hot-head, I can tell you."

"I am *not* hot, I am only speaking and considering everything from the point of justice. But he will get it from me yet, the red-mug; I shall complain to the superintendent of division. We shall see!"

And he did in fact complain.

One day the superintendent of the division came to make a preliminary inspection of the line. In three days' time very important gentlemen were expected from St. Petersburg to make an inspection of the road: everything had to be made ship-shape; some new gravel was ordered before their arrival, added, levelled, and smoothed out, the sleepers were examined, the nuts tightened, the verst-posts newly painted, and the order was given that some fine yellow sand be strewn over the crossings. A wife even drove her old man out of the nearest cabin, which he almost never left, in order to trim a little tiny grass-plot. Semen worked a whole week to bring everything into first-rate order, even mended his coat and burnished his brass badge till it shone. Vasili also worked hard. At last the superintendent arrived in a buzzing hand-car, worked by four men and making twenty versts an hour. It came flying toward Semen's cabin, and Semen sprang forward and reported in military fashion. Everything appeared to be correct.

" Have you been long here ? " asked the official.

" Since the second of May, Your Honour."

" Very well, thank you. And who is at Number 164 ? "

The inspector, who rode with him on the car, replied : " Vasili Spiridov."

" Spiridov, Spiridov—— Oh, the one you reported ? "

" The very same."

" Very well, let us have a look at Vasili Spiridov. Go ahead."

The workmen leaned upon the handles and the car sped away down the line. " There will be a fight between them and the neighbour," thought Semen, looking after the disappearing car.

About two hours later Semen went on his rounds. He saw that some one was coming toward him, walking along the line, and there was something white visible on his head. Semen strained his eyes to see. It was Vasili ; in his hand he carried a stick ; a small bundle was slung across his shoulders, and one cheek was tied up with a white handkerchief.

" Where are you going, neighbour ? " Semen shouted to him.

When Vasili approached him closer, Semen saw that he was as pale as chalk and wild-eyed ; and when he began to speak his voice broke.

" I am off to the city," he said, " to Moscow—to the head office of the administration."

" To the administration—— Is that it ? You are going to make a complaint, are you ? Better not, Vasili Stepanich. Forget it——"

" No, brother, I will not forget it. It is too late to forget. You see, he struck me in the face, struck me till the blood flowed. As long as I live, I will not forget it, nor let it go at this."

" Give it up, Stepanich," Semen spoke to him, taking hold of his hand. " I speak truth : you will not make things better."

" Who speaks of better ! I know myself that I will not make them better ; you spoke truly about fate—you did. I shall not do much good to myself, but one has to stand up for justice."

"But won't you tell me how it all came about?"

"How it all came about——? Well, he inspected everything, left the car on purpose to do so—even looked inside the cabin. I knew beforehand that he would be strict—so I had everything in first-class order. He was just going to leave when I came out with my complaint. He immediately burst forth: 'Here,' he said, 'is to be a Government inspection, and you dare come forward with your complaints about your vegetable garden! We are expecting privy councillors, and you come with your cabbages!' I could not control myself and said a word—not so very bad either, but it seemed to offend him, and he struck me—— And I stood there as if it was the most usual thing in the world to happen. Only, when they went off, I came to my senses, washed off the blood from my face and came away."

"And what about the cabin?"

"My wife is there, she will take care of the work; and, besides, the devil take their road, anyway! Good-bye, Ivanich," he said to Semen on taking leave of him; "I don't know if I shall find justice for myself."

"You don t mean to tell me that you will go on foot?"

"I shall ask them at the station to let me ride in a goods train; to-morrow I shall be in Moscow."

The neighbours took leave of each other and each went his way. Vasili stayed away for a long time. His wife did all the work for him, sleeping neither night nor day, and looked very worn and exhausted. On the third day the inspectors passed: an engine, guard's van, and two private cars, and Vasili was still absent. On the fourth day Semen saw Vasili's wife; her face was swollen with incessant weeping and her eyes were very red. "Has your husband returned?" he asked her. She only waved her arm, but did not utter a word.

. . . .

When still a little boy Semen had learned how to make willow pipes. He burnt out the pith, drilled out where necessary the tiny finger-holes, and finished the whistle of the pipe so artistically that almost anything could be played on it. At odd moments he now made lots of such flageolets and sent them by an acquaintance of his, a guard, to the city, where they were sold at a penny each. On the third day after the inspection he left his wife at home to meet the six o'clock train, took his knife and went into the woods to cut his willow sticks. He came to the end of his section, where the road made a sharp turn, descended the embankment and went up the hill. About a half verst farther was a large bog, around which grew splendid shrubs for his pipes. He cut a bundle of sticks and went home, again walking through the wood. The sun was already low; and a death-like quiet reigned all about; only the chirping of the birds could be heard and the crackling underfoot of the wind-fallen wood. A little more and he would reach the railway line; suddenly it seemed to him as if he heard coming from somewhere the clang of iron striking on iron. Semen hurried his steps. "What can it be?" he asked himself, knowing that no repairs were going on in that section at that time. He reached the edge of the wood. Before him rose high the embankment of the railway; and he saw on the top, on the line, a man squatting down at work on something. Semen began to ascend the embankment very quietly, thinking that some one was trying to steal the bolt-nuts. He saw the man rise; in his hand he held a crowbar; he quickly shoved the crowbar under the rail and gave it a push to one side. Semen felt everything grow dim; he tried to shout, but could not. He saw that it was Vasili, and made a dash for the embankment, but Vasili was already rolling down the other side of the embankment with spanner and crowbar.

"Vasili Stepanich! Little father, friend, come back! Give me the crowbar! Let us put the rail in place; no one will ever know. Come back, save your soul from a great sin!"

But Vasili did not even turn round, and went on into the woods.

Semen remained standing over the dislocated rail, his sticks lying in a heap at his feet. The train which was due was not a goods, but a passenger train, and he had nothing to stop it with: flag he had none. He could not put the rail into its right place; with bare hands one cannot fasten in the rail spikes. He had to run, run for dear life to his cabin for the necessary tools! God give him strength!

And Semen started to run breathlessly toward his cabin. He ran—now, now he would fall—at last he left the wood behind, he had only about seven hundred feet left to his cabin—suddenly he heard the factory whistle. Six o'clock, and at two minutes past six the train would pass. Great God! Save the innocent souls! And before his eyes he seemed to see how the left wheel of the engine would strike the cut rail, quiver, slant to one side, and tear the sleepers, knock them all to splinters; and just here is the rounded curve, and the embankment; and the engine, the cars, all would go pell-mell down, down from the height of seventy-seven feet, and the third-class cars were crammed full of people, little children among them. Now they were sitting tranquilly, not thinking of anything. O Lord, teach him what to do! No, he would not be able to get to the cabin and return in time.

Semen gave up his intention of running to the cabin, turned and ran back quicker than he had come, his head in a whirl. Not knowing himself what would happen, he ran up to the cut rail: his sticks lay scattered all around. He bent down and took one of the sticks, not understanding himself why he did it; and ran farther. And it seemed to him that the train was already approaching. He heard a far-away whistle, heard the rails begin to quiver measuredly and quietly: he had no more strength left to run. He stopped about seven hundred feet from the fatal spot: suddenly he became illumined, as it were, by a thought. He took off his hat, took from it a handkerchief; took out his knife from his boot-leg and crossed himself. God's blessing!

He slashed his left arm a little above the elbow with his sharp knife; the blood spurted down in a hot stream; he dipped his handkerchief in it, smoothed it out, tied it to his stick, and displayed his red flag. He stood waving the flag; the train was already in sight. The driver did not see him, he would come nearer, but at a distance of seven hundred feet he would not be able to stop the heavy train!

And the blood was pouring and pouring—— Semen pressed his hand to his side, but the blood would not stop; evidently he had made too deep a cut into the arm; his head was beginning to turn; he was getting dizzy, as if black flies were swimming in his eyes; then everything became altogether dark, and loud bells were ringing in his ears—— He no longer saw the train, no longer heard the noise: only one thought predominated: "I shall not be able to keep on my feet, shall fall down, drop the flag; the train will pass over me!—— Dear God, help, send some one to relieve me——" His soul became a void, and he dropped the flag. But the bloody flag did not fall to the ground: some one's hand caught it and raised it aloft in front of the oncoming train. The driver saw him and brought the engine to a stop.

. . . .

The people came rushing from the train; soon they gathered into a crowd; before them lay a man, unconscious, covered with blood; another man stood beside him with a bloody rag tied to a stick.

Vasili surveyed the crowd and lowered his head.

"Arrest me," he said; "it was I who cut the line."

ATTALEA PRINCEPS

VSEVOLOD M. GARSHIN

IN a certain large town there was a botanical garden, and in this garden was a large glass-house. The house was very beautiful, with its tall graceful columns and delicately wrought arches, particularly in the evening when the setting sun bathed it in rosy light and the fiery reflections danced and mingled together like the colours in some large precious stone. The plants within could be seen through the thick transparent glass, and though the house was large they were very crowded in it. Their roots were massed and tangled together, and they all fought one another for every available drop of water and every scrap of nourishment. The trees pushed their branches in among the palm leaves, bending and breaking them, and in their turn being bent and broken against the iron frames.

Though the gardeners were always busy, cutting, pruning, and training, they accomplished but little ; for the growth, space and freedom were necessary. The plants were beautiful delicate things, natives of the hot countries ; they dreamed of their homes and longed to be there. No matter how transparent the roof, it was not the blue sky. In winter, when the glass was covered with frost and snow, it was quite dark in the house. The wind would hoot and beat against the frames, making the plants tremble with fear. They would listen to the roar, and think of another wind, warm and moist, the wind of their beloved home countries. They longed to feel it fanning them once more, shaking their branches and playing with their leaves. But the air in the house was still ; unless perhaps some heavy storm would break the glass and let in a cold, sleety draught that made the leaves turn pale, shrivel up, and die.

The glass, however, was soon mended. The director of the gardens was a learned botanist of great repute, who would not permit of disorder, though actually he spent most of his time in a little glass laboratory, over his microscope.

Among the plants there was a lovely palm, more beautiful than all the rest. The director in his little laboratory gave it the Latin name of " Attalea." This was not its real name, but then, the botanists did not know its real name, so a little wooden label bearing the name " Attalea " was attached to its trunk.

One day there came to the garden a native of the country where this palm grew. When he caught sight of it he smiled, for it made him think of his home.

" Ah ! " he exclaimed, " I know this tree," and mentioned its proper name.

" I beg your pardon," the director called out from his laboratory, though he was at the moment engaged in dissecting some little stalk, " there is no such palm as you have just mentioned ; the one you are referring to is ' Attalea Princeps,' a native of Brazil."

" Oh, yes," the Brazilian said, " I daresay the botanists call it Attalea, but it has a real name of its own."

" A real and proper name is one that has been given by science," the director said drily, shutting the door of his laboratory, so as not to be disturbed by people who were too stupid to understand what was said to them.

The Brazilian stood for a long time gazing at the palm. A feeling of sadness came over him. He thought of his own country, of her lovely woods and sun and sky, of her wonderful beasts and birds, her vast pampas and glorious southern nights. It seemed to him that he had never been happy anywhere but at home, and he had been all over the world. He touched the palm with his hand, as though bidding it good-bye, then left the garden, and on the following day took ship for home. But the palm remained behind. She felt lonelier and sadder than ever.

For thirty feet she soared above the tops of the other trees, who did not like her, but envied her and considered her proud.

Attalea's height was only a source of grief to her : and besides, they were all together while she was quite alone. She remembered her home more than did the others, perhaps because she was nearer to the hateful glass roof that had taken the place of her home.

Occasionally she would get a glimpse of something blue. It was the sky, though strange and pale, yet it was the real blue sky.

When other trees gossiped among themselves Attalea would remain silent. She was always thinking how nice it would be to be out, even under that pale blue sky.

" I wonder whether they are going to water us soon," said a

sago palm, who was very fond of moisture ; " I am simply parched to-day."

" I am surprised at what you say, neighbour," said a large cactus ; " I should have thought the quantities of water you get every day would have been enough for you. Just look at me ; I get very little, and yet I am always fresh and succulent."

" We are not so frugal ; we cannot grow on poor, dry soil like you cacti ; we are not accustomed to living anyhow. Besides, no one asked your opinion."

The sago palm felt hurt and lapsed into silence. " As for me," the cinnamon remarked, " I am fairly contented with my position. It is dull here, of course ; but at any rate one is not afraid of being skinned."

" We are not all of us skinned, you know," a stately fern observed. " To some people I daresay even this prison must seem like a paradise after the miserable existence they have been accustomed to outside."

The cinnamon was offended and began a dispute. Some took her side, others that of the fern, and a quarrel ensued ; had they been able to move from their places a battle would have followed.

" I wonder why you all quarrel like this ! " Attalea interposed. " It is so senseless ! All this bitter feeling and irritation merely adds to your misfortunes. You had much better leave off and listen to me. I have a suggestion. Let us begin growing taller and broader ; let us spread our branches and lean against the frames with all our weight, so that the glass will be shattered into a thousand pieces and we can get out into the open. Of course, if we send out one little shoot, it is soon cut off, but what could they do against a hundred strong, determined branches ? We have only to work together in a friendly manner and we are sure to succeed."

No one interrupted the palm. All were silent, not knowing what to say. At last the sago palm gained courage.

" What nonsense ! " she said.

" What nonsense ! What nonsense ! " they all echoed in one voice, each endeavouring to show Attalea how absurd the plan was.

" An unheard-of idea ! Absurd ! Ridiculous ! "

" The frames are very strong ; we could not possibly break them. And even if we did, what then ? Men would come with choppers and knives and cut off our branches. They would mend the frames and everything would go on as before. The only difference would be that we should lose some of our limbs."

"As you please," Attalea replied. "Now I know what to do. I shall not trouble you any more. You can live as you choose; go on grumbling at each other and quarrelling about the amount of water you get, and remain for ever under this glass roof. I will find a way for myself. I am determined to see the sun and the sky, not merely through this iron grating and glass, and I shall certainly see them." And the palm looked down haughtily from her green summit on to the mass of foliage spread out beneath her. No one ventured to speak, only the sago palm whispered to a neighbour.

"We shall see how they will cut off her big stupid head, and then she will not be quite so conceited." Though they remained silent, one and all were angry with Attalea for her proud words. Only a little creeper approved of what she had said. It was the poorest, humblest little plant in the whole house, and had pale, flabby, little drooping leaves. It had no distinguishing feature of any kind; its only use in the house was to cover up the bare soil. It wound itself about Attalea's feet as it listened; her words seemed to be right. It had never known the south, but it also loved air and freedom, and looked upon the glass-house as a prison. "If an insignificant little creeper like myself can suffer through the loss of my grey sky, pale sun and cold rain, what must be the feelings of such a beautiful, powerful tree like Attalea?" it thought, as it wound itself caressingly about the palm.

"If I were a big tree, I would take her advice. We would grow up together and attain our freedom. The others would see that Attalea was right."

Unfortunately it was not a big tree, but only a humble, drooping little creeper. It could only wind itself still closer about Attalea's trunk, whisper words of love, and express a desire for the success of her undertaking. "Of course, it is not so warm with us, the sky is not so clear nor the rains so invigorating as in your country, but even we have a sky and sun and wind, such as they are. We have no such stately trees like you and your neighbours, with such large leaves and beautiful flowers, but we have some very nice trees like the fir, the yew, and the silver birch. A poor little creeper like myself can never hope to attain freedom, but you are so big and strong. Your trunk is firm and you have not much further to grow before you reach the glass roof. You will easily shatter it to pieces and once more see God's world. Then you must tell me if it is as beautiful there as it used to be. I shall be quite satisfied even with that."

" But why won't you come out with me, little creeper ? My trunk is firm and strong ; lean on it and climb up to me. I can carry you easily."

" Oh no ! How could I ? See what a sickly, weak, little thing I am ! I cannot even lift one little shoot. No ! I am not fit to be your comrade. Go on growing ! I wish you happiness ! The only thing I ask of you is that when you are free you will sometimes remember your little friend." Then the palm began to grow. Former visitors to the house were amazed at her enormous size, and with each month Attalea grew higher and higher. The director of the garden put this down to his excellent treatment, and was proud of his knowledge and the success of his work.

" Why, look at Attalea Princeps," he would say. " A specimen of her size is rarely met with even in Brazil. We apply all our knowledge so that the plants may develop here just as freely as in their native lands, and I think we have attained some measure of success." And with a self-satisfied expression he tapped the trunk of the tree with his cane, the blows resounding through the whole house. The leaves of the palm trembled. " He imagines that I grow for his pleasure," she thought. " Let him go on thinking so " ; and had she been able to express her thoughts aloud the director would have been surprised at her pain and wrath.

She continued growing, using up all her sap to increase her height, and denying the nourishment to her roots and leaves.

Sometimes it would seem to her that the distance between her and the roof remained the same, then she would strain with all her might. The frames were getting closer and closer, and at last a young leaf came into contact with the cold glass and iron.

" Look ! Look ! " the other plants exclaimed ; " see where she has got to ! Will she really do it ? "

" How she has grown ! " a stately fern remarked.

" I do not see anything to wonder at. If she had only grown as stout as I am that would have been another matter," observed a plant which had a trunk like a barrel.

" What is the use of stretching ? She will not accomplish anything by that. The iron gratings are strong and the glass is thick."

Another month went by and Attalea was still growing higher and higher, until at last she was leaning against the iron frames. There was no more room for her to grow. Her trunk began to bend, her foliage at the top doubled up, the cold iron joints cut into the tender flesh of her young leaves, destroying their beauty. But the palm had no pity for her leaves, and notwithstanding the discomfort she pressed heavily against the iron frames until at last they began to give way, though they were made of solid iron. Trembling with excitement, the little creeper watched the proceedings.

" Does it not hurt you ? " she asked the palm. " As the frames are so strong would it not be better to abandon your project ? "

" Hurt me ! what does that matter when I *want* my freedom ! Did you not encourage me ? " the palm replied.

" Yes, I did encourage you, but I had no idea how difficult it would be. It pains me to see you suffer like that."

" You need not pity me, little weakling. I am determined to be free or die."

At this moment there was a loud crash. The thick iron frames had given way at last. There was a shower of glass splinters, and one struck the director's hat as he was coming out of his laboratory.

" I wonder what has happened ? " he exclaimed nervously, when he saw the pieces of glass flying through the air. He stepped back a little and looked up at the roof. Attalea's beautiful crown, now straight once more, stood out proudly at the top.

" Is this all ? " she thought. " Was it for this that I worked and suffered for so long ; this that I considered my highest goal ? "

It was about the middle of autumn when Attalea put her head out of the hole she had made in the roof. There was a fine drizzle, half rain, half snow ; the wind was chasing the low-hanging clouds, and it seemed to Attalea that they would carry her away with them. The trees were already bare and looked like terrible ghosts. Only the firs and the yews were still green. They looked solemnly at the palm, as much as to say, " You will freeze to death. You do not know what frost is ; you are not hardy like us. Why did you come out of your warm house ? "

And Attalea realised that this was the end.

She began to freeze. " Should she go back under the roof again ? " But it was too late. She would have to stay there in the cold wind and snow, look out at the grey sky, the poor country, the dirty yard belonging to the garden, the huge dull town that could be seen through the mist, until, down there in the warm, men would decide what to do with her.

The director ordered the palm to be cut down.

"Of course, one could build a dome over her," he said, "but what would be the use? She would only break it again. Besides, it would cost too much. She had better be cut down." Attalea was tied up with ropes, so that she should not fall and break the walls of the house, then she was cut down very low, right by the roots. The little creeper wound about her trunk did not want to part with its friend and also fell under the axe. When the palm was removed, lying near her roots were the bruised little shoots and leaves of the creeper. "Take away that rubbish!" the director said. "It is getting yellow, and the axe has cut it up too much. Put something else in its place."

One of the gardeners pulled the little creeper out by the roots with one skilful stroke of his spade. He put it in a basket, took it out to the yard, and threw it on the dead palm that was lying in the dirt, already half-covered with snow.

IGNATI N. POTAPENKO

BIGGER THAN YOURSELF

FROM the wide-open gate of a tall many-storeyed house a man walked out into the street. It would be more correct to say that he shot out. Turning to the right, he did not walk along the pavement as people do ordinarily, but strode along.

As a matter of fact there was nothing particularly striking about the man. He was of middle height, broad-shouldered though not stout, and very healthy looking—his broad chest in particular bearing witness to that. His face was insignificant, one that would not attract attention or be easily remembered. The features were neither large nor small, neither handsome nor ugly, just medium—so to speak. He wore a beard—dark, with a red tinge in it, as though burnished by the sun; had side-whiskers on his cheeks, and a thin moustache. Notwithstanding the commonplace features of this man who had shot out of the gate of the tall house, all the passers-by stopped and stared at him curiously as he strode along.

He seemed, for the amusement of the public, to have gathered together purposely the strangest collection of apparel. He wore high boots with thick soles, that resounded loudly on the stone pavement. The boots came right over his knees, and his trousers were tucked into them. His broad pea-jacket, made of some strange home-spun the colour of camel skin, was open, and even when the air was still, its skirts standing out on either side of him looked as though they were blown out by the wind. Large glass buttons sparkled on his velvet waistcoat, and his neck was enveloped in a bright red shirt with a slanting opening. His thick, unkempt hair hung over his shoulders, and to crown the whole effect, he wore a black felt hat with an unusually wide brim. If we add that in his right hand he carried a thick stick which he had himself cut recently in the nearest wood and that he flourished his clenched left hand—that he wore a frown and two severe wrinkles on his forehead, it will be understood why the passers-by stepped to one side and stared at him so curiously.

His name was Fiesov, and there was hardly an inhabitant of the town that did not know him. It is true that he had been bred and born in that town and had lived there for twenty-four years, yet in all this time he had not accomplished anything outstanding. Yet he had a name and fame that no one would have dared to impugn.

Before he had shot out of the gate of the tall house and stalked along the street, Fiesov had had a certain interview. It took place on the fourth floor of the tall house, and inadvertently had a fateful significance.

In addition to the usually fierce expression of his face—which seemed as though he wished, with one blow of his hand, to strike all mankind on the cheek—two things were plainly visible: unwavering resolution and sarcasm. Fiesov showed his teeth and raised his clenched fist. Every one could see that.

For the sake of clearness and the full explanation of subsequent events, we will describe the scene that took place on the fourth floor of the tall house. It had happened only a quarter of an hour before. Fiesov had gone through the gate, also with resolution in his face, but without sarcasm. One might have noticed even that there was less resolution in his legs than there was in his face. But when he had walked through the yard, entered the hall, and was walking up the stairs, firmness entered his legs and chest, a thing, as is known, that always happens in the last moment before a decisive battle.

Getting up to the fourth floor he rang the bell without the slightest hesitation, and when the door was opened, he asked the maid with assurance:

" Is Varenka at home ? "

He was told that she was, and entered. He put his stick in a corner of the miniature hall, took his hat with him, and followed the maid into the drawing-room. No one was there, and the two doors, one to the left and one to the right, were firmly shut. It was a tiny room, long and narrow, and had one window. There was a small couch in a loose cover of sail-cloth to protect the upholstery beneath, one arm-chair, several other chairs, and a table. Poverty glanced out of every corner and from every crack of the floor, from which the stain was wearing. On the shelf stood some cheap objects of art, such as clay jugs, glass baskets, sea-shells, and empty scent-bottles. In the midst of them was a round mirror that distorted the face of any one that happened to look in it.

Fiesov paced the room, and the old floor groaned and trembled beneath his tread. Passing the mirror he glanced at it and became convinced that his face was pale. He grew angry with his face for being pale.

The bright rays of the summer sun streamed into the window from the street. It was hot and stuffy. His forehead shone with perspiration.

When the door to the right opened, he stopped suddenly and stared at the girl who entered. His eyes were small, sharp, and penetrating. The girl looked very young. There was something childish about her rather pale face. Small and thin, she wore a grey knitted shawl that hid her neck, shoulders, bosom and both hands.

" Oh, it is you, Misha ! " she said in amazement, opening wide her large blue eyes, and she seemed not at all pleased to see him.

" Yes . . . yes . . . I ! " Fiesov replied, remaining in his original attitude with his original expression.

" But why ? " she asked, looking away. " You told me that you would not come for a long time and would avoid me until . . . this would pass."

She had a soft caressing voice, but she was apparently trying to make it softer still in her anxiety not to offend her visitor.

" Yes, I thought I could, but later I became convinced that I couldn't . . . " Fiesov said, in the tones of a man sentenced to death. " And so I have come for the last time. I tell you, Varenka, that you alone are capable of bringing me to that broad path of useful social activity to which I am so strongly drawn. . . . And without you, without your support, I shall fall into an abyss from which I shall never rise. . . ."

A faint smile, that instantly vanished, appeared on the girl's thin lips.

" You exaggerate, Misha. Isn't that so ? . . ." she said simply.

" You will soon be convinced that I don't ! "

She shook her head.

" But, really, Misha . . . let us put this aside. . . . I can't. . . . What can I do ? I like you very much, but not in the way you want me to. I know you too well, Misha."

" You do not know me if you prefer some foppish nonentity in a fashionable coat and grey gloves to me ! "

Varenka blushed faintly.

" I assure you, you are mistaken. I don't prefer any one else at all. . . . You are quite mistaken."

" But I shall perish without you. . . . Do you hear ? . . . I have decided . . . yes, I have decided to die ! " Fiesov said, trying to make his rather thin voice sound deeper.

" Oh, don't ! " Varenka said, with a sweet smile. " That will never be ; you are not capable of it, Misha ! And really . . . it only seems to you . . ."

" Is this your last word ? "

" I have told you so already, Misha ! . . . When a few weeks have gone by, you too will see that you did not love me. You too cannot love me, just as I cannot love you. We know each other too well. You will only thank me . . ."

" No . . . perhaps some one else will say that for me. . . ."

" Really, Misha, you are quite incorrigible ! "

" Yes, I am incorrigible . . . incorrigible because I cannot enjoy an empty, commonplace life, because my soul is guided by ideals, and because even those nearest to me, those whom I value most on earth, either cannot or will not understand me. . . . But you will understand, Varenka, you will understand when it is too late. . . . Good-bye ! "

This small speech was made with warmth, with sparkling eyes and trembling voice. Fiesov was about to turn and go out, when he suddenly noticed a smile on Varenka's lips, a smile that she took no pains to hide.

" You are amused ! In vain, I assure you ! " he said.

" Not at all. I simply recalled what mother said about you. She said that you were very nice but had one failing—that you wanted to be bigger than yourself."

" Well, soon your mother and all of you will see that you were mistaken ! . . . Good-bye ! "

He turned right round and, seizing his stick in the hall, went out. He ran madly down the stairs and into the street in the manner in which we met him.

He flew home as fast as possible. He had a mother and sister in the town. They possessed a small income on which they lived free from want. But Fiesov did not live with them. It was already seven years since—being about to pass from the seventh to the eighth form—he left school and took rooms for himself. He considered the life led by his mother and sister too bourgeois.

" In the morning there is tea, at mid-day coffee and cream, dinner at three, tea again at seven, supper at ten, and bed at eleven, and so on every day of one's life! The devil knows what it all means!" he said, and decided to live by himself. He had, by the way, a little money of his own, the interest on which was sufficient to keep him. This act of his grieved his mother and sister, but that was of little consequence, since all his acts grieved them. The first grief he caused them was when he threw up his school. It was an inexplicable decision on his part, as he had passed the seventh form, and well, too.

"Why?" he was asked.

"Because, had I remained in the eighth form, it would have looked as though I were trying for a diploma, and that is commonplace. Every one does that."

And all these griefs came largely because "that is commonplace, every one does that." Settling in a furnished room, he at once introduced an order that was not at all like the order maintained by the rest of the world. There was a bed, but he ordered it to be removed, and slept on some kind of animal skin. He kept his books in the chest of drawers, while his linen was strewn about on the window-sill, on the writing-table, and sometimes even on the floor. The first thing in the morning, he ate a large piece of meat, and thus fortified himself until the evening, considering it a low occupation to spend much time over food—"a commonplace that everybody does." Then he eliminated from his toilet all the appurtenances considered necessary by ordinary folk, and made himself into such a scarecrow that his poor female relatives fainted at the sight of him. In the course of time he toned down some of the extremes and made his toilet more seemly, but his compromise did not carry him far enough to wear a starched collar, ordinary boots, or a hat with a less startling brim. Later, he began to reject practically everything that people considered comfortable, and as a result suffered real privations.

With it all he was quite sincere, and did everything from pure motives. From the time he was fourteen, there had grown in his heart a vague feeling that always kept him in a nervous state. Nothing satisfied him, and he was always hankering after something. As the years went by, this feeling grew to a painful degree, but became no clearer. It seemed as though an ulcer had grown in his breast and threatened all his body. Sometimes he was possessed by a feeling of universal love, and wanted to perform some act that would instantly save all mankind. However, he had no clear idea from what evil mankind was to be saved. Sometimes a fury seized him and he would be possessed with the desire to commit some great evil, also of a kind that would shake the earth and startle all its inhabitants. As a result, he would pursue his studies by fits and starts; sometimes he would abandon books for weeks at a time, at others seize them and learn his lessons so well as to astonish his masters. His capabilities were not very great, but determination helped them considerably.

There were not a few incidents in his life when glory seemed to approach him as it were, and he was separated from it only by the smallest interval. Once when he was walking by the river-bank he heard the cry of a drowning boy who was battling with death. The quick current was bearing him away to the depths. Our hero overflowed with benevolence. His eyes lit up, he rushed towards the river and began to take off his clothes. He removed his coat, his hat, his waistcoat, and by the time he got to his shirt, decided that it was not worth while risking his life for such an insignificant act, for the sake of saving the life of some perhaps worthless boy. Meanwhile a crowd had gathered, and a long-bearded workman stepped out, and without stopping to consider for a moment, plunged into the water as he was and began to swim. The workman saved the boy, while Fiesov remained on the bank waiting for the great deed with which he would save all mankind in one effort.

And as the occasion for such a deed did not arrive, and the ulcer in his bosom grew larger, he was constantly tossed from side to side: committed eccentricities; quarrelled with the police in the street when he was informed that "strangers were not admitted," when they "insulted his human dignity"; entered into disputes with neighbours at the theatre when they did not approve of an actor over whom he was in ecstasies; spoke excitedly, nervously, and loudly everywhere, of everything, and to every one, stamping his feet, banging his stick, and waving his arms. The only thing he accomplished was that he was considered an incorrigible crank by some, and a madman by others.

But all were mistaken in him. The real trouble was that he was very vain; he wanted to accomplish something great, whereas his powers were small. Nature frequently produces such contradictions, endowing with brilliant abilities a man who desires nothing of life but dinner, supper, and a warm bed, and putting into the heart of a weak "average man" the desire for great deeds.

Fiesov had many friends who were sincerely fond of him, but all thought of him with a smile. In reality he was a good fellow, sensitive to every kindly impulse, ready to give up anything to a man in want; all knew and valued this quality in him.

With Varenka he had been friendly from childhood, when suddenly a misfortune happened to them; he fell in love with her, and so violently that life without her seemed unbearable. There were long conversations, heated explanations, when with the heat of a lover he proved to Varenka how she must love him, how she was destined to make his life fruitful, that from that very moment he would give up his indefinite wanderings and begin his great work—though what it was to be he could not say. But that did not matter, it would become clear of itself. Love illuminates everything. Love is the most powerful lever in life!

But Varenka could not convince herself of this. She looked on Fiesov as a spoilt child that kindled itself with words but was incapable of any definite work. She fully shared her mother's opinion, that he was a good man, but that it was a pity he wanted to be larger than himself. The most important thing, though, was that Varenka, while appreciating his good qualities, did not love him. She told him so, and we witnessed their last resolute explanation.

Fiesov reached home. The maid who opened the door noticed something peculiar about him, but paid no special attention. She announced in the kitchen that "Fiesov has just come in furious. . . . As soon as he got in his room he began pacing up and down, from corner to corner, stamp, stamp, stamp, like the blows of a hammer." But in the kitchen they paid no attention to that. The housemaid and the other members of the kitchen could scarcely guess that the peculiar thing in Fiesov's face was nothing less than resolution, final and irrevocable.

Yes, he had decided. And what if he were pacing his room instead of sitting down to his writing-table, that looked more like a shop counter? Of course, he had many things to think over, very many. To disappear from the face of the earth without expressing himself from the depths of his soul, was far from his intention. If they could not value his life (he had Varenka in his mind), then they should value his death. But all this must be thought over so as to express his soul in a few words. He had no worries of any kind. His belongings and small capital would naturally go to his mother. There was no need to bother about that. He would have liked to bequeath it to mankind, but nothing would have come of it. Besides, humanity might go to the devil, since it did not appreciate his strivings (here too he meant Varenka).

At last he sat down by the table and began to write. The first letter was addressed to Varenka, and we give it, word for word :

" VARENKA—I should have desired my death not to cause you pain. I should have liked you to greet the news with a smile ; I should have liked your whole life to be one constant smile. I loved you. I speak as one dead, because, though the hand that pens this letter is still moving, I am already dead—yes, dead. You alone could have awakened me to life, but you did not wish to. God be with you ! Reviewing my whole life, I see that no one understood my aspirations. I had friends, but they liked me superficially. No one knew my soul, no one could look into it and see the impetuous strivings after the Ideal that never gave me peace. Oh, Varenka ! I dreamt that you were an exception. I dreamt that you were more clear-sighted than the rest, but I was mistaken ; you are just as short-sighted as the others. What is the use of living when your beloved refuses you support ? Life consists of days and days, of breakfasts, dinners, suppers and sleep, of commonplace interests, commonplace occupations and commonplace conversations. Is it worth while living only for this ? Humanity ? Oh, my God ! Humanity ! It prizes its commonplaces and is ready to stone its prophets. No, there is nothing great in life, and it is not worth while living for pettiness, that is, to spend life's energies in rising from bed, dressing, eating and cooking food, moving about, wagging one's tongue, and so on. And so it is settled. The thing you would not believe has happened. Varenka, I loved you with a holy love of which only the chosen are capable. But when you read this letter, I shall no longer be on this earth. Forgive me, and may God forgive you. Be happy.—Yours, M. FIESOV."

His hand flew swiftly over the paper. His bruised soul overflowed in phrases, naturally and easily. Having finished it, he re-read the letter once, twice, and a third time. It was expressive and strongly put. Varenka would be sorry and realise what she had lost.

Then he began a letter to his mother and sister. This was shorter :

" Because interests that were incomprehensible to you prevented me from expressing my feelings, do not imagine that I did not love you. I love you tenderly and fear more than anything that this news will drive you to despair, since I know that you, too, loved me. But alas, that love could not bind me to life! There is a higher love that lives only in the hearts of a few, but it does not meet with sympathy and dies with those hearts. All my belongings in things and money I bequeath to you. When you read this letter, I shall no longer be on the earth. Gather together all your strength to bear your loss bravely.—Your MICHAEL."

This letter, too, he read more than once, and found it touching and noble. Then he took several sheets of paper, and writing a few lines on each, addressed them to his various friends. All these letters had the same contents, and merely stated the bare facts of the case. They said:

"MY FRIEND H.—When you read this letter I shall no longer be on this earth. Life without love and glory, life without great deeds is not worth a movement of the finger, and so I die as simply and easily as I sit down to dinner.—Yours, FIESOV."

When he had finished all the letters to his friends (and there turned out to be two dozen of them) and got up from the table, his forehead and neck were bathed in perspiration, but he never even thought of taking his handkerchief from his pocket and wiping it off. When one has decided to die, one does not think of such nonsense.

He put the letters into envelopes, addressed them, and went out into the street. There was a post-office near by where he bought a number of stamps, which he fixed on to the envelopes. Then going up to the letter-box he dropped them in, one by one, unhesitatingly and with a firm hand. When one has made an irrevocable resolution, one does not stop at trifles. Then he returned home. . . .

People meeting him on the way walked past him without taking the slightest interest in him. He felt that the world, with its commonplace, empty life, seemed to walk away from him; he no longer felt himself to be a member of that big family called humanity.

He went home, entered his room, and locked the door. Pulling out the table-drawer, he took out a revolver, wiped it, examined it carefully, and being convinced that it was in perfect order, loaded it with six cartridges and put it on the table.

"And so all is ready! All is ready!" he thought. "One movement of my hand, a light pressure on the trigger, and life, with all its enigmas and enthusiasms, is over! How simple it is!"

He was very pleased with the idea that the question should be decided so simply. He took the revolver, put it against his temple, then removed it some distance and . . . for the time being, did not shoot; he was only trying it, so as not to make a mistake, and through some negligence, remain alive. "So," he said, and again put the revolver on the table.

For some reason he wished to review all the events of his life. However, this was always done on such occasions. When you finally take leave of something, you try to see clearly what it is you are losing. He paced up and down the room. Picture after picture rose before his eyes. There were many absurdities and stupidities, but so much noble fire, so much persistency and determination, so much strength. And it would all be wasted, go down to eternity with him at his last breath.

He walked up and down for two hours. The sun rose and the street lamps were extinguished. He felt hungry. It was somewhat strange. . . . But, after all, there was really nothing strange about it. His organism had gone through a terrible ordeal; in a few hours it had lived through a lifetime! Besides, he never ate anything after his morning beef-steak.

At first he wanted to deny his organism the satisfaction of this purely animal desire, in which there was nothing lofty. It was even incongruous, somehow, to be thinking of food a few hours, perhaps minutes, before death. But he was so irresistibly drawn towards the little low cupboard where his provisions were kept, that he could not control himself. He opened the door, and suddenly, in a terrible fright, jumped back against the opposite wall. A mouse had jumped from the cupboard and scampered into its hole in a corner of the room. He was unutterably afraid of mice.

It flashed through his mind that to be afraid of such a silly thing in his position was somewhat unseemly. All the same, he was afraid of mice and remained by the wall until his last enemy, his enemy at death's door, had disappeared into its hole.

Then he again approached the cupboard, took out some sausage, an open tin of sardines, a half-empty bottle of beer and a small bottle of vodka. He put all these things on the table, drank a little vodka, and began to eat with excellent appetite.

" Of course this does not change the facts of the case at all," he thought, and lit a candle. Feeling a little tired, he sat down in an arm-chair and became lost in thought. He was thinking of the same thing, that is, his past life as well as the future did not exist for him. . . .

. . . .

At nine o'clock in the morning of the following day there was a large concourse of people in the corridor of the house where Fiesov lived. All those friends of Fiesov's who had received his letter appeared there with peculiarly anxious faces; Varenka ran up, pale and excited; Fiesov's mother and sister drove up in a cab, both in a half-fainting condition. The landlord was also there, as well as a policeman and the district inspector.

As the fatal event was known to every one, they dispensed with preliminary attempts to get the door open and immediately employed a locksmith. While the locksmith was engaged on the lock, a restrained whispered conversation went on in the corridor. The landlord of the house expressed the opinion that the event was to be expected, and that in general Fiesov was capable of anything. The district inspector agreed with him. " Oh yes," he said, " he was bound to come to some such end; you know he has long been under observation at the police station." He was evidently of the opinion that every one who was under police supervision was bound to commit suicide. Varenka was crying and blaming herself as the chief cause of the catastrophe. The rest were perplexed, growing gradually accustomed to the idea that Fiesov was bound to have acted in that manner.

The locksmith turned to the district inspector. " It is ready, sir."

The inspector put his hand on the handle of the door, opened it cautiously, and walked in, followed by all the people gathered in the corridor.

For a moment all were dumbfounded at the picture before them. No one understood anything. Fiesov was sitting in an arm-chair, his long legs in their big boots being stretched out beneath the table. His head, resting against the back of the chair, hung to one side. On the table near him lay a revolver. The only strange thing was that there was no sign of blood anywhere, and his face was red and not pale, while it even seemed that there was perspiration on his forehead. His long hair fell untidily to one side.

" He still breathes!" some one remarked, noticing that Fiesov's powerful shoulders rose and fell like a wave on the sea.

" He breathes ! He breathes ! " they all cried out in chorus under the presidency of the district inspector, who, being by his calling unafraid of dead men, moved towards the table, and suddenly jumped back.

Fiesov rose up to his full height, and rubbing his eyes, looked at his guests.

He evidently could not make out what it was all about.

" What the devil is the matter ? " he said at last, in a sleepy voice. " Or am I dreaming ? "

" Mr. Fiesov, you informed your friends that you were going to lay hands on yourself," the district inspector said. " It is not fitting to make a jest of such a thing. You may even have to answer for it. . . ."

Fiesov suddenly remembered everything.

" The devil ! Of course ! How is it I went to sleep ? Eh ? " he said, seizing his head. " Well . . . well . . . I suppose it is fate."

To-day he hadn't the slightest desire to die. A good sleep had, like a hand, taken from him his mood of yesterday.

The inspector walked out, severely followed by the policeman, while Fiesov's friends stayed behind to congratulate him on his fortunate and miraculous escape from death.

. . . .

Five years later, Fiesov might have been met every morning at nine o'clock making his way to a certain office, and at three o'clock on his way back. He was smartly dressed, wore short hair and a bowler hat. Being at last convinced that you cannot make yourself bigger than you are, he resigned himself, took a place in a business office, and began to live as all do.

There were rumours that Varenka was no longer averse to accepting a proposal from him if he made it now, and as he still preserved his former attachment towards her, there is no doubt that the proposal was made and that the marriage took place.

ANTON P. CHEKHOV
1860–1904

DARLING

OLIENKA, the daughter of the retired civil servant Plenianikov, sat musing outside in her little porch. It was hot; the tiresome flies were very persistent; it was pleasant to think that it would soon be evening. Dark, rain-laden clouds were coming up from the East, whence every now and again the distant rain could be seen.

In the middle of the yard stood Kukin, theatrical producer and proprietor of "The Tivoli" pleasure gardens, who lodged in a wing of the house. He stood looking out on the sky.

"Again!" he said in a tone of despair. "It is going to rain again! Every day, rain! rain! It seems to rain out of sheer perversity. It spells ruin to me! Every day of it means a terrible loss!"

He clasped his hands and turned to Olga Semionovna:

"It is enough to make a man cry! You work and strive and worry; you lie awake at night, thinking out ways and means of improving things, and what is the result? First you have the stupid ignorant public; you give it the best little operettas, cantatas, beautiful duets, but do you think it appreciates them? Do you think it understands them? Not a bit. What it wants is low comedy. Give it something vulgar. And then, look at the weather! Every evening it rains. It has been raining steadily from the 10th of May and all through June. It is simply dreadful. The public does not come, but the artists will not forgo their pay nor the landlord his rent."

On the following day, when, towards evening, the clouds began to gather again, Kukin held forth with a hysterical laugh:

"Well, let it rain! Let the garden get flooded with water, and may I drown in it, so that I shall have no more happiness in the next world than in this. Let the actors sue me! I don't care! Let them sentence me to hard labour in Siberia! To the scaffold! Ha! Ha! Ha!"

The same thing was repeated on the third day.

Olienka would listen seriously to Kukin, not saying a word, and sometimes her eyes would fill with tears. In the end she was touched by Kukin's misfortunes and fell in love with him. He was small and thin, had a reedy Jewish voice, a waxed moustache, and a yellow face that bore a perpetual expression of despair, but still he inspired in her real, deep love. She could not exist without love, and was always in love with some one or other. Once it was her father, who was now an invalid in an arm-chair, who sat in a dark room battling for breath. Then it was her aunt, who lived at Bransk, and came to visit them twice a year, and earlier, when she was still at school, she had been in love with her French master.

Olienka was a healthy, quiet, good-natured, kind-hearted girl. Looking at her plump rosy cheeks, her soft white neck with the mole on it, her good-natured smile that never failed to appear when something pleased her, men would say to themselves, " Yes, she is quite pretty," and respond to her smile, while lady guests would sometimes, in the middle of a conversation, seize her by the hand and exclaim, in an outburst of affection, " You darling ! "

The house (in which she had lived since her birth) was situated on the outskirts of the town, in Gipsy Lane, not far from the " Tivoli " gardens. In the evenings she could hear the music in the gardens and the noise of the fireworks in the air, and it seemed to her that there Kukin was battling with his fate and assailing his principal foe—the indifferent public. A sweet trembling would come over her heart, the desire for sleep would leave her, and when, towards morning, Kukin returned home, she would tap gently at her window, put out her head and give him a gentle smile.

Soon he proposed to her and they were married. When he was privileged to see her white neck and full round shoulders, he clapped his hands and exclaimed, " You darling ! "

He was happy in his own way, but as it rained on his wedding day, the look of despair did not leave his face.

After the wedding they lived together very happily. She would sit in the box-office, see that the gardens were tidy, keep the accounts, and pay the wages ; her rosy cheeks and sweet naïve smile now shining from the little box-office window, now from the wings of the stage, now from the buffet. And she went about telling her acquaintances that there was nothing more necessary or important in the world than the theatre, and that it was the only thing that afforded true pleasure and made one cultured and humane.

"But do you think the public sees this ?" she would ask. "What it wants is low comedy ! Yesterday we gave a performance of *Faust*, and would you believe it, all the boxes were empty. If Vanotchka and I had put on some vulgar piece the theatre would have been packed. To-morrow Vanotchka and I are producing *Orpheus in Hell*. You must come and see it."

Everything that Kukin said she repeated. Like her husband, she too despised the public for its boorishness and indifference to art. She would interfere at rehearsals, correct the actors, supervise the behaviour of the musicians, and when an adverse criticism appeared in the local paper, she would cry bitterly and rush off to the editor to protest and explain.

All the actors liked her ; they used to call her "Vanotchka and I," or "Darling." She was very good to them, would lend them small sums of money, and if it so happened that she was sometimes deceived in one of them, she would indulge in a good cry all by herself, but would never complain to her husband.

In the winter, too, they lived together happily. They took the town theatre for the season and let it out for short periods to little Russian touring companies, to conjurors, or to local amateurs. Olienka filled out and literally shone with contentment, while Kukin grew thinner and more yellow, and would go about complaining of his losses, though in reality his affairs went remarkably well the whole winter. He used to cough at night, and his wife would give him raspberry syrup, lime-flower tea, or she would bathe his forehead with eau-de-Cologne and wrap him up in her soft shawls.

"What a dear you are !" she would say quite sincerely, stroking his hair. "How handsome you are !"

In Lent he went to Moscow to get together a company, and she, left alone, could not sleep at nights, but would sit at the window gazing at the stars. At such times she would compare herself to the hens that were restless and could not settle down at night without a rooster.

Kukin was detained in Moscow. He wrote saying that he would return by Holy Week, and made arrangements regarding the "Tivoli." But on Monday of Passion Week, late at night, there was a loud ominous knock at the gate—Boom ! Boom ! Boom ! The sleepy cook, shuffling along in her bare feet, went to open it.

"Open, please !" a deep voice said from the other side of the gate, "there is a telegram for you."

This was not the first time Olienka had received a telegram from her husband, but, somehow, she grew cold all over. With trembling hands she tore open the telegram and read the following words, "Ivan Petrovitch died suddenly to-day. We await instructions for funeral on Tuesday."

The signature was that of the manager of the company.

"My darling!" Olienka sobbed aloud. "My own dear Vanotchka! Why did we ever meet? Why did I get to know and love you? Why have you left your poor unfortunate Olienka? . . ."

Kukin was buried on Tuesday in Moscow at Vagankov cemetery. Olienka returned home on Wednesday, and reaching home, she threw herself on her bed, crying so loudly that her plaints could be heard in the street.

"Darling!" said the neighbours, crossing themselves; "Darling Olga Semionovna is bewailing her husband."

One day, three months later, when Olienka was returning from church dressed in deep mourning, one of her neighbours, Vassily Andreyitch Pustovalov, who was also returning from church, happened to be walking at her side. He wore a straw hat and a white waistcoat, across which hung a gold chain, and looked more like a country squire than a merchant.

"Everything has its meaning," he said gravely, with a sympathetic tone in his voice. "If some one near to us happens to die, it is by the will of God. We must think of ourselves and bear our sorrows humbly."

He accompanied Olienka right to her door and there left her. For the rest of the day she could hear his steady voice, and she had only to close her eyes in order to see his dark beard. She had taken a great liking to him. Apparently she, too, had made an impression on him.

Not many days later, a certain old lady whom she knew but little, came to take coffee with her, and no sooner was she seated than she began talking of Pustovalov, saying what a good, respectable man he was, and that many women would be only too glad to get the chance of marrying him. Three days later Pustovalov himself came to visit her. He did not stay for more than ten minutes or so, and said very little, but Olienka fell in love with him, so deeply, that she lay in a fever the whole night and could not close her eyes. The following morning she sent for the old lady. Soon she was engaged and not long after she married.

After the wedding Pustovalov and Olienka lived together happily. He would work in his office until dinner-time, after which he would go out on business and Olienka would take his place until the evening, making up accounts and attending to the despatch of goods.

" Timber is getting twenty per cent dearer every year," she would say to her customers and acquaintances. " Why, not long ago we used to sell local timber entirely, now Vasitchka has to go and buy it in the government of Mogilev. And what an awful tariff we have to pay ! " she would exclaim, holding her hands up in horror. " What a tariff ! "

It seemed to her that she had dealt in timber for years and years, and that the most important and necessary thing in the world was timber. She would pronounce the technical terms, like beam, plank, joist, deal, batten, etc., with a touching sense of kinship.

In her dreams at night she would see mountains of boards and planks, and long chains of carts carrying timber out of the town. Once she dreamt that a whole regiment of beams invaded the yard, and a fierce battle ensued. The planks and beams struggled with one another, falling in heaps with a tremendous crash and getting up again. She cried aloud in her sleep, and Pustovalov said gently, " Olienka, dear, what is the matter with you ? Cross yourself ! "

What her husband thought, she thought also. If, for instance, he thought that it was too hot in the room, or that business was slack, she thought so too. Her husband did not care for outside amusements, and would stay at home even during holidays, and she would always stay with him.

" You are always at home or at the office," her friends would say to her. " Why don't you go to the theatre or the circus occasionally ? "

" Vasitchka and I have no time for the theatre," she would reply solemnly. " We are hard-working folk, and have no time to waste on nonsense Besides, what good is there in a theatre ? "

On Saturday evenings Pustovalov and Olienka would go to church, and on all feast days to early service. They would return home from church side by side, their faces the embodiment of kindliness. They were both slightly perfumed, and Olienka's silk dress rustled pleasantly. When they got home they would have tea and milk-bread, with various jams, and afterwards pies. Always about mid-day an appetising smell would issue from their door, past the gate, into the street,—a smell of soup, roast lamb or duck, varied on fast days by that of fish. One's appetite was always whetted on passing their gate. In the office a samovar was always ready, and the customers were given tea and rolls. Once a week husband and wife would go to the baths and return side by side, both very red.

"We have nothing to complain of: we live very well, thank God!" Olienka would say to her acquaintances. "God grant every one such happiness as Vasitchka and I have."

When Pustovalov went away to Mogilev to buy timber, she felt very lonely, and would lie awake, crying, the whole night. Sometimes, in the evening, Sinerdin, a young army veterinary surgeon who lodged in the wing of her house, would come and sit with her. He would talk or play cards, and amuse her for a while. She was especially interested to hear about his own private life. He was married and had a little boy. He did not live with his wife, for she had deceived him, but sent her a monthly allowance of forty roubles for the boy. When he talked of his family Olienka would sigh, shake her head, and feel very sorry for him.

"God be with you," she would say as she bade him good-night and accompanied him to the top of the stairs with a candle. "Thank you for trying to amuse me. God grant you health. Our holy Mother . . ."

She expressed herself in the same grave, solemn manner as her husband. When the veterinary surgeon had gone down the stairs and was already out of the door she still called after him:

"Do you know, Vladimir Platonitch, you should try to get reconciled to your wife. You should forgive her, if only for your boy's sake. Boys understand so much."

And when Pustovalov returned, she told him in a whisper about the veterinary surgeon's unhappy married life, and they both sighed and shook their heads, and talked about the boy, whom they feared must miss his father. Then, by some strange bond of sympathy, they both fell on their knees before the holy image, bowed down to the ground, and prayed that God would bless them with children.

Thus the Pustovalovs lived quietly and peacefully in love and concord for six years, when one winter day, Vasily Andreyitch having gone out without a hat on after drinking some hot tea, caught a chill and took to his bed. The best doctors attended him, but the illness ran its course, and he died after four months. Olienka was again a widow.

Why did you leave me, my darling!" she sobbed at the funeral.

" How can I live without you, poor unfortunate wretch that I am ? Good people pity me, a poor orphan. . . ."

She dressed herself in deep mourning and gave up wearing a hat and gloves. Rarely did she go out of the house, and then only to church or to visit her husband's grave, and she lived at home like a nun. It was not until six months after her husband's death that she put off her widow's weeds and opened the shutters of her windows. Sometimes, in the morning, she would be seen marketing with her cook, but as to how she lived at home and what was happening there, people could only guess. They guessed by such signs as, for instance, that she was seen taking tea in the garden with the veterinary surgeon, and that he read the paper aloud to her ; that once, when she met an acquaintance in the street, she was reported to have said :

" We have no adequate veterinary supervision in our town, and as a consequence disease is frequent. For instance, one hears of people falling ill through drinking bad milk, or by being infected by horses and cows. We ought to be just as careful about the health of our animals as we are of our own health."

She repeated the veterinary surgeon's words and held all his opinions about everything. It was clear that she could not live without an attachment, and had found her happiness in the little wing of the house. Neither she nor the veterinary surgeon spoke to people about their new relations, and tried to keep it secret, but they were not successful, for Olienka could have no secrets. When his colleagues from the regiment came to visit him, she would give them supper and pour out their tea ; at the same time she would talk about the plague that had attacked the cattle, and complain about the town slaughter-house, while the veterinary surgeon would feel very uncomfortable, and as soon as the others had gone would seize her by the hand and whisper angrily :

" I've told you not to talk about things you don't understand ! When my colleagues and I are talking, I must ask you not to interfere. This is too much ! "

She would look at him in amazement and ask anxiously :

" But, Volodotchka, what can I talk about ? " and with tears in her eyes she would put her arms round him, beg him not to be angry, and they would make it up.

However, this happiness did not last long. The veterinary surgeon departed with his regiment, departed for ever, as he was stationed far away, near Siberia. And Olienka was left alone.

Now she was quite alone. Her father had died some time before, and his chair, covered with dust and with one leg broken, reposed somewhere in the garret. She grew thin and plain, and when people met her in the street they no longer looked at her nor greeted her with a smile as of old. Clearly her best years had gone by, and she had begun some new kind of life, strange and unknown, about which it was better not to think.

In the evenings Olienka would sit at her little porch and listen to the music and the fireworks at the " Tivoli," but it meant nothing to her. No longer did it inspire thoughts. She would look out on her empty yard, thinking of nothing, desiring nothing, and when night came she would go to bed and dream of the empty yard. She ate and drank almost mechanically.

And what was worse than all, she no longer had any opinions. She saw the objects around her and understood all that went on, but she could not form any opinion about these things, and did not know what to talk about. How awful it is not to have opinions! For instance, you see a bottle, or it rains, or a peasant drives by in a cart, but why the bottle stands there, or the rain falls, or the peasant passes, what meaning there is in these things, you could not say for a thousand roubles. In the days of Kukin and Pustovalov, and later, in the time of the veterinary surgeon, Olienka would have explained everything and given her opinions on any subject, but now her mind and heart were as empty as her yard. It was as bitter and painful as gall.

Little by little the town expanded on all sides. Gipsy Lane was now called a street, and in place of the " Tivoli " gardens and the timber yards there were little streets of houses. How quickly time flies! Olienka's house was no longer white, the roof was rusty and the garden filled with weeds. Olienka herself grew old and plain. In the summer she would sit at her little porch, her soul as sad and empty as ever, and in winter she would sit by the window and look out upon the snow. With the coming of spring, when the wind carried the sound of the church bells towards her, a gleam of memory would remind her of the past. A sweet pain would come over her, and her tears would flow abundantly, but this would be only for a moment. Again there was emptiness, and she did not know why she lived.

Briska the black cat would purr and rub herself against her mistress, but Olienka was not moved by these caresses. That was not what she desired. She wanted the kind of love that would absorb all her being, her soul, her reason; give her thought and an understanding of life; the kind of love that would warm her aged blood. She pushed Briska from her with annoyance, saying:

" Go away! Go away! I don't want you here!"

And so the days and the years went by without so much as a single joy, idea, or even opinion. What Mavra the cook said was quite good enough for Olienka.

One fine hot day, towards evening, when the cattle were being driven home and the yard was filled with clouds of dust, some one knocked at the gate. Olienka herself went to open it, and when she looked out she stopped short, bewildered. Outside stood the veterinary surgeon Sinerdin, already grey, and in civilian dress. Suddenly she remembered everything, and bursting into tears embraced him. She did not say a word, and was so excited that she did not know how they got into the house and sat down to tea.

" My dear Vladimir Platonitch!" she murmured, trembling with joy, " whence did the Lord send you?"

" I want to settle down here for good," he began. " I have retired and want happiness in freedom in my old age. Besides, it is time my boy went to school; he is growing up. You know, of course, that I am reconciled with my wife."

" Where is she?" Olienka asked.

" She is at the hotel with the boy, and I am hunting for lodgings."

" But, my dear, you can have the whole of my house! What do you want with lodgings? And I will not take anything from you," Olienka went on excitedly, and burst into tears again. " You can live here; the little wing will be enough for me! What joy, my Lord!"

The next day the roof was being painted and the walls whitewashed. Olienka went about with her arms akimbo, giving orders. On her face shone the former smile—she seemed to have become alive again, grown younger, as if awakened from a long sleep.

The veterinary surgeon's wife arrived, a thin, ugly, disagreeable woman with short hair, and with her the boy Sasha, a chubby little fellow of nine, with clear blue eyes and dimpled cheeks. He had scarcely entered the yard when he ran up to the cat, and soon there was heard his merry laugh:

" Auntie, is this your cat ? " he asked Olienka. " When she has kittens will you give us one of them ? Mamma is afraid of mice."

Olienka talked to him and gave him tea ; a sweet emotion pervaded her, just as if he had been her own son. And when, in the evenings, he used to sit at the table repeating his lessons, she would look at him with affection and pity and whisper :

" My darling beautiful boy . . . little one . . . how clever and pretty you are ! "

" An island," he read out, " is a piece of land surrounded entirely by water."

" An island is a piece of land . . . ." she would repeat, and this was the first opinion she had expressed with conviction after all those years of silence and absence of thought.

She had her opinions now, and at supper would talk to Sasha's parents about how difficult it was for children at school nowadays ; that still scholastic training was better than home teaching ; that after passing out of school one could do what one liked, go in for medicine or engineering.

Sasha was sent to school. His mother went off to Kharkov to her sister's and never returned, and his father was out every day seeing cattle and would sometimes not come back for two or three days at a stretch. It seemed to Olienka that the boy was quite neglected, that he was superfluous in the house, and that he would die of hunger, so she took him to her side of the house and installed him there in a little room.

Six months had gone by since Sasha came over to her wing of the house. Every morning Olienka goes into his room while he is still asleep with his cheek on his arm. She scarcely breathes, and it pains her to wake him.

" Sasha ! " she says at last, softly, " get up, dear ; it is time to go to school ! "

He dresses himself, says his prayers, and then sits down to breakfast. He drinks three cups of tea, eats two rolls and some French bread and butter. He is not quite awake yet, and feels a little cross.

" Sasha, dear, learn your fable properly," Olienka says, with a look as though she were sending him off on a long journey. " What a trial you are to me ! Try, dear, and do well. Obey your masters . . ."

" Oh, do leave off ! " answers Sasha.

Presently he is on his way to school, a little boy in a big cap, with a satchel on his back. Olienka follows him softly. " Sashinka ! " she calls after him. He turns round and she thrusts a date or a caramel into his hand. When he turns the corner of the street leading to his school, he feels ashamed that a big, tall woman should be following him ; he turns round and says :

" Auntie, you had better turn back now ; I can go on alone from here."

She stops and watches him until he disappears within the school gates. Ah ! How she loves him ! Not one of her former loves has been as deep, nor was her soul ever so utterly subjected with such disinterestedness and consolation as now, when more and more there awakened in her the feeling of motherhood. For this strange boy she would have given up her life with the greatest of pleasure, thankfully. Why ? Who can tell ?

She goes home after having seen Sasha safely to school, so quiet and peaceful and contented ; so full of love. Her face, that has grown younger in the last six months, shines radiantly. Acquaintances meeting her feel a pleasure at the sight of her and say :

" Good morning, darling Olga Semionovna ! How are you getting on, my dear ? "

" Lessons are so hard for children at school nowadays," she says on meeting an acquaintance marketing. " It is no joke. Yesterday in the first form they had to learn a fable off by heart, as well as do some Latin translations and a problem. . . . What do they expect of a child ? "

And she begins to talk of the masters, the lessons, the text-books, repeating Sasha's opinions.

At three o'clock they have dinner together ; in the evening they do the home work, and cry together. Putting him to bed, she makes the sign of the cross over him many times, murmuring a prayer, and when she herself goes to bed, ponders over the future, distant and vague, when Sasha will have finished his education and become a doctor or an engineer ; when he will have his own house and carriage, marry and have children. . . . She begins to doze, still worrying over these things, the tears running down her cheeks from out her closed eyelids. The black cat is lying at her side, purring.

Boom ! Boom ! Boom !

Suddenly, there is a knock at the gate. Olienka starts up and can scarcely breathe for fear ; her heart is hammering. A few seconds go by and the knocking is repeated.

" It must be a telegram from Kharkov," she thinks, shaking like a leaf. " The mother wants Sasha back. . . . Ah, God ! " She is in despair ; her head and hands and feet have gone quite cold. It seems to her that she is the most unfortunate being in the whole world. Another minute goes by and voices are heard. It is the veterinary surgeon returning from his club.

" Thank God ! " she says to herself.

Gradually that oppressive feeling leaves her ; again she feels light-hearted. She lies down, thinking of Sasha, who is sleeping soundly in the next room, and every now and again she hears him talking in his sleep :

" I'll give it to you ! " " Get away ! " " Don't fight ! "

THE ENCASED MAN

ANTON P. CHEKHOV

IN a shed belonging to Prokoffy the elder, on the outskirts of the village, the belated hunters were preparing for bed. There were two of them, a veterinary surgeon, Ivan Ivanitch, and Burkin, a schoolmaster. Ivan Ivanitch had a curious double surname, " Chimsha Gimalaisky," and as it did not fit him, he was known over the whole country merely by his Christian name and patronymic. He lived near the town, at the stud, and had come down to enjoy the fresh air. Burkin, the schoolmaster, stayed with Count P—— every summer, and therefore was quite at home in the place.

They could not sleep. Ivan Ivanitch, a tall gaunt old man of sixty, with a long moustache, was sitting by the door of the shed, smoking his pipe. The moon shone full on his face. Burkin lay inside on the straw, and in the darkness could not be seen.

They touched on various topics. Among other things, they talked about the elder's wife, Mavra. She was healthy and not at all stupid, yet she had never in her life been out of the village, nor had she seen a town or a railway train. For the last ten years she had sat at home by the stove all day and come out only at night.

" There is nothing astonishing in that ! " Burkin remarked. " There are many people in the world who are solitary by nature and who try to withdraw into their shells like a crab or a snail. It may be a type of atavism, a reversion to the time when our forefathers were not yet social animals, but lived alone in caves ; or perhaps it is merely one of the many aspects of human character—who knows ? Of course, I am not a scientist, it is not my business to bother about such questions, but it seems to me that people like Mavra are not rare in this world. Here is an example. About two months ago, there died in our town a certain man by the name of Belikov, a Greek master and colleague of mine. Perhaps you have heard of him. He was distinguished by the fact that even in fine weather he invariably went about wearing goloshes and a padded overcoat, and carrying an umbrella. His umbrella was always in a sheath, and his watch in a grey leather pocket. When he brought out his pocket-knife to sharpen his pencil, that too was in a case ; even his face seemed to be in a case, as it was always hidden inside his high collar. He wore dark spectacles, a comforter, and cotton-wool in his ears. When he took a cab he always asked the driver to put up the hood. In a word, this man was constantly striving to envelop himself, to make a case for himself, so to speak, that would protect him from all outside influences. Reality irritated and frightened him, and held him in a perpetual state of anxiety. It may be, that in order to justify his timidity, his dislike for reality, he always praised the past and things that had never existed. The dead languages that he spoke were at bottom no more than the goloshes and umbrellas in which he hid himself from the realities of life.

" ' How beautiful and musical the Greek tongue is ! ' he would say, with a sentimental expression ; and as though to give proof to his words, he half closed his eyes and raised one finger when he pronounced the word ' Anthropos ! '

" His thoughts too, Belikov tried to enclose in a case. The only things he could clearly understand were circulars prohibiting something or other and articles of the same nature. If a circular forbade a boy to be out in the street after nine o'clock in the evening—or an article spoke against the love of the flesh, then for him it was quite clear and definite—something was forbidden and there was an end to it. To him there was always a doubtful element about positive decision and permission—something unutterably lazy. If a theatrical society was formed in the town ; if a reading were arranged or a tea-party made up, he would always shake his head and say quietly :

" ' This is all very fine, but I am afraid something or other may happen.'

" Any transgression or departure from the ordinary rules of convention made him feel wretched, though one might have wondered what it could possibly matter to him. If one of his colleagues happened to be late for morning prayers ; if he heard of the pranks of some boy or other ; if one of the mistresses was seen walking in the evening with an officer, he became hugely excited and would go about saying something or other was sure to happen.

" At our staff conferences he oppressed us all with his cautiousness and suspiciousness, his stereotyped precautions regarding the boys' and the girls' school.

" He would complain that the boys behaved badly and were noisy in class ; that it might get to the ears of the principal and that something or other would happen ; that if Petrov of the second form and Yegorev of the fourth were expelled, then things might be better. What did we think ? With his sighs and lamentations, his smoked glasses on his tiny pale face—a face as small as that of a polecat, he oppressed us all. Petrov and Yegorev were taken in hand, put under arrest, and in the end both were expelled from school. He had a curious habit of visiting us regularly in our own quarters. He would come to a man's rooms, sit down silently as though on the look-out for something, stay like that for an hour or two, and then go away without a word. This is what he called ' maintaining good relations with his colleagues.' One could see that these visits were irksome to him, and that he only kept them up out of a sheer sense of duty.

" All the masters stood in awe of him, and so did the principal too. Imagine our men, fairly clever, respectable fellows, all brought up on Turgeniev and Schedrin, and then this man who always went about with his umbrella and goloshes, ruling the school with an iron hand for the space of twenty-five years ! And not only the school ; he ruled the whole town ! The ladies would be afraid to arrange private theatricals or Saturday evening parties for fear that it should get to his ears ; they were actually afraid to indulge their palate or to join a game of cards in his presence. Owing to the influence of such people as Belikov, for the last ten or fifteen years every one was afraid of doing anything at all in our town. One was afraid of talking too loudly, of writing letters, of making acquaintances, even of learning to read and write. . . ."

Ivan Ivanitch, wishing to make a remark, cleared his throat, puffed at his pipe, and said hesitatingly :

" Yes ; clever, respectable men who read Schedrin, Turgeniev, Buckle, and so on, yet they gave in, submitted. . . . That is the point."

" Belikov lived in the same house where I did," Burkin continued. " His door was opposite mine ; we saw a good deal of each other and I knew all about his domestic life. It was the same thing at home, dressing-gown, night-cap, shutters, bolts, a whole heap of restrictions and limitations, and oh ! if something or other should happen ? Fast fare was supposed to be bad for him, rich fare impossible, so they said he used to eat fish cooked in butter—a diet that could hardly be called plain on the one hand or rich on the other. He was afraid of having a woman servant in the house for fear of getting a bad name, so he kept a man-cook, Afonasy by name, an old fellow of sixty who was a drunkard and half-witted, and had been an officer's servant and could cook after a fashion. He would stand by the door with arms crossed, constantly mumbling the same sentence:

"'How they do increase nowadays!'

"Belikov's bedroom was very small, just like a box, and his bed was enclosed by curtains. When he got into bed at night, he would pull the bed-clothes right over his head. It was hot and stuffy, the stove roared, the wind shook the tightly-closed doors; sighs came from the kitchen, ominous sighs. . . .

"He lay in bed under the bed-clothes trembling with fear. He was afraid that something or other would happen; that Afonasy would cut his throat or that thieves would get in; even when he went to sleep he was troubled by unpleasant dreams. When in the morning we walked to school together, he was pale and depressed, and one could see that the idea of going into the school with its many people was a source of terror to him, was repugnant to his whole being. Even my presence was irksome to his solitary nature. 'The class-rooms are very noisy,' he would say as if trying to find an excuse for his depression. 'I don't know what things are coming to.' And would you believe it, this Greek master, this encased man, very nearly got married!"

"Not really! You're joking!"

"Yes, he nearly did, though it may seem remarkable to you. A new master was appointed for history and geography, a fellow from Little Russia by the name of Michael Savitch Kovalenko. He did not come alone, but brought his sister Varenka with him. He was a tall young man, with a swarthy complexion and large hands; you could tell from the look of him that he had a bass voice, and it really was as deep as though it issued from a barrel—Ber! Ber! Ber! His sister was no longer young—about thirty—tall and graceful, with red cheeks and dark brows, as pretty a girl as one could wish to see. She was jolly and boisterous, very fond of laughing. At the smallest trifle she would burst into a ringing laugh—'Ha! ha! ha!'

"I remember that the first occasion on which we really had an opportunity of becoming acquainted with the Kovalenkos was at a birthday party given to the principal. Amidst the dry, uncomfortable pedagogues who even go to parties out of a sense of duty, we suddenly saw a new Aphrodite born out of the foam. She came in with her arms folded, laughed, sung, danced. She sang 'The Winds Blow' with great feeling; then another song and another until we were all charmed, even Belikov. He sat down near her and remarked with a sentimental smile:

"'The tongue of Little Russia by its softness and its music reminds one of ancient Greek.'

"She felt flattered by this and began talking enthusiastically about her Province of Gadvansk; of the farm-house where her mother lived; of the lovely cherries they grew, and melons and pumpkins (melons and pumpkins she called by their quaint Little Russian names), and of the delicious soups they made—so delicious that they made your mouth water.

"As we sat listening to her, suddenly, for some unknown reason, the same thought came into our minds.

"'It would be nice to get them married!' the principal's wife whispered to me.

"It was brought home to us immediately that Belikov was not married, and it seemed strange to me that we had not been conscious of this till now; and had completely overlooked this important possibility in his life. 'How does he bear himself towards women, and what does he think of marriage?' Formerly, this had not interested us in the least; it may be because it never occurred to us that a man who always wore goloshes and always slept in a curtained bed could possibly fall in love.

"'He is well over forty and she is thirty . . .' the inspiration of the principal's wife began taking shape. 'I think she would accept him.'

"You don't know the things we do in the provinces out of sheer boredom, what unnecessary, stupid things! I daresay it is because we never do what is necessary. For some reason we were all seized with an irresistible desire to see Belikov married, though he was the sort of man you could not imagine with a wife. The principal's wife, the inspector's wife, all the women connected with the establishment became immensely interested, got to look brighter even, as though they had suddenly discovered an aim in life.

"The principal's wife took a box at the theatre, and there was Varenka with a lovely fan, smiling and happy, and by her side Belikov, small and bent, looking as though he had been dragged from his house. I gave a party; the ladies insisted that Belikov and Varenka should be invited. In a word, the machine was set in motion. Varenka was very nearly married. Life at her brother's was not very gay—it was generally known that they were always bickering and quarrelling. This is a typical scene. Kovalenko would be striding down the street, a tall lanky fellow in an embroidered shirt, his hair crowding out from under his cap on to his forehead; in one hand would be a parcel of books, in the other a thick knotted walking-stick.

" Behind would follow his sister, also carrying an armful of books. ' But, Michael, you've not read this one!' she shouts after him, ' I'm sure you haven't!'

" ' I tell you I have!' Kovalenko shouts back angrily, banging his stick on the pavement.

" ' Oh dear, Minchick, why will you get angry! Our discussion is merely a matter of principle.'

" ' I tell you I've read it!' Kovalenko bawls still louder, again banging his stick on the pavement.

" As you may imagine, it was much worse at home. The girl of course got tired of such a life, and longed for a home of her own; and besides, she was getting on in years. There was no chance for her; she had to marry whom she could, and even the Greek master was not to be despised. I daresay most of our girls marry merely for the sake of marrying. However, be that as it may, Varenka began to show a distinct preference for Belikov.

" As for Belikov, he used to visit Kovalenko in the same way that he did us. He would arrive and sit down without speaking. He would keep silent while Varenka sung to him ' The Winds Blow ' or gazed pensively at him with her dark eyes, or suddenly burst out with her ' Ha! ha! ha!'

" In love affairs, particularly when there is a question of marriage, suggestion plays an important part. All of us—my colleagues and the ladies—took to proving to Belikov that he ought to marry—that there was nothing to do in life but marry. We congratulated him, and with serious mien would utter such commonplaces as that marriage was a serious step. Besides, Varenka was not a bad-looking girl, was the daughter of a councillor of state, and, most important of all, was the first girl who had been nice and kind to him. In the end his head was turned and he decided to marry."

"At that stage you ought to have taken his goloshes and umbrella from him," Ivan Ivanitch remarked.

"We found that impossible. He put Varenka's photograph on his table, and used to call on me often to talk about her, about family life, about what a serious step marriage was. He visited Varenka frequently too, but did not change his mode of life one atom. On the contrary the thought of marriage seemed to have a depressing effect on him; he got thin and pale and retreated still further into his shell.

"'I like Varvara Savishna,' he would say to me with a faint smile, 'And I think every man should marry, but . . . it all happened so suddenly . . . I must consider.'

"'What is there to consider?' I said to him. 'Marry and get it over!'

"'No, marriage is a serious step; one must weigh carefully all the duties and responsibilities it implies—so that nothing untoward should happen afterwards. I am so disturbed I cannot sleep at nights. To tell the truth, I am afraid she and her brother have such queer ideas, they look at things in such an unusual way. . . . And then, she is so rash. You may marry, and, without foreseeing it, let yourself in for something or other.'

"He kept on deferring the proposal, much to the disgust of the principal's wife and all the other ladies, while he duly weighed his future duties and responsibilities. At the same time he used to walk with Varenka every day, perhaps because he thought it was expected of him, and would call on me every evening to talk about family life.

"As far as one can conjecture he would have proposed to her in the end, and there would have followed one of those absurd marriages that take place by the thousand in our midst, either because people are bored or that they have nothing better to do. But suddenly there happened a tremendous scandal. I must first tell you that Varenka's brother Kovalenko took a deep dislike to Belikov the first time he met him, and could not endure the sight of him.

"'I can't understand why you want to talk to that spy, that little worm. How can you fellows live here? The very atmosphere is suffocating. Do you call yourselves teachers? You are too hide-bound. You do not worship at the temple of science, but at the court of decorum—you reek with stagnation like one of our policemen's sentry-boxes. No, brothers! I'll stay another six months with you and then return to my farm to fish for crabs and relearn to talk Little Russian!'

"Another time he would laugh till the tears came to his eyes; first in a deep and then in a thin voice.

"'Why does he come to my house?' he would ask me. 'What does he want of me? He just sits and stares.'

"He even nicknamed Belikov 'The Spider,' and when one day the principal's wife hinted that it would be a good thing for his sister to marry such a 'reliable' man whom every one respected, he frowned and muttered, 'It's not my business. She can marry a viper if she chooses. I don't like meddling in other people's affairs.'

"Now listen to what happened later. Some mischievous person made a caricature of Belikov walking along with an open umbrella, turned-up trousers, and goloshes; on his arm was Varenka, and underneath was written 'Anthropos in love.'

"The artist had seized his expression wonderfully well. He must have spent many nights at the work. Every one received a copy—all the masters and mistresses, the civil servants—even Belikov himself got one. The caricature had a very depressing effect on him.

"We had come out of the house together. It happened to be the first of May, and we had all—masters and boys—agreed to meet at the school and then go out of the town into the woods. He was gloomier than ever.

"'What horrid, spiteful people there are in the world,' he said, his lips trembling.

"I felt quite sorry for him. As we walked along, who should overtake us but Kovalenko on a bicycle, followed by Varenka, also on a bicycle, flushed and red, but jolly and happy. 'We'll go on ahead,' she called out to us. 'What awfully jolly weather!' Both passed out of sight. Belikov turned from green to white and appeared quite stunned. He stood still and looked at me. 'What is the meaning of that?' he asked; 'or do my eyes deceive me? Is it proper for schoolmasters and women to ride bicycles?'

"'What is there improper about it?' I asked. 'Why shouldn't they cycle if they want to?'

"'But how is it possible?' he exclaimed, amazed at my coolness. 'What are you saying?'

"He was so overcome that he refused to go any farther and returned home.

"On the following day he was continually rubbing his hands together nervously, and from his face one could see that he was not well. He even absented himself from his work, a thing that had never happened to him before. He had no dinner either. Towards evening he clad himself warmly, though it was quite hot summer weather, and set out for the Kovalenkos'. Varenka was not at home, but her brother was in.

"'Won't you sit down, please?' said the brother coldly, with a frown. He had been roused from an after-dinner nap and was sleepy and in a bad humour.

"Belikov sat silent for about ten minutes and then began: 'I came to unburden my heart to you. I am very unhappy. Some libellous person has had the audacity to make a caricature of me and of some one else who is very dear to us both. I consider it my duty to inform you that I am not to blame in the matter. . . . I have never given the least occasion for such an insult. On the other hand, I have all along behaved as an honourable man should do.'

"Kovalenko almost boiled over with rage, but said nothing. Belikov, too, sat silent for a moment, and then continued in a soft sad voice:

"'I have another thing I want to say to you. I have been at my work now for a long time, while you are only just beginning. I consider it my duty as an older colleague to advise you. You ride a bicycle, and such an amusement is not proper to one who has the education of children.'

"'Why, may I ask?' Kovalenko said in his bass voice.

"'I should have thought it was unnecessary to explain, Michael Savitch, the reasons are so obvious. If the masters ride bicycles, what must one expect from the boys? Nothing remains for them but to walk on their heads. Besides, when a thing is forbidden by a circular it stands to reason it is impossible. I was horrified yesterday when I saw your sister. I could scarcely believe my eyes. For a lady to ride a bicycle is positively dreadful.'

"'May I ask what it is you want?'

"'I only want to advise you, Michael Savitch. You are a young man; your future is still before you. You should conduct yourself with caution. You make many, many mistakes. You wear embroidered shirts, always go about the streets carrying bundles of books, and then there is the bicycle! The principal is sure to get to know that you and your sister cycle, and from him to the governors . . . what good is there in it ? '

" ' That my sister and I cycle is nobody's business but our own ! ' Kovalenko said, turning purple with passion. ' And whoever dares to meddle in my domestic and private affairs does so at his own risk ! '

" Belikov turned pale and rose from his chair.

" ' If you adopt that attitude I cannot continue,' he said. ' And I must ask you never to express yourself in such terms about the principal and governors in my presence. You should be respectful to your superiors.'

" ' Did I speak ill of my superiors ? ' Kovalenko asked, looking at him with rage. ' Please leave me in peace. I am a plain honest man and have no desire for further intercourse with men of your stamp. I do not like sneaks.'

" Belikov fidgeted nervously and began to put on his coat quickly, an expression of horror on his face. It was the first time in his life he had been spoken to so rudely.

" ' You can say what you like,' he observed, as he walked out on to the staircase landing. ' But I must warn you that in case by chance any one may have overheard our conversation, I must repeat its contents to the principal . . . the chief points, that is. It is my duty to do so.'

" ' Get along then ! Make haste and tell him ! '

" Kovalenko seized him by the collar and pushed him out ; Belikov rolled down the stairs, his goloshes clattering as he fell. The staircase was steep and winding, but he reached the bottom unhurt. When he reached the bottom he immediately felt to see whether his spectacles were safe.

" As luck would have it, just as he rolled down, Varenka and two ladies happened to come in, and they stood at the bottom and watched him fall. To Belikov this was worse than anything. He would far rather have broken his neck, or his legs, than have appeared ridiculous. The whole town would know now ! Something or other was sure to happen ! Some one would draw another caricature, and the upshot would be that he would be requested to resign ! . . . When he got up, Varenka recognised him, and seeing the absurd expression on his face, his crushed coat and goloshes ; not understanding what had happened and thinking that he had slipped accidentally, she could not contain herself but burst out laughing, ' Ha ! ha ! ha ! '

"With this jolly 'Ha! ha! ha!' everything was ended; the engagement, even Belikov's earthly existence. He did not hear what Varenka said; did not see anything. When he got home, the first thing he did was to remove her portrait from the table, then he went to bed and never got up again.

"Two or three days later Afonasy came and asked me whether the doctor had not better be sent for as something or other was wrong with his master. I went into Belikov's room. He was lying inside the curtained bed, muffled in the bed-clothes and perfectly silent. When I asked him a question, he would reply 'Yes' or 'No' and not another word. He lay in bed and Afonasy circled round him, solemn, gloomy, and smelling of vodka like a public-house.

"In a month Belikov died. We all went to his funeral; that is, the two schools and the seminary. When he lay in his coffin he had a gentle, pleasant, almost happy expression as though he were glad that at last he had been put into a case which he need never leave. Yes, he had attained his ideal! And, as if in his honour, it rained on the day of the funeral, and we all had goloshes and umbrellas. Varenka, too, was present, and when the coffin was lowered she sobbed aloud. I have noticed that at a funeral people either laugh or cry, a halfway mood is unknown. I must confess that to bury people like Belikov is a great pleasure. When we returned from the cemetery we tried to look humble—no one dared to give expression to this feeling of joy—a feeling akin to that we experienced as children when our elders went away and we were left to roam about the garden in perfect liberty for hours on end. Ah, liberty! liberty! A mere suggestion, a faint hope of her, gives wings to the soul! Don't you think so?

"We returned from the cemetery in a good frame of mind, but scarcely a week went by before life went on exactly as before, uninteresting, wearying, senseless; a life with no restrictions printed in circulars, yet with no proper freedom. We were no better off than before. Belikov was buried, but how many other men in cases remained in the world, and how many more were yet to come!"

"That is just the point," Ivan Ivanitch said, lighting his pipe.

"How many more are to come!" Burkin repeated.

The schoolmaster came out of the shed. He was a stout little man, quite bald, with a long beard that reached nearly down to his waist. Two dogs followed him out.

"What a moon!" he said, looking up. It was midnight. On

the right the whole village could be seen ; a long street that stretched out for about four miles. Everything was immersed in a quiet, deep sleep ; not a movement or sound ; it was hard to believe that nature could be so still. When, on a moonlit night, you see a broad village street with its huts, hayricks, and willows, a tranquil feeling pervades you. In this quietude, hidden by the shadows of night from labour and worry and grief, the village looked peaceful and sad and beautiful, and it seemed that the stars looked down at it affectionately, that there was no evil in the world, and that all was well.

To the left, on the edge of the village, a large field stretched out ; it continued in the distance, as far as the horizon, and in its breadth, filled with moonlight, there was also no movement or sound.

" That is the point," Ivan Ivanitch repeated. " And we who live in stuffy crowded towns write unnecessary articles, play bridge—aren't we in a kind of case ? If you like, I will tell you a story illustrating this."

" No, thank you ; it is time for bed ; to-morrow will do," Burkin objected.

They went into the shed and lay down on the straw. As they were dozing off came the sound of light footsteps : tap, tap . . . some one was walking near the shed—walking a few steps, then stopping, and then again tap—tap.

The dogs growled.

" That is Mavra," Burkin said.

The footsteps ceased.

" See how people lie," Ivan Ivanitch went on, turning on his other side ; " and then to be called a fool for enduring the lie ; bearing the insult and humiliation, not daring to assert that you are on the side of honesty and freedom, but to lie and smile yourself ; all for the sake of a piece of bread and a warm corner, or for some office that isn't worth a penny—no, it is impossible to go on being like that ! "

" How you do wander off, Ivan Ivanitch ! " the schoolmaster said. " Let us go to sleep."

In ten minutes Burkin was asleep, but Ivan Ivanitch kept sighing and tossing from side to side. After a little while he rose and, sitting down again outside the hut, lit his pipe.

IN EXILE

ANTON P. CHEKHOV

OLD Semion, nicknamed the Wiseacre, and a young Tartar whose name nobody knew, sat by the fire on the river-bank. The other three ferrymen lay in the hut. Semion, an old man of sixty, gaunt and toothless, though broad-shouldered and healthy, was drunk. He would have gone to bed long ago had it not been for the flagon in his pocket and the fear that his companions in the hut would ask him for vodka. The Tartar was ill and tired. Wrapped in his rags, he was expatiating on the glorious life at Simbirsk, and the beauty and wit of the wife he had left behind him.

" Of course, you can hardly call it paradise here," the Wiseacre remarked. " You can take it in at a glance—water, bare banks, and clay everywhere, nothing more. Holy Week has long gone by, and there is still ice on the river, and this morning it snowed."

" Misery ! Misery ! " the Tartar moaned as he glanced around apprehensively.

Ten paces below lay the river, cold and dark, beating against the high clay bank as it wended its way swiftly to the distant sea.

Close to the bank lay a barge. On the other side little fiery serpents crept along, now dying out, now blazing up. It was last year's grass burning. And behind the serpents of fire darkness again.

The Tartar looked up at the sky. There were as many stars as in his own country, just the same darkness about him. But there was something lacking. At home in Simbirsk the stars were brighter and the sky was different.

" Misery ! Misery ! " he moaned again.

" You will get used to it," the Wiseacre said with a laugh ; " you are young and foolish still. Your mother's milk has scarcely dried on your lips. It is only your folly makes you think there is no one more unfortunate than you. A time will come when you will say, ' God grant every one such a life as this ! ' Look at me now. In a week's time the river will be open ; we will launch the small ferry-boat, and you will all go wandering off over Siberia, while I shall stay here rowing from bank to bank as I have done for twenty-two years day in, day out. And nobody here except the fish under the water and I above it. Yet, thank God, I do not want for anything. God grant every one such a life!"

The Tartar heaped wood on the fire, huddled closer to it, and said: " My father is ill. When he dies my mother and wife are coming to join me here. They promised me they would."

" What do you want with a wife and a mother?" the Wiseacre asked. " It is folly, brother. The devil put these notions into your head. Do not listen to him. If he talks to you of women, say you do not want them; if he begins about freedom, answer in the same way. You need nothing; neither father nor mother nor wife, nor freedom, nor hearth, nor home; you want none of these things, curse them!" Wiseacre took a sip from his bottle and continued: " I am not a common peasant, brother. My father was a deacon, and when I lived in freedom at Kursk I went about in a frock-coat, but now I have brought myself to such a point that I can sleep naked on the bare earth, and eat grass if necessary. God grant every one such a life! There is nothing I want, no one that I fear, and I know that there is no richer or freer man in the whole world. As soon as they sent me here from Russia, I made up my mind from the very first day not to want anything. The devil talked to me also about wife, home, freedom, but I answered back persistently: 'I don't want anything!' I stuck to that view and, as you see, I live well and am contented. Give way to the devil one inch, and you are lost beyond salvation; you will sink in the slough and never emerge. It is not only our brother the peasant who goes under, but even men of birth and education. About fifteen years ago a certain gentleman was sent here from Russia. He would not share up with his brothers, and there was some trouble about a forged will. Some said he was a prince's or a baron's son, but perhaps he was only an ordinary civil servant—who knows? Anyhow, he came here, and the first thing he did was to buy himself a house and some land in Mihortirsk. 'I want to live by the sweat of my brow,' he said, 'I am no longer a gentleman, but only a settler.' 'Well, God help you,' I said. 'It is a good wish!'

" He was a young man then, and loved to fuss and worry. He did his own farming and fishing, and would think nothing of riding sixty miles on horseback. But then came the misfortune. From the very first year he began to make a practice of riding into Girino to the post-office. He would stand on my boat, sigh, and say, 'Oh, Semion! why are they so long sending me money from home?' 'You have no need of money, Vassily Sergeyevitch,' I would say. 'What is the use of it to you? Give up your past, forget that it ever existed, and begin life anew. Do not listen to the devil!' I warned him; 'he means no good and will only put a halter round your neck. Now it is only money you want, later you will look round and desire something more; then another thing will occur to you and another. . . . If you want to ensure happiness to yourself, take my advice and desire nothing. If fortune has treated us badly, we must not bow down before her and beg for charity, we must despise her and laugh at her, and presently she will laugh with us.' So I would speak to him. . . . A year or two later I was again ferrying him across. He was laughing and rubbing his hands! 'I am going to Girino to meet my wife,' he said. 'She has taken pity on me and has come over. How good and kind she is!' He could scarcely contain his joy.

"A day or so later he returned with his wife. She was a young, beautiful woman, wore a hat, and had a little baby girl in her arms. There were stacks of luggage of all kinds. Vassily Sergeyevitch was fussing round her. He could not take his eyes off her; could not praise her enough.

"'Well, brother Semion,' he said to me, 'life is not so bad even in Siberia!' 'You won't always think so,' I said to myself. And from that time onward he used to go every week to Girino to see whether money had been sent him from Russia. Of money he wanted no end. 'For my sake,' he said to me, 'she is burying her youth and beauty in Siberia, and is sharing my miserable life. In return I must procure her every enjoyment possible.' To make things gayer for her, he sought the acquaintance of the officials, and of all kinds of people. And, of course, all this company had to be provided with food and drink. A piano was installed, and a little lap-dog for the sofa—curse it. In a word, luxury, extravagance. The lady did not stay long with him. How could she? Everywhere was mud and water; it was cold; there was no fruit or vegetables, and the people were ignorant, drunken persons with no culture. Of course she got tired of it; she was a lady spoiled by the city life. And her husband, too, was no longer a gentleman, just a settler—no honour in that.

"Three years went by. I remember on Assumption Eve I heard some one calling from the opposite bank. I rowed across, and there was the lady wrapped up to the ears and accompanied by a young man, one of the officials. They had a troika! I rowed them across; they got into the troika and rode off. There was no one else in sight. Next morning Vassily Sergeyevitch rode up in haste. 'Semion, did my wife cross over with a man in glasses?' he asked. 'Yes,' I answered; 'you may as well seek to capture the wind in the field.' He followed them for five days. When he returned he dropped into the boat and beat his head against the side. 'This is what you get,' he sobbed. 'Life is not so bad, even in Siberia!' I reminded him with a smile. And he continued to wail. After this he wanted his liberty. His wife had returned to Russia, and he wanted to see her, to persuade her to return to him. Well, brother, from that day he spent his time riding from the post-office to the town authorities. He sent off petition after petition, begging to be allowed to return to Russia. One telegram alone cost him a hundred roubles. He sold his land, mortgaged his house to the Jews. His hair grew grey, his shoulders bent, and his face grew as yellow as though he had consumption. When he was speaking to you, a lump would rise in his throat, and the tears would come into his eyes.

"Thus he lived for eight years until at last he forgot it all and came to life again. He had found a new consolation. His daughter, you see, was growing up. He simply doted on her. And truth to tell, she was not at all bad looking—pretty, dark-browed, high-spirited. Every Sunday he would take her to the church at Girino. They would stand in the boat side by side, she smiling and he not able to take his eyes off her. 'Yes, Semion,' he would say, 'life is not so bad in Siberia. Even in Siberia one can be happy. See what a pretty daughter I have! You won't find a prettier lass within a thousand miles.' 'Yes, she is certainly pretty,' I replied, while to myself I thought, 'You wait a bit . . . she is young and hot-blooded, she wants to live: and what kind of a life is there here?'

"Anyway, brother, the girl began to pine. She grew listless and ill, and now she can scarcely stand on her legs. Consumption, they say it is. There, brother, is your Siberian happiness. That is how people live in Siberia. The father took to hunting after doctors and bringing them to see his daughter. If he only hears of a doctor or quack, no matter if he has to go two or three hundred miles, he instantly sets off to fetch him.

"I cannot tell you how much money he has spent on doctors. It would have been more worth while to have drunk it all away. She will die just the same. Nothing can save her. And then he will be utterly lost. He will either hang himself in despair or try to escape to Russia. If he runs away, they are certain to catch him; then there will be a trial, penal servitude, perhaps a halter. . . ."

"It was fine: it was good," the Tartar murmured, shuddering with cold.

"What was fine?" the Wiseacre asked.

"Wife, daughter. . . . What does despair or penal servitude matter when he has had his wife and daughter? . . . You say a man should want nothing; that is misery. His wife lived with him for three years—that was a gift from God. To have nothing is misery—but those three years were good. You don't understand."

Shivering with cold, and trying to find the correct Russian words to explain himself, the Tartar went on to say how he hoped God would never let him fall ill and die in a strange land to be buried in that cold red earth; that if his wife came to him, even only a single day, a single hour, for such happiness he would be prepared to undergo untold tortures and would thank God for them. One day of happiness was better than nothing at all.

And again he talked of his beautiful, clever wife whom he had left at home until he bowed his head in his hands and burst into tears. He assured Semion that he was not guilty and was unjustly sentenced. It was his brothers and his uncle who had stolen the person's horses and half killed the old man. But he had been accused unjustly. The three brothers had been sent to Siberia while the rich uncle remained at home.

"You will get used to it," Semion drawled.

The Tartar said nothing but, through eyes full of tears, gazed at the fire. His face bore a perplexed, hunted expression as though he did not understand why he found himself there in the darkness and cold among strangers, far from his own people in Simbirsk. Wiseacre lay down by the fire, smiling to himself and humming an air.

"What happiness can she have with her father?" he continued after a while. "She is a consolation to him and he loves her, it is true, but he must be none too easy to get on with, a crotchety, severe old man. And a young girl does not want severity. She wants kisses, ha! ha! ha! and perfumes and pomades. Yes, it's not an easy business!" Semion sighed, as he got up with difficulty. "The vodka is all gone, that means time for bed. Eh, brother? I'm going. . . ."

Left alone, the Tartar heaped more wood on the fire and, gazing into the flames, dreamt of his native village and his wife. If she would only come to him for a month, for a single day, he would not mind if she went back again. A month, or even a day of happiness was better than nothing. Suppose she kept her promise and came out to him, how would he support her? Where could she live? "If you have nothing to eat, how can you live?" he asked aloud. Working a whole day and night at the oar he only made ten kopeks. It is true he sometimes got extras in the way of tips, but the ferrymen pooled all such money and shared it out among themselves. They gave the Tartar nothing, however, and only scoffed at him. And it was terrible to suffer from hunger and cold. . . .

Now, when he was trembling with cold, and every bone in his body was aching, he should have gone into the hut to sleep; but it was even colder there in the hut, for he had nothing wherewith to cover himself. Here he had no protection, but there was at any rate the fire. In a week, when the waters would have quite fallen, they would begin to use the small ferry-boat, and none of the ferrymen, except Semion, would be wanted. Then the Tartar would tramp from village to village begging for food and work. His wife was only seventeen. She was pretty, and spoilt and shy. Would she, too, have to tramp from village to village, brazenly, and ask for bread? No, no, it was too terrible to think of. It was getting light; the barge, the trees and the water stood out plainly. Turning round, you could see the clayey slope with the thatched hovel at the bottom, and beyond that the village huts. The cocks in the village were already crowing.

The red clayey slope, the barge, the river, the strange unfriendly people, hunger, cold, sickness — perhaps these things were not— perhaps it was all a dream, the Tartar thought. It seemed to him that he was asleep and heard the sound of his own snoring. Of course he was back at home at Simbirsk; he had only to call out to his wife and she would answer . . . and his mother was in the next room. . . . What terrible dreams people have! How do they come? The Tartar opened his eyes. What river was that? The Volga? It was snowing.

"Hi, there!" some one shouted from the opposite bank. "Ferry, please!"

The Tartar woke with a start and went for his mates. Pulling on their torn coats and swearing in their hoarse, sleepy voices, the ferrymen hurried down to the bank. Called from their sleep, the river, over which a cold wind was blowing, seemed very uninviting to them, and reluctantly they got into the boat. The Tartar and three of the others took the oars that in the darkness looked like the claws of a crab. Semion threw himself on his stomach across the helm. From the other bank the shouting continued, and twice a revolver shot was heard. Whoever it was must have thought that the ferrymen were either asleep or had gone to the village public-house. " All right, you've plenty of time ! " Wiseacre said in the tone of a man who was convinced that there was no need to hurry in this world—that there was no sense in it anyhow.

The huge clumsy barge left the bank and moved along slowly between the overhanging branches of the willow. Except for the passing of the trees the barge seemed to be at rest. The ferrymen pulled at the oars with a measured stroke. Wiseacre, lying across the helm and making a bow in the air, swayed from one side to the other. In the half light it seemed as if they were sitting on some enormous prehistoric beast with huge claws and floating away with it into the cold, desolate country that one sees in nightmares. The trees were left behind ; they gained the open water. The measuring of the oars could already be heard from the further bank.

" Quicker ! Quicker ! " the stranger shouted across the water. Ten minutes later the barge bumped heavily against the landing stage. " It snows, snows all the time," Semion grumbled, as he wiped the snow from his face. " God knows where it all comes from."

On the bank stood a frail little man wearing a short fox-skin coat and a white lambskin cap. He stood immovable, a little way from his horse. He had an absorbed, gloomy expression as though he were trying to recollect something and was angry with his disobedient memory. " I am hurrying to Anastasevka," he said, when Semion approached him and took off his cap with a smile. " My daughter is worse. They say a new doctor has been appointed there."

The cart was dragged into the barge and the ferrymen started back. The man whom Semion called Vassily Sergeyevitch stood stock still all the time, biting his full lips and staring straight before him. When the driver asked him for permission to smoke, he made no reply, just as if he had not heard.

"Life is not so bad, even in Siberia!" Semion said maliciously, as he lay over the helm. Wiseacre's face wore a triumphant expression, as though he were rejoicing that things had turned out as he had predicted. The miserable, helpless expression of the man in the fox-skin coat seemed to afford him great delight. "You will find it muddy, travelling in this weather," he remarked when the horses were being harnessed. "You should have waited another week or so till it got drier. Or better still, not go at all. What is the use of going? People rush about, year in year out, and nothing ever comes of it. Don't you think so?" Vassily Sergeyevitch tipped the ferrymen without a word, got into the cart, and drove off.

"Gone for the doctor again!" Semion said, slapping his hands to get them warm. "You can as easily get a doctor worth anything as capture the wind in the field or catch the devil by his tail—curse him! Lord! How stupid people are. Forgive an old sinner!"

The Tartar walked up to Wiseacre and, for a moment, stood looking at him with hatred and disgust. Shivering with cold, and in his excitement bringing in Tartar words, he burst out: "He is a good man—good—and you are vile—wicked. He has a good soul and you are a beast! A vile beast! He is alive while you are dead! God made man that he might know joy and sorrow and despair, but you desire nothing. . . . You are a stone, a piece of clay. A stone needs nothing and neither do you. . . . You are a stone! God loves that poor man, but not you!" They all laughed, and the Tartar, with a forlorn movement, drew his rags closer round him and went back to the fire. Semion and the others went towards the hut.

"It's cold!" one of the ferrymen said in a hoarse voice, as he stretched himself on the straw that covered the damp clayey floor. "To be sure it is!" another agreed. "A convict's life!"

All lay down. The wind burst the door open, driving in the snow. No one was inclined to get up and shut it—they felt too cold and lazy. "I'm all right!" murmured Semion, as he dozed off. "God grant every one such a life!"

"You must be a convict seven times over, even the devil would not have you!" From without came a sound as of a dog whining.

"What's that? Who is there?"

"It is the Tartar, crying." "What a fool!"

"He will get used to it!" said Semion, and dropped off to sleep. The others quickly followed his example. The door remained open.

AT HOME

Anton P. Chekhov

"SOME one called from Gregorev's for a book, but I told them you were not at home. And by the way, Yevgeny Petrovitch, I really must ask you to talk seriously to Serioja. Both to-day and the day before yesterday I discovered him smoking, and when I attempted to scold him, he put his hands over his ears and shouted so loudly as to drown my voice."

Yevgeny Petrovitch Bikovsky, the district public prosecutor, who had only just returned from a sitting and was taking off his gloves in his study, looked up at his boy's governess and laughed. "Serioja smoking!" . . . He shrugged his shoulders. "I can imagine the little imp with a cigarette! How old is he?"

"Seven. Of course you may not think it serious, but smoking at his age is a bad, injurious habit, and such habits should be eradicated from the very beginning."

"I quite agree. Where does he get tobacco from?"

"From your table."

"Really? In that case you had better send him to me."

When the governess had gone, Bikovsky sat down in his arm-chair by the table, closed his eyes and fell to musing. His imagination pictured Serioja with a huge cigarette about a yard long, enveloped in clouds of tobacco smoke. The picture brought a smile to his lips. At the same time the anxious, serious face of the governess reminded him of a time long gone by in the half-forgotten past when smoking in the nursery or at school inspired in parents and masters a strange and somewhat puzzling feeling of horror. The word horror exactly describes it. Such boys were flogged or expelled from school; their lives were made a burden to them; yet not one of the masters nor the parents could have told you exactly what harm there was in smoking, nor why it was considered such a crime.

A great many clever grown-up people, too, fought against the tobacco habit without precisely knowing why.

Yevgeny Petrovitch recalled how the headmaster of his school, a learned and kind-hearted old man, would turn quite pale with fright if he discovered a boy smoking. He would instantly summon a council of masters, and the culprit would forthwith be expelled.

Such seems the law of everyday life! The more intangible the evil, the more fiercely it is combated.

Yevgeny Petrovitch brought to mind the cases of two or three victims, and could not help thinking that the punishment wrought consequences far more evil than did the crime. A living organism is capable of adapting itself to any environment, else otherwise human beings would realise at every turn how normal activities were based on hypotheses that could not be proved; and how little was really known of the fundamental truths in such branches as education, law, literature. . . .

These and similar thoughts, the workings of a tired brain that craved for rest, began to float through his mind. They came crowding one after another, disconnected, remaining only on the surface without penetrating the depths.

To a man whose whole time is taken up by legal affairs and whose mind is constantly set in one direction, such homely, wandering thoughts as these produce a comfortable, soothing effect.

It was nine o'clock in the evening. In the flat above, on the second floor, some one was pacing the room, to and fro, from corner to corner, and in the flat above that, two people were playing a duet on the piano. The man who was pacing the floor—judging by his nervous tread—must have been tortured by some tormenting thought, or perhaps by a toothache, while the monotonous duet embued the evening stillness with a certain drowsiness that was conducive to lazy thinking. In the nursery Serioja and the governess were talking together. "Papa has come!" the boy sang. "Papa has come! Papa! Papa!"

"*Votre père vous appelle*, go at once!" the governess piped in a thin little voice like that of a frightened bird. "Do you hear?"

"What can I say to him after all?" Yevgeny Petrovitch asked himself. But before he had time to invent anything to say to his son, Serioja, a boy of seven, entered. It was only by his clothes that one could distinguish that he was a boy and not a girl. He was frail, fair-skinned, and fragile. He seemed like some exotic flower, and everything about him was soft and gentle; his looks, his gestures, his curly hair, even his little velvet coat. " Good evening, papa ! " he said in a soft voice, climbing on to his father's knee and kissing him. " Did you want me ? "

" One minute, Sergey Yevgenitch," the father began, gently disengaging the boy's arms. " Before we can think of kissing, you and I must have a serious talk. I am very angry with you and don't love you any more. Understand that I don't love you—you are no longer my son—yes . . ."

Serioja looked intently at his father, then transferred his gaze to the table and shrugged his shoulders.

" What have I done to you ? " he asked in perplexity, blinking his eyes. " I did not go into your study once to-day and have not touched anything."

" Natalia Semionovna has just informed me that you smoke. Is it true ? Do you smoke ? "

" Yes, I smoked once. It is true ! "

" There now, you are telling a lie into the bargain," the public prosecutor said, frowning in order to hide a smile. " Natalia Semionovna caught you twice. You have been discovered in three bad actions—smoking, taking another person's tobacco, and lying. Three bad faults."

" Oh, yes ! " Serioja recollected, his eyes dancing. " It is quite true ; I did smoke twice, once to-day and once before that."

" You see, you yourself admit it was not once but twice. . . . I am very angry with you. You used to be a good boy ; and now you appear to have become bad."

Yevgeny Petrovitch rearranged Serioja's collar, thinking, " What else shall I say to him ? "

" It is not right," he continued. " I did not expect it of you. In the first place you have no right to take tobacco that does not belong to you. Every man has the right of enjoying his own property, but if he takes something that is not his own, then he is a bad man ! For instance, Natalia Semionovna has a trunk full of dresses. It is her own trunk, and that means that we—that is, you and I—have no right to touch it as it does not belong to us. Do you follow ? Again, you have little horses and pictures . . . I do not take them, do I ? Perhaps I should like to have them . . . but I know they are yours and not mine."

" You can take them if you like ! " Serioja said, raising his eyebrows.

" Don't mind me, papa, take them! That little dog you have on the table is mine, but I don't care . . . let it stay there!"

" You don't understand," Bikovsky said. " You gave me the dog, so now it is mine and I can do what I like with it, but I did not give you the tobacco. The tobacco is mine." (I shall never be able to make him understand this way, the public prosecutor thought. Impossible! It's quite useless!) " If I want to smoke tobacco that does not belong to me, then first of all I must ask permission." Lazily connecting his sentences, choosing childish words, Bikovsky set out to explain to his son the meaning of private property.

Serioja fixed his gaze on his father's chest, listening attentively. He loved to sit talking with his father in the evenings. Then he rested his elbows on the table, half closed his eyes, and transferred his gaze to the paper and ink-pot. Then it wandered round the room and settled on the paste-bottle.

" Papa, what is paste made of?" he asked suddenly, lifting the bottle up to inspect it.

Bikovsky took the bottle from him, put it back on the table, and continued: " And secondly, you smoke. . . . That is not good. Just because I happen to smoke, it does not mean that you may do so. I smoke, knowing that it is bad for me. I scold myself for it. . . . (What a subtle teacher I am! thought the public prosecutor.) Tobacco is bad for the health, and a man who smokes dies sooner than he would otherwise have done. Smoking is particularly bad for a little boy like you. You have a weak chest, you are not strong yet, and in delicate people tobacco causes consumption and all sorts of diseases. You remember Uncle Ignaty? Well, he died of consumption. Had he not smoked he might have been alive to-day."

Serioja gazed at the lamp pensively, touched the shade with his finger and sighed.

" Uncle Ignaty played the violin well!" he remarked. " The Gregorevs have his violin now."

Serioja put his elbows on the table, rested his head on his hands and grew thoughtful. By the expression on his face one could see that he was following the trend of his own thoughts. A look of sadness mingled with terror appeared in his large blinking eyes. No doubt he was thinking of death that had so recently taken his mother and his uncle Ignaty. Death bears mothers and uncles away to the other world, but their children and their violins remain. The dead live in heaven, somewhere near the stars, and look down on the earth. Do they feel the separation ?

" What else can I say to him ? " Yevgeny Petrovitch was thinking. " He is not listening to me. Obviously he does not consider his action or my arguments as serious. How can I make him understand ? "

The public prosecutor got up and began to pace the room.

" In my young days these questions were settled very simply," he reflected. " Every boy found smoking was whipped. This cured the poor spirited and cowardly ; but the braver and more intelligent of them took to hiding their tobacco in their boots, and smoking in the sheds. When discovered there and punished a second time, they went off to the river to smoke, and so on until the small boy grew into a man. To keep me from smoking my mother used to bribe me with money and sweets. Now such methods are considered immoral and are despised."

Taking his stand at the very base of reason, the modern pedagogue strives to make the child realise the idea of " good," not as connected with fear or vanity, but as an end in itself.

While he was thus pacing up and down, Serioja knelt on his chair, and leaning over the table began to draw. Some drawing-paper and a blue pencil always lay ready for him on the table, so that he should have no temptation to touch his father's papers, or the ink.

" When cook was chopping the cabbage to-day she cut her finger," he remarked, while drawing a house. " She screamed so loudly that we were all terrified and rushed into the kitchen. She was stupid ! Natalia Semionovna told her to put her finger in cold water, but she would suck it. . . . How could she put her dirty finger into her mouth ! It's not nice, is it, papa ? "

Then he went on telling his father how at dinner-time a barrel-organ man had come with a little girl who had danced to the music.

" He has his own thoughts," the public prosecutor mused. " He lives in his own world and sets his own standard of what is important and what is not. To fix his attention and awaken his consciousness, it is not sufficient to imitate his words, one must know and understand his way of thinking. He would have understood me easily enough had I really been sorry about the tobacco, or had I been hurt, or cried. . . . Mothers bringing up their children know unconsciously how to feel with them, to cry with them, to laugh with them. . . .

You can achieve nothing with logic and moralising. Well, what shall I say to him now? What?"

And it seemed strange and absurd to Yevgeny Petrovitch that he, an experienced lawyer, who had spent half his life cross-examining and sentencing, should be at a loss what to say to the boy.

"Listen; give me your word of honour that you will never smoke again," he said.

"Word of honour!" Serioja sang out, pressing hard on his pencil and bending over his drawing. "Word—of—hon—our—word . . ."

"I wonder whether he knows what 'word of honour' means?" Bikovsky asked himself. "No, I am a bad mentor! If a teacher, or one of my colleagues, could only look into my mind just now, they would consider me soft and suspect me of too much theorising. . . . At school or in court these troublesome questions are settled much easier than at home. Here you deal with people whom you love with all your soul, and love is exacting; it complicates the question at issue. If the boy were not my own son—say a pupil, or a prisoner, I should not be afraid; my thoughts would not wander like this."

Yevgeny Petrovitch sat down by the table and pulled one of Serioja's drawings towards him. The drawing represented a house with a crooked roof and showed a column of smoke that zigzagged like forked lightning to the very top of the paper. Beside the house stood a soldier, with two dots for eyes placed in the middle of his face, and holding a gun that looked like the figure 4.

"A man cannot be taller than a house," the public prosecutor said. "Look, the roof of the house only reaches to his shoulder." Serioja climbed on to his father's knee and snuggled into a comfortable position.

"But, papa," he said, looking at his drawing. "If you draw the soldier smaller, you cannot see his eyes."

Should he correct him? From daily observation of his own son the public prosecutor was convinced that children, like savages, have their own conceptions in art, which in their various forms are quite incomprehensible to adults. Judged by adult standards, Serioja would have appeared abnormal. He thought it proper and reasonable to draw men taller than houses, and to portray by means of his pencil not only objects but also sensations. Thus he represented the sound of an orchestra as sphere and smoke; and the sound of a whistle as a spiral thread. In his mind sound was intimately connected with form and colour ; thus, when colouring the letters of the alphabet, he invariably made L yellow, M red, A black, and so on.

Throwing down his drawing, Serioja settled himself comfortably once more and began toying with his father's beard. At first he smoothed it down carefully, then, parting it, he arranged it in the form of side whiskers.

" Now you look like Ivan Stepanovitch," he said. " And now you will look like our Swiss. Papa, why does a Swiss always stand by the door ? Is it to frighten thieves away ? "

The public prosecutor felt Serioja's breath on his face, and his beard touched the boy's cheek. A warm, gentle feeling arose in his heart, as though not only his hands but his whole soul was lying on Serioja's velvet coat. He gazed into the boy's large dark eyes, and it seemed to him that out of those deep wells there looked out at him his mother, his wife—all that he had ever loved.

" How could I whip him ? " he thought. " Of what use to think out a punishment for him ? I am no good as an educationalist. At one time people were simpler, theorised less and decided things boldly. Now we think too much—logic has conquered us. . . . The more developed a man is, the more he speculates and falls into subtleties, the more undecided and doubtful he becomes, the less confidence he has ; he approaches questions more timidly. And really, what courage a man must have in order to teach, judge, write ponderous tomes. . . ." The clock struck ten.

" Well, boy, time for bed ! " he said. " Say good-night and go along."

" But, papa," Serioja said, making a move. " I want to stay a little longer. Tell me something. Tell me a story."

" Very well, only you must go to bed directly I have finished."

On fine evenings Yevgeny Petrovitch would often tell Serioja stories. Like most busy men he did not know a single poem or story by heart, so that he had to improvise each time. He would always begin with the formula, " Once upon a time in a certain kingdom," and then would follow some innocent nonsense or other. He never knew what the middle or end of the story was going to be. The scenes and characters came at random impromptu, while the plot and moral came of their own accord, so to say. Serioja loved these improvisations, and his father had noticed that the simpler the plot the more strongly it impressed itself on the boy.

" Listen," he began, raising his eyes to the ceiling. " Once upon a time, in a certain kingdom, there lived an old king with a long grey beard and . . . and such a long moustache. Well, he lived in a palace of crystal that shone and sparkled in the sun like a huge mass of clear ice. The palace, my boy, stood in a large garden where you must know grew oranges . . . figs and cherries . . . tulips, roses, lilies of the valley—and brilliantly-coloured birds sang all day. On the trees there hung little glass balls that tinkled in the wind so sweetly that it was a pleasure to listen to them. Glass gives a softer sound than metal. Well, what else was there? There were also fountains . . . you remember there was a fountain in Auntie Sonia's garden in the country? Well, the fountains in the king's garden were exactly like that, only ever so much larger, and the spray from them reached to the very top of the highest poplar."

Yevgeny Petrovitch thought a moment, and then continued: " The old king had an only son and heir to his throne—a little boy, just like you. He was a good boy. He was never cross, went to bed early, never touched anything on the table—and . . . was altogether a clever boy. He had only one fault . . . he smoked."

Serioja listened attentively, his eyes blinking as they gazed straight into his father's. " What next? " the father asked himself. Then, after a little uncertainty, ended the story thus: " Through smoking the king's son fell ill with consumption, and died when he was only twenty. The infirm and aged monarch was left alone, utterly helpless. There was none to govern the kingdom nor to protect the palace. Enemies came and killed the old king, and destroyed the palace, and now in the garden there are no longer any cherries or birds or little glass balls . . . you see, boy. . . ."

Such an end appeared to Yevgeny Petrovitch as too naïve and absurd, but on Serioja it created a great impression. Again an expression of sadness and fear came into his eyes. For a moment or two he sat gazing pensively at the dark windows, then shuddered and said in a lowered voice:

" I will not smoke any more . . ."

When the boy had bidden him good-night and had gone to bed, the father began pacing quietly up and down the room, a contented smile on his face.

" People would say it was beauty and the artistic form that affected him," he thought. " Even if that were so, it is no consolation. After all, it was not a fair means . . . why must truth and morals be presented, not in the naked form, but gilded and sugared like a pill ? It is not rational. It is falsehood, deceit, trickery . . ."

He recalled how, when he had to make a speech to a jury, instead of giving them an analysis of the facts, he gave them a vivid account of the case ; and how people get their ideas on life, not by reasoning and self-analysis, but by reading novels and historic romances.

Medicine must be sweet, truth beautiful. . . . Man had accustomed himself to that since the days of Adam. . . . However . . . perhaps that was natural and was as it should be. . . . There are many delusions and illusions in nature. . . . He sat down to work, but these idle homely thoughts long strayed through his mind. Above, the piano had stopped, but the inmate of the second floor was still pacing from corner to corner. . . .

IN THE COACH-HOUSE

ANTON P. CHEKHOV

I

IT was ten o'clock at night. Stepan, the coachman, Michael, the dvornik,[1] the coachman's little grandson, Aleshka (who had come from the village on a visit to his grandfather), and Nikander, an old man of seventy whose nightly custom it was to call at the house on the chance of selling his herrings, were seated around a lantern in the great coach-house, and playing at korol.[2] Through the open doors of the coach-house there could be seen the spacious courtyard of the mansion in which the gentry lived, the gates of the courtyard, some outbuildings, and the dvornik's lodge. All was shrouded in darkness, except that four windows in a wing tenanted by lodgers were brightly lit up, and causing the shadows thrown by the upturned shafts of a number of carriages and sledges to mingle with the shadows thrown by the card-players where they hovered and darted over the walls and doors of the coach-house. Behind a thin partition-wall which divided the coach-house from the stable there were standing several horses, and everything was redolent with the smell of hay, added to a not over-pleasant odour of herrings which proceeded from old Nikander.

" He is lying unconscious," said the dvornik. " Without doubt he will die. Aleshka, you little pig, do not look at my cards, or I will box your ears for you! Yes, the doctors have gone, and his father and mother have arrived. They did so but a short while ago. 'Tis a most pitiful affair, and I pray to God He may avert it! 'Tis said the gentleman is an only son. What a misfortune, to be sure!"

All except Aleshka, who was absorbed in the game, glanced at the brilliantly lighted windows in the wing.

" To every man his fate," pursued the dvornik. " Of course, there will be an inquest held. Yet what do *I* know about the affair? What did *I* see? This morning the gentleman sent for me, and, handing me a letter, said: ' Put this in the post.' Even as he spoke

[1] Gatekeeper or porter.

[2] " King "—a card game.

his eyes were full of tears. Neither his wife nor his children were at home—they had gone for a walk. Well, while I was gone with the letter he shot himself in the temple with a revolver, and I returned to find the coachman's wife shouting the news about the courtyard ! "

" Then the gentleman has committed a great sin," said the herring merchant hoarsely, with a jerk of his head. " Yes, a very great sin."

" It must be that he had lost his reason through over-study," added the dvornik, taking a trick. " He used to sit up whole nights over his books. Play away, peasant. He was a good-looking gentleman, too—tall, fair-haired, and dark-eyed. Also, he was a most respectable lodger."

" 'Tis the female sex which brings such things about," remarked the coachman as he capped the king of diamonds with the nine of trumps. " Maybe he loved some woman other than his wife ? Or maybe his wife had grown cold to him ? Such is often the way."

II

Suddenly a wailing voice resounded through the stillness.

" He is gone," said the dvornik laconically. " They have sent to the hospital for the layers-out."

" The Kingdom of Heaven and eternal rest be with him ! " whispered the coachman, crossing himself.

Glancing at his grandfather, Aleshka did the same.

" Nay, 'tis not right to remember such folk," put in the herring merchant.

" Why not ? "

" Because 'tis a sin to kill oneself."

" True," assented the dvornik. " Therefore his soul will go straight to Hell, to the Unclean One."

Rising, the old man picked up his pack. " The same thing happened to our mistress, the general's lady," he continued, as he settled the pack more comfortably over his shoulders. " In those days we were her serfs. Well, her eldest son went out of his mind, and shot himself in the mouth with a pistol. According to the law such persons are to be buried outside a graveyard, and without priest or requiem ; but, to avoid such a scandal, our mistress bribed the police and the doctors to give her a paper which said that her son had committed the deed in a fit of delirium, and without knowing what he was doing.

Yes, such things *can* be done for a consideration. So they buried him with priests and full rites and music, and he was laid beneath the church. A month went by—two months—yet nothing happened. Then, during the third month, it was reported to the general's lady that the watchmen of the church had come to see her. What could they be wanting? As soon as they were brought into her presence they fell down upon their knees before her. 'Your Excellency,' they cried, 'we cannot go on with our task. All night your son lies wailing beneath the church!' "

Aleshka shuddered, and pressed his face close to his grandfather's back, that he might not see the windows.

"At first our mistress would not listen to the watchmen," continued the herring merchant. "Yet after a while the watchmen came to her again, and with them came the deacon of the church, for he too had heard the wailing. Then the general's lady perceived that it was going to be a bad business; so, having called the watchmen into her private room, she said to them: 'Here are twenty-five roubles for you, my friends. Do you, in return, go quietly by night, and dig up my unhappy son again, and bury him outside the graveyard.' Yes, and probably she handed them also a glass apiece. Well, the watchmen did as she had bidden them; and though the gravestone, with its inscription, remains in the church to this day, the general's son himself lies buried without the precincts. May the Lord pardon us for our sins! Only one day in the year may one pray for such folk, and that day is Trinity Sunday. Also, though one may not give alms for them, one may feed the birds to gain rest for their souls. So every third day the general's lady used to go to the cross-roads for that purpose; and one day she beheld there—though whence come no one knows—a black dog! It leapt upon the bread and devoured it, and what that dog was there can be no doubt. For the next five days our mistress remained as one distracted—she ate and drank nothing whatever. Then suddenly, when in the garden, she fell upon her knees, and prayed, and prayed. . . . Well, good-night, my friends, and may God and the Queen of Heaven be with you all! Come along, good Michael, and open me the gates."

So saying, he departed with the dvornik, and the coachman and Aleshka also stepped outside, rather than be left alone in the coach-house.

III

" A man has lived, and a man has died," said the coachman as he glanced at the lighted windows with their hovering shadows. " This morning the gentleman was walking about this very yard, and now he lies there a corpse ! "

" Yes ; and for us, too, the time will come to die," added the dvornik, moving away with the herring merchant. Presently the pair became lost to view in the darkness.

Not without some diffidence, the coachman, followed by Aleshka, approached the lighted windows. A very pale lady, with large, tear-filled eyes, was helping a grey-headed, handsome gentleman to move a couple of card-tables into the centre of the room—probably to serve as a resting-place for the body. On the green baize of the card-tables figures, written in chalk, were still visible, while the coachman's wife—the same woman who, in the morning, had run screaming about the yard—was standing a-tiptoe on a chair, and endeavouring to cover over a mirror with a sheet.

" Grandfather, what are they doing ? " asked Aleshka in a whisper.

" They are about to lay him on those tables," answered the coachman. " But let us go, little one ; it is bedtime."

Grandfather and grandson returned to the coach-house, said their prayers, and pulled off their boots ; after which Stepan lay down in a corner on the floor, and Aleshka betook himself to one of the sledges. The doors of the coach-house had been closed, and a strong smell of oil was proceeding from the extinguished lamp. After a while Aleshka raised his head, and looked around him. Through the crack between the doors the four lighted windows were still visible.

" Grandfather, I am afraid ! " the little boy called out.

" Nay, nay. Go to sleep ; go to sleep."

" I tell you I am afraid ! "

" What are you afraid of ? Oh ! the little fool ! "

For a moment there was silence. Then Aleshka leapt from the sledge, and, weeping loudly, ran across to his grandfather.

" What is it ? What is the matter with you ? " asked the startled coachman as he too rose to his feet.

" He is wailing, grandfather ! He is wailing ! "

" Who is wailing ? "

"The gentleman, grandfather! I am afraid! Do you not hear him?"

The coachman listened.

"'Tis only the women mourning," he said. "Run away, little fool. Yes, 'tis only the mourners lamenting the dead man."

"Nay, but I want to go back to the village," continued the boy in a paroxysm of sobbing and trembling. "Grandfather, *do* let us go back to the village, to mamma's! *Do* let us go, grandfather dear, and God will send you the Kingdom of Heaven in return!"

"Oh, the little donkey! But nay, nay. Say no more, say no more. Hold your tongue for a moment while I light the lantern. The little idiot!"

The coachman felt for his matches, and lit the lantern. Yet even then the light failed to reassure Aleshka.

"Grandfather, *do* let us go back to the village!" he begged again through his tears. "I am so frightened here! Why did you take me away from the village, you bad man?"

"What? *Whom* are you calling a bad man? How dare you address your grandfather in such a manner? I shall have to flog you for it!"

"Flog me, grandfather—flog me as hard as Sidor's goat if only you will be kind to me and take me back to mamma's!"

"Now, now, little grandson," whispered the coachman, soothingly. "There is nothing to be afraid of, or I, too, should be afraid. Say a prayer to God."

IV

The doors creaked, and the dvornik's head showed itself.

"What? Not asleep yet, Stepan?" he asked as he entered. "I myself am not likely to get much sleep to-night. All night long it will be a question of opening and shutting the gates. But what are you weeping for, Aleshka?"

"He is afraid," the coachman answered for his grandson.

Once more a short, wailing cry sounded through the air.

"They are mourning the dead man," commented the dvornik "His mother cannot believe her eyes. Truly 'tis a terrible thing for a man to kill himself!"

"Is the father there too?"

"Yes; but he sits quietly in a corner. As for the children, they have been sent away to some relatives. . . . Well, Stepan, shall we cut for trumps again ? Eh ? "

" I'm your man," replied the coachman, scratching himself. " And do you, Aleshka, run away and sleep. You are nearly old enough to get married, yet there you stand blubbering, you little rascal ! Now, run away, little grandson—run away and sleep."

The dvornik's presence had partially reassured Aleshka, so he returned—though not over-boldly—to the sledge, and lay down. Until sleep overcame him he could hear occasional whisperings of :

" It is I to play. I go so much."

" It is I to play. I go so much."

Then in the courtyard a bell rang, and a door creaked as though it were saying, in its turn, " It is I to play. I go so much." When at length Aleshka saw the dead man in his dreams, and, terrified at his eyes, leapt up in a renewed fit of weeping, morning had dawned, his grandfather was asleep and snoring, and the coach-house no longer seemed a place to be afraid in.

THE CHORUS GIRL

ANTON P. CHEKHOV

ONCE, when she was younger, prettier, and had a better voice, her admirer, Nikolai Petrovitch Kolpakov, was sitting in the entresol of her summer cottage. It was unbearably hot and stifling. Kolpakov had just dined and had drunk a full bottle of cheap port; he was out of sorts and not very well; they were both suffering from ennui and were waiting until it should become a little cooler, so that they could go for a walk.

Suddenly and unexpectedly the bell rang. Kolpakov, who was in his shirt-sleeves and slippers, sprang from his seat and looked questioningly at Pasha.

" Probably the postman—or maybe one of the girls," she said.

Kolpakov would not feel embarrassed in the presence either of the postman or of Pasha's friend; but, to guard against a possible emergency, he caught up his clothes and boots in one hand and went into the next room, while Pasha ran to open the door.

To Pasha's great surprise she found there an unknown, young and beautiful woman, dressed with exquisite taste and evidently a lady.

The stranger was very pale and breathed hard, as if she had just climbed a very long flight of stairs.

" What can I do for you ? " Pasha asked.

The lady did not reply at once. She made a step forward, slowly looked around the room and sat down in a way that clearly showed she was tired out. Then she moved her pale lips in an effort to say something.

" Is my husband here, at your house ? " she asked at last, lifting to Pasha a pair of large eyes with lids red from weeping.

" Whose husband ? " Pasha whispered.

" My husband—Nikolai Petrovitch Kolpakov."

" No, no, madame—I—I do not know any husband."

A moment passed in silence. Several times the stranger touched her pale lips with her handkerchief and held her breath, as if to repress an inner shivering. Pasha stood riveted before her and looked at her in perplexity.

" So you say he is not here ? " asked the lady, with a stronger voice and smiling with a strange kind of smile.

" I—I do not know whom you are asking about."

" You are a nasty, odious, vile creature," the stranger began, looking at Pasha with hatred and disgust. " Yes, you are abominable, and I am glad, very glad, that at last I have the opportunity to tell you so ! "

Pasha felt that she was making an impression of something nauseatingly ugly on this lady, all in black, with her thin, white fingers.

" Where is my husband ? " continued the lady. " But, after all, what does it matter if he is here or not ? But I must tell you that his embezzlements have been discovered and they have begun a search for Nikolai Petrovitch, and he will be arrested. See what you have done ! "

The lady rose to her feet and walked about the room in great excitement.

" To-day he will be found and arrested," she went on, with a sob, and the sound showed how grieved and outraged she was. " I know who brought him to this horrible pass ! You odious, low, miserable, lewd, mercenary creature ! " The lady's lips curled and her nose wrinkled in disgust. " I am helpless—listen to me, you low woman ! —I am helpless, you are stronger than I ; but there is One who will defend me and my children ! God sees everything ; He is just ! He will call you to account for every one of my tears, for all my sleepless nights ! There will come a time when you will remember my words ! "

Again there was silence. The lady walked to and fro wringing her hands, and Pasha stood and stared at her as stupidly as before, not understanding what it all meant and awaiting something terrible at her hands.

" I do not know anything, lady," she said at last, and suddenly burst into tears.

" You lie ! " cried the visitor, her eyes flashing angrily. " I know all. I know he has spent every day of the last month at your house ! "

" Well, what of that ? I receive many guests at my house, but I do not compel anybody to come. They come of their own accord."

" I tell you that his swindle has been discovered ! He has spent other people's money—for such as you! For *you* he has committed a crime! Listen to me!" the lady cried, stopping determinedly before Pasha. "You cannot have any principles; you live only to bring misfortune—that is your aim; but I cannot think that you have fallen so low that you have lost every vestige of human feeling! He has a wife and children; if he should be found guilty and sent to Siberia, I and his children will die of hunger. Do you understand what it means? But there is a way to save him and all of us from poverty and disgrace. If I should bring them to-day the nine hundred roubles he has embezzled, they would leave him alone. Only nine hundred roubles!"

"What nine hundred roubles?" Pasha asked in a low voice. "I —I do not understand—I have not taken——"

"I do not ask you for the nine hundred roubles. You have no money, and I do not want what belongs to you. I ask you for something else. Men generally give costly presents to such as you. Return me only those trinkets which my husband has given you!"

"Madame, your husband has never given me any trinkets!" screamed Pasha, who was at last beginning to understand.

"Then where is the money? He has squandered all I had, and has taken that of others. Where has it all gone to? Listen to me, I beg of you—I was excited and said many unpleasant things, but I beg your pardon. You must hate me, I know; but if you are capable of feeling pity you will understand my situation. I implore you to return the things to me!"

"Ah, yes—" said Pasha, shrugging her shoulders. "I would gladly do so, but may God punish me if I have taken anything from him. Upon my conscience! But let me see," and the chorus girl suddenly became confused. "Some time ago he did bring me two trinkets—if you care to have them I will return them to you."

Pasha pulled out a toilet-table drawer and took out a tawdry gold bracelet and a thin gold ring set with a cheap ruby.

"Please take them!" she said, handing them to her visitor.

The lady flushed deeply and her lips quivered. She was very much offended.

"What is this you are giving me?" she asked. "I have not come here for charity. I have come for what does not belong to you —for what you, taking advantage of your position, have forced out of my husband—the weak, unfortunate man! On Thursday, when

I saw you with him in the harbour, you wore costly brooches and bracelets, so it is no good playing the innocent with me! I ask you for the last time: will you or will you not give me the things?"

"Lord, how funny you are!" said Pasha, beginning, in her turn, to feel offended. "I assure you that I have not received from your Nikolai Petrovitch anything other than this bracelet and little ring. He used to bring me only sweet tarts."

"Sweet tarts!" The stranger smiled bitterly. "At home the children have nothing to eat, and here we eat sweet tarts! Then you refuse finally to return the trinkets?"

There was no reply. The lady pressed her handkerchief to her face and burst into tears.

"I implore you!" she cried through her sobs. "You have been the ruin and undoing of my husband; I implore you to save him. You have no pity for him; but the children, the children—what have they done that this misfortune should fall upon them?"

Pasha pictured to herself the little children standing in the street and crying with hunger, and began crying herself.

"What can I do, madame?" she said. "You say that I am a wretch and that I have ruined Nikolai Petrovitch, and yet I swear to you, as if I were standing before God Himself, that I have not in any way benefited by your husband's visits. In all our chorus there is only Moti who has a rich admirer."

"I ask you for the things! It is the things I want of you! I weep, lower myself—if you wish I will fall on my knees to you!"

Pasha cried out in sudden fear and wrung her hands. She felt that this pale lady, who spoke in the high, refined language in which people generally express themselves on the stage, would make good her threat and really fall on her knees before her. She would do that out of pride and nobleness, knowing that it would elevate herself and degrade the chorus girl.

"Well, I will give you the things." Pasha began to bustle about, wiping her eyes. "You can have them. But they are not from your Nikolai Petrovitch. I got them from my other guests. But, as you please!"

She pulled out the top drawer of the bureau and took from it a brooch set with diamonds, a string of coral, several rings, and a bracelet, and handed them all to the lady.

"Take them if you want to, but I tell you again, I had no benefit whatsoever from your husband. Take them, and get rich on it!" continued Pasha, who was deeply offended at the lady's threat to fall on her knees to her. "And if you are an honest and lawful wife to him, you had better keep him in hand near yourself, that's all! I did not call him—he came himself."

The lady looked at the jewellery through her tears. "These will not do," she said. "There is hardly five hundred roubles' worth here."

Pasha impetuously threw out of the bureau a gold watch, a cigar-case, and a pair of cuff buttons, and cried, with a fling of her hands:

"And now I have nothing more left! You may even search me!"

The visitor sighed and with trembling hands wrapped the trinkets in a handkerchief, and without saying a word, without even the slightest bow, she left the room.

The door of the next room opened and Kolpakov appeared. He was very pale, and his head shook nervously, as if he had just swallowed something bitter, and tears were in his eyes.

"What kind of things have you given me?" Pasha fell upon him. "When, I ask you?"

"Things—nonsense, who speaks of things!" said Kolpakov, shaking his head. "My God! She cried before you, lowered herself——"

"I ask you: what things have you given me?" screamed Pasha.

"Good Lord! She, noble, proud, pure, she wanted to go down on her knees before—before this hag! And I brought her to this! I allowed it!"

He caught his head in his two hands and groaned.

"No, I will never forgive you this! Never! Get out of my sight, you dirty beast!" he shouted, backing away from Pasha with disgust. "She wanted to go down on her knees, and to whom? To *you*! Oh, my God!"

He dressed himself quickly, avoiding contact with Pasha, and turning to the door went out.

Pasha lay down and began to cry bitterly. She was already regretting the trinkets she had so thoughtlessly given away, but she felt, too, deeply offended. She remembered how a merchant, about three years before, had given her a beating without any provocation, and cried still more bitterly.

THE AVENGER

Anton P. Chekhov

As soon as Fedor Sigaev found out that his wife was unfaithful to him, he decided to revenge himself, and for that purpose he paid a visit to the shop of Schmucks & Co., dealers in all kinds of fire-arms, and asked the man to show him a good revolver. His face expressed anger, sorrow, and irrevocable decision.

"I know what I am about to do," he thought. "My honour has been trodden in the mud, the sanctity of the family outraged, and wickedness is triumphant; therefore I, as a good citizen and an honest man, must appear as the avenger. First I shall slay my wife and her lover, then myself——"

He had not, as yet, bought a revolver, nor had he shot any one, but his imagination already pictured to him the ghastly wounds he would inflict, the crowds of people and the scenes at the inquest. With the malignity of a deeply offended man he imagined the horror of his relatives and the public in general, the mortal agony of his faithless wife, and even saw in his mind's eye the large headings in the papers and the long editorials treating of the breaking up of family life.

The shopman, an active little man with a paunch and white vest, displayed before him on the counter several revolvers, and with a deferential smile upon his lips, continually scraping with his feet, said:

"I would advise you, sir, to take this splendid revolver. The newest make of Smith-Wesson. It is the latest thing in fire-arms; it has six chambers, with an extractor. Just look at its beautiful workmanship. The very latest, sir. We sell dozens every day for defence against marauders, wolves, and the wreckers of family happiness. The bullet strikes surely and powerfully, can hit at a considerable distance, and kills outright the faithless wife and her lover. As to suicides, I can assure you, sir, that I know of no better make——"

The man lowered and lifted it in the air, pulled the trigger, took aim, and handled the weapon lovingly as if he could not contain his enthusiasm. Looking at his rapturous face one could think that he would gladly have sent a bullet through his head if he only possessed a revolver of such beautiful workmanship as Smith-Wesson's.

"What is the price of one?" asked Sigaev.

"Forty-five roubles."

"M-m! It is too expensive!"

"In that case I will offer you one of another make, a cheaper one. We have a large assortment at different prices. For instance, this revolver is of a French make. The price is only eighteen roubles, but—(the man's face expressed contempt)—this make is an old-fashioned one, it is bought now only by intelligent proletarians and by women cranks. To commit suicide or to shoot one's wife with such a revolver is considered now a sign of vulgarity. Polite society recognises only Smith-Wesson."

"I am not going to kill any one or to commit suicide. I simply need a revolver to frighten away thieves from my summer cottage," Sigaev gloomily lied.

"It is none of our business what you are buying a revolver for," said the man, modestly lowering his eyes. "If we should try to find out the reasons in every case we should be compelled, sir, to close our shop. For frightening away thieves this revolver is no good, sir, because it produces a dull, weak sound. I would suggest that you buy one which is generally used, the Mortimer pistol or, as it is commonly known, the duelling pistol."

"Would it not be a good idea to call him out?" ran through Sigaev's head like lightning. "But no, that would be too much honour—such a beast ought to be killed outright like a rabid dog."

The man, gracefully turning and scraping his feet, put before him a whole heap of revolvers without ceasing to smile and to chat. But somehow a Smith-Wesson seemed to Sigaev more desirable and imposing than the rest. He took one of them in his hands and sank into thought. His imagination pictured to him how he would fire through her head and the blood would pour in torrents from the wound, over the carpets and parquet-floor, and how the dying traitress would writhe in mortal agony.

"That would not do," he thought. "I should do much better to kill him and myself—her I will spare. Let her live and suffer all the harrowing pangs of remorse, and suffer the contempt of all who come in contact with her. That would be much worse for a nervous, over-sensitive nature like hers than death."

And he pictured to himself his funeral: he, the offended one, was lying in his coffin with a gentle smile on his lips, and she, pale and worn-out with remorse, walked in his funeral cortège like a veritable Niobe, and did not know where to hide from the contemptuous glances the highly indignant people threw at her.

"I see, sir, that you like Smith-Wesson best," the clerk suddenly disturbed him in his dreams. "If the price seems too high to you, I am willing to let you have it five roubles cheaper. Besides, we have still other makes, slightly cheaper."

The little man turned gracefully to the shelves and took down another dozen revolvers.

"Here is one for thirty roubles. That is not dear, if you consider that our currency has fallen terribly and the import duty on foreign makes is becoming higher with every day. 'Pon my honour, sir, I am a conservative by nature and even I begin to grumble! Judge for yourself, sir, things have come to such a pass that only the rich can allow themselves the luxury of a good revolver! The poor must satisfy themselves with revolvers of cheap Russian make, namely, those which are made in Tula, and the Tula make is a—misfortune! You fire at your wife with such a revolver and hit your own shoulder."

Sigaev suddenly felt very sorry that he would not live to see the sufferings of the traitress. Revenge is only sweet when one can see and gloat at one's enemy's sufferings. What good would his revenge do him when he would lie in his grave and not see the havoc it had wrought?

"Would it not be better," he thought, "to kill *him* first, be present at *his* funeral and only kill myself afterwards? But I should be arrested long before that and my revolver would be taken away from me. And so: I will kill him, her I will spare, and I—I will not commit suicide at first, but will let myself be arrested instead. There is always time enough to kill oneself. An arrest would give me an opportunity to show the jury and society in general the whole baseness of her conduct. If I should be fool enough to kill myself she would probably succeed, with her characteristic boldness and natural aptitude for lying and prevaricating, to clear herself of all guilt and put all blame on me, and society would perhaps justify her action, and—who knows ?—probably laugh at me ; if, on the contrary, I should remain alive, then——"

A moment later he thought :

" Yes, and besides, if I should kill myself I should probably be accused and suspected of being prompted by a petty impulse. And, in truth, why should I kill myself ? Besides, to shoot oneself would be to confess cowardice. And so : I will kill him, and will leave her alive. As to myself, I shall be arrested. On the trial she would have to figure as a witness. I can easily imagine her confusion when questioned by my lawyer ! The sympathy of the press and the public would in such a case undoubtedly be on my side."

He considered, and the salesman continued to display before him his goods and dutifully to entertain his customer.

" Here are some revolvers of English make which we received but a short time ago, but I assure you that they pale to nothing before the Smith-Wesson. The other day—you, of course, have seen it in the papers—an army officer bought from us a revolver of the Smith-Wesson make. He fired at his wife's seducer and—what do you suppose ?—the bullet went right through his chest, then it went through a bronze lamp, then the piano, from the piano it rebounded, killing a spaniel and wounding the wife. A splendid feat, and one which does honour to our firm. The officer is now under arrest. Of course, he will be found guilty and sentenced to a number of years of penal servitude in Siberia. That is, first, because our laws are too antiquated, and, secondly, because the jury is almost in every instance over-partial to the seducer. Why ? Because the judges, jury and public prosecutor all have a weakness for breaking the tenth commandment, and they do not care in the least if there be one husband less in Russia. As to society—I really believe it would enjoy nothing better than the deportation of all husbands to Saghalin. Oh, sir, you cannot imagine what a feeling of indignation fills my heart when I think of the deplorable state of our contemporary morals ! Why, to love the wife of another is just as much in vogue as to smoke some one else's cigars or to read some one else's books. Our trade is falling off every year more and more—that does not mean that family life has become purer and the breaking of the tenth commandment rarer—but simply that the husbands are reconciled to their fate and are afraid of the courts and of penal servitude."

The clerk looked about cautiously and whispered :

" And whose fault is it, sir ? Why, only the Government's ! "

" Where is the wisdom of going to Saghalin on account of such a hog ? " thought Sigaev. " If I should be sent to Siberia my wife would be free to marry again, and to betray her second husband ; she would be triumphant. And so : her I shall not kill ; myself, also not ; *him* I shall also not kill. I must find another way to revenge myself—one more sensible and more painful. I will pay them with contempt and will institute against her divorce proceedings in which her scandalous conduct will be shown before all the world and she will be for ever disgraced."

" Here, sir, is still another make," said the man, taking down a new dozen of revolvers. " I ask you to turn your attention to the peculiar mechanism of the lock."

Sigaev, after his decision, no longer needed a revolver, and wished nothing better than to get out of the shop. The salesman in the meanwhile waxed more and more enthusiastic, and did not tire of displaying his goods.

The offended husband felt conscience-stricken at the sight of the salesman, who was giving himself so much trouble displaying his wares, smiling, turning, scraping, and trying with all his might to please him, the customer.

" Very well, in that case," he muttered, " I will call later on, or—or will send some one."

He endeavoured not to see the expression on the shopman's face, but, to smooth out at least a little the awkward position to which he had brought himself, he felt it necessary to buy something. But what ? He looked around the walls of the shop, wishing for something cheap, and his eyes rested upon a net which hung near the door.

" This—what is this ? " he asked.

" That is a net for catching quail "

" What is the price of it ? "

" Eight roubles, sir."

" I will take one." The offended husband paid the eight roubles, took the net, and left the shop.

NATALIA VLADIMIROVNA

ANTON P. CHEKHOV

I

ONE evening, nine years ago, at the time of the hay harvest, a friend of mine—Peter Sergeitch, a lawyer—set out with me to ride to the station for letters.

The weather had been perfect, but on the way home we began to hear distant thunder, and to perceive an angry black cloud advancing to meet us. Against its dark background the church and the house gleamed white, and the tall poplar-trees silver. All the air was full of the scent of rain and of new-mown hay. My companion seemed to be in the best of spirits, and, among other things, observed that it would be a fine stroke of luck if suddenly we were to come upon some old mediaeval castle, with castellated battlements and moss and owls complete, where we could take shelter from the rain, and let the storm beat upon us until the close of eternity.

Then a first spurt of rain came sweeping over the fields of rye and oats, and the wind plucked at us, and the dust circled high in mid-air. Peter Sergeitch laughed, and spurred his horse forward.

" Splendid ! " he cried. " Splendid indeed ! "

Infected by his gaiety, I, too, laughed, without giving a thought to the matter of whether or not I might be soaked to the skin or killed by a stroke of lightning. How the whirlwind and the gallop caught one by the throat, and made one feel as though one were moving swifter than a bird ! How they fired and tickled one's breast ! Yet by the time we had reached home the wind had fallen, and great drops of rain were pattering down upon the grass and roofs.

II

In the stable-yard not a soul was to be seen.

Peter Sergeitch himself unsaddled the horses, and led them to their stalls. Meanwhile, I stood at the door of the stable, and gazed at the rain-soaked ridges of hay. The luscious, rousing scent of the crop was even stronger here than in the open. Everything had become a blur of mist and damp.

" What a peal that was ! " said Peter Sergeitch as he approached me just when a particularly loud, reverberating clap of thunder had seemed to split the very heavens in twain. Panting with the swift motion of the ride, he stood beside me on the threshold, and looked at me. And as he did so I could see that he was in love with me.

" Natalia Vladimirovna," he began, " I would give the whole world to stand here for ever and gaze at you ! You look to me so beautiful to-night ! "

His eyes were full of mingled rapture and entreaty, his face was pale, and on his beard and moustache there were glistening raindrops which, to my fancy, seemed also to be gazing at me with eyes of love.

" I love you ! " he went on. " Yes, I love you, and the very sight of you makes me happy. I know that you can never be my wife, but I wish for nothing, I have need of nothing, except that you should *know* that I love you. Do not speak, do not answer me, do not take the least notice of what I say. Only learn that you are very dear to me, and permit me to continue looking at you as I am doing now."

His passion communicated itself to me, and as I gazed back into his inspired face, and listened to the murmur of his voice as it mingled with the sound of the rain, I felt as though I were bewitched, and could not stir. Nevertheless, I could have remained there for ever—for ever I could have looked at his shining eyes and listened to the sound of his voice !

" Do not utter a word," he said again. " Continue only to be silent, and all will be well."

And, indeed, all was very well with me just then. For sheer joy I laughed—then started to run towards the house through the pouring rain. He, too, laughed, and, darting forward, pursued me. Noisily as children we clattered, wet and panting, up the stairs, and flew into the drawing-room. My father and my brother, who were not used to seeing me full of laughter and gaiety, stared at me in astonishment—then joined in our merriment.

III

The storm-cloud had passed away, and the thunder had ceased to roll ; yet on Peter's beard there were still glistening a few raindrops. All that evening, until supper-time, he sang, whistled, and played with the dog—chasing it from room to room until he came near to upsetting a servant who happened to be entering with the tea-urn. At supper-time, too, he ate enormously, talked a great deal of rubbish, and assured us that to eat fresh cucumbers during the winter season gave one a foretaste of spring.

When I went to bed I put out my candle, and opened the bedroom window. My soul was full of a vague, indefinite feeling. I recalled the fact that I was free, healthy, rich, and well-born, as also the fact that I was beloved. Yes, above all things I recalled that I was rich and well-born. My God, how good that seemed! Then, shivering slightly with the chill which was rising from the garden, I endeavoured to decide whether or not I loved Peter Sergeitch; and, without deciding either way, fell asleep.

Next morning, on seeing the sunbeams and the shadows of the lime boughs playing over my bed, the events of the previous evening returned vividly to my recollection. Life seemed to me bounteous, varied, and full of delight. Singing softly, I dressed myself in haste, and ran down into the garden.

IV

What happened afterwards? Nothing happened. True, next winter, when we were living in town, Peter Sergeitch paid us an occasional visit; but country acquaintances are interesting only in the country and in summer-time, whereas in town, and during the winter, they lose half their charm. Should they be taking tea with you, they seem to be wearing strange garments, and to be stirring their tea overlong with the spoon. Though Peter Sergeitch would discourse in a general way on love, he was quite a different being from what he had been in the country. In town we were more conscious of the barrier which stood between us. I was rich and well-born, whereas he was poor, and not even of gentle rank—a mere deacon's son who had happened to attain the post of a public prosecutor. Both of us—I through youthful ignorance, and he for God knows what reason—looked upon the barrier in question as too high and too broad ever to be surmounted. When visiting us, he would laugh in a forced manner, and criticise Providence; yet, should any one else chance to enter the room, at once he would become moodily silent. True, no barrier existed which could not have been broken through; but the heroes of contemporary romance, as I know them, are too timid, too unenterprising, too slothful, too diffident of their own powers, ever to perform such a feat. They are too ready to accept the idea that they never will succeed, and that life has cheated them; wherefore, instead of striving, they criticise, and call the world base—forgetting that, through that very criticism, they themselves are merging into baseness.

For myself, I had kinsfolk who showed me affection, and prosperity lay all around me. I lived hand in hand with happiness, and sang as I pursued my way through life. Never once did I try to understand myself, or to know what I was looking for or wanted in life. I simply let time pass by. Affection hemmed me about, bright days succeeded warm nights, the nightingales began to sing, and soon the hay was giving forth its sweetness. Yet all these things, astonishing and delightful to the senses though they were, passed from me as they pass from all human beings, and vanished as a cloud might do.

V

At length my father died, and I found myself growing old. What, that summer evening, had so pleased me, and charmed me, and bidden me hope—the sound of the rain, the pealing of the thunder, the thoughts of happiness, the talk of love—had now become for me a mere memory. Before me there lay only a dreary, empty waste, on the horizon of which not a living soul was visible. Yet on that horizon there was looming something dark and terrible!

A ring at the bell! . . . Peter Sergeitch had called! . . . When, in the winter-time, I see the trees, and remember how, in the summer-time, it was for me they donned their greenery, I whisper to them, "My dear ones!" Similarly, whenever I chance to encounter some one who has been with me in the spring-time of my life, my heart feels sad, yet warm, as I whisper to that person words of like import. . . .

Not long before, my father's influence had procured for Peter a post in town. He had grown a little older and a little greyer. Also, he had ceased to hold forth on the subject of love, or to talk nonsense. He had no great enthusiasm for his work, but seemed to be ailing, to be disillusioned, to be shaking his fist at life, to be living against his will.

Entering the room, he seated himself by the fire, and gazed silently into the flames. And I, not knowing what to say, asked him:

"Well—what?"

"Nothing," he replied; and again the firelight played upon his sorrowful face.

Then I remembered the past; and suddenly my shoulders began to heave, and my head to sink forward, and I burst into a storm of tears. I felt sorry beyond measure both for him and for myself. I felt a passionate yearning for what was gone, for what life had denied me. Nor had I a thought in my head about my being rich and well-born.

Continuing to sob convulsively, I pressed my hands to my temples and murmured:

"My God, my God! I have ruined my life!"

Meanwhile he sat without speaking. Yes, he forbore to say to me, "Do not weep"; for he knew that I *must* weep, and that the time had come for me to do so. Yet by his eyes I could see that he was sorry for me. And I too was sorry for him, as well as angry with him for having been so faint of heart—for having so little understood how to order my life and his own.

VI

When, later, I saw him to the door, he seemed purposely to be a long time putting on his overcoat. Twice he kissed my hand in silence and gazed into my tear-stained face. I have an idea that during those few moments he was recalling to his memory the thunder, and the rain-soaked ridges of hay, and our laughter, and my face as it had looked that day. Lastly, he tried to say something—something which he seemed very much to desire to say—but he could not do so. He just nodded his head and pressed my hand. May God be with him!

After seeing him depart, I returned to the study, and seated myself upon the hearthrug in front of the fire. The red coals had turned to ashes, and were beginning to die out, and the frost was knocking louder and louder at the window-panes, and the wind was singing in the chimney.

A maid-servant entered, and, thinking that I was asleep, called me by name.

THE CHAMELEON

Anton P. Chekhov

THE police sergeant Achumyelof, wearing his new cloak and with a bundle under his arm, is walking across the market-place. He is followed by a red-haired policeman carrying a sieve filled to the brim with confiscated gooseberries. Quiet reigns all around. Not a soul in the market-place. The open doors and windows of the shops and public-houses gaze out sadly upon God's world like hungry mouths wide open. Not even beggars are hanging around.

Suddenly Achumyelof hears some one shouting: " So you want to bite, you accursed beast! Children, don't let him! Nowadays dogs are not allowed to bite. Stop him! Oh, oh! "

The howling of a dog is heard. Achumyelof looks in the direction from which the sound comes and sees a dog, limping on three legs, run out of Pichugin's timber-yard. A man in a starched calico shirt and with a vest unbuttoned is chasing him. The man is close at the dog's heels; suddenly he lurches forward, falls to the ground, and takes hold of the dog's hind feet. Again the dog's howling is heard and the cry, " Do not let him! " Sleepy faces appear at the windows of the shops, and at the timber-yard a crowd quickly gathers as though it had grown out of the ground.

" Do you think it can be a riot? " asks the policeman.

Achumyelof turns to the left and walks toward the crowd. Near the gate of the timber-yard he sees the man with the unbuttoned vest holding up his right hand and showing the crowd a bloody finger. On his half-drunken face there is an expression as though he were saying: " Wait, I will make you pay for this, you scoundrel! " And the finger itself looks like a trophy. In this man Achumyelof recognised Khriukin, the goldsmith. In the centre of the crowd, with his forefeet spread out and trembling from head to foot, sits the author of the whole row—a young white greyhound, with a pointed muzzle and a yellow spot on his back. In his watery eyes there is an expression of distrust.

" What is the matter? " asks Achumyelof, making his way through the crowd. " Why are you here? What is the matter with your finger? Who has been screaming? "

" I was just walking along, sir, not touching anybody," says

Khriukin, coughing into his fist, " to see about the wood for Dimitri Dimitriyevitch, when suddenly this vicious cur bites my finger. You will excuse me. I am a man who works; I have very particular work to do, and somebody will have to pay me, for I won't be able to use this finger maybe for a week! There is nothing in the law, sir, about having to stand things from animals! If they are all going to bite it would be better not to live in this world!"

" Now," says Achumyelof sternly, moving his eyebrows up and down, " now, whose dog is this? I shall not allow this matter to rest. I will teach you people not to let your dogs run about loose! It is time that something were done about people who won't obey regulations. When I punish the scoundrel he will find out what it means to let dogs and other animals roam about. I will show him who I am! Yeldyrin," turning to the policeman, " find out whose dog it is and draw up a report. The dog will be killed. Make short work of it! He is probably a mad dog anyhow. Whose dog is it?"

" He looks like General Yigalof's dog," says some one in the crowd.

" General Yigalof's? H-m! Yeldyrin, take off my cloak; it is terribly hot! It is probably going to rain. There is one thing that I do not understand: how could that dog bite you?" says Achumyelof, turning to Khriukin. " He does not come up to your fingers. He is such a little dog, and you are such a big man. You have probably torn your finger on a nail, and afterwards the idea of the dog occurred to you and you are trying to extort money. I know you people; you are devils!"

" He teased the dog by putting a cigarette in his face; but the dog is no fool and went for him, sir."

" You lie, squint-eye! He did not see it, sir! What does he want to lie for? You, sir, can tell whether a man is lying or talking according to his conscience as in the sight of God. But let the judge decide whether I am lying! The law says that nowadays we are all equal. I have a brother myself among the gendarmes. If you——"

" Stop talking!"

" No, that is not the general's," observes the policeman pensively. " The general does not have dogs like that. His dogs are mostly setters."

" Are you sure of that?" " Yes, sir, quite sure."

" I know it myself, too. The general has high-priced thoroughbred dogs, but this is—the devil knows what! He has neither hair nor shape—just a common cur. For any one to keep a dog like that! What are you people thinking of? If such a dog should show itself in Petersburg or Moscow, do you know what would happen? They would not stop to look up the law, but just simply—and that is the end! Khriukin, you have suffered pain, and I will not let this matter rest. I must give them a lesson! It is about time!"

"But perhaps it is the general's dog after all," the policeman thinks aloud. "It is not written on his muzzle. The other day I saw a dog like that in the general's yard."

"Of course it is the general's," says a voice in the crowd.

"Yeldyrin, help me put on my coat. It is draughty around here; I am shivering. Take the dog to the general's and find out there. Say that I found him and sent him. And tell him not to let the dog out in the street. It is probably an expensive dog, and if every fellow is to hit him on the nose with his cigar, he will soon be ruined. A dog is a delicate creature. And you, blockhead, put down your hand! It is not necessary to exhibit that stupid finger of yours. It is your own fault!"

"There is the general's cook. Let us ask him. Hello, Prokhor, come here a minute! Look, is that dog yours?"

"That dog? We never had such a dog in our lives!"

"He is not worth asking questions about," says Achumyelof. "He's a tramp dog. There is nothing more to be said. If I say he is a tramp dog, he *is* a tramp dog! He will be killed."

"That is not ours," continues Prokhor. "That dog belongs to the general's brother, who has recently arrived. My master is not a lover of greyhounds, but his brother is fond of them."

"So his brother, Vladimir Ivanovitch, has arrived?" asks Achumyelof, and a rapturous smile spreads over his face. "Well, well, and I did not know it! He is here on a visit?"

"Yes, sir, on a visit."

"Well, well, he probably was home-sick for his dear brother. And I did not know it! So it is his dog, you say? I am very glad. Take him! A nice little dog! A quick little dog—*Snap*, and he has hold of the fellow's finger. Ha-ha-ha! Why are you trembling, you dear little thing? That man is a villain!" Prokhor calls the dog and walks away with him from the timber-yard. The crowd laughs at Khriukin. "I will catch you some time!" Achumyelof threatens him, and wrapping himself in his cloak, he continues on his way across the market-place.

A WORK OF ART

Anton P. Chekhov

SASHA SMIRNOV, only son of his mother, entered the office of Dr. Koshelkov, carrying under his arm something wrapped up in No. 223 of the *Bourse Gazette.*

"Ah, my dear lad!" the doctor greeted him. "Well, how do we feel? Anything new?"

"My mother sends her respects, Ivan Koshelkov, and commands me to thank you," said Sasha Smirnov in a highly excited voice, placing his hand on his breast. "I am the only son of my mother, and you have saved my life—cured me of a dangerous illness, and—we, both of us, do not know how to thank you for it."

"That is enough, young man!" the doctor interrupted him, beaming with pleasure. "I did only what every one else would have done in my place."

"I am the only son of my mother," Sasha continued. "We are poor people and of course cannot pay you for your services, and—we are pained—our conscience is not at ease, doctor, and we, that is I and my mother, whose only son I am, beg you to accept as a mark of our esteem and gratitude—this object—which object is very valuable, of antique bronze—a work of art."

"There is really no necessity," the doctor frowned. "Now, where is the need of it?"

"No, but you must not refuse it, please," Sasha continued to mutter, unwrapping the parcel. "You will greatly mortify us, my mother and myself, by a refusal. It is a nice thing, this—of antique bronze. It was left us by my late father and we kept it as a dear heirloom, a remembrance. My father used to deal in old bronzes, you know, buying them when chance offered, and selling them to lovers of fine art. My mother and myself are now in the same business."

Sasha took the object out of its paper wrappings and solemnly placed it on the table. It was a very small candelabrum of old bronze and of very artistic workmanship. It represented a group: on a pedestal stood two female figures in the costume of Mother Eve. The figures smiled coquettishly and, on the whole, gave one the idea that if they were not in duty bound to support the candlestick they would at once jump down from the pedestal and turn the room into such a scene of revelry as would make you, reader, blush with shame at the mere thought of it.

After the doctor had examined his present he scratched his ear, chuckled and blew his nose.

" Yes, it is really very beautiful," he continued ; " but how shall I best express myself ? It is that—You know what I mean—improper —This is no longer what they call décolleté, but the devil only knows what——"

" I do not know why you should think so."

" Why, the Arch-Tempter himself could not have invented anything worse ! To put a thing like this upon a table means to pollute the whole dwelling ! "

" How curiously you look upon art, doctor ! " Sasha said in an offended tone. " Why, this is a *chef-d'œuvre* ! Just look at it more closely—why, it is of such an exquisite beauty that the heart is filled with a feeling of deep reverence and tears well up to the eyes. When you see such loveliness you forget everything earthly ! What grace ! What expression ! "

" I understand that very well, my dear boy," the doctor interrupted ; " but I am a family man ; the children are always running about and ladies often visit me——"

" Of course, if one looks at it from the standpoint of the crowd," said Sasha, " then, of course, this highly artistic work appears in a different light. But, doctor, you must rise above the crowd, all the more so because by your refusal you will deeply grieve myself and my mother whose only son I am—you have saved my life—and we present you with the most valued object in our possession, and—I am only sorry that we have not the companion to this candelabrum."

" Thank you, my dear boy. I am very grateful—and wish that you greet your mother for me. But, really, 'pon my honour ! Judge for yourself—my little ones are always running about these rooms and ladies are often calling. But, well, let it stay ! You are not to be convinced ! "

" And there is nothing of which to be convinced," Sasha said joyously. " Just place the candelabrum right here near this vase. It is too bad that there is no mate to it! Such a pity! Well, good-day, doctor."

After Sasha left, the doctor contemplated the candelabrum for a long time, scratched his ear, and thought.

"The candelabrum is a splendid piece of workmanship—that cannot well be denied. It would be a great pity to throw it away. But it is quite impossible to leave it here! M-m! There is a nice problem for you! To whom could I present it?"

After he had considered the matter for a long time he suddenly remembered a great friend of his, the lawyer Ukhov, to whom he was indebted for conducting a law-suit.

"Why, that is a splendid idea," decided the doctor. "It is kind of awkward for him on account of our friendship to take money from me, and it will be only proper on my part to make him a present. I will take this piece of devilry to him myself. By the way, he is a bachelor and very giddy."

Without letting the grass grow under his feet, the doctor dressed, took the candelabrum, and went to see Ukhov.

"How are you, comrade?" he greeted the lawyer, glad to have found him in. "I called upon you to thank you, little brother, for the service you did me, and as you do not care to accept payment in money, you must at least accept a present. This, little brother, is an object of art—a veritable gem!"

At the sight of the candelabrum the lawyer was transported with joy.

"Oh, what darlings!" he laughed. "Ah, the devil take them all, what won't they invent! Why, it is marvellous! Delightful! Where did you get such a beauty?"

After he had admired the candelabrum to his heart's content and poured out his rapture, he looked fearfully at the door and said:

"Only, brother mine, you must take this thing back with you. I will not accept it!"

"Why not?" the doctor asked in affright.

"Because—my mother comes to see me sometimes, and the clients—besides, I would not like the servants——"

"No, no, you must not refuse my gift!" The doctor waved his hands. "I will not hear of it! Why, it is a work of art! Just look how much feeling and expression! I do not want to consider a refusal at all! I'll feel very offended!" And the doctor almost ran out of

Ukhov's house, glad to have got rid of the unwelcome present, and went home.

After the doctor left, the lawyer looked attentively, from every side, at the candelabrum, and even touched it with his finger. Then he began to rack his brains over the question of what to do with the present.

"The thing is really beautiful," he reflected. "It would be a great pity to throw it out, but it is not at all a proper object to keep in one's house. The best thing to do in such cases is to present it to some one. I will take it this evening to Shishkov—the comedian. The rascal loves this sort of thing, and, as luck will have it, to-night is his benefit."

Ukhov was as good as his word, and that same evening the carefully wrapped up candelabrum was presented, among many flower offerings, to the comedian. The whole evening the artist's dressing-room was besieged by men who came in to admire the present.

After the performance the comedian shrugged his shoulders, gesticulated and harangued:

"Now, what in the world am I to do with this thing? I am living in a private family! Actresses often come to see me! And this is not a photograph—you cannot hide it away in a bureau-drawer!"

"Do you know what I would advise you to do, sir?" said the hair-dresser, who was just then helping him to divest himself of his wig. "There is an old woman by the name of Smirnov—every one knows her. She deals in old bronzes, I would sell it to her."

Some two days later Dr. Koshelkov sat in his study and, with his finger to his forehead, was thinking deeply upon the bile-pigments. Suddenly the door was thrown open and in flew Sasha Smirnov. He smiled and his whole figure breathed forth happiness. In his hands he held something wrapped up in a newspaper.

"Doctor!" he began breathlessly. "Just picture my joy! As your luck would have it, we succeeded in obtaining the mate to your candelabrum! Mother is so happy! I am the only son of my mother; and you have saved my life!"

And Sasha, trembling with the feeling of gratitude, placed the candelabrum before the doctor. The doctor opened his mouth, wishing to say something, but could not utter a word; he had lost the use of his tongue.

THE SLANDERER

ANTON P. CHEKHOV

SERGEY KAPITONITCH AKHINEYEV, the teacher of calligraphy, gave his daughter Natalya in marriage to the teacher of history and geography, Ivan Petrovitch Loshadinikh. The wedding feast went on swimmingly. They sang, played, and danced in the parlour. Waiters, hired for the occasion from the club, bustled about hither and thither like madmen, in black frock coats and soiled white neckties. A loud noise of voices smote the air. From the outside people looked in at the windows; their social standing gave them no right to enter.

Just at midnight the host, Akhineyev, made his way to the kitchen to see whether everything was ready for the supper. The kitchen was filled with smoke from the floor to the ceiling; the smoke consisted of the odours of geese, ducks, and many other things. Victuals and beverages were scattered about on two tables in artistic disorder. Marfa, the cook, a stout, red-faced woman, was busying herself near the loaded tables.

"Show me the sturgeon, dear," said Akhineyev, rubbing his hands and licking his lips. "What a fine odour! I could just devour the whole kitchen! Well, let me see the sturgeon!"

Marfa walked up to one of the benches and carefully lifted a greasy newspaper. Beneath that paper, in a huge dish, lay a big fat sturgeon, amid capers, olives, and carrots. Akhineyev glanced at the sturgeon and heaved a sigh of relief. His face became radiant, his eyes rolled. He bent down, and, smacking his lips, made a sound like a creaking wheel. He stood a while, then snapped his fingers for pleasure, and smacked his lips once more.

"Aha! The sound of a hearty kiss! Whom have you been kissing there, Marfushka?" some one's voice was heard from the adjoining room, and soon the closely cropped head of Vankin, the assistant school teacher, appeared in the doorway. "Whom have you been kissing here? A-a-ah! Very good, Sergey Kapitonitch! A fine old man indeed! Alone with a woman!"

" I wasn't kissing at all," said Akhineyev, confused ; " who said I was, you fool ? I only smacked my lips with pleasure at the sight of the fish."

" Tell that to some one else ! " exclaimed Vankin, whose face expanded into a broad smile as he disappeared behind the door. Akhineyev blushed.

" The devil only knows what may come of this ! " he thought. " He'll go about tale-bearing now, the rascal. He'll disgrace me before the whole town, the brute ! "

Akhineyev entered the parlour timidly and cast furtive glances to see what Vankin was doing. Vankin stood near the piano, and deftly bending down, whispered something to the inspector's sister-in-law, who was laughing.

" That's about me ! " thought Akhineyev. " About me, the devil take him ! She believes him ; she's laughing. My God ! No, the matter mustn't be left like that. No ! I'll have to make it so that no one will believe him. I'll speak to all of them, and he will only appear a silly gossip in the end."

Akhineyev scratched his head, and, still confused, went up to Padekoi.

" I was in the kitchen a little while ago, arranging things there for the supper," he said to the Frenchman. " You like fish, I know, and I have a sturgeon that long. About two yards. Ah, ha, ha ! Yes, by the way, I had almost forgotten. There was a good joke about that sturgeon in the kitchen. I entered the kitchen a little while ago and wanted to look at the food. I glanced at the sturgeon and, for pleasure, I smacked my lips—it was so piquant ! And just at that moment the fool Vankin entered and says—ha, ha, ha !—and says : 'A-a ! A-a-ah ! You have been kissing here ! '—Marfa ! Just think of it, the cook ! What an invention, the blockhead ! The woman is ugly, she looks like a monkey, and he says we were kissing. What an absurd fellow ! "

" Who's an absurd fellow ? " asked Tarantulov, as he approached them.

" I refer to Vankin. I went out into the kitchen——"

The story of Marfa and the sturgeon was repeated.

" That's what makes me laugh. What an absurd fellow he is. In my opinion it would be more pleasant to kiss the dog than to kiss Marfa," added Akhineyev, and, turning round, he noticed Mazda.

"We have been speaking about Vankin," he said to him. "What a queer fellow. He entered the kitchen and noticed me standing beside Marfa, and immediately he began to invent different stories. 'What?' he says, 'you have been kissing each other!' He was drunk, so he must have been dreaming. 'And I,' said I, 'I would rather kiss a duck than kiss Marfa. And I have a wife,' said I, 'you fool.' He made me appear ridiculous."

"Who made you appear ridiculous?" inquired the teacher of religious knowledge, addressing Akhineyev.

"Vankin. I was standing in the kitchen, you know, and looking at the sturgeon——" And so forth. In about half an hour all the guests knew the story about Vankin and the sturgeon.

"Now let him tell," thought Akhineyev, rubbing his hands. "Let him do it. He'll start to tell them, and they'll cut him short: 'Don't talk nonsense, you fool! We know all about it.'"

And Akhineyev felt so much appeased that he drank, for joy, four glasses of brandy over and above his fill. Having escorted his daughter to her room, he went to his own and soon slept the sleep of an innocent child, and on the following day no longer remembered the story of the sturgeon. But, alas! Man proposes and God disposes. The evil tongue does its wicked work, and even Akhineyev's cunning did him no good. A week later, on a Wednesday, after the third lesson, when Akhineyev was standing in the teachers' room discussing the vicious inclinations of the pupil Visyekin, the director approached him, and, beckoning to him, called him aside.

"See here, Sergey Kapitonitch," said the director. "Pardon me. It isn't my affair, yet I must make it clear to you, nevertheless. It is my duty—You see, rumours are on foot that you are on intimate terms with that woman—with your cook. It isn't my affair, but—You may be on intimate terms with her, you may kiss her—You may do whatever you like, but, please, don't do it so openly! I beg of you. Don't forget that you are a schoolmaster."

Akhineyev stood as though frozen and petrified. Like one stung by a swarm of bees and scalded with boiling water, he went home. On his way it seemed to him as though the whole town stared at him as at one besmeared with tar. At home new troubles awaited him.

"Why don't you eat anything?" asked his wife at their dinner. "What are you thinking about? Are you thinking about Cupid, eh?

You are longing for Marfushka. I know everything already, you Mahomet. Kind people have opened my eyes, you barbarian ! "

And she slapped him on the cheek.

He rose from the table, and staggering, without cap or coat, directed his footsteps toward Vankin. The latter was at home.

" You rascal ! " he said to Vankin. " Why have you covered me with mud before the whole world ? Why have you slandered me ? '

" How ; what slander ? What are you talking about ? "

" Who told everybody that I was kissing Marfa ? Not you, perhaps ? Not you, you—murderer ? "

Vankin began to blink his eyes, and all the fibres of his face began to quiver. He lifted his eyes toward the holy image and ejaculated :

" May God punish me, may I lose my eyesight and die, if I said even a single word about you to any one ! May I have neither house nor home ! "

Vankin's sincerity admitted of no doubt. It was evident that it was not he who had gossiped.

" But who was it ? Who ? " Akhineyev asked himself, going over in his mind all his acquaintances, and striking his chest. " Who was it ? "

FEÓDOR SOLOGUB
B. 1863

THE WHITE MOTHER

I

EASTER was drawing near. Esper Konstantinovitch was in a perplexed, weary mood. It began, seemingly, from the moment when at the Gorodischevs he was asked: "Where are you greeting the festival?"

Saksaulov for some reason delayed his reply.

The hostess, a stout, short-sighted, bustling lady, said: "Come to us."

Saksaulov was annoyed. Was it with the girl who, at her mother's words, gave him a hasty glance and instantly averted her gaze as she continued her conversation with the young professor's assistant?

Mothers of grown-up daughters saw a possible husband in Saksaulov, and this irritated him. He looked upon himself as an old bachelor, and he was only thirty-seven. He replied coldly: "Thank you; I always spend this night at home."

The girl looked at him and asked with a smile: "With whom?"

"Alone," Saksaulov replied, with a shade of surprise in his voice.

"You are a misanthrope," observed Madame Gorodischev, with a somewhat sour smile.

Saksaulov valued his freedom. It seemed to him strange, whenever he thought of it, that at one time he had been very near to marriage. He had grown accustomed to his small but tastefully decorated flat, to his own valet, the aged, sedate Fedot, and to the latter's no less aged wife, the good Christine, who cooked his dinner for him, and tried to convince himself that he did not marry out of a desire to remain true to his first love. In reality his heart had grown cold from indifference, born of his lonely, purposeless life. He possessed an independent income, his father and mother were both dead, and he had no near relations. He lived a quiet, regular life, was attached to some Government department, was intimately acquainted with contemporary literature and art, took an epicurean pleasure in the good things of life, while life itself seemed to him empty, meaningless.

Were it not for one pure, bright dream that visited him at times, he would have grown quite cold, like so many others.

II

His first and only love, that had ended before it had time to blossom, would sometimes, in the evenings, wrap him in strange, sweet fancies. Five years ago he had met the young girl who had produced such a lasting impression upon him. Pale, delicate, with slender waist, blue-eyed, fair-haired, she seemed to him almost a superhuman creature, born of the air and mist, and blown by fate for a brief space into the city din. Her movements were slow; her clear, tender voice was soft, like the murmur of a brook rippling gently over stones.

Saksaulov—was it accident or otherwise?—always saw her dressed in white. The impression of white had become inseparable from his thought of her. Even her name, Tamara, always seemed to him white, like the snow on the mountain-tops.

He began to visit at the house of her parents. More than once he had resolved to say those words to her that bind one human being's fate to another's, but she would never let him speak. Fear and anguish were reflected in her eyes. She would get up and leave him.

What did she fear? Saksaulov saw in her face the unmistakable signs of maidenly love. Her eyes would light up at sight of him and a faint blush would spread over her face.

But on one memorable evening she listened to him. The time was early spring, soon after the river had broken up and the trees had clothed themselves in soft green leaves. In a flat in town Saksaulov and Tamara were sitting by an open window that looked over the Neva. Without considering what he was to say and how to say it, he began to speak tender and what seemed to her terrible words. She turned pale, gave a wan smile and rose. Her delicate hand trembled on the carved back of the chair.

"To-morrow!" she said softly, and left him.

Saksaulov sat for a long time in tense expectancy, staring at the door that had hidden Tamara. His head was in a whirl. A sprig of white lilac caught his eye; he picked it up and went away, without so much as taking leave of his hosts.

That night he could not sleep. He stood by the window staring into the dark street, that grew lighter with the dawn. He smiled and kept on pressing the sprig of lilac in his hand. In the morning he noticed that the room was strewn with petals of the white lilac, and this struck him as both naïve and absurd. He took a bath and felt refreshed; then he went to Tamara.

They told him she was ill—had taken cold somewhere. And Saksaulov never saw her again. In two weeks she was dead. He did not go to her funeral. Her death left him almost unmoved, and already he wondered whether he had loved her, or if it had merely been a passing fascination.

He would muse about her sometimes in the evening; then he began to forget her. Saksaulov had no portrait of Tamara. It was only last spring, after several years had gone by, that he was reminded of her by a sprig of white lilac in the window of a restaurant, sadly out of place among the rich eatables. And from that day he again loved to think of Tamara in the evening.

Sometimes he would fall into a light sleep and dream that Tamara had come. She would sit down near him and look at him with caressing, longing eyes. And it was painful to feel Tamara's expectant gaze upon him and not know what it was she wanted.

Now, as he left the Gorodischevs, he thought timidly: "She will come to give me the Easter greeting." Then a feeling of fear and loneliness took such hold of him that he thought, "It might be well to marry, so as not to be alone on holy mysterious nights."

Valeria Michailovna—the Gorodischev girl—came into his mind. She was not a beauty, but her dress always suited her to perfection. She was well disposed towards Saksaulov, and would hardly refuse him if he proposed.

The noise and crowd in the street distracted him, and his thoughts of the Gorodischev girl soon became tinged with the usual shade of irony. And could he be false to Tamara's memory? The world seemed to him so petty and vulgar that he longed for Tamara—and Tamara only—to give him the Easter kiss. "But," he thought, "she will again look at me with that strange expectancy. The white, gentle Tamara, what is it that she wants? Will her soft lips kiss me?"

III

With tormenting thoughts of Tamara, Saksaulov wandered about the streets. The coarse faces of the grown people disgusted him. He reflected that there was no one with whom he would gladly exchange the Easter kiss. There would be many kisses on the first day—coarse lips, knotted beards, an odour of wine.

It was much more pleasant to kiss children. The faces of children became very dear to him.

He walked for a long time, and when he grew tired he went into a church garden off the noisy street. A pale boy, sitting on a seat, looked up at Saksaulov apprehensively, then continued sitting motionless, staring straight before him. His blue eyes were sad and caressing like Tamara's. He was so small that his feet projected in front of the seat. Saksaulov sat down beside him and began observing him with a pitying curiosity. There was something about this lonely little child that created sweet, stirring memories. And he was the most ordinary boy, in ragged clothes, a white fur cap on his fair little head, and worn, dirty boots on his feet.

For a long time he sat on the seat, then he got up suddenly and began to cry pitifully. He ran out at the gate into the street, then stopped, set off in another direction and stopped again. It was obvious that he did not know which way to turn. He cried quietly to himself, the big tears rolling down his cheeks. A crowd gathered and a policeman came up. They asked the boy where he lived.

" Gluhov House," he lisped, in the manner of very young children.

" What street ? " the policeman asked.

But the boy did not know and only repeated : " Gluhov House."

The policeman, a good-natured young fellow, reflected for a moment. He knew there was no such house in the immediate neighbourhood.

" With whom do you live ? " asked a gloomy looking workman. " With your father ? "

" I have no father," the boy replied, looking up at the crowd with his tearful eyes.

" No father ! dear, dear ! " the workman said solemnly, shaking his head. " But you have a mother ? "

" Yes, I have a mother," the boy replied.

" What is her name ? "

" Mother ? " the boy replied ; then, after a moment's reflection, added, " Black mother."

Some one in the crowd laughed.

" Black ? I wonder if that is their surname ? " the gloomy workman suggested.

" First I had a white mother and now I have a black one," the boy attempted to explain.

" We shall never make head or tail of you, my boy," the policeman said decisively ; " I had better take you to the police station. They will make inquiries on the telephone."

He went up to a gate and rang, but the house porter had already caught sight of him and was coming towards the gate, broom in hand. The policeman ordered him to take the boy to the police station, but the boy bethought himself and cried out : " Let me go ; I will find the way myself ! "

The porter's broom may have alarmed him, or perhaps he had indeed remembered something ; at all events, he ran away so quickly that Saksaulov nearly lost sight of him. After a while, however, the boy slackened his pace. He walked from street to street, running from one side to the other, searching in vain for his home. Saksaulov followed him silently. He was shy of talking to children.

At last the boy grew tired. He stopped by a lamp-post and leant his shoulder against it. The tears glistened in his eyes.

" My dear boy," Saksaulov began, " haven't you found it yet ? "

The boy looked at him with his sad gentle eyes, and suddenly Saksaulov realised what had made him follow the boy so persistently. In the face and glance of the little wanderer there was something wonderfully like Tamara.

" What is your name, my dear ? " Saksaulov asked in a tender, agitated voice.

" Lesha," the boy replied.

" Do you live with your mother, Lesha, dear ? "

" Yes, with mother. Only she is a black mother ; before I had a white one."

Saksaulov concluded that the black one was the step-mother.

" How did you manage to get lost ? " he asked.

" I was walking with mother, a long way ; then she told me to sit and wait and she herself went away. I began to get frightened."

" Who is your mother ? "

" Mother ? She is—so black and cross."

" What does she do ? "

The boy reflected.

" She drinks coffee," he said.

" And what else does she do ? "

" She quarrels with the lodgers," Lesha replied. reflecting for a moment.

" And where is your white mother ? "

" They took her away. They put her in a coffin and took her away. And father, too, they took away." The boy indicated the distance with his hand and burst into tears.

" What shall I do with him ? " Saksaulov thought. But suddenly the boy ran on further. After passing several houses he slackened his pace and Saksaulov caught him up again. In the boy's face there was an expression of mingled fear and joy.

" Here is Gluhov House," Saksaulov said, indicating a hideous five-storeyed building.

At this moment, from the gate of the " Gluhov House " a dark-haired, dark-eyed woman appeared, in a black dress and black shawl with a white pattern. The boy shrank back apprehensively.

" Mother," he whispered.

The step-mother stared at him in astonishment.

" What are you doing here, you little scamp ? " she shouted. " I told you to sit on the seat. Why have you come back ? "

She was about to strike the boy, but observing that a gentleman was looking at them, very severe and grave of aspect, she softened her tone.

" Can't I leave you for half an hour but you must run away ? I have run myself off my legs, looking for you, you young scamp ! I feel fit to drop."

She seized the child's little hand in her broad one and dragged him into the yard. Saksaulov made a note of the address and went away.

Saksaulov liked to listen to Fedot's sound judgments. When he returned home he told him about the boy Lesha.

" She left him on purpose," Fedot announced. " What a vicious woman, to take the boy so far from home ! "

" But what was her motive ? " Saksaulov asked.

" Who can tell ? The stupid woman must have thought that the boy would wander about the streets until some one or other would pick him up. After all she is a step-mother. What is the child to her ? "

" But the police would have found her," Saksaulov said incredulously.

" That is possible, but then she may be leaving the town, and how could they find her then ? "

Saksaulov smiled.

" Really," he thought, " my Fedot should have been an examining magistrate."

Sitting near the lamp with a book that evening, he fell asleep. In his dreams he saw Tamara—gentle and white—she came and sat beside him. Her face was wonderfully like Lesha's. She gazed at him steadily and persistently, as though expecting something. It was painful for Saksaulov to see her bright, pleading eyes and not know what she wanted. He rose quickly and walked over to the chair where Tamara appeared to be sitting. He stood before her and demanded imploringly, in a loud voice : " What do you want ? Tell me ! "

But she was no longer there.

" It was only a dream," Saksaulov thought, sadly.

V

Coming out of the Academy exhibition on the following day Saksaulov met the Gorodischevs. He told the girl about Lesha.

" Poor boy," Valeria Michailovna said softly ; " his step-mother simply wants to get rid of him."

" One can hardly say," Saksaulov replied, annoyed that both Fedot and the girl should take such a tragic view of a simple incident.

" It seems obvious," Valeria Michailovna went on warmly. " There is no father ; the boy lives with his step-mother, to whom he is simply a nuisance. She will get rid of him one way or another."

" You take a very gloomy view," Saksaulov said with a smile.

" Why don't you adopt him ? " Valeria Michailovna suggested.

" I ? " Saksaulov asked in surprise.

" Why not ? " she persisted ; " you live alone and have no one belonging to you. A good deed at Easter is well done. You will at least have some one with whom to exchange the Easter greeting."

" But, Valeria Michailovna, what could I do with the child ? "

" You could get a nurse. Fate seems to have sent the child to you."

Saksaulov looked at the flushed, animated face of the girl in wonder and unconscious tenderness.

When Tamara appeared to him that evening he seemed to know what it was she wanted, and in the stillness of his room he heard her clearly pronounce the words : " Do as she bids you."

Saksaulov got up, rejoicing, and passed his hand over his sleepy eyes. On the table lay a sprig of white lilac. Where had it come from ? Had Tamara left it in token of her will ? And suddenly it dawned on him that in marrying the Gorodischev girl and adopting Lesha he would be fulfilling Tamara's wish. He breathed in the fragrant perfume of the lilac joyously.

Suddenly he recollected that he had bought the sprig of lilac himself that day. " But it makes no difference," he thought. " It is significant that I should have wanted to buy it and should have forgotten afterwards that I had done so."

VI

In the morning he set out to find Lesha. The boy met him at the gate and took him to his home. Lesha's mother was drinking coffee and quarrelling with her red-nosed lodger. Saksaulov learnt something about the boy's story from her.

He had lost his mother when he was three years old. His father had married this dark woman and died too, within a year. The dark woman, Irina Ivanovna, had a year-old child of her own. She was about to marry again. The wedding was to take place in a few days, and immediately afterwards they were to go into " the provinces." Lesha was a stranger to her and in her way.

" Give him to me," Saksaulov suggested.

" With great pleasure," Irina Ivanovna said with a malignant joy. " Only you must pay for his clothes," she added, after a pause.

And so Lesha was installed in Saksaulov's house, and the Gorodischevs' girl helped him to find a nurse and in other details relating to the boy's comfort. This necessitated her presence in Saksaulov's apartments. Seeing her thus busy with these homely cares, she seemed a different being to Saksaulov. The door of her soul opened to him. Her eyes grew tender and radiant and she was permeated with almost the same gentleness that was so characteristic of Tamara.

VII

Lesha's stories about his white mother touched Fedot and his wife. When putting him to bed on Easter Eve they hung a white sugar egg at the head of his bed. " This is from your white mother," Christine said; " only you mustn't touch it, darling, until the Lord has risen and the bells begin to ring."

Lesha lay down obediently. He stared at the lovely egg until he fell asleep.

And Saksaulov was sitting alone. Near midnight an unconquerable drowsiness closed his eyes, and he was glad that he would soon see Tamara.

And she came, radiant, all in white, bringing with her the joyous distant sound of church bells. With a gentle smile she bent over him and—unutterable joy !—Saksaulov felt a light touch on his lips, and a gentle voice pronounced softly: " Christ has risen ! "

Without opening his eyes Saksaulov stretched out his arms and embraced a slender, gentle body. It was Lesha, who had climbed on to his knee to give him the Easter kiss.

The church bells had awakened the boy. He had seized the white egg and run in to Saksaulov.

Saksaulov awoke. Lesha laughed and held up his egg.

" The white mother has sent it," he lisped. " And I will give it to you and you must give it to Auntie Valeria."

" Very well, my dear, I will do as you say," Saksaulov replied.

He put Lesha to bed, then went to Valeria Michailovna with Lesha's white egg, a gift from the white mother, which at this moment seemed to him a gift from Tamara herself.

THE INVOKER OF THE BEAST

FEÓDOR SOLOGUB

I

IT was still, tranquil, neither joyous nor sad. There was an electric lamp in the room. The walls seemed impregnable. The windows were covered with heavy dark green curtains, darker in tone even than the green of the wall-paper. Both doors, the large one to the side and the small one at the other end, opposite the window, were tightly shut. And there, behind them, it was dark and empty—in the broad corridor, as well as in the spacious cold and desolate drawing-room, where drooping plants yearned for their native soil.

Gurov was lying on the couch. A book was in his hand. He was reading. Now and again he would pause. He mused and meditated during these pauses, and it was always about the same thing; always about *them*.

They were all around him. This he had noticed long ago. They were hiding. They were incessantly near him. They rustled quietly. For a long time they were not visible to the eye. But one day, when he awoke tired, pale and suffering, and wearily turned on the electric light to banish the dense gloom of an early winter morning, he suddenly saw one of them.

Small, grey, lightly alert, he flashed above his head, muttered something—and vanished. From that day, in the morning and in the evening, Gurov would see these small, elusive house-sprites running past him. To-day he was certain they would come.

From time to time he felt a slight headache, then a sudden flash of heat and then cold again. Then from the corner emerged the long, gaunt Fever, with her ugly yellow face and dry bony hands which she entwined about him, as she lay down beside him, and began laughing and showering him with kisses. And these quick, passionate kisses of the cunning Fever and these slight periodical headaches were both pleasant.

Weakness and languor spread over the whole body. This, too, was pleasant. The turmoil of life seemed to have receded into the distance.

And people, too, seemed far away, uninteresting, unnecessary. He wanted to be alone with these sly, timid house-sprites.

Gurov had not been out for some days. He had locked himself securely in the house. No one was allowed in. He was alone, thinking of them, awaiting them.

II

The weary waiting ended in a strange unexpected manner. There was the slamming of a distant door and from the drawing-room Gurov could hear the sound of measured footsteps. Some one was coming, drawing nearer, with light, assured tread.

Gurov turned his head towards the door. A cold draught came into the room. Before him stood a boy of a strange and wild aspect. He was draped in a linen cloak. He was half nude, barefooted, swarthy, and sunburnt. He had black, wavy hair and bright black eyes. A wonderfully perfect, handsome face; so handsome that it was almost awe-inspiring to gaze at its beauty. The face expressed neither good nor evil.

Gurov was not surprised. A powerful sensation took hold of him. He could hear the house-sprites running away to hide themselves.

And the boy began to speak.

" Aristomachos, have you forgotten your promise, or is this the way of valiant men ? You left me when I was in mortal danger, you made me a promise which you seemingly did not intend to keep. For a long time I have been seeking you, and now I find you living in idleness and in luxury."

Gurov looked at the handsome, half-nude boy in perplexity; a confused recollection awoke in his soul. Something long since submerged and forgotten began to assume vague form, and tormented his memory that could find no solution to this strange apparition; a solution that seemed so near and so intimate.

And what had become of the invincibility of his walls ? Something had happened around him, some mysterious change had taken place. But Gurov, absorbed in his vain exertions to recall something that was kindred to him, yet was slipping away into the tenacious clutch of ancient memory, was not yet fully conscious of the change that he felt had taken place. He turned to the wonderful boy.

" Tell me, dear boy, simply and clearly, without unnecessary reproaches, what is it that I promised you, and when did I leave you in time of mortal danger ? I vow by all that is holy that my honour would never have permitted me such a black deed as that of which you accuse me."

The boy shook his head. In a voice as musical as the sound of a stringed instrument, he said :

" Aristomachos, you have always been a man skilful in words, and no less skilful in matters requiring daring and prudence. If I said that you left me in time of mortal danger, it was not to reproach you, and I do not understand why you speak of your honour. Our undertaking was a daring and dangerous one, but who can hear us now ? Before whom do you seek to prove with your crafty, wily words and your dissembling ignorance of what happened this morning before sunrise that you had not made me a promise ? "

The light of the electric lamp grew dim. The ceiling seemed dark and lofty. There was a smell of grass—its forgotten name had at one time been soft and joyous. A cool breeze blew.

Gurov rose and asked : " What is it that we two had undertaken ? I deny nothing, dear boy, only I do not know what you are speaking of. I cannot remember."

It seemed to Gurov that the boy was looking at him and yet not looking at him, that some one else was present, some one as foreign and wonderful as this curious stranger, and that the form of this marvellous person was in some way inseparable from his own. Some ancient soul seemed to have entered Gurov's body and enveloped him in the long-lost freshness of his vernal impressions.

It was dark ; the breeze grew fresher and colder ; in his heart arose the joyous ease of pristine existence. The stars shone brightly in the dark sky. The boy spoke.

" We had undertaken to kill the Beast. I tell you this under the multitudinous gaze of the all-seeing heavens. It may be that your fear confounded you. And no wonder ! We were going to do a mighty daring deed so that our names should be famous through the generations."

The soft, monotonous, gentle murmur of a stream could be heard in the nocturnal stillness. The stream was not visible, but the sense of its nearness was sweet and refreshing. They stood under the broad shelter of a tree and continued their conversation begun at some other time.

Gurov asked : " Why do you say that I deserted you in your

moment of mortal danger? Who am I that I should get frightened and run away?"

The boy laughed. The sound of his laugh was like music, and like music were the words that he uttered, the laughter still rippling in his voice.

"Aristomachos, how cleverly you pretend to have forgotten everything! What is your motive in doing it, and doing it so well as to bring reproaches on yourself that I had not even intended? You left me in a moment of mortal danger because it had to be; you could not have helped me otherwise than by forsaking me at that moment. And will you still persist in your denial when I remind you of the words of the Oracle?"

Gurov suddenly remembered. A brilliant light seemed to illuminate the dark domain of things forgotten. In a wild ecstasy, loudly and joyously he cried out:

"One shall kill the Beast!"

The boy laughed, and Aristomachos asked:

"Did you kill the Beast, Timarides?"

"With what?" Timarides exclaimed. "However strong my hands, I am not the one who can kill the Beast with a blow of my fist. We were imprudent, Aristomachos, and unarmed. We were playing on the sandy bank when the Beast fell upon us suddenly and pinned me with his heavy paw. It fell to my lot to offer up my life as a sweet sacrifice to glory and a noble cause, and to you to carry out our plan. And while the Beast was rending my defenceless, unresisting body, you with your long legs, Aristomachos, could have run for your lance and killed the blood-intoxicated Beast. But the Beast did not accept my sacrifice. I lay beneath him quiescent and still, looking into his bloodshot eyes. He held his heavy paw on my shoulder; his breath was hot and quick, and he growled softly to himself. Then, with his broad, hot tongue, he licked my face, and went his way."

"And where is he now?"

Strangely tranquil, and in a voice that sounded strangely melodious in the gentle stillness of the humid air, Timarides replied:

"He followed me. I do not know how far I have come to find you, but he followed me. I led him on by the scent of my blood. I do not know why he has not touched me. But I have enticed him to you. Get your weapon that you have hidden so carefully and kill the Beast, and I in my turn will run away and leave you alone in your moment of mortal danger, eye to eye with the infuriated Beast. Rejoice, Aristomachos ! "

With these words Timarides set off at a run. For a short while his white cloak glimmered in the darkness. Already he was out of sight. And at this moment the terrible roar of the Beast could be heard, and the sound of his heavy tread. The bushes parted, and the enormous, hideous head of the Beast appeared, a livid fire flashing out of its huge flaming eyes. And in the dark stillness, beneath the nocturnal trees, the black and furious Beast bore down on Aristomachos.

Aristomachos' heart was filled with terror. " Where is my lance ? " flashed across his brain.

And at this moment, by the sense of the cool night air that beat against his face, Aristomachos knew that he was running away from the Beast. Its heavy bounds and broken roars grew closer and closer. And when the Beast reached him, a loud cry rent the stillness of the night. It was Aristomachos who had cried out. And recalling some weird ancient words, he began an incantation to the walls.

And thus conjured, the walls began to rise about him. . . .

III

The bright, enchanted walls stood firm, and the wan light of the electric lamp seemed dead against them. Gurov was in his usual surroundings.

Again the Fever came lightly and kissed him with her yellow, dry lips, and caressed him with her dry, bony hands, which diffused heat and cold. The same thin little book with the white leaves lay on the table by the couch on which Gurov had lain contentedly before in the arms of the amorous Fever, while she showered quick kisses upon him. And again the tiny little house-sprites laughed and rustled around him.

Gurov pronounced loudly and indifferently : " The spell of the walls." He stopped. But what was the spell ? Had he forgotten the words, or had they never existed ?

The little grey mischievous house-sprites danced around the little book with the deadly white leaves, repeating in their silky little voices :

" Our walls are strong. We are in the walls. No harm can come to us from outside."

In the midst of them stood one just as small as the rest, but different from them. He was black all over. His garments fell about him in folds of smoke and flame. His eyes flashed like lightning. Gurov was seized by terror and then by a sudden joy. He asked: "Who are you?"

The black guest spoke.

"I am the Invoker of the Beast. In a long past existence, on the banks of a forest stream, you abandoned the lacerated body of Timarides. The Beast gorged himself on the beautiful body of your friend—he ate of the body that should have tasted to the full of earthly happiness; a creature of superhuman perfection had perished to satisfy for a moment the ever ravenous and insatiable Beast. And the blood, the wonderful blood, the sacred wine of joy and happiness, the wine of superhuman bliss—where is this blood? Alas! the thirsty, ever thirsty Beast drank of it for a moment and is thirsty anew. You abandoned the lacerated body of Timarides on the banks of a forest stream, you forgot the promise made to your valiant friend, and the words of the ancient Oracle failed to banish the fear from your heart. And do you imagine that you are safe, that the Beast will not find you?"

His words were harsh and cruel. While he was speaking the house-sprites ceased their dancing; the little grey creatures stopped to listen to the Invoker of the Beast.

And Gurov said: "What do I care for the Beast! Have I not put a spell on my walls for ever? The Beast cannot penetrate to me here."

The little grey creatures rejoiced; their voices rang out in a merry laugh. Again they took hands and made ready to form a ring, when the Invoker of the Beast spoke, and his voice sounded harsh and austere:

"But I am here. I am here because I have found you. I am here because the spell of the walls is dead. I am here because Timarides is waiting, incessantly imploring. Do you not hear the gentle laugh of the valiant, trusting boy? Do you not hear the roar of the Beast?"

From without the walls the threatening roar of the Beast could be heard drawing nearer.

"The Beast roars without the wall, the invincible wall!" Gurov exclaimed in terror; "my walls are enchanted for ever and their barrier is impenetrable."

And the Dark One spoke in a commanding voice:

"But I tell you that the spell of the walls is dead. If you wish to save yourself by the spell why not try and repeat the incantation?"

A cold shiver ran down Gurov's back. The incantation! But the ancient words were forgotten. And what did it matter? Was not the ancient spell dead—dead?

And every object in the room confirmed with irrefutable evidence that the spell of the walls was dead, because the walls, and the light and the shadows, all grew dim and wavering. The Invoker of the Beast went on speaking terrible words. Gurov's head ached and ached, and the importunate Fever tormented him with her hot, passionate kisses. The terrible words rang out, scarcely reaching his consciousness; and the Invoker of the Beast grew larger and larger, diffusing hot vapours and grim terror. Fire flashed from his eyes, and when at last he grew so tall as to screen the light of the lamp, his black cloak suddenly fell from his shoulders. And Gurov recognised him—it was the boy Timarides.

"Will you kill the Beast?" Timarides asked in a ringing voice. "I have enticed him, brought him to you, destroyed the spell of the walls. The base gift of a hostile god, the spell of the walls had turned to naught my sacrifice and shut you out from your deed. But the ancient spell of the walls is dead; be quick and take up your sword and kill the Beast. I was only a boy before, now I have become the Invoker of the Beast. The Beast drank of my blood and is thirsty anew; he ate of my flesh and is hungry again, the cruel insatiable Beast. I have brought him to you and you must fulfil your promise and kill him; or die yourself."

He vanished. A terrible roar shook the walls. A damp cold draught filled the room.

The wall, exactly opposite the spot where Gurov lay, opened, and out came a ferocious, monstrous, hideous Beast. With a savage growl he walked up to Gurov and laid his heavy paw on his breast. The pitiless claws penetrated to the very heart. A sharp pain pierced through his body. With flaming, bloodshot eyes the Beast bent over Gurov, and crunching his bones with his teeth, began to devour his palpitating heart.

A SOOTHING DREAM

Feódor Sologub

SERIOJA died.

It was Passion week. In the house, preparations were being made as usual for the festival—preparations that were a joy to the children and pleasant to the adults. Eggs were coloured with cochineal, saffron was prepared for the rolls, and cream whipped for Easter visitors; there was a smell of vanilla and cardamom.

The floors were polished, dirt and dust was everywhere removed, the windows were cleaned. The servants were tired out. The girls, Serioja's sisters, dreamt of pleasant kisses, and shuddered at the thought of the unpleasant ones.

And Serioja lay in his room, which was bare, so that the furniture should not absorb the fresh air in the room where there was a sweet smell of tallow.

He was only fifteen, bright and gay, and loved by the family. It was the beginning of Spring, just before Easter Sunday, and Serioja's sisters wanted pleasures only, and were afraid to think of death.

Serioja's death was so out of keeping with the rush and bustle of preparation for the festival, that they wanted to deceive themselves and imagine that he was recovering for it.

He had been ill for some time, and they had decided to take him away somewhere, but it was put off because they could not make up their minds where to take him. And suddenly, no one knew why, his lungs got worse quickly, and he grew so weak that it was impossible to move him; the journey would have been too tiring, and besides, the warm climate could not then have saved him.

The young doctor said to Serioja's distracted father:

"Not more than a month, now."

The old doctor said wearily and indifferently:

"Six weeks at the most."

Serioja's father conducted them politely to the door. His face was red and confused. His mind would not grasp the fact that Serioja was about to die. His thoughts were slow and dazed.

He stood by the fireplace in the dining-room, and mechanically looked at himself in the mirror hanging above it, straightened his tie that had slipped to one side, and with trembling fingers stroked his moustache that was beginning to grow grey.

In an awkward, apologetic manner he walked up to the table where his wife was peeling almonds. Thrusting his hands into the pockets of his short house-jacket, he stood behind her back, and suddenly, by some intuition, by the manner in which she bent over, by her suppressed bodily suffering, by the trembling of her lips, he realised that she knew the worst.

It struck him painfully that she was not lying among her soft pillows weeping bitterly, but was sitting there with the young boys, apparently so calm, yet suffering cruelly. And the boys, helping their mother, laughed and talked carelessly.

The sight of her lonely suffering sent an acute pain through him. A lump rose in his throat, and with small, quick footsteps he walked away from her, the tap-tap of his heelless shoes resounding on the polished floor. Small and grey he went along the empty corridor to his study—to throw himself on the couch, his face to the high back, and toss about with sighs and groans on the dark green leather.

Hearing his footsteps behind her, his wife grew redder than before, and her face twitched, but she sat straight and calm. The almonds were all finished ; she wiped her soft white hands on a towel, and went slowly into her husband's study.

And there they sat, side by side, weeping bitterly in their despair, no consolation in sight. . . .

II

It was the Saturday before Easter. Serioja was asleep. He was dreaming—a strange but soothing dream.

It was a sultry day, he dreamt. Before his eyes there stretched a valley golden in the bright rays of the sparkling sun. He sat on the threshold of a poor hut. The broad leaves of two palm-trees threw a shade on his sunburnt legs and on his white linen clothes. He was small, as he used to be ten years ago, and very happy. His tiny body, scarcely covered by the white linen, was as light as that of an earthly angel. Everything made him gay—the earth so hot and firm beneath his bare feet—the air so sultry yet fresh,—the sky so blue and high, yet so near that it seemed to touch the earth—the quick flight of the birds—the cries of the children playing by the neighbouring huts—his mother's mellow, unexpected voice as she chatted merrily with other women by the well in their white garments, swarthy and barefooted.

Now she was returning. On her shoulder was a long narrow-necked pitcher. Her bare, swarthy arm was raised to support it. The sunlight played on her rosy cheeks, her lips were half-parted in a smile, her eyes gazing at the child from beneath long lashes sparkled and shone with pleasure. She was proud of her boy while he ran, laughing and joyful, to meet her. In his hands was a toy he had made himself out of clay—a bird,—a clay bird, but it seemed alive.

The wonderful little artist had modelled it out of heavy clay—his fingers had been quick and deft, and the clay seemed to wish to come to life, and the little bird trembled in the warm, childish fingers full of the will that creates life.

The mother passed him in her haste to relieve herself of her burden. Smiling, without a bend of her neck or a motion of her head, she cast a glad look at her son from her deep black eyes.

The boy put out his left hand, and catching hold of her sunburnt foot, cried:

"Look, mother!"

He was a little surprised at his foreign speech, but soon forgot it, and left off wondering at the strange tongue and the fact that he was understood.

His mother stopped and laughed. She asked:

"Well, what is it, my son?"

The boy raised the clay bird and said gaily:

"Look, mother, here is a bird I made myself; it sings like a real one."

He put his lips to the tail of the bird where it was formed like a whistle and blew into it, and from the clay back of the bird there issued a soft whistle. Modulating his breath, the boy blew into his clay whistle creating real musical sounds.

The mother laughed and said:

"What a clever boy to make such a wonderful bird! Look after it, hold it firmly in case it should fly away."

She went into the hut and about her work. And the boy sat on the perch gazing pensively at his bird, and stroking its feathers with his slender fingers.

"Do you want to fly away?" he asked softly.

The little wings moved slightly.

The boy asked again:

"Do you want to fly away?"

The little heart began to beat in the bird's breast.

For the third time the boy asked:

"Do you want to fly away?"

The little body trembled all over, it spread its feathers and flapped its wings—the bird twittered and turned its head from side to side.

The boy opened his hand and the bird flew away. And in the light blue sky its joyful song receded farther and farther.

The sultry sun rose higher and closer grew the still air.

III

Serioja awoke bathed in a cold sweat.

There was a horrible pain in his chest and breathing was difficult. But where was the little bird, the little bird that he had made?

There it was by the window, twittering, beating its wings and flying away.

"My bird!"

"And who am I?"

Serioja raised himself, but fell back on the pillows again. He murmured in his delirium:

"And who am I?"

The mother bent over him, but Serioja did not see her. He did not see the walls of his room, they had gone off again and left him alone.

IV

He was on the top of a hill.

The country spread out before him sparkling in the sultry noonday sun. His clothes were poor and worn, his weary feet were covered with dust, and dust was in his short, golden beard.

His companions remained below in the shade of the olives, sleeping off their fatigue.

Around him the light grew brighter, and more majestic grew the broad sparkling heavens. Floating through the transparent air, and bringing a cool heavenly breeze with them, two men in resplendent flowing garments came up and spoke to him. He asked them:

"Who am I?"

"Do not be afraid," they answered him. "On the third day you will arise."

His clothes were already a fiery red, and a fiery halo was over his head, and the fire in his blood made his blood course through his veins, and a shout of unutterable joy escaped him.

V

He awoke. His cry brought them, frightened, to his bedside. A thin stream of blood flowed from his mouth, coming out from the left side of his pale lips. His face was deadly white, the frightened eyes gazed above the dear ones gathered at his deathbed, wide-open eyes motionless with terror.

Black and sightless, with terribly shiny white teeth, there approached an inexorable figure bringing with her an eternal cold and eternal darkness. She was enormous. She took all the air from Serioja, and like a dark cloud, shaking the heavy folds of her garments, she bore down straight on Serioja.

But, loud as thunder, the voice of the resplendent man was heard:

"On the third day you will arise."

And behind the black mantle of the deadly guest could be seen the golden lighting of the Resurrection day, a glad sight to Serioja's eyes. His pale face lit up with the joyous golden lighting, and in his eyes was a quiet triumphal look. He whispered, catching his breath:

"On the third, I will arise."

And he died. . . .

VI

On the third day he was buried.

THE HOOP

Feódor Sologub

EARLY one morning, in a deserted street on the outskirts of a town, there walked a lady and a boy of four. The boy was gay and rosy, the lady was young and well-dressed. She smiled in her happiness and looked anxiously at her son. The boy was bowling a hoop, a large, new, yellow one. He ran after it with awkward childish movements, laughing joyfully, stamping his chubby feet, displaying his bare knees and waving his stick. It was not at all necessary to raise the stick so high, but what would you have!

What joy! A short while ago he had no hoop, and now there it was bowling along so swiftly! And everything was so jolly!

There was nothing there before—for the boy—it was all new—the morning street, the bright sun, the distant murmur of the town. To the boy all was new, pure and joyful.

Yes, all is pure; children never see the impure side of things until their elders show them where to look.

II

A shabbily-dressed old man, with coarse hands, stood at the crossing and drew himself up against the fence in order to let the lady and her son pass. The old man looked at the boy with dim eyes, and smiled dully. Slow, vague thoughts began to creep into his bald head.

"A gentleman's son," he thought. "A nice little fellow. How he enjoys himself. A child—a gentleman's child, mind you!"

There was something he could not understand, something that seemed strange to him. A child: but children are pulled by the hair. Petting indulges them: children are always in danger of being spoilt.

And the mother did not repress her son—did not shout or threaten. How well-dressed and beautiful she was! What did she want for? She evidently lived in peace and comfort.

When he—the old man—was a boy he had led a dog's life! It was not too sweet even now, although he was no longer beaten or went hungry. In those days it was hunger, cold, and blows. In those days there was no such indulgence as hoops or other such toys of the gentry. Thus his whole life had passed in poverty, care, and bitterness. There was nothing to remember—not a single joy.

Smiling with toothless mouth at the boy, he grew envious. He thought: "A stupid amusement." Envy made him weary. He went to his work—in the factory where he had worked from childhood, where he had grown old. All day he kept thinking about the boy.

Effortless thoughts: it was so easy to remember the boy running, laughing, stamping, chasing his hoop—and his legs were so chubby and his knees so white. . . .

The whole day, amidst the din of the factory machines, he thought of the boy and the hoop. And at night he dreamt of the boy in his sleep.

III

Next morning dreams again possessed the old man. The machines rattled, the work was mechanical, and it was not necessary to think about it. The hands performed the accustomed task, the toothless mouth smiled at the absorbing dream. The air grew cloudy with dust, near the ceiling the belts with a sharp hiss glided from pulley to pulley. The far corners were enveloped in noisy gloom. People moved about like ghosts—human speech was drowned in the resounding song of the machines.

And it seemed to the old man that he was a little boy, that his mother was a lady, that he had a hoop and stick with which he was playing, bowling the hoop with his stick. He was dressed in white—his legs were fat and his knees bare. . . .

Day after day the same work and the same dream.

IV

When returning home one evening, the old man saw in the street a hoop from an old barrel—a rough, dirty hoop. The old man trembled with joy, and tears started to his dim eyes. A sudden, almost unconscious desire entered his soul. He looked round cautiously, bent down, and with trembling hands seized the hoop and carried it home, smiling shamefacedly.

No one saw him, no one asked questions. Besides, what business was it of anyone's? A little ragged old man carrying an old hoop of no use to anybody—who would notice him?

But he carried it stealthily—in fear yet smiling. Why he had picked it up, why he was carrying it home he himself did not know. It was so like the boy's toy, so he had taken it.

To see, to touch, was more real than that dream, dimmer than the din and roar of the factory, hazier than the noisy gloom. . . .

For several days the hoop lay under the old man's bed in his poor crowded corner. Sometimes he would take it out and look at it—the dirty grey hoop comforted him, and the ever-present dream of the happy boy became more real.

V

On a clear, warm morning, when the birds in the shelter of the town trees were singing more gaily than usual, the old man rose very early, took his hoop and walked out of the town.

Coughing, he wound his way among the old trees and clinging branches through the woods. The silence of the sombre trees with dark, dry barks was incomprehensible to him. The scents were strange, the insects amazed him, and the pearly dew was as in a fairy tale. There was neither din nor dust, and a wonderful soft darkness lay behind the trees. The aged legs glided over the carpet of leaves and stumbled against the ancient roots.

The old man broke off a dry twig and put it through the hoop.

A meadow, bright and still, lay before him, the many-coloured, countless dewdrops sparkling on the blades of the newly-mown grass.

Suddenly the man struck the hoop with his stick and set off at a run ; the hoop rolled softly over the meadow. The old man laughed with joy and ran after the hoop like the boy. He threw out his legs, caught the hoop with his stick, and raised the stick high above his head as the boy had done.

It seemed to him that he was a little boy once more, gentle and happy. His mother was following him and watching him with a fond smile. Like a child he felt a little chilly at first in the dark wood, on the gay grass and the soft moss.

The grey, goat-like beard on the worn tace shook and laughter and coughs issued together from his toothless mouth.

VI

The old man loved to come to the wood in the morning and play in the glade with his hoop.

Sometimes he feared that someone might see him and laugh, and at this thought an unbearable sense of shame possessed him. The shame was akin to fear ; his legs grew weak and gave way under him. He looked around cautiously and shamefacedly.

But no—no one saw him—no one heard him. . . . And having

played to his heart's content he walked peacefully back to town, a light glad smile on his lips.

VII

And so, no one saw him ; and nothing more happened. He played peacefully for several days, and one dewy morning caught cold, took to bed, and died. When dying in the factory hospital amid strange, indifferent people, he smiled serenely.

He was comforted by the thought that he, too, had been a child, had laughed and gambolled on the fresh grass under the shady trees while his dear mother looked on.